# The

# Last Thing

# She Said

Who will believe her?

Also by Rachel Walkley

The Women of Heachley Hall

# The Last Thing She Said

## Rachel Walkley

Spare Time Press

Published by Spare Time Press
Copyright © 2018 Rachel Walkley
All Rights Reserved

ISBN 978-1-9996307-3-7

To N.

~ ♫ ~

Use what talents you possess; the woods would be very silent if no birds sang there except those that sang best.

~ Attributed to Henry Van Dyke

Accept the things to which fate binds you, and love the people with whom fate brings you together, but do so with all your heart.

~ Marcus Aurelius, *Meditations*

# Chocolate with marble fondant

## Naomi

## 2008

Every June the first, Naomi's eldest sister visited their grandmother, insisting whoever was available on the day be towed along to watch Gran blow out a candle on her birthday cake and fall asleep with feigned exhaustion.

'I've baked a cake,' Rebecca announced over the telephone to Naomi. 'You're coming, and we'll pick up Leia on the way to the house.'

Naomi behaved exactly as Rebecca would expect – like a grumpy teenager impatiently waiting to turn twenty. 'Oh, God, do we have to take her? You know Leia hates all the mumbo jumbo that Gran spouts. She'd have her in one of those sheltered housing places.'

'Gran's not that old. If it wasn't for Granddad passing away, she'd still be sprightly and full of beans.'

'And in her right mind. Why do we put up with all this nonsense? Her clairvoyance? This "I can see the future" business?'

'She doesn't see it. She hears it,' Rebecca corrected with infuriating precision. 'It doesn't do anyone any harm, so leave her to it.'

'Harm? No, I suppose not.' Naomi hung up and closed her bedroom door, blocking out the scrape of bow against string. She'd taken up residence with an ambitious violinist who preferred to practise in the hallway, sandwiched between the front door and the bottom of the stairs, where she claimed the acoustics were good. The budding Nicola Benedetti was in full flight of the bumble bee mode and unlikely to stop practising for a few days due to her impending recital. Naomi preferred the hallowed practice rooms of the university.

A trip to Gran's cosy house wasn't a bad idea.

During the journey across the southern Fens to Chatteris, the three sisters ignored the flat fields flooded with golden rapeseed and isolated ribbons of trees and twisted thickets. Rebecca sighed a few times, Leia dozed, and Naomi wished she was spending the day with Kyle.

When Rebecca opened the sunroof, a slice of cold air cut through the car's interior. Leia jerked in her seat.

'What the—,' she muttered.

'Leia!' Rebecca said.

Naomi smiled. 'Isn't this jolly, eh? All of us together.'

'Don't be so negative, Naomi,' said Rebecca.

Leia's head lolled from side to side. 'Wake me when we're there.'

'No appreciation, you two. I keep this family going, you know that?' Rebecca drummed her fingers on the steering wheel. A lock of hair flew across her face. Her hand brushed against her eyes. Tears? Rebecca wasn't jolly in the slightest. However, she wasn't visiting Gran's house under duress. Their parents never required them to visit Rose on her birthday and Rose wasn't bothered with gifts or cards.

Rebecca always wanted to go, as had her father, Paul, who'd visited his mother on a regular basis. As the only child, he'd been quite aware of his filial duties. After his career had taken off, he'd handed the reins over to Rebecca, who'd then dragged her siblings along to witness something that had become an obsession: Rose's enigmatic premonitions. None of them had ever come true, a fact that Leia laboured frequently. Ignoring the lack of enthusiasm, Rebecca led the pilgrimage to the heartlands of the bleak Fens to pay tribute to an aging woman who was both disconnected from the outside world and constantly grieving her lost husband.

Rebecca's empathy was legendary. She cried over television dramas whether the ending was happy or sad, she melted when told a love story and dreaded watching the news for fear it might upset her. Prone to nightmares, when she was a child she often sleepwalked, and tested her parents' patience with her ghoulish dreams and horrible visions. Were the two things tied together, Rose's profound belief in fate and Rebecca's fear of the unknown destroying what she loved? Naomi, emerging from her adolescent years, and finding the adult view of the world more daunting than she'd anticipated, wanted a simple life that removed her from her family's quirky way of living apart from each other, yet often interfering as if suffocatingly close in proximity.

'Why did they go, do you think?' Naomi said, thinking out loud.

'Who?' Rebecca asked, closing the sunroof and turning up the heater. Summer was tardy this year.

Leia snored softly.

'Mum and Dad. Why did they go to live in the States?'

'Because they had the chance.' Rebecca never begrudged them the decision.

'I should have gone, shouldn't I?' Naomi said, lowering her chin and examining her clasped hands. 'I've held you back.'

'Nonsense.' Rebecca managed a swift glance over her shoulder to the rear seat. 'I don't regret you living with me. I'd do it again. Watching you turn into a young woman has been deeply satisfying. Any man who snaps you up will have found a nugget of gold.'

Naomi stared at the back of Rebecca's head. The compliment caused a swell of unbearable guilt at her behaviour over the past year and her attempts at shaking herself free from Rebecca's maternal grasp.

'I'm sorry,' she whispered, struggling not to cry.

The air-conditioner blasted into her face; Rebecca might not have heard the apology. Naomi sank into the misery of silence.

'Wake up, sleepy head.' Rebecca prodded Leia. 'We've arrived.' The car stopped outside of Rose's tired house with its bay window and lace net curtains.

The three of them trooped up to the faded front door. 'Now, girls,' Leia said after a lengthy yawn, 'let's do this one more time.'

'One more time?' Rebecca asked in alarm. 'What do you mean?'

'I'll tell you later. And as for you, Naomi, chin up. Rebecca loves playing big sister. She was born to watch over us.'

'You were awake!' Rebecca glared at Leia.

The rebuke ended abruptly. Rose opened the door and held open her arms, welcoming in her granddaughters with a cheerful smile.

\* \* \* \*

Rose puckered her lips and slowly expelled a stream of air. The diminutive flame flickered for a second then died. Through the threads of smoke that lingered above the birthday cake, Rose's pale eyes fixed on Naomi. When she spoke, her warbling voice was stretched, but the revelatory words were enunciated clearly.

'Beware of a man named Frederick and his offer of marriage.' Rose blinked and gave a small satisfactory nod. 'Cut a slice for me, love.'

Naomi glanced to her side. Rebecca was poised, holding the fake ivory handle of the cake knife with a white-knuckled grasp.

'I don't know anyone called Frederick,' Naomi whispered into Rebecca's ear. She'd no plans to marry gaming geek Kyle, or any other man for that matter, at least not until she could see the benefit outshine the exuberant cost and extensive planning needed.

Rebecca pressed the knife through the layer of marble icing. 'She's done it. That's all that matters,' she said quietly.

'What's that?' Rose cocked an ear towards her granddaughters. Even if Naomi bothered to ask questions, Rose, with a humorous twinkle in her eye, would likely shrug dismissively. Sometimes she claimed it was a spirit that dropped the thought into her head, other times she implied the eruption of a whispering voice was due to the revitalising energy of her birthday. The lack of consistency significantly weakened Rose's sage advice.

On the other side of the stained kitchen table, Leia removed the plate from Rose's hand.

'Here, Gran, let me help you.' She thrust the plate at Rebecca. 'Just slice the cake. She's had her moment.'

Her moment, as Leia put it, was something of a tradition on Rose's birthday. The sugary-topped sponge, which Rebecca had baked that morning, the solitary pink candle and the customary extinguishing of the flame, were a necessary precursor to the miniature party. Without fail, every year, Rose, with her salt and pepper hair swept back from her face into a bun, leaned toward the candle, and spoke her words of prophecy. The only difference this time was she had said them directly to Naomi instead of to a spot on the far wall.

'Why don't you go and sit down, Gran,' Rebecca said, 'and we'll bring you the cake and cuppa. Make yourself comfortable.'

'Right oh.' Rose smiled, and tottered out of the kitchen, her wide hips rocking from side to side. She liked cake.

'With luck, she'll be asleep soon.' Leia brushed the crumbs to one side with a sweep of her hand.

Naomi's appetite shrivelled. 'Why did she speak to me? She usually has this glazed expression and never refers to somebody in the room.'

Leia retrieved the teapot from underneath the hedgehog cosy. 'Forget it, Naomi. How can you possibly know if she meant you or not? If Mum and Dad were here, they would shrug off this silliness.'

Not quite true. The level-headed father of the three women hadn't frowned upon Rose's gift of foresight and he had heard many birthday prophecies prior to his departure overseas.

Rebecca glared at Leia and not at the anxious Naomi. 'Well, I've nearly always visited on Gran's birthday, and Naomi's right. This one is different. She was definitely looking at Naomi.' She poured the milk into the cups and selected the prettiest china one for Rose. 'But honestly, Naomi, don't dwell on it. If you do meet a man called Frederick, you'd have to go back in time to find him. I mean, who calls a boy Frederick these days.' She chuckled half-heartedly.

'I suppose,' Naomi murmured. Had she not been at school with a Freddy? The nastier kids had called him Freddo.

Leia poured the steaming tea into the cups. She had a ring on every finger. None of them worked well together, but at least she'd not worn the one with the skull and crossbones, which, she claimed, had something to do with an anatomy club. Rebecca hated it and blamed Leia's morbid fascination with disease. Naomi preferred the serpent ring, coiling its way up to Leia's knuckle.

'You said you're getting serious with Kyle,' said Leia.

'I am.' Naomi really liked him: he had a nice laugh, and he paid for half of everything, like a thoroughly modern man should. He'd turned a hobby into a job and made good money from it.

Leia loaded the tray with slices of cake and cups. 'So, let's just brush Gran's annual descent into melodrama to one side. She has these funny turns and that's it.'

Naomi opened the door to the sitting room. 'Funny turns? What was the one she made years ago, Becca, something about trying hard and failing or something like that, wasn't it?'

'Yes,' Rebecca said softly. 'Something like that. Nine years ago.'

Leia laughed. 'Trust you to remember.'

Naomi tried hard to relax. Her sisters were right – Rose's peculiar declarations were harmless. If they came true, nobody had seen or heard anything. The anxiety refused to abate, though. Regardless of her calm delivery, why had Rose stared right into Naomi's eyes?

Rose maintained a startlingly minimalist house. The clutter-free existence was reflected in each room and, barring the stack of magazines and a few books on the bookshelf behind the television, she declined any gifts that might clutter the tidy scene. Since the death of their grandfather, she'd emptied the house of his lingering presence, box by box, and, over four years, she'd dispatched his possessions to charity shops, starting with the clothes in the wardrobe and ending with his fishing hooks and bait enshrined in a small glass-topped souvenir cabinet. The empty cavities created inside cupboards and the bare shelves were devoid of dust, because Rose kept things spick and span in an unending cycle of cleaning. She refused the offer of hired help.

She was in her usual armchair, which was positioned directly in front of the television and in handy reach of the tall side table. Upon her knee, the lazy ginger cat, Samwise, was curled into a seamless ball of fur. Rose's head was tipped to one side and her shoulders sagged into the seat. A tiny woman, she wore bulky layers of clothing.

Naomi unbuttoned her jacket and slipped it off. The heat pumped out by the radiators was too much for her.

'See,' Leia remarked, 'already asleep. She doesn't care two hoots about this gift of hers. Hardly a convincing case for ESP, is she?'

From between Rose's lips, a gentle snore escaped. Leia placed the tray on the coffee table and the sisters arranged themselves on the long sofa, tea cups in one hand, cake in the other.

If they didn't share some common features – rosy lips, high-bridged noses and greyish eyes – an observer might not believe the twins were sisters. Leia and Rebecca, born within hours of each with Rebecca claiming the honour of first out, were far from identical and it showed in every mannerism. Slender and angular, classically beautiful Leia was a graduate of medicine who preferred not to bother with patients, and had gone straight back to university to study deadly diseases. The fashionable stonewashed jeans and logo splattered t-shirt exemplified the look she maintained even off campus. In contrast, regal Rebecca wore a dapper solicitor's uniform – black trouser suit with a garnet brooch on the jacket's lapel. She daintily picked at the cake with a fork, swallowing a morsel before sipping on her tea.

They drank tea and ate the rich cake in silence, waiting for the appropriate moment to stir from their compartmentalised trains of thought and initiate a conversation; they'd lost the inclination to chatter years ago. By the time they'd finished eating, Rose's snores were rattling through her teeth.

Leia cleared her throat. 'I've decided to go to America and join Mum and Dad. I've been offered a post as research associate at Harvard School of Public Health.'

Rebecca wrapped her arm around her twin and squeezed her. 'Congratulations. It's what you wanted.'

'Yes,' Leia said, wriggling free. 'It is. Seems they want my brain for a big breakthrough project. I guess I'm going to have to deliver it.'

'And I'm thinking that I'll be engaged soon,' Rebecca said, blushing.

'Really?' Naomi said. 'He's keen, isn't he?'

'I caught him measuring one of my rings. Ever since he moved in, Howie's been checking dates with me, asking what my favourite time of year is, who my best friends are. I reckon he's costing it all out.'

'He is a bank manager,' Leia said.

'He's a good one,' Naomi said. 'And if he does ask?'

'I'll say yes. I'm happy.' Rebecca collected the plates.

Naomi had no doubt that Rebecca would fit right in with the roles of wife and mother. She was born to nurture, unlike Leia, whose idea of fun was analysing data and peering at things under a microscope followed by a spell in a pub. Naomi wasn't rushing into anything just because Kyle was now part of her life. She smiled, thinking about his shockingly poor taste in music and the spike of tufted hair that rose above his forehead. Kyle was perfect – so laid back, he was flat on his back and unlikely to bother with something as uncool as marriage.

'If Kyle agrees, I might,' she said. 'One day. Not for a long while, though.'

'You're only nineteen,' said Leia. 'Play the field a bit more.'

Rebecca coughed loudly and glared at Leia. 'She's not like you. Or me, for that matter.'

Naomi rolled her eyes and stared at the corner of the room. They were doing it again, managing her life as if she wasn't there. 'I'm happy, thank you very much. We're all fine. All that angst when Mum and Dad decided to leave England and settle abroad was a storm in a teacup. Here we are, working, studying, roofs over our heads and perfectly okay. Even Gran coped. She'll miss you, Leia,' Naomi added, almost apologetically.

Leia snorted. 'No she won't, at least not like you and Becca. If she thought for one minute I believed in all her nonsense, she might show a jot of interest in my work, but she doesn't. She thinks science is too... concrete, too inflexible. I need to be more arty.'

'That's harsh,' Rebecca said. 'She was a nurse.'

Naomi remembered Rose's uniform, the snug fit around the waistline. 'Look at her now, though. She's aged so much in the last couple of years.'

'People age differently.' Leia said with a shrug. 'She should probably exercise more.'

'Oh, please stop judging, Leia,' said Rebecca. 'She's just tired and feeling a little frail. She might be catching something.'

Rose stirred, and her snoring abruptly stopped.

'Shh, she's waking up.' Naomi crept over to the armchair. 'Gran, you've cake and tea. It's getting cold.'

Rose's eyes flickered, and she opened them. 'Oh, Naomi, there you are. I was just dreaming about you.'

'You were?' Naomi handed her the plate and a fork, then bent over to listen.

'Yes. I hope I haven't upset you.'

Rose's string of tiny pearls coiled around the folds of her neck. Real pearls, Rose liked to boast, and given to her by an unidentified friend after the death of her husband four years earlier. Rebecca had speculated whether the person was somebody from Rose's art appreciation club, whereas Leia thought Rose had simply found the forgotten necklace after their grandfather, Frank, had died. Naomi believed Rose when she claimed their true value wasn't intrinsic but something of a secret between her and this friend. Rose's compulsion to harbour secrets infuriated her family.

'Upset. About what?'

Rose drove the prongs into the icing; her hand shook. 'You know,' her dry lips wrinkled as she frowned, 'I think I said something I wish wasn't going to come true. I want you to be happy. All of you.'

'We are, Gran,' Rebecca said.

Naomi kissed Rose's forehead. 'Don't you worry, Gran. We're all big grown up girls now and can look after ourselves. You enjoy your birthday cake and, when you're ready, we'll put on the TV and you can pick a show or film.'

Rose's wan expression turned pink. She was easily satisfied. 'That would be lovely.'

Naomi returned to the sofa. She wished Rose had forgotten what she'd said over the cake, because Frederick, whoever the bloke was, had an air of misfortune about him. The last thing she needed was bad luck.

Rebecca returned from the kitchen where she'd deposited the crockery. She clapped her hands and jolted Naomi out of her daydreams. 'I brought some DVDs with me – how about a musical?'

Rose picked *Enchanted*.

Leia whispered in Naomi's ear, 'More fairy tales.'

'Don't ruin things, Leia,' Naomi snapped, annoyed by Leia's ability to dampen anyone's enthusiasm. 'Sometimes real-life experiences are disappointing.'

Leia folded her arms across her chest and leaned back in her seat. Rebecca shuffled her bottom between them and aimed the remote at the television. 'Let's sing, shall we? Something we can all do without upsetting each other.'

Naomi leaned against her big sister and sighed. 'Thanks,' she said softly. 'Next year, it'll be just you and me on her birthday. In the meantime, I'm going to forget Gran ever said anything to me.'

'You do that, Naomi,' Rebecca said sympathetically. 'Concentrate on your music. It's time for you to discover your audience, isn't it?'

Naomi stared at the screen. Fat chance of that. She needed pupils to teach. *One thing at a time, Becca.*

# one
## Rebecca
## 2010

There were fruit buns, ham sandwiches and red velvet cake, Rose's favourite, which Rebecca had baked at dawn while Howard slept. Rebecca had covered the dining room table with a lacy white cloth and platters of nibbles including spicy sausages on cocktail sticks. She was pleasantly surprised by the number of mourners who'd driven to the house for the wake.

Leia, clad in black jeans and shirt with her knobbly elbows tucked in, circulated with a tray of soft drinks and duly slipped something alcoholic in hers, glancing sideways a couple of times as she poured. Rebecca had noticed and said nothing. She yearned for a drop of vodka in her orange juice. Instead of succumbing, she sustained her sobriety out of necessity.

Her father, who'd survived the service at the crematorium with his eyes drowning in grief, held a cup of cold coffee in one hand and an untouched flapjack in the other, staring out the window at the half-constructed pool house. Rebecca hoped the builders finished it by the time the baby was due. Howard joked about using it as a birthing pool. The thought of giving birth brought with it bursts of anxiety. The fuss and indignity of labour with its long hours of panting and pushing filled her with dread more so than the pain. She'd told the midwife she wanted the whole package: epidural and gas and no birthing pool. She'd rather keep some clothes on.

Nancy, Rose's unflappable daughter-in-law, dished out unremarkable platitudes to the gathering with as much sympathy as she could muster. She and Rose had never seen eye-to-eye. At least they'd maintain civility. Sometimes Rebecca wondered if her mother had forced her husband to leave England to escape Rose. A wicked thought, and unlikely given Nancy had had to re-create her career from scratch. Nancy passed close to Paul and handed him another tissue, something she'd not required herself during the funeral service.

Rose had wanted a humanist funeral, according to Leia, who previously hadn't expressed a jot of interest in how Rose wanted to be packaged and sent off into the next world. Something had happened to Leia on the day of Rose's death and it had left her unusually withdrawn and reflective. However, the tears had dried up, and she had embraced black clothing and refused to acknowledge the extraordinary timing of her visit coinciding with Rose's passing.

With Leia already in the country – she'd been alone with Rose when she'd died of her aneurysm – the three of them had aired the differing options over a meal cooked by Rebecca. Howard had escaped into his study when their voices grew heated. Having struggled to book last minute flights, Paul and Nancy hadn't arrived, leaving the decision-making to the sisters. Rebecca was sure the funeral was supposed to be Church of England, and Naomi insisted it should be pagan, or something spiritual with plenty of music.

The humanist viewpoint, brought up by Leia, reflected her scientific slant on life. Nothing happened after death, there was no hereafter, and Rose, with her no-nonsense approach to life, wanted nothing said at her funeral other than a few thank-yous.

'But she gave Granddad a church funeral,' Rebecca said.

'Because his mother, according to Dad, wanted it. Made her promise it.' Leia quaffed the Barolo like water, further annoying Rebecca. She slid the bottle out of her sister's reach.

Naomi wore a dejected expression. 'What if there's more than one way to find God?' she said quietly, picking at her food. 'Any god.' As usual she sought the middle ground.

'Quite,' said Rebecca. 'Which includes Jesus, so why not stick with tradition.'

Leia spluttered. 'Oh please. It does not.'

'Why didn't she specify the details in her will?' Naomi asked, her face painfully white. She clutched a napkin into a ball.

'Her will asked for her house and contents to be sold and given to charity,' said Rebecca. 'It wasn't drawn up by me.' The solicitor was based in Peterborough and as old as Rose.

'Can't we just skip over the words and songs.' Leia leaned over the table and snatched the bottle back. 'Keep it short and sweet.'

With Leia hogging the wine, Rebecca retrieved the bottle once again. 'What about everyone else who'll be turning up? Mum and Dad. Her friends. Those strange cousins from Scotland that she talks about but rarely meets. They'll be coming down.'

The notorious Scottish second cousins had descended for Rebecca's wedding and drank everyone under the table. She'd wished she'd not invited them, although Howard hadn't complained; they'd brought a single malt in a casket.

'They're not really Scottish,' Naomi said. 'They just migrated north.'

'Does it matter?' Leia scowled, spinning her plate around on the placemat. 'Do people really care?'

Rebecca gasped, wrenched the plate out of Leia's hands and put it next to the nearly empty wine bottle – it was her favourite tipple and she wanted more than anything to down the whole lot. 'Yes, most people do, Leia. Please try. We're saying goodbye to a special person in our lives.'

'I didn't mean the funeral. I mean the religious stuff,' said Leia indignantly. Her porcelain skin seemed stretched thinly over her cheekbones. There were shadows under her eyes. Had she slept much over the last couple of weeks? Leia wasn't as robust or as insensitive as she liked to pretend, neither was she a superhuman. The paramedics had tried and failed to resuscitate Rose, according to Leia, who wasn't a proper doctor. However, the family didn't blame her; nobody had said a thing. An aneurysm was impossible to detect, and Leia's limited clinical experience had no bearing on the outcome. Rebecca had reiterated this fact to Leia several times. Leia denied it was the reason for her outbursts and bouts of tears.

'Can we please stop arguing.' Naomi rubbed her watery eyes. 'Why can't we just do a little of everything? A hymn, she always liked "Morning has Broken"; I heard her humming it once. We could light a candle instead of a prayer – we can say silent ones to ourselves, then Rebecca can read a eulogy.'

'Me?' Rebecca nearly dropped the plate. 'You know I don't like public speaking.'

'Don't look at me,' muttered Leia. 'I can give a conference paper, but speaking from the heart…'

'Dad can't, he's far too upset,' Naomi said.

'You do it then.' Leia swivelled on her seat and folded her arms across her chest.

Naomi shook her head. 'I'm going to play something on my flute, a bagatelle. Something jolly to send her off to … the other place.'

'Oh, that's sweet of you.' Rebecca patted Naomi's hand. 'Look, I'll ask somebody else to do it. What about somebody from that art group she attended? Or the vicar might know someone. She might not have gone to church regularly but she helped do the flower arranging now and again. There has to be somebody who knew her well enough. We can feed them a few anecdotes to help.'

A silence enveloped the gathering. A tired Rebecca was resigned to organising the whole thing. She pushed the bottle across the table and Leia emptied it into her glass.

'Good,' Rebecca murmured. She'd called Howard back into the dining room and suggested he served dessert. Such a patient man. She'd given him a loving smile and he'd stroked her warm belly.

After briefing her unflappable parents, Rebecca had deduced nobody, especially Rose, cared less what was said at the funeral and, due to its simplicity, the service pleased everyone. The unassuming pensioner who gave the eulogy turned out to be something of a revelation when it came to knowing Rose's life. Rebecca was determined to find out more about him, but he'd disappeared straight after the funeral and not appeared at the wake. She planned to ask around and find out if anyone knew where he lived, and why the vicar had suggested his name.

Satisfied there was enough food on the dining room table, Rebecca mingled with the guests. Entering the L-shaped sitting room, she spotted the clan of cousins parked in one corner, talking softly. Unlike her wedding, when they'd been rowdy, they had offered polite commiserations at the crematorium and occupied a long line of chairs at the back. Being the descendants of Rose's uncle, they had come out of respect for Paul.

Across the room, huddled in an armchair with a humped back, was Naomi. Her eyes still weepy, she clutched her hands into a prayer grasp and stared at the cold fireplace. Rose's departure had hit her hard. Behind her, wearing a streamlined black suit and tie, was her boyfriend, Kyle, with his usual spiky hair flattened over his forehead. Tentatively, he touched her shoulder and squeezed it. His supply of tenderness sapped, he stepped back and perched his bottom on the windowsill, seemingly lost as to what to do to console her.

Rebecca failed to isolate what it is what about Kyle that warranted her disapproval. He wasn't uncouth or slovenly; he was slick and facile – the up and coming gaming enthusiast who couldn't decide if he wanted to critique computer games or design them and instead had found a niche market making review videos, which she considered such a waste of an education. He needed to carve out a career because Naomi, having just completed her music degree, was hardly going to pay a mortgage with her teaching. Until that day came when Naomi realised the generous potential she harboured, Kyle was supposed to be the rock in her life, like Howard. Rebecca maintained an expression of neutrality. Kyle hardly ever spoke to Rebecca and avoided her parents, so she had no opportunity to pin him down. In any case, a full assault on the young man wasn't appropriate at a funeral.

Naomi's shoulders shuddered as another wave of tears trickled down her face. Before Rebecca could intercede with a box of tissues, Kyle helped her to feet and whisked her away to the dining room to coax her into eating.

Continuing her circuit, Rebecca arrived in the kitchen, her favourite room and one she'd designed herself and had fastidiously overseen in its construction. The room was solely occupied by a ginger-haired woman in sensible heels washing up dishes in the sink. Rebecca hurried forward.

'You don't have to, we've a dishwasher,' she said.

The woman turned, sopping dishcloth in one hand. 'I don't mind. I like to keep busy. I used to work as a school dinner lady.'

Her rosy cheeks were mottled and slightly wrinkled, but otherwise, she had an attractive face.

'I'm sorry, I can't remember your name.' Rebecca had tried hard to individually welcome everyone at the crematorium. The generous turnout had surprised her. Rose had left a legacy of kindness that had touched many, including acquaintances from her childhood, the street she and Frank had lived in for decades, and the wider community of the small town. Even her old nursing colleagues had read the obituary in the newspaper and come to say farewell.

'I'm Barbara Charnwood, Rose's neighbour. I live opposite.' Barbara held out her wet hand and Rebecca graciously shook it. A fan of soapy suds sprayed outward. 'Oh, I am sorry, I've made you wet.' She pointed at Rebecca's prominent bump. 'Due soon?'

Rebecca groaned. 'You'd think. But no, three months.'

'I never had kids. Couldn't, you see.' She held up her hand. 'Don't go giving me a pity party. I've been blessed in many other ways.'

'Rose would have appreciated your help. But you don't need to.' Rebecca passed her a tea towel.

'We both lost our husbands within a few months of each other.' Barbara dried her hands. The bones of her knuckles were swollen and the skin hung loose on the backs of her hands. The rings on her fingers contained clusters of diamonds. Barbara's clothes were of exceptional quality, too. Rose's neighbourhood wasn't that well-off.

Barbara followed her gaze. 'Good fortune comes to those who wait.' She grinned.

Rebecca blinked. 'I'm sorry?' The lucky expression echoed in her head, awakening other thoughts, other sayings. 'Did something miraculous happen to you?'

'You could say that. Why don't I tell you? Let's go sit in the sun outside, and I'll tell you all about your lovely grandmother and how she helped old Babs.'

'Babs?' Rebecca was convinced she was remembering it correctly. She collected her wits, trying not to appear overly curious. For a few minutes, she'd ignore her guests and rely on her sisters and parents to play host. Howard, who tolerated social gatherings, could hold the fort while she and Babs chatted. She appreciated the privacy offered by sitting outdoors, although before crossing the threshold of the door she had to take a few deep breaths. At least the cursed affliction hadn't trouble her much recently.

Outside on the swing bench, sheltering under its canopy shade, Barbara began her story. As Rebecca listened, she closed her eyes, clasped her hands together, as if praying that what she was about to hear would finally prove that her faith in Rose was warranted. She overlaid Bab's voice with Rose's lyrical one and, gradually, that was all she heard. The tale ceased to belong to Barbara and it became Rose's, which seemed sweet justice, since Rose had anticipated it.

# Babs will get her numbers right and win a fortune.

Rose often waved at Babs through her bay window, and if Frank was in the front garden, he shouted a greeting across the street to Babs as she swept the leaves off her driveway. But after the death of her husband, Babs shut herself away. Neither Rose nor Frank thought it healthy for the widow. It took several months of gentle persuasion to convince her to come over for a cup of tea. Frank offered to mow the overgrown meadow at the back of her house. Rose lent Babs her collection of musicals on DVDs, and passed on her favourite cake recipes and discarded cookery magazines.

Gradually, Babs accepted their help and explained she worried about money. Her husband's company had only paid her a frugal pension. Frank suggested she consult a solicitor because excessive workload might have contributed to Phil's heart attacks, especially successive ones.

Babs, however, confessed to Rose with a soggy tissue crushed into her palm that her husband had drank a little too much and had gambled a significant proportion of his savings on horses and other things.

'He played the pools every week, the slot machines, and when he said he was going for a walk in the park, I knew he detoured to the bookies. I'm surprised he managed to keep up on the mortgage payments.'

Rose patted Babs's bony hand. 'He could have done better, dearie, but if he didn't want help, what could you do?'

'I should have got a job. But I've no qualifications. I left school with one O Level in domestic science. I'm wondering if anyone wants alterations doing on their clothes. Or curtains. Do you think I could advertise in the local press and find some work that way?' Babs's heavily-lined curtains were homemade and she'd hand-stitched the covers of her embroidered cushions. She'd sewed her summer dresses using her own designs and collected the leftover scraps to make every quilt in the house.

'You could try,' Rose said, unsure if anyone wanted their trousers turned up or curtains adjusted. Probably not these days when tailor-made curtains were the norm and clothes came in all manner of sizes.

A few weeks later Babs appeared on Rose's doorstep, her sharp eyes sparkling. 'I've got a job at St Winfred's primary school. I'm a dinner lady and I'm helping with the costumes for the nativity play.'

'Good for you.' Rose welcomed her in.

'No Frank?' Babs joined Rose in the kitchen where a lemon drizzle cake sat on the rack waiting for Frank and his sweet tooth. Babs licked her lips.

'He's refereeing a footie match at the playing fields.' Rose had tried hard to convince Frank not to take up the hobby, but he'd been adamant that she'd been mistaken about what she'd heard and that she should try to extract more clarity when she blew out the candles. But Rose was quite aware that what she'd told him a decade ago was perfectly accurate.

Babs chatted away incessantly, ignoring pale-faced Rose, who repeatedly checked the clock on the kitchen wall.

'He should be home by now.' Rose almost missed Babs's other news.

'I'm playing the pools. I know it's daft, but I really find it therapeutic, like I'm making a connection to Phil. It's only a few pounds – can't do any harm, can it?' Babs stirred her tea and nibbled on a slice of lemon drizzle. 'Rose? Are you alright?'

The policeman knocked on the door two minutes later and broke the news. 'I'm so sorry, Mrs Liddell. The first aider tried CPR, so did the paramedic, but it seems his heart was too weak.'

Babs held Rose's trembling hand in hers. 'It's been so hot today, hasn't it? All that running around…' Her voice tapered into a tiny murmur at the back of Rose's mind.

Over the next few weeks, as the turmoil of losing her husband swept Rose into a dismal place, it was Babs's turn to help her. While Rose's son and daughter-in-law did the best that they could, they weren't there when Rose woke at the crack of dawn to an empty house and a cold oven. She couldn't face baking anything, so Babs brought around muffins and flapjacks; small offerings to keep her from wasting away.

The two women learnt how to cope, to share their fears and deal with the lonely anniversaries and those little loving memories that slipped in when they least expected them.

'The pools haven't paid out a thing,' Babs announced on the day of her wedding anniversary and a year after Frank's untimely death. 'So I bought a lottery ticket. It's a rollover week.'

Rose smiled. 'I think you've picked the right one today.'

'You and your optimism. I wish I could believe in fate the same way you do.' Babs returned to her house across the street to watch Launcelot deliver the winning numbers.

Rose waited for a few days and heard nothing. A handful strangers came and went at Babs's house, including a man in a smart suit carrying a black suitcase. Babs kept the curtains drawn throughout his visit as if something profane or audacious might be happening behind them. Rose knew it wasn't anything that terrible, but she felt sorry for Babs. Money wasn't everything and it wouldn't necessarily heal Babs. But it might help if Babs used it wisely. Rose lay awake at night trying to think of how to help her friend and neighbour.

The following weekend, a strangely stiff-backed Babs appeared at her door. 'I've resigned from the school job.' She chewed nervously on her lip and declined the tea and cake on offer.

'I don't know what to do, Rose.' Babs battered away the tears that were forming. 'I can't get my head around it. What am I going to do with all this money? I have no children. A couple of cousins somewhere. Do you think they'll pester me? Or should I just give them some money and hope they'll leave me be?'

Rose gasped. 'You're talking millions, aren't you? Not thousands.'

Babs blinked a few tears away and nodded. 'I don't want to sell my house. These advisors say I should sell and move. Phil is still there with me. They say I should invest in funds. I've told them no press, no publicity.'

'That's for the best, isn't it?'

'I'm not telling anyone else. Not yet. Please say nothing, Rose. I don't want Tracy next door and that ghastly husband of hers stalking me. They say people will beg for money off me.' Babs dug into her handbag and retrieved a handkerchief. 'I never thought I'd feel like this. Miserable and worried. I should have stuck to the pools.'

'You just need time, dearie,' Rose said. 'Like you did after Phil passed on.' And Frank too. She was starting to cope much better now that she'd removed a few of his things from the wardrobes and shelves. While Babs liked mementos, Rose wasn't as keen.

A couple of days later, Rose posted some holiday brochures through Babs's letterbox with a note suggesting she might escape and find herself someplace where nobody knew her humble origins. Babs often lamented the fact Phil hated travelling abroad. 'Splash out and treat yourself to something exotic,' Rose wrote on the note.

Rose wasn't sure if Babs would really do it, but she did. She asked Rose to keep an eye on her house while she went first to Spain then Italy. The travel was extended to include Morocco, followed by a safari in Kenya. She returned with rosy cheeks, a fresh outlook on life and a string of little pearls that she insisted Rose have as a thank you present.

'I'm going to give some money away. I visited this orphanage in Kenya and I want to do something for those poor kids. I'm going to extend this house into the back garden and stay put. Why should I move? I like living here.' Babs stabbed enthusiastically at the chocolate cake with a fork.

'Sounds… admirable,' Rose said.

'I'm going to India to see what I can do to help those women stuck in sweat shops.'

From the front window, Rose watched the house across the road expand and swallow up half the garden. The driveway was resurfaced, the privet hedge trimmed and the curtains replaced with new ones that came from some posh department store in London.

The transformation continued for a year and, throughout, Babs travelled, until eventually she turned up on Rose's doorstep.

'I'm back,' she sang, wearing an elegant dress, her face glowing with the remembrance of some hot climate.

'Come in.' Rose ushered her into the sitting room.

Babs halted on the threshold. 'You've got a visitor—'

'Don't mind Neil. He's an old school friend. Why don't you sit down there,' Rose pointed at the sofa, 'and I'll go fetch the tea. Or coffee, isn't that what you prefer these days, Neil?'

Rose hummed to herself in the kitchen. She had a good feeling about Babs and Neil. She hated how things had turned out for Neil and wished she'd been able to warn him, but sometimes what she heard whispering in her head when she blew out the candle didn't make much sense. With Neil, it had been particularly vague.

# two

## Rebecca

The swing rocked gently to and fro, like a pendulum. Rebecca opened her eyes. The seat tipped back and the warmth of the sun swept across her face. Although Barbara had finished telling her tale, Rose's words continued to echo in Rebecca's mind as if the story wasn't quite complete, which was probably true. Over the years, Rose would have accumulated many fragmented stories that matched the things she had heard. If Rose had kept records, she had said nothing to anyone or even hinted at their existence. According to Paul, the cupboards in the house were almost bare; stripped of clutter and ready for the next phase. The clearance company engaged to finish the task were delighted.

Rebecca was certain that Barbara's account referred to an entry in the notebook hidden in her bedroom. She itched to run upstairs, find it and read the things she'd written down all those years ago when she was a young girl and barely able to join her letters together.

'She was a good friend,' Barbara said softly, staring over the heads of the roses to the pile of bricks waiting to be turned into a pool house. 'You're busy here,' she said, pointing to them.

'Yes,' Rebecca said. 'So much has happened since we moved in three months ago and we're trying to renovate some of the rooms. It's a bit of a mess. It's such a big house compared to our flat in Cambridge.'

'I couldn't move. I'm happy where I am.'

Rebecca pressed her feet into the patio slab and the swing froze. 'Barbara, the man you met in Rose's house is the same Neil who gave the eulogy, isn't he?'

She smiled. 'Yes. The very same.'

Before the funeral service, Paul had spoken to Neil over the telephone, giving him facts and dates, significant moments in Rose's life. Neil had then painted those strokes into an affectionate portrait of Rose by adding extra pieces of information from his own experiences.

'He didn't come back here,' Rebecca said.

'No, he's not one for mixing socially. He was very happy to talk about Rose and wish her peace, but he's not going to sit and eat sandwiches.' Barbara checked her wristwatch. 'My taxi will be here shortly.'

'You came all this way by taxi?'

Barbara's eyes twinkled like the diamonds on her fingers. 'It's hardly an inconvenience. I go everywhere by taxi.'

'Would you mind if we stay in contact? I'd like to meet Neil again. I rushed back here to set up the food and never got to say thank you. I didn't realise he wasn't coming.'

'I'll ask him,' Barbara replied. A gentle smile creased her face. 'It was lovely talking to you. I'm so glad I had the chance to tell you my little story. It's bothered for me for some time that her family didn't know how she helped me. She was precious.'

'Yes,' Rebecca murmured. 'She was.'

They walked to the front of the house and there on the drive was a private car with blacked out windows and a chauffeur – not really a taxi. Rebecca accepted a kiss on the cheek and waved Barbara goodbye.

An hour later, the tick tock of the mantel clock in the sitting room was discernible; most of the mourners had departed with comfortably full stomachs and their reminisces of Rose's gentle life completed. Rebecca wondered how many of those often humorous anecdotes and touching accounts had been foretold by her visionary grandmother. No, not visionary. Rose frequently like to correct; she heard things.

Naomi left clutching Kyle's hand. She refused the comfort of her parents – she'd adapted to not needing it. But Rebecca doubted Kyle was an adequate substitute. Naomi's need for companionship hinged on astute masculinity, something that her sisters couldn't provide. However, two-dimensional Kyle lacked it, too; he allowed Naomi to sink far below her potential. Musicality was her innate gift and Rebecca believed it hadn't been fully exploited by her overly cautious sister.

Leia helped tidy up. 'It's a bit like cleaning up the lab after the undergrads have trashed it.' She mopped the surfaces down with a disinfectant wipe. 'Do you want me to stay?'

'Oh, gracious, no. If you want to take Mum and Dad back to the hotel, then that's fine. Howard is ferrying a few to the train station.' Leia had driven her parents across from Cambridge in a hire car. The three of them preferred the hotel to Rebecca's slightly chaotic house with its walls stripped of paper and a partially functional bathroom.

Saying goodbye with nearly dry eyes and cracked lips, Paul hugged Rebecca to his chest, almost crushing the bump. 'Dear Becca, thank you.' The gymnastic baby kicked back.

Her mother's maudlin embrace, the kind that ended before it began, was due to jet-lag, Rebecca generously assumed. Nancy had left Boston in a middle of a crucial project. 'Not a very convenient time. You would have thought Rose could have warned us,' her mother half-heartedly chuckled. Nobody joined in.

With the house finally empty, Rebecca left the stacks of dirty dishes in the kitchen and hurried up the stairs; Babs' story required immediate attention. Rebecca's destination was the antique oak dressing table in the bay window of her bedroom. Perched on the little velvet topped stool, she opened the lowest drawer. Inside, buried beneath a heap of monogrammed handkerchiefs that had belonged to her grandfather, was the old school exercise book with its tatty blue cover and lined pages.

Each page carried a headline; one of Rose's premonitions, carefully recorded underneath the year. Always the same day, naturally, June the first. The first entry was in 1990, when Rebecca had been seven years old. The handwriting was barely legible, although it had improved with time, evolving from a lopsided string of enlarged letters that failed to sit on the line into a cursive flow. Sometime around the age of ten, she'd developed a decorative style with flourishes and loops – her fountain pen and calligraphy days. With each passing year, Nancy's criticisms of Rose had heaped higher, so as a child, the reason Rebecca gave for her interest for capturing those odd sentences was suitably immature and easy to ignore.

'I'm going to write stories about them,' she'd told her parents.

Underneath each entry, a young Rebecca had speculated what her gran's sayings had meant and the research had embodied two broad assumptions, which she now realised were misleading and a waste of time and effort. The first conjecture was that Rose had predicted some important event, perhaps one that involved celebrities or politicians, and certainly nobody Rose knew. With hindsight, such a thing seemed ludicrous, especially after hearing Barbara's story, but the reasoning had to do with the family's tendency to treat Rose as a comical Nostradamus.

The second mistake was more understandable. She wanted the premonitions to be instantaneous, or at least current and traceable through newspapers and later when technology changed, retrievable via the Internet. The immediacy was a crucial anomaly, and in retrospect, terribly misplaced. Rebecca had wanted that facet to be real more than anything else.

She thumbed through the pages and found the relevant entry.

*Babs will get her numbers right and win a fortune.*

Rose had foreseen Barbara's winning lottery ticket years before it happened. She counted on her trembling fingers – ten years. The date was explicit – June the first, 1995, when Rebecca was a skinny twelve-year-old with a crush on Take That. Barbara had won the lottery in the summer of 2005. Ten years! No wonder she'd abandoned the notebook in the back of the drawer.

Rebecca tried to imagine the birthday cake and candle, the wisp of smoke and Rose's pursed lips. The trouble was all those birthdays had blurred into a montage of cakes and candles. If she hadn't written everything down verbatim, the sayings would have turned into a jumble of words. Thank goodness, she had a good memory for the written word, something she'd relied on in her work.

The preceding page was blank. Little Rebecca had drawn a huge question mark on it. In 1994 she'd missed Rose's birthday due to illness. Paul usually provided her with the prophecy when she missed a birthday, but not that time; he'd said he had forgotten it.

The need to be there on Rose's birthday and witness for herself the brief act of precognition had remained a compulsion right up to the end of her gran's life. When she was at university and unable to attend, Paul rang her, asked her to fetch a pen and paper, then without preamble told her. The small mission completed, he'd then talk about other things, usually Leia's "mishaps". In her final year of university, Rebecca acquired a fancy phone and he'd sent a text. After her parents moved to Boston, she had to make sure to be with Rose. Whether Naomi or Leia came along hadn't mattered, although she successfully twisted their arms on many occasions. With Leia also gone, she had planned to go on her own and not trouble Naomi. Except two weeks ago, Rose had failed to reach her birthday.

Rebecca never did pen any tales of her own. She wasn't sure what to write. Even at that tender age, those strange sentences didn't belong to her. It was like those invasive visions – they were always somebody else's.

Before she found out she was pregnant, she'd had a particularly stressful week at work. 'They're worse when I step outside,' she'd told Howard. 'It's like they come over invisible radio waves and sometimes from afar. I saw Dad last week writing in his journal. When I asked him how his book was going, I knew what he'd written before he told me. I can't concentrate on my cases.'

Howard had sympathised with a mutually beneficial kiss.

To some extent, the pregnancy had calmed her; something she hadn't anticipated. However, she feared that once the baby arrived she wouldn't be able to take it for walks in the park. If Howard wasn't there with her, rescuing her sanity … she dreaded the thought of losing him.

She'd never told anyone about her peculiar happenings, apart from the man she loved with a deep passion. Not a soul, not even Rose when she'd been alive. If she could pluck up the courage to tell anyone it would be Naomi. Her little sister was tolerant and less inclined to judge compared to sharp-tongued Leia, who'd gleefully recommend a good shrink and a bottle of wine. While Leia with her innate sense of scepticism refused to countenance a world of mysticism or magic, the pragmatic Naomi might just believe it possible. As for herself, Rebecca remained, for the most part, the happy housewife. Albeit one with a secret.

Back to the notebook.

* * * *

*Ludlow Palace at four o'clock is a guarantee.*

Recorded on June first, 1998, when Rebecca had been sixteen and on course to study law. She'd been on a school trip or something and had been unable to visit Rose. She'd relied on her father's recollection and concluded he had meant the castle or town and told her the wrong thing. At the time, Rebecca had conjured up a bomb scare or some other terrible crime, but nothing happened in Ludlow of any significance for days, then weeks. She'd checked the papers regularly.

Pangs of nostalgia kept her turning the pages. The next one was especially vague.

*And he tried so hard and still failed.*

1999. Ten-year-old Naomi had already demonstrated her talent for flute playing, setting her on a different path to the one Nancy had envisaged – accountancy, because Naomi had won a maths competition.

Rebecca chewed on her lip and stared out of the bedroom window at the yawning hole in the lawn. Ten years – could that time span be significant? Constant? She racked her mind for the events of 2009. She'd married Howard. Rose had her first spell in hospital for her heart problems. Leia was established in her new post at Harvard University, living with her parents and driving them crazy with her erratic lifestyle.

What else? Who had tried? Somebody close to them or a person on the fringe of Rose's life?

She returned to the kitchen and finished tidying up. Howard was due back. He never criticised her, but she felt obligated to keep on top of the housekeeping, especially as she no plans to go back to work. Once the baby arrived she'd tell the partners at her law firm.

Bending over, the canon ball weight of the baby dropped with her. She loaded the dishwasher, slowly and woefully disorganised in arrangement. The smell wasn't helpful. To her relief, Howard bounded in and tossed his keys on the worktop.

'Oi, let me do that.' He nudged her out of the way. 'Go put your feet up, love. You look awfully pale.' He began to reorganise the racks of plates.

'Do I?' She touched her cheeks; they felt flushed. 'Baby's having a good kick.'

He turned and rested his palm on the spot above her belly button. 'Wow, that's an acrobat in there.'

'Howie?'

'Mmm,' he said, returning to stacking the dishwasher.

'Do you remember last year, anything special happening or unusual?'

'To who?'

'Well, anyone we know.' She eased her bottom onto one of the kitchen stools.

'Can't think of anything. Of course, I ruined my chances of promotion, didn't I?' He snorted and dropped a spoon in the cutlery pen.

He straightened up as he recalled reporting a colleague for some dubious trade deal, believing it was the right thing to do. The man had been frogmarched out of the office. Unfortunately, Howard's promotion, which he was convinced was a shoo-in, never happened, leading him to wonder whether to change jobs.

'Yes,' Rebecca said, the word catching on a dry throat. 'You did try hard for it.'

'Damn right,' he muttered, shutting the dishwasher door. The motor whirred and there was a whoosh of water. He washed his hands in the sink. 'Why are you asking?'

Now wasn't the right time to tell him about the notebook. She was too tired and shocked to burden him with another Liddell revelation. She'd leave it to when the baby was safely in the rosewood crib. She planned to do it one quiet evening. The notebook would rest upon his knee and she'd explain how a young girl had discovered things that transported her beyond the realms of imagination. He should know the truth about Rose's clairvoyance; they shared everything. But not today.

'Nothing, darling. I'm going to have a bath,' she said.

'Right-ho.'

Before she reached the door, he caught up with her and took her hand, drawing her towards his mouth for a kiss.

'It went well today, didn't it?' he said, releasing her from his embrace. 'I mean, as good as these things go.'

'Yes, it did. Everyone said nice things, and I met people I'd like to get to know. I feel a connection to them because of Rose. I liked getting to know them. I don't want to be a recluse.' She tracked his thin nose until she greeted his dark eyes. He blinked, startled by her searching gaze.

'You aren't,' he said, quietly. Trying hard again, she thought, but she wasn't convinced he understood. She was a recluse. He must know by now that she was.

'I'm scared,' she whispered.

'Please, don't be. You're so strong, Becca. You can't let this thing of yours break you. I thought, you know, that you had it under control.' He looked worried; she'd made him anxious. She hated being the cause when he had so many other things to worry about at work.

She forced a smile onto her face for his benefit. Under control? Yes for now, but after the baby came? 'You're right. I'm just emotional.'

In the bath, the water lapped around the island of her risen belly. She'd confirmed two of Rose's cryptic predictions and the solution to the last had been right under her nose. She flicked a bubble with a ruby fingernail and wondered how many others were that simple to solve.

After the bath, she pored over the notebook in the sanctuary of a warm bed, sipping the hot chocolate Howard had left on the bedside table. She couldn't relax or allow her mind to settle. With the spiral bound book resting on her knees, she returned to the first page, back to 1990. Seven-year-old Rebecca had taken several attempts to spell the last word correctly. Her mother had helped her, explaining what it meant.

'Why are you writing it down?' Nancy had asked.

'Because Gran asked me to.' Had she? Maybe she had; Rebecca couldn't remember, but she did recall the tricky word.

*Poor man, framed by a terrible artist. The ignominy.*

She traced her finger along the sentence and paused at one word – artist. She clucked her tongue; what a fool she'd been to overlook him. She sat straighter and ignored the stomping foot of the baby. The connection to Neil was right there on the first page of her notebook. What had happened to Neil and when?

There was only one way to find out – go and see Barbara.

# Poor man, framed by a terrible artist.
# The ignominy

In Rose's class at school sat a small boy with coal black hair and milky skin reading a book on Picasso. His name was Neil and he'd rather read than talk to the other children. He excelled at writing, loved history, but cared little about maths or science. He stared glumly out the window during geography and when he should be studying French, he doodled on the corner of his exercise book. The only time he seemed to come out of his shell was during art lessons.

An accomplished mimic, he had an eagle's eye for detail and put it to good use. The teacher was impressed and encouraged him to continue with art after he left school and went to college. He wasn't especially keen, finding the hustle and bustle of student life painful and relentless. However, he excelled at the subject and undertook a second degree in art history. After graduating with a first-class degree, he travelled to several European cities, and met Carlos in Madrid. The two men fell in love.

For twenty years, he lived beneath Carlos's atelier and, rather than paint or draw, he bought and sold the produce of other local artists. Good things don't last forever, and nor does young love. With Neil losing interest in making art and preferring to deal in it, the couple drifted apart and accepted that they wanted different things in life. Neil preferred the excitement of a rising bank balance; Carlos lived in a mess of acrylic paints and brushes.

Returning to London in 1984, Neil set up his business and was quickly approached by a man with reputable credentials and deep pockets. After a swift sale, Neil's confidence grew; he was in the right place. Wealthy businessmen invested in the artwork as an alternative to stock and shares for long term investments.

Neil fed their hunger by hunting across Europe and locating unusual artwork. Those busy years consolidated his reputation.

It was Carlos who told him about a rare impressionist painting in the house of a retired spinster with growing debts. Neil snapped up the picture, buying it significantly below its value and sold it to his hungry banker at an inflated amount. Now he could relax a little and spend some time painting and reading. He even dated a few men, hoping to re-kindle the cold hearth of his heart. None of them replaced Carlos.

Drawn back into the game of buying and selling, the lure of money was irresistible. The contacts he made during the 1990s dragged him into a murkier world. However, he convinced himself that he had never crossed the threshold into full-blown criminal activities. Or so he thought.

After a few lucrative deals involving Medieval pieces of dubious providence, he fell for the charms of Carlos once again. His friend came to visit during the millennium year. An unexpected reunion and full of promise, Carlos was effervescent with excitement.

'This one is a cubist—'

Neil wasn't so sure. He gave Carlos the benefit of the doubt, which proved to be a poor decision. The documents seemed too good to be true; the exhibition's stamp on the back of the frame a little fresh perhaps; the brush strokes… well, he couldn't quite pin down what was wrong with them, but they were a reasonable match to another work by the same artist and that particular picture hung in a national gallery.

With Carlos's encouragement, Neil arranged the deal. He sold it to a twitchy man who owned a gallery and he in turn shifted it on again to a Russian. Then Carlos suddenly disappeared. A cold shivery sweat clung to Neil's back in those dark hours of remorse and anger, and an ominous wave of nausea filled his empty belly.

The special detectives from the serious fraud squad arrived the next day. They'd watched the deal from afar, ready to pounce. Neil accepted his stupidity; he'd not paid enough attention to the nature of his clients. The art world was rather notorious for laundering money. The cash used to buy the picture was dirty and once it came out the other end in the hands of the Russian it was clean. What truly upset Neil was the accusation of forgery.

The police took one look at his mimicking skills, something of a hobby he pleaded, and they charged him with forging the painting. Neil, through his lawyer, tried to trace Carlos, but Carlos had vanished. Bitter at the betrayal, and overcome with depression, Neil pleaded guilty. He pieced it all together while on remand: not only had Carlos painted the picture, during his abrupt visit, he left behind evidence in Neil's small studio: paints, canvas, pieces of wooden frames.

The judge was surprisingly sympathetic and showed some pity. The sentence could have been much worse, and prison wasn't as hellish as Neil feared. He was given books to read, a cell which he shared with another quiet individual who'd committed some other white-collar crime, and when he proved he wasn't any trouble, they let him give art lessons to the other prisoners.

Leaving prison after six years was the real soul crushing moment in his life. He had nothing left – no home, no business and no friends. He struggled to find work and, as the weeks drifted into months, he frequently wondered if he should reach out to Carlos and discover the truth. But Carlos's disappearance was permanent and Neil had no money.

He moved out of London to sleepy East Anglia and for a while lived in a caravan in a farmer's field. With his nerves nearly crippled by depression and anxiety, he lit a match one evening and came close to burning himself and caravan down. The local farmer, who had noticed the decline in his health, suggested giving a talk to his wife's art appreciation group in the village hall.

Neil arrived at the hall next to the parish church with no idea what to say. Ashamed, he nearly left, all too aware of his inadequacies. But on the way out, he bumped into the farmer's wife.

'Neil, love, you look frozen. Come in. There's plenty of cake and tea.' She chivvied him through the door and the lure of food assisted her.

He was hungry, always. The cake smelt delicious. Casting aside his fears, he spoke about his life. The rise and fall of an art dealer, he called his talk, which he presented without notes. At the end, the small gathering applauded and raised their hands for questions. Their generosity astounded Neil.

They weren't just farmers' wives. There were teachers, a retired pharmacist, the local GP, and a magistrate, which horrified Neil until the elderly gentleman spoke to him afterwards and agreed that it was a setup. There was a familiar face too – the woman with the weeping strands of hair and pinched nose. He couldn't put a name to her. She stared at him, throughout his presentation.

She'd brought the cake, and, after cutting him a slice, she handed it to him on a paper plate. 'You remember me, don't you, Neil?'

'I think so,' he said. 'But I can't think where.'

'School. Class 4A. You'd sit in the corner reading. You were very shy back then, too.'

The memory slotted into place. 'Rosemary? Rosie?'

'Rose, these days.' She smiled, then slowly allowed it to dissipate. 'I'm sorry about what happened to you.'

Neil shrugged. 'It's done.'

'And now you have so little. You have such talent, though. People of talent shouldn't hide away, not if they can share it. Why don't you come back and teach a few of us? Some of us like to do watercolours. Moira over there, the one with the dark hair, does damn fine charcoal sketches.'

'I don't know…' He had enjoyed teaching the prisoners, but he had no qualifications.

'Just us,' she repeated. 'A few of my friends. We do nice cake.'

She persuaded him and the following week, he gave a class on Turner and it went down well. His reputation grew, and he was invited to other groups in the area. He sold a few pictures, too.

The money was enough for a deposit on a small one-bedroom flat. Life was returning to his blood and he put on weight. By now, his celibacy was unbreakable. Carlos had stolen his heart away to some distant place; he couldn't trust any man anymore, maybe anyone. Or so he thought.

Rose invited him to her house. While he examined the wedding photograph on the bookshelf, he found out Rose had recently lost her husband.

'I'm sorry.' He shifted uncomfortably on the sofa, wondering if this was some kind of date. 'You know, I should tell you, that...' He tried to squeeze the word out.

'That you're gay?' she said. 'Of course. Please don't worry, your secret is safe.'

'I'm not ashamed of my sexuality. In prison, I had to hide it. But it was never a secret.' He maintained a pride in some things.

'Then, let's be friends.' The doorbell rang. 'That will be Babs. She lives across the road. Lost her husband too. We can all be friends.'

Neil wasn't sure it would work out so easily, but perhaps he wasn't the best judge of people. With Rose's confidence infecting him, he rose to greet the rosy-cheeked Babs and noted her dress was of good quality, her shoes expensive and her hair arranged immaculately. Money still charmed Neil, as it did Babs.

They never married. Neither of them was interested in that kind of relationship. Companions was how Rose described them. They travelled together every year for an extended period. Babs provided the finances and Neil brought along his knowledge. The benefits were mutual: Babs discovered education late in life, while Neil found peace and a purpose that suited his needs.

Rose had solved a mystery. Neil was her poor man, framed by an artist and cheated by a lover.

# three

## Rebecca

Barbara welcomed Rebecca into her home two days after the funeral. Rebecca had provided no reason for her visit, other than she wanted to know more about Rose and her friends, especially Neil, who it turned out lived with Barbara. The conversation began with the cat, Samwise. Barbara had been going across the road to feed him. However, with the clearance company waiting in the wings to strike, the cat needed a new home. Barbara had volunteered to adopt him.

'The poor chap will have to go in the cattery when we travel, won't he, Neil?'

Neil stroked Samwise's back and a puff of ginger dander floated away. 'He's probably not got long left.'

Rebecca waited, masking her impatience, as the couple talked about their next holiday destination: China.

'I'm fascinated by their brush strokes,' said Neil.

The remark provided Rebecca the opportunity to broach the subject of his life as an artist. He happily chatted, speaking with a soft, undulating voice accompanied by the odd prolonged pause, as if he was re-living things vividly. By the time he finished, Rebecca wished he had known what Rose had said when she blew out her birthday candle in 1990.

'You went to prison in 2000?' Rebecca asked.

'Yes. Came out in 2006.'

Wisps of white hair criss-crossed his forehead. He brushed them aside, unfazed by Rebecca's questions. Finding Neil had proved easier than she'd anticipated.

'Then you met my grandmother again?'

'Yes. I got involved in her art class at the church hall.'

That explained how the vicar knew him. Things were slotting into place. The moment she'd stepped through the door of Barbara's modest house and saw Neil's paintings lining the walls, she knew she'd found "the artist". The charming couple sat side by side on the brocade sofa, although their styles clashed. Babs wore a floral-patterned dress with a gold buckle belt and puffed sleeves which was in stark contrast to Neil's checked shirt and jeans. While Barbara's skin was stretched smoothly over her cheekbones, Neil had narrow cheeks, aged and leathery after many years of living in Spain's dry heat. He interwove his long fingers into a knot on his lap and occasionally they twitched, especially when he spoke about life in prison.

His mannerisms were not effeminate in any way; there was nothing to suggest that his heart would never bend towards Barbara in the way perhaps she wanted. But given their ten years of co-habiting, they'd come to some arrangement that worked. Her house and money had re-established his status as an upstanding member of society and, in return, Neil chaperoned her around the globe. Rebecca envied them, the freedom to go anywhere without the hindrance of responsibilities.

Barbara, who'd been pottering in the background pouring out the tea and arranging biscuits on what looked like a silver plate, chipped in with a question. 'Are the dates important?'

'Neil.' Rebecca leaned forward, her bump hampering her, and accepted another refill of her teacup. 'Do you often wonder if, if you'd known about Carlos's betrayal, you would have changed anything, perhaps avoided dealing with certain people?' She wasn't sure if she was making sense to him.

He pursed his lips. 'You mean, changing the course of history, like a time machine?'

Barbara chuckled. 'Now, Rose was a big fan of Doctor Who. Loved the idea of going back and forward in time.'

Rebecca hadn't known. It saddened her to think of her gifted gran, unable to influence or alter the course of the future she'd predicated.

'I suppose,' she said.

Neil's face brightened. 'Fascinating,' he said. 'But it's something of a paradox. If I knew what would happen with me and Carlos, the forgery, it wouldn't be the future anyway, just one possibility among others. That's why the Doctor never made sense to me. I never did like science fiction.'

'Rose had an uncanny ability to bring people together,' said Barbara. 'We're very grateful to her.'

Rebecca nodded. But had all of Rose's birthday babbles resulted in happy endings? She was determined to find out. Now that she had Neil and Babs's story straight, she knew that what Rose heard in her head were prophecies that took years to come true. Ten years, it seemed. So all she had to do was focus on that ten year gap and the people Rose knew or had known at some point in her life.

It sounded easy, but it wasn't; the time delays had yet to fully resolve themselves and Rose had met so many people through her line of work in the nursing home. Especially troubling was knowing that it might be a few years before a Frederick appeared on the scene. And whose scene in particular? She really hoped it wouldn't involve Naomi, because life was complicated enough.

\* \* \* \*

Between giving birth to her two children, saddling herself with the unending worry of motherhood, she spent four years seeking out people who were connected to Rose, at least those that were still alive. From them, she pieced together a few stories that were possible solutions.

The one about Ludlow Palace turned out to be the winner of the Cheltenham Races – ten years after the racing tip had been made and of little use to a bookie. The horse had been trained at Newmarket by the son of Rose's cousin, one of the Scottish gang who'd returned south.

The saddest tale was "The junction was never wide enough; what a tragedy." The accident had happened opposite the care home where Rose had once worked. A resident with dementia had wandered into the path of a car taking the tight corner too quickly. Rose had retired after she made the prediction, but she must have been alive when the accident happened a decade later. She'd never said a word to anyone, it seemed, not even a warning or a passing remark of regret. She was still fondly remembered by the staff at the home and they'd erected a plaque on the wall in her memory.

Each connection between premonition and event revealed another part of Rose's life. Unravelling Rose's past brought joy to Rebecca and alleviated some of her fears that nobody directly related to Rose was ever the "victim" of her prophecies. Although Rebecca continued to worry about Naomi, she concluded that Kyle wasn't Frederick, and how could he be? In fact, she agreed with Naomi; Rose hadn't been referring to her youngest granddaughter in the haze of the candle smoke. Her grandmother, whose old mind had altered in some way, had hallucinated as she spoke and possibly believed she was addressing somebody else and certainly not Naomi.

Rebecca was disappointed that she'd not found the answers to all of Rose's predications. With the kids growing fast, she simply hadn't the time to investigate. The notebook remained in the drawer, buried under the handkerchiefs and forgotten. Howard, aware of its existence, accepted her findings with the same mild-mannered faith he'd demonstrated when she'd revealed her own psychic trait. With Rose gone, there weren't any new ones to add to the yellowing pages, and as the years ticked by, the chances of uncovering the truth behind the remaining ones diminished.

In the meantime, she was distracted by more pressing matters.

Abruptly, when Eleanor reached school age, the visions increased in frequency. They had a tendency to stalk her, forcing her to see things. She was blinded by them, left feeling frightened and vulnerable because they gave her fresh nightmares. When Howard went on business, he hated leaving her.

When the episodes first started, years ago, she was convinced she'd hit her head and suffered a concussion. It had taken a while for her to work out she was seeing things through other people's eyes. Remote sensing, she discovered, was another form of extra sensory perception, like Rose's precognition. A gift? Not in the slightest. She had a spy network in her head and she used it to invade people's privacy, without them knowing. But for what purpose?

The random invasions into other people's space were downright frightening. She couldn't hear or touch what she saw; she might as well be watching a television show with the sound muted. If witnessing other people's viewpoints was supposed to be advantageous, it wasn't apparent why. What point was there in seeing things, sometimes events that were happening thousands of miles away, as if she was right there? Clairvoyance in any form was at best annoying and at worst terrifying. Her body responded by going cold, her limbs often froze and, for a few seconds, she was paralysed. Out on the streets, people bumped into her, cursing her stupidity, or they issued an embarrassed throaty cough. A few laughed.

As for her sisters, she had failed to see the world through their eyes; they had an aura around them, protecting them, she assumed. Rebecca hoped it remained that way, because otherwise the complications it might create would be unbearable.

She'd tried to explain her happenings, as she called them, to Howard when they'd first dated. He'd called them a funny migraine or something similar, suggesting she visited a doctor. But when she described what he alone and nobody else could see, he'd stopped scoffing. Naturally, he had also been astounded. She wondered if he was a little proud of his special wife and her secret life.

'Don't tell anyone, Becca,' he'd warned. 'They'll cart you off. And I know you're not crazy.'

Leia, being medically trained and brilliant, should have been the obvious choice to act as confidante. However, the consequences of divulging anything supernatural to the sceptic would maybe fracture their strained relationship further. Rebecca was so envious of her twin's freedoms, her exciting life and prestigious job. It was not fair, at all; she'd given up on her own career as a solicitor.

Howard's rock steady support was the reason why she'd said yes to his proposal – besides from being head over heels in love with him. However, neither of them had anticipated that those images, which replaced her own vision with flashes of somebody else's, would become more frequent and invasive, as if flicking from one TV channel to another without warning.

'I will find a way to control them,' she told him. 'They never tell me anything useful. One or two seconds of a snap shot that most of time makes absolutely no sense. And when they do, it's too late; I can't help anyone. Why choose Rose and me? Why isn't anyone else in my family afflicted?'

Howard didn't have any answers. Instead, he reached out to touch her.

Irritated by his calmness, she brushed his hand off her shoulder. 'What about the kids? I don't want them to have a crazy mum. And what if they've inherited it?'

'Try your yoga again.'

'It won't work. It's like a volcano waiting to erupt. Something is forcing these visions on me, like bad karma. What have I done wrong?'

Rediscovering the notebook had been a mistake. The pages revealed the extent of Rose's clairvoyance and, although a little trivial sometimes, those voices had visited Rose for most, if not all of her adult life, without skipping a year. But unlike her grandmother, Rebecca's visions weren't annual; they were random and intensifying. If she couldn't find a way to control them, she feared her isolation would drive her to the brink of madness.

Howard's glum face offered her no comfort.

# four

## Rebecca

## February 2018

Due to the kids' noisy request for pancakes and marshmallows, an unscheduled trip to the local supermarket was required. All the ingredients were in the cupboards, but by the time they'd gobbled up three pancakes each, Rebecca realised there wasn't a drop of milk left in the house. She packed the children off to bed.

'I'll go,' Howard said from behind the amber pages of the Financial Times.

'No, I can do this,' she said, picking up her purse. 'I'll walk.'

He lowered his newspaper to under his chin. 'Sure?' His eyebrows knotted together, showing his habitual concern.

She didn't need mollycoddling; she was a little tired of it. 'I've been fine for a month now. I'm not an epileptic, you know.'

He sighed. 'I know. It's just the way you describe these happenings of yours, you'd think you've been blinded by them.'

'Tosh. They last seconds and I'm not incapacitated. They're annoying. And, as I said, I'm fine.' She doubted her definition of fine matched his. She bent over and kissed the corner of his square forehead next to a streak of grey hair. He shook out his newspaper and disappeared inside the world of financial markets.

Fifteen minutes later, she'd nearly reached the shop when she spotted Eveline Draycott from number sixteen walking her two Cocker Spaniels on the opposite pavement.

'Hi, Rebecca.' She waved and strode past in her gym outfit, yanking on the lead attached to the two mischievous dogs. They ran her ragged, ate the Persian carpets and peed on the bathroom mat. Rebecca knew those things, because she watched the dogs from afar. She witnessed Eveline in her rubber gloves and latex catsuit clean their mess up. The woman had clothing for every occasion. If it was raining on collection day, her husband wore a striking sou'wester to put out the bins.

Rebecca smiled and waved back. The next person she met was Gerald, who went for a stroll most evenings, ostensibly to escape his wife, according to Howard, which Rebecca had to agree was right. They briefly made eye contact. Gerald flinched, his silly little rabbit nose twitching. He muttered something, possibly a greeting, or more likely 'Bugger off'. Grumpy old sod.

So far nothing unusual had happened. There were hardly any pedestrians. The streetlights illuminated the cracks in the pavement and the rainwater in the puddles. Everything was normal. She wasn't alone though; a few yards away at the end of driveways were front doors. The row of houses included a few grandiose dwellings, all neighbours who politely ignored each other, except when called upon in a crisis. Unsurprisingly, Rebecca and Howard were often at the forefront of those rescues.

The last one had involved Deidre Wilberforce and an unfortunate incident with a malfunctioning step-ladder. Unknown to Deidre, Rebecca had been right with her when she tottered on the top step and fell awkwardly. The poor woman almost died of fright when Howard appeared on the doorstep, red-faced from the sprint up the road.

'But I've not even called an ambulance. How did you know?'

The explanation was painfully pathetic and quite rightly unbelievable – Rebecca had been hanging out the washing in her garden, and heard her scream from the other side of the street. The washing part was true, the rest was a lie. Fortunately for Howard, the pain distracted Deidre from asking further awkward questions.

Deidre had fractured her wrist and returned home the next day. Rebecca graciously accepted the bunch of flowers on Howard's behalf, while saying nothing of her own involvement. As far as Rebecca was concerned, and she told Deidre the same, it was a relief to know that the neighbourhood watch functioned correctly; people continued to mind their own business.

Would any of them know she wasn't what she seemed? Probably not. Even her own family were clueless as to the reasons why she was suffering with agoraphobia.

Naomi thought Rebecca was the conventional wife, striving to tick all the boxes of motherhood and far too busy with wiping mucky chins and cooking to have a "life". If it wasn't for the fact she struggled to concentrate, Rebecca would have gone back to work six years ago. Instead, fearing she was going to achieve nothing in life, she'd set herself the goal of being good at something, and that meant being a good wife and mother. She despised herself, not because it wasn't an honourable role to perform, but because she hadn't worked damn hard for years to end up cooped up indoors armed with a mop, wooden spoon and ironing board.

She had Howard's sympathy. He sometimes had to tread carefully around her when she got into one of her dark moods. What she lacked was an empathetic ear to listen to her woes. Rose would have been the obvious choice. However, she'd left it too late to reveal her secret; she'd assumed Rose had years to go. The vacant spot in Rebecca's soul would need more than sympathy to fill the emptiness. She needed somebody who wasn't afraid of the unknown, of taking a risk.

She picked up a shopping basket. Two pints of milk. A box of free-range eggs – how she envied the hens. She added a bar of chocolate for herself. She scanned the barcodes at the self-service and paid in cash. It was as she crossed the threshold of the exit door that she came over slightly fuzzy. And cold. The brush of iciness sent goose bumps scurrying along her arms and shoulders.

The young woman smiled. Shiny white teeth. She had a glass of clear liquid in one hand and a glittery backed mobile in the other. She laughed, her glossy pink lips glinting under the lights. The man, whose eyes Rebecca had stolen, reached out and touched the back of the girl's hand.

Who was he?

Rebecca, still partially frozen in the doorway, was blocking the exit.

'Oi, don't stand there, love,' somebody shouted from behind her.

'Sorry,' she muttered, steering her blinded body forward into cool evening air.

She recognised the pub. Naomi had taken her there once when she'd visited Bury St Edmunds a few years back, a rare solo trip out to hear Naomi play in her penultimate concert. Much to Rebecca's disappointment, Naomi had given up playing concerts. The pub, she recalled, was the King's Head.

The laughter on the woman's lips died as the man stroked his hand along her wrist, touching her sleeve. The gesture was desired. The girl slowly blinked and her face started to fade.

Rebecca read her lips: 'Leave her.'

The vision abruptly ended. Kyle was the obvious suspect for the tryst. She remembered his slender fingers; neatly trimmed fingernails and hairless knuckles. She had cultivated an eye for detail.

She rested against the bicycle railings, breathing heavily. What now? Should she tell Naomi what she'd seen, call right now and ask, 'Where do you think Kyle is? Because I know he's in the pub with another woman.'

What if Naomi for one minute believed her? How would things pan out if Naomi marched into her local pub and confronted her boyfriend? Later, there would be questions – have you been spying on me, Becca? How long have you known? How did you find out? And they would tear Rebecca apart. She'd no plausible answers and even if Howard backed her up, Naomi would never believe she'd actually been with Kyle, seeing what he saw. Ludicrous. Crazy, just like Gran.

The happenings didn't always involve a head hop. Sometimes, she found herself on the ceiling, the proverbial spider, staring down at bald patches and hair buns. Or she was a lowly cat or a dog, looking up. If she did land in somebody's head, which happened rarely, it was because the connection to that person was strong; it was somebody she knew. The context was often poor and confusing, the colours blurred into a washed-out palette, similar to a dream. And like a silent movie, there were no sounds to aid her interpretation. No smells, either. If she made sense of any of these visitations, it was those related to her father, with whom she had a strong bond, even across an ocean. Her mother, who had never adapted to life with children, had less of a presence. Sometimes, she wondered if she was with Leia, because the scene was garish and fast moving, as if she was in a nightclub with strobe lighting. The company Leia kept wasn't good. It couldn't be, given the clothing worn. She worried about Leia more and more.

She never made a connection with Naomi. This seemed odd, because Rebecca had fulfilled a particular role in Naomi's life; she had to protect Naomi, an instinct that remained strong years after Naomi had left the nest Rebecca had maintained on their parents' behalf.

'Oh dear,' she murmured. 'Oh dear.' She attempted to run home, the bagged milk cartons banging against her thighs.

She rushed into the living room. 'Howie, Kyle is cheating on her.'

Howard, who'd abandoned his newspaper, ceased tapping on his iPad, and raised his eyebrows into bemused arches. 'You mean Naomi?'

She nodded. 'He's in the pub with this other woman. What should I do? I can't do anything, can I?' She slumped into the armchair with her purse and the shopping bag heaped by her feet.

'It's definitely him?'

'Oh, gosh, yes.' She pressed her hand to her mouth. Her heart continued to gallop, her palms tingled. 'This is awful, Howie.'

'And Kyle is with somebody else?' He folded his arms across his chest, clearly angry.

'Pink lipstick. Naomi doesn't wear anything like that. Kyle touched her and she said, "Leave her".' The words nearly stuck in her dry throat.

Howard rose to his feet and went to the drinks cabinet. He poured himself a whisky and another for Rebecca. 'Drink.' He held it out to her.

Rebecca took it, understanding the significance. She was to do nothing. She swallowed the burning liquid and tears pricked her eyes.

'Why me?'

He shoved the bags to one side and crouched by her legs. Taking her trembling hand, he squeezed it. 'You're a special lady and I believe you. You know I do. But you're not her guardian angel. You're nobody's angel but mine, Eleanor and Toby's. If you were to try to save everyone, where would it take you? It would screw you up.'

She rested the glass on her knee. He was right; calm, sensible Howard generally was. 'One day, I'll tell her,' she said quietly.

'But not today. If what you saw is true, then Kyle is going to leave her and she's going to find out the hard way. Better it comes from him. If she's going to feel enraged and bitter, better at him and not you.'

'It's alright.' She smiled softly. 'I know what you mean. Oh, darling. I want to be free of this affliction. I hate it. It serves no purpose other than to confine me here. Why couldn't I be normal? Or at least talented like my sisters. Naomi was playing concertos at the age of ten. Leia's giant brain—'

'You have a gift. Gifts are given for a reason, a purpose. Talents have to be nurtured, don't they? I mean, Naomi has to practise to maintain hers and Leia spends hours reading, thinking. You have to find a way of controlling yours… contain it. Then you'll be free of its constraints.'

Such wise words, almost insightful for a man of numbers, a risk taker who expected success and banked on it. But his expectations scared her. He anticipated something unachievable especially as things were worsening, getting harder to bear. She said nothing of her fears for the future.

He cocked his head to one side. 'If you want to see somebody—'

The shrink option terrified her. 'Absolutely not.' She'd declined the offer numerous times. 'I will not be turned into some experiment or spectacle. I am not a magician or a freak. Rose understood the dilemma… I wish…' She wished for many things and having Rose back was chief amongst them.

'What, darling?' He leaned closer.

'Nothing. I'm tired.'

He stood, helping her to her feet, and removed the glass from her hand. 'Tell you what. I'll make you a nice hot chocolate with the rest of this whisky shot and you go lie in bed and listen to some music.'

It wasn't a solution. But in the absence of a cure for her malady, it was the next best thing.

The call came three weeks later, the one she'd been expecting. Naomi was on her way over. Kyle had split up with her and, through the sobbing, it was apparent she intended to cry in person on her big sister's shoulders. The girl who had left nearly ten years ago was returning; Rebecca was needed once again.

By the time Naomi arrived in her kitchen with red eyes and flushed cheeks, Rebecca had made up her mind. She'd not drop one hint of what she'd seen in the pub and instead, she would try her best to stay neutral. Naomi wanted to stand on her own two feet and Rebecca had no intention of interfering in her affairs. Unless asked, of course.

# five

## Naomi

## March

Naomi gripped the steering wheel and tried hard not to imagine Kyle filling boxes with all his things, objects that once she might have considered clutter but in reality were fixtures of their life together. She'd left a list of untouchables pinned to the refrigerator, believing he would honour their agreement. If he didn't, then what little amicability that remained between them would die an abrupt death.

Her bravery with dealing with his departure didn't last long. By the time she reached Rebecca's house in Huntingdon, she had cried twice and hated herself for the duration of each mini-breakdown.

Leia called Rebecca's home "the palace". The immodest house with its five bedrooms and pool house was hidden behind neat privet hedges and a pruned curtain of fir trees. Approaching the driveway, the gate automatically swung open. She parked her humble car next to a pristine Discovery. The perfect world of Rebecca was further illustrated by the row of hanging baskets with their artistic arrangements of in-season flowers and the immaculate lawn that swept around the whole house, creating a sea of tranquil green.

Rebecca greeted Naomi at the door, swept her into her arms and squeezed her against her soft bosom. 'Oh, darling, I'm so sorry.'

The "darling" had crept into Rebecca's vocabulary in an insidious fashion; she also added "gosh" frequently and unnecessarily. Ever since Howard had moved out of general banking and into hedge funds, she'd adopted a new personality that she believed fitted the role of a high-flying investment banker's wife. Naomi envisioned Rebecca holding the most elegant dinner parties and hosting numerous charity coffee mornings. Her sister was destined for the part and had rehearsed it numerous times as a child with tea sets and dolls, forcing Naomi and Leia to participate when both of them preferred sticking their heads in a book. Naomi often though Leia was the odd one out, but thinking back over the years they'd spend under the same roof, it was always Rebecca who'd diverged from their games.

Naomi followed her into the hall, past the vase of roses, and the welcoming gallery of photographs arranged to present a stream of smiley faces. Starting at the door with the baby ones – wrapped around canvas with gentle pastel backgrounds – they continued to the kitchen door where seven-year-old Eleanor and Toby, a boisterous five-year-old with two missing teeth, hugged each other in a school photograph. Naomi dearly loved her niece and nephew, especially as she wasn't required to be anything but the doting aunt who turned up on their doorstep with sweets. When she paused to inspect the latest photographs, Rebecca cleared her throat.

'Howie has taken the kids to the park so we can talk.'

The ivory kitchen shone in the morning sunlight. Each of the flat surfaces emitted a dazzling glare that criss-crossed the room. Naomi hid in the shade by the tallest cupboard until Rebecca waved her over to the breakfast bar and an uncomfortable high stool.

Howie's absence was appreciated. Naomi had never quite got him, nor understood exactly what Rebecca saw in him. Stiff, boring and nailed to an office chair was how Leia described him, and while Naomi recognised handsomeness – especially the neat goatee beard – he lacked a flair for doing anything other than handling numbers. But he'd done well and who could blame Rebecca for enjoying the privileges of marrying a man who made money so easily. After the children were born, she'd given up work. 'How can I find joy in conveyancing and divorces after my babies have brightened up my life so much.' Naomi wondered if that implied life before kids hadn't been that thrilling with Howie or if there was some other nefarious reason why she'd jacked in a good career.

Surveying the construct of married life with its potted herbs on the windowsill and the family calendar hanging from the utility room door showing columns of predetermined activities and appointments, Naomi wasn't the slightest bit envious. Money she might covert, but not this humdrum pattern of life. When she hit the road each morning to visit a school and complete a roster of music lessons, she returned home knowing that the busy part of the day was done. Selfish perhaps, almost superficial in its lack of complexity, Naomi had the advantage of spontaneity when it came to her time. Where she went, what she did each evening wasn't dictated by children or a husband. Thinking about it, as she stirred her coffee, Kyle had often sulked when she turned down a night out.

She frowned and Rebecca, misunderstanding the gesture, reached over and patted the back of her hand. 'How are you coping?'

Naomi ignored the question. 'How did you know Howard was the one?' she asked.

Rebecca's hand slid away and circled her mug. 'I imagined being ninety and waking up to find him in bed with me. It felt good. Reassuring. We're friends first and foremost, and he's a great dad.'

There was nothing original about her answer. Spouses by default had to be friends.

'I thought Kyle was my best friend and he seemed to treat me the same.'

When Rose had died, he'd prepared her for the news by pouring a glass of her favourite red, putting the tissue box out, and holding her hand throughout the call from Leia. When Kyle was thoughtful, he was really sweet. The break-up hadn't been handled with the same delicacy.

He hunched his shoulders, as if making himself smaller lessened the impact. He didn't look at her directly. A casually constructed man, Kyle possessed an uncultivated charm blended with a boyish, almost elfin, look and yet when he spoke, he usually delivered undulating words with bright sparkles of wit. Sat on the couch in their cluttered living room – the games consoles scattered around – he made his intention clear with no preamble, no gentle build-up, and stumbled over his poor choice of words.

'I'm leaving you; I think it's for the best; you know we've been living apart for a long time.'

Was she surprised? No, that wasn't what she felt. Disappointed, definitely. She added bitter and annoyed. Kyle, with his hands clasped on his lap, exhaled an unnecessary sigh. All the tension he embodied in his stiff back evaporated within seconds of making his announcement. Perhaps this apparent display of relief was the reason she lost her temper.

Naomi had always known Kyle was a bit of lazy sod. He could have earned a degree in procrastination if any university offered one. For the early years of their co-habiting, his lassitude hadn't especially bothered her. Kyle slowed her down, kept her from racing away, hell bent on delivering some whimsical idea. They made a great team of opposing symmetry, a kind of comfortable yin and yang. She consumed energy, he emitted it by doing as little as possible. That was what she thought, now she wished she'd kicked him in the butt. Something had changed him. He'd gone out for long walks with his earpieces glued into his ears and his woolly hat pulled down to his neck.

'What have I done wrong?' she asked, staring down at him.

He sprang to his feet, but remained rooted to the spot, uncertain and awkwardly posed, hands stuffed in his pockets where he jangled the loose coins that he always kept in the depths.

'Nothing really. I mean, it's us, whatever made us stick together, it's gone.'

She knew he wanted more, but the thought of marriage still left her cold. The whole idea of being co-opted into his family gave her the creeps, especially his snarky sister and her rude friends. Naomi liked equal partnerships; independence coupled with friendship and a life that ticked over gently without the chains of wedlock. She thought she'd had it with Kyle, but he was right, they weren't a couple any longer and hadn't been for a while.

Kyle's laid back attitude, something she once found endearing, slowly evolved into an infuriating habit of disinterest in her life, especially her music. Yet, Kyle had worked to be the more affectionate half of the two of them, while she had done nothing other than give him the comforts of home, a decent sex life –

although recently something they'd paid scant attention to – and the odd joint adventure, but otherwise, he was right, they led separate lives.

'And having kids, was that an easy decision?' she asked Rebecca, who fidgeted with everything in sight, as if things weren't in their correct place or alignment.

'Remember that ragdoll I kept on my bed? You used to tease me about it.'

Yellow wool for hair and a stitched mouth, the doll had gone everywhere with Rebecca until she finished primary school. 'Leia teased you, too,' Naomi said defensively. Leia preferred Play-Doh while Naomi threaded beads onto string. The sisters weren't the best playmates.

'The moment Mum dropped that doll into my lap, when I was five years old and before you arrived, I was destined to be a mother.' She rocked her arms from side to side.

The link Rebecca had created in her mind would hardly withstand a critical psychological evaluation. Ragdolls were nothing like babies and if she'd treated it as such, it was in her mind only. The doll sat on her bed all day, if Naomi remembered correctly.

'I don't feel like that,' she said. 'Sometimes. Maybe.' Rarely, was more accurate. 'I don't go gooey near baby things.'

'Good grief, Naomi, half of my friends only came round to the idea after they met their husbands… partners,' she added belatedly.

'Kyle wants kids, or so he says. I'm not burning inside for a baby and I work with children.'

'Sure that's not putting you off, the kids in school?'

'No, not those kids, They're teenagers, mostly. Sensible kids. Their parents pay for the lessons, so if they waste my time, they must have a good reason. I've got a good pass rate when it comes to exams.'

However, structured lessons with school children was quite a contrast to the real world of kids. The more she thought about it, Kyle was the archetypal dad in the making and she'd pushed the decision away for years.

'You're a good teacher, Naomi.'

A sweet compliment, but it wasn't helping her. She bit her lip, struggling to keep her anger in check. The conversation with Kyle was fresh in her mind. 'And I asked him if he had another woman.'

Naomi thought Rebecca was unnecessarily pale given it was an obvious question to ask him. Kyle hadn't looked especially aghast at the accusation. Although, in hindsight, he'd started to sweat a little by then.

Rebecca squeezed the dishcloth and water dripped onto the floor tiles. 'He denied it?' She hurried to clean up the spillage.

'Yes. Just things not working out as he thought.' A lame excuse, in retrospect, but in character.

'Why now, I wonder.' Rebecca's neat eyebrows perched a little higher, the colour returning to her cheeks. Naomi didn't mind the curiosity. She needed to purge Kyle.

'Kyle went on and on about how I didn't appreciate him, that he's unhappy. Frankly, he wants an uneventful life. And babies,' she said, begrudgingly.

Kyle had strung more sentences together than she'd heard him speak in weeks. He had every right to want to be a father and marry, and play happy families, but she couldn't go there. When they were both fresh and hungry for each other, she'd come close to feeling broody, especially when Rebecca's firstborn had slept in her arms. Eleanor's little hands and feet were adorable and tempting. Naomi had accepted the advice of her family and they'd told her not to rush; the young Naomi, whose career as a music teacher was just beginning, shouldn't snatch to her chest the first eager man she met. She had waited too long, though. Way too long.

'Well, perhaps you're better off without Kyle then.' Rebecca pursed her lips and slurped on her coffee. She'd never taken to his hedgehog hairstyle or glib sense of humour. 'He isn't the man you thought he was,' she said, without glancing up.

Naomi slammed her mug down and the coffee spilt over her hand. She shook off the drops. 'You never liked him, so why am I not surprised by—'

'Naomi! I never told you to leave him, not once. I simply offered advice about taking your time, which you clearly did.'

'But you looked down on him.' Defending Kyle came easily, she had done it a few times with her mother. Poor Kyle, during her parents' annual visits, had hunkered down out of sight.

Rebecca used a dishcloth to remove the spots of coffee on the worktop. 'I. Did. Not. You assume I don't like him because he's not sophisticated in some way.'

'Leia didn't,' Naomi mumbled. 'Mum—'

'I can't speak for them.'

'He connects with people, young people. He knows his business. He's got over two thousand subscribers on—'

Rebecca rolled her eyes. 'I've no idea what that means, but did I ever say that was a bad thing?'

Words weren't always necessary when facial expressions revealed opinions; Rebecca wore a thin mask and Naomi saw the disappointment through it.

'He's going to a friend's house, some guy he knows. It doesn't matter anymore.'

Rebecca leaned forward. 'So why do you speak as if you're defending him? He was uncomfortable with me, us. He frequently had an excuse not to come when you visited.'

Naomi plucked at her sleeve and scowled. 'He's not exactly Howard's type.'

'And he's yours?'

Once, probably, but no longer. Right now, Kyle was clearing his things out of their house without a hint of remorse. Regret came in many guises; Naomi had yet to find a suitable form for her own regrets.

'What next?' Rebecca asked.

'I'm selling the house, I suppose.' She felt numb, tired and a little afraid. Tomorrow was bin day. Kyle sorted the recycling. He mowed the postage stamp-sized lawn, he washed her car. When the valve burst, he fixed the leaky shower and he sorted the Wi-Fi whenever it went dead. Living alone was something she'd never really done; the thought of an empty house terrified her.

'It's only your name on the deeds, isn't it?'

'He couldn't get a mortgage because he's freelance and I was the one with a regular income. But he's always paid up every month, so... I'll sell and split it fifty-fifty.'

'Where will you live?'

'I like Bury St. Edmunds. It's compact and well-connected. I might not find anywhere else that gives me everything I need. It would be nice to find somewhere that isn't a terrace.' She'd practise her flute and re-establish her connections with musical friends and groups. Out there was a community she had neglected for too long and blaming Kyle was a weak excuse.

'Of course.' Rebecca smiled. 'I'd love to see you perform again. You've missed out on quite a bit these last few years. I often hear you playing in my head, and it's comforting to know—'

There was a squeal of laughter from one of the children. Rebecca's sentence hung incomplete in the air as she hurried to welcome her husband back from the park. 'Off with those filthy shoes,' she called.

Naomi remained in the kitchen, savouring the last episode of quiet before Eleanor and Toby raided her handbag for the inevitable bags of sweets. Tonight would be about playing games and watching cartoons. Tomorrow, she'd return to a partially empty house and start again. Dejected, her appetite crushed into nothing, she couldn't imagine anyone taking on with a thirty-year-old music teacher with a flabby belly and tousled hair.

'Auntie!' The cry shook off the misery and she bent over to kiss the grubby cheek on offer.

Howard brushed a kiss along Naomi's cheek. 'Becca told me,' he murmured. 'I'm sorry.'

'I think I'm in shock,' Naomi said. 'It feels unreal.'

Toby charged up and down until Rebecca carried him off. 'You're filthy, young man,' she said.

Eleanor held Rebecca's hand. 'Where's Uncle Kyle?'

The word uncle caused a lump to form in Naomi's throat. 'He's not coming today, sweetie.' Or ever again. She turned away from Howard and wiped a tear away.

Over dinner, with the kids safely tucked up in bed, Naomi steered the conversation away from Kyle and the anguish he'd caused. Howard said little. Rebecca maintained an awkward sympathetic expression.

'Gran would have been sixty-nine tomorrow; she went too soon,' Rebecca said abruptly.

Naomi fingered the stem of her wine glass. 'I wonder if she ever predicted where we'd all end up? I don't mean now, but in a few years' time.'

Rebecca scraped her knife across her plate and shot a glance at Howard, who blinked. She was on the verge of saying something, but her husband hushed her with a minute shake of his head.

'What?' Naomi asked.

Rebecca shrugged. 'Oh, she was hardly Nostradamus, was she?'

Naomi smiled, the first one of the evening. 'True. I always thought you believed her the most.'

Rebecca blushed. 'It would be nice, wouldn't if, if she'd had some kind of gift?'

'Gift?' Naomi sipped her wine. 'I don't think it was anything other than an entertaining way to spend her birthday, wasn't it?'

'Quite,' Howard said. 'Now if she could have predicted the stock market, you could have written that one down.'

Rebecca laughed weakly into her glass and her cheeks glowed. She brought her cutlery together with a loud clatter, signifying the end of the meal and the conversation, and collected the dishes.

Naomi stayed out of the kitchen as the couple loaded the dishwasher. She discerned strained voices over the running water, but the words failed to make it as far as the dining room, only the tone of their conversation reached where Naomi sat waiting. She folded her napkin and sighed. She'd stirred up something, but what? If she'd developed her own gift, it seemed it was the art of making people uncomfortable with her presence.

It was something of a relief that Howard excused himself to do something important elsewhere and Toby came downstairs with toothache. Naomi, seeing an escape route, retired to bed.

\* \* \* \*

Rising as early as the children, she joined them for breakfast, while Howard went to play a round of golf and Rebecca sorted the laundry. The domestic harmony was uninspiring for the grouchy Naomi, who collected her bag and said goodbye to her sister.

'You're welcome to stay for lunch—'

'I should go and check that Kyle hasn't taken the kitchen sink.' He wouldn't but she wanted to see what he'd left behind.

A lot, it turned out. His clothes, computing stuff and the important brewery kit had gone, as had his photographs and camera equipment. Wherever he'd gone didn't require furniture or pots and pans; he was moving in with someone. Had he lied to her about finding somebody?

There was a note on the fridge door. *With Mike.* She'd no clue who Mike was or whether he actually existed. Downhearted and unable to practise her flute, she mooched around the house, picking up things, wondering how she'd managed to collect so many decorative objects that served no purpose.

Checking her watch, she decided the day had progressed enough for her to contact Leia in the States. She couldn't stomach talking to her sister, hearing the sarcasm – messaging was bearable.

Leia wasn't the least bit smug about the break-up. However, she supported the view that Kyle lacked depth; he cruised through life at a low altitude when what the Liddell sisters were supposed to do was reach for the stratosphere.

*I've split up from so many men, I've lost count* – Leia's boyfriends rarely lasted more than a few months. Her soulless message didn't help. Naomi plunged into the doldrums. She tried a different tactic.

*When are you coming back here? You can take me out somewhere.* Leia was a man magnet. Her beautifully defined, symmetrical face and trendy clothes pulled men out of the crowd and maybe Naomi could take advantage of it. There again, rebounding off Kyle onto one of Leia's rejects was hardly the best way to regain her confidence. She had to cope on her own, salvage her pride. Leia provided the excuse.

*I'm at a critical point of the study. I've a paper to write, too.*

The academic life belonged to Leia and her father. She thrived in an intellectual bubble of conferences and spells in the laboratory performing a battery of experiments. She'd finally gained her doctorate and found her niche. What she failed to do was soften her acerbic voice and direct manner. Naomi's long spell with Kyle might have ended but she had at least lived with him; Leia lived in an annexe joining her parents' house.

Chalk and cheese was how Naomi described her twin sisters to those who had never met them. Alike in appearance to some extent and both pale in complexion, the similarities ended there. Leia, although versatile in nature, was hard and abrasive and unlikely to crumble under pressure. Rebecca had a soft, smooth exterior, almost mellow in tone and behaviour yet able in a moment to turn and sharpen herself into something just by using a cutting riposte. However, since Rose's death, she'd retreated and reluctantly dished out her pearls of wisdom. Something must have happened to the genteel Rebecca; she'd become a recluse, distancing herself from the affairs of others unless prodded into action by Leia or their father, whose occasional interest in family affairs only served to heighten tension between the sisters and not relieve it.

The trio of women, whose diverse lives mainly converged around birthdays, graduation ceremonies, and funerals, had never recovered from the shock of the family break-up. While some families had to contend with parental divorce, the Liddell sisters had been left to their own devices as if orphaned. The consequences rippled on in silence, since none of them wanted to apportion blame.

# six

## Naomi

## June

With reluctance, Naomi put her house on the market. For weeks, she'd clung onto the idea that Kyle might decide he'd made a mistake and move back in as if nothing had happened. However, Kyle, other than the occasional message to sort out financial necessities and requests to forward his mail, resolutely kept his distance from Naomi.

The real kick in the teeth came when she'd spotted him walking down the street with a woman. Although they weren't holding hands, Naomi knew an established couple when she saw one. The unknown companion sashayed from side to side, tottering on her high heels and she wore the kind of skin-tight jeans Naomi gave up on years ago – they'd never suited her. The girl chatted exuberantly, her hands flying about in all directions. Kyle responded by smiling and nodding in an animated manner that Naomi recognised from their early days; he was happy.

Naomi had hid from them in a shop doorway and ground her teeth. Anger replaced appeasement.

She'd expected him to mope about for weeks, hopefully miserable and disappointed, like her. Reality hit hard; he'd moved on. Worse still, she suspected he'd met this woman before their breakup. She swore down the phone at Rebecca, who agreed it was a terrible discovery, but in a voice that clearly meant she wasn't surprised.

While Rebecca feigned comfort, Leia played the bitter card – Anger is okay, Naomi, use it. Leia's almost sympathetic email arrived on the morning of Naomi's meeting with her accountant: a lacklustre woman with a serious face, who offered her advice in one sentence. 'You need to release capital if you want to put a deposit down on a new place.'

Naomi returned home despondent. She'd have to move out into rented accommodation until she freed up some cash and paid off Kyle's share. With the summer approaching – she typically relied on a private lessons to tie her over until the autumn – she added another school to her roster, arranging to cover a teacher on maternity leave.

She set off early for Ely. The first lesson was arranged for nine o'clock and the familiar route provided her with a little nostalgia trip. As a child, the family had lived in north Cambridgeshire, in easy reach of Cambridge University, where her father taught, and the small cathedral city of Ely where her mother worked as a legal consultant. She hadn't attended the school she was due to visit. Her parents sent her, and the twins, to another one with ridiculous fees and a pin-striped blazer, which all of them had detested wearing. She stuffed the fledging memory back before it blossomed too far. Childhood wasn't going to cure her of the blues.

The heat of summer persevered, turning the kerbside grass limp and yellow. As she cut across the county along a minor road, the car abruptly swerved and deaccelerated. The steering wheel and the car seemed misaligned. She pulled over, blocking the entrance to a farm lane, and switched off the engine. The reason became clear when she inspected the car. The rear passenger tyre was flat.

She swore. Unless she was willing to fork out for a call-out charge, she'd have to change the tyre herself. A couple of cars raced by, paying her no heed. The spare tyre was in the boot, along with the jack and wheel locks. She stared at them – she'd no clue how to use the jack. The manual for the car was in the glove compartment and she thumbed through it, hunting for instructions.

An Audi pulled up behind her Seat Ibiza, its huge wheels churning the dirt into ruts. The driver climbed out and slammed the door shut. He was a strikingly tall man with a neatly trimmed bronze beard. The creased waxed jacket he wore was slightly ill-fitting and unable to cope with his broad frame, whereas the blue jeans and gnarled leather boots, which like his car were muddy, were more in tune with his stature. He wore a plain baseball cap and its shadow hid his eyes; only the triangular apex of his thin nose peeped out from beneath.

Naomi froze to the spot.

'G'day. Can I help you?' He stepped forward, tilting his head to one side to catch a glimpse of the flat tyre. 'Puncture?'

'Probably. Just happened.' She clutched the manual to her chest. 'Am I blocking your access?' She looked over her shoulder to the farm track.

He smiled – the whiskers shifted upwards and she spotted two thin lips. 'No. I'm sorry. I didn't mean to scare you. I can help, if you like. Of course, if you want to change—'

'I don't know how,' she said, rapidly. 'I've never had a puncture before.'

He peered into her open boot. 'You've got a spare at least. Not one of those stupid repair kits.'

Her attentive ears picked up on something. He wasn't English, nor European. He'd the drawl of a Canadian or American, yet he'd greeted her with a distinctive Australian accent. The confused mess of dialect continued as he offered to change her tyre. 'I'm not in a hurry. I don't mind.'

'That would be very kind of you,' she said, still standing by the passenger door. 'Do you do this often?'

He laughed. 'I lived a while in Australia's outback. You don't leave people alone on the roadside. People can die out there if nobody helps.' He picked up the jack.

'This is England, I can call somebody.'

'It's okay. I really don't mind.'

He crouched by the tyre and examined it. 'It's a bit worn. You should check the others.'

Kyle had done those kind of things with her car: the oil, the tyres, he'd even arranged for services. She'd paid the vehicle little attention other than to run it through a car wash every few weeks.

'Gosh, is it?' she said, then cringed. She sounded like Rebecca. 'I mean, thank you for letting me know. I'm in a hurry. I'm supposed to be in Ely at nine.'

He looked at his watch. 'I'll get you there. Just.' He started to crank up the car and she watched, making mental notes. She had to learn to take better care of herself and her things.

She returned the manual to the glove box. 'Are you sure I'm not holding you up?'

He shook his head, straining to loosen a bolt. 'I'm on my way to Spalding. I'm not expected until this afternoon.'

'Work, I take it?' Watching him, Naomi felt equally superfluous and curious. No rings on his fingers and clean nails. 'What do you do?' The question slipped out.

'I sell farm machinery. Beet harvesters. So, lots of travel up and down the country.' He gritted his teeth and the bolt finally loosened. 'What about you?'

She hesitated, and he swivelled to look over his shoulder. He smiled, quite a lovely smile. Why shouldn't she talk to a stranger by the roadside? Cars came by every now and again, and he didn't look like the kidnapping type. Not that she knew what a kidnapper might look like, but if he was going to drag her into the hedges, he would have done it by now before any more witnesses spotted them together. This would be Leia's analytical approach to the situation. Rebecca relied on her natural instincts which generally meant being overly cautious and staying in the car with the doors locked.

'I'm a music teacher. Peripatetic.'

'Meaning?'

'I travel from school to school and teach woodwind instruments to kids. Mainly the flute. I'm supposed to start at this school in Ely today and I'm not going to make a good impression if I turn up late.' She checked her watch again.

The wheel came off, landing in his capable hands. 'I'll put this in the trunk. I don't think it's repairable. Music? Like classical?'

She spotted the odd word: trunk. He was American. Or did they say trunk in Australia too? The man was intriguing. And strong; he lifted the tyres with ease.

'Mostly. Popular songs too.'

He aligned the spare tyre and shoved it into place. 'Cool,' he said, focusing on the task and not her. 'You must be good if you teach.'

The compliment tickled her and her scalp, which tingled with a juvenile response that once might have triggered a girlish giggle.

With the jack extracted and back in the boot, he slammed the door shut. 'All done.' He stared at the wheel. 'It's not supposed to go far on that.'

'No. It's one of those thingy ones. Temporary. I'll get it fixed once I'm back in Bury.'

'That's where you live? I'm near Newmarket. Look, I really don't like the look of that wheel now that it's on. I'll drive behind you until you get to Ely. Make sure you arrive safe.'

Naomi wasn't sure the wheel was that unreliable. 'I'll be fine.'

'No, honestly. Just let me make sure.' He stared right at her until she knew she was blushing.

What harm could it do? 'Okay.' She explained where she was going.

'I know the street.' He fished his car keys out of his pocket.

The car handled fine. The Audi kept a reasonable distance, although she could still see her rescuer in the rear view mirror, his face once more obscured by his cap. What a decent bloke – who else would have stopped? He was good with his hands. A man who was good with his hands... Tiny shivers travelled down her arms and reached her fingers.

She pulled up just short of the school gates. She wondered if he might drive off, but he didn't, which was a relief; she wanted to say thank you properly. Before she could get out of her car, he was by the driver's window, tapping on the glass. He moved fast.

'Car handled okay?'

'Absolutely,' she said. 'Steering's fine. Th—'

'If you're worried about driving back to Bury, just call me.' He thrust a business card through the open window.

'I'm sure—'

'I know, but humour me. I happen to think it's fate that we met and we should perhaps meet up again. If you like.' He pulled off his cap. Two grey eyes, as light as the moon, and hooded eyelids. The hairs on the back of her neck stood up on end again and in a nice kind of way.

'Fate?' She almost laughed. It was the kind of thing Rose would say. Naomi quickly glanced at the name on the card: Ethan O'Reilly. She emitted a quiet sigh of relief. How silly that at that precise moment she should remember what Rose had told her nearly ten years ago; the words of warning about Frederick. She gave Ethan O'Reilly her full attention. He'd maintained a partially serious expression throughout her little mental detour. He liked to stare, but it wasn't invasive.

'Well, thank you so much for your help. Hopefully, I'll make it back to Bury with no problems and get a proper tyre.' She hesitated, pressing the card between her finger and thumb. 'My name is Naomi. Naomi Liddell, just in case I do ring.'

'I don't think I'll forget your voice.'

She checked the rear view mirror – she was blushing again; how embarrassing. She dropped the card into the unused ashtray.

The clock on the dashboard said a little past nine o'clock. 'I really need to—'

Ethan straightened up. 'Sorry, I'm holding you up. Go rock,' he said, stepping back, nearly into the path of an oncoming car.

'Watch out!'

He gave a thumbs up. 'Or should I say, go Mozart or something?'

She laughed and was still chuckling as she parked in a space outside the school's main entrance.

Nobody in the music department commented on her tardiness. She hurried into the practice room to find a small boy holding a tarnished flute in one hand and a crumpled sheet of scales in the other.

The journey home was uneventful. Throughout it, she kept bursting out into fits of giggles. The realisation she'd unintentionally kept Rose's dramatic prophecy in the back of her mind all this time was disconcerting, as was the relief that it was insignificant. Picking up the business card, she swivelled it around in her fingers. Why not ring him? He might have a tale or two to tell about where he'd come from and why he was in England. Meeting Ethan had been a mini-adventure and she fancied another to break the monotony of teaching; a distraction from her failings.

# seven

## Naomi

Ethan's card made it into her purse, then onto the little coffee table by sofa. Something had happened. A new feeling of optimism had been born. Embryonic, and lacking form, it needed fuelling. She poured a small glass of wine, picked out a few chocolates from a box gifted to her by one of her pupils and dialled Ethan's number.

'Hello?' His voice lifted cautiously, its ambiguous dialect locked into those two syllables. Not a howdy or a g'day, but definitely not a British hello.

'Er, it's me—'

'Naomi,' he said cheerfully. 'You're home safe and sound?'

'Sure.' She licked a little wine off her lower lip and sat straighter. He'd answered. She'd half-expected him not to for some inexplicable reason. 'Thank you, again, for your help.'

'My pleasure. I'm glad I was there to help you.'

So deliciously polite and... there it was, that strange feeling pinging inside her tummy.

'I'm not troubling you... ringing now, am I?'

'Actually, I'm just finishing off a heap of paperwork.'

'Oh, I'm sorry.' She'd read him wrong. He'd played the gallant gentleman for no other reason than to help her out and, given his attractive features, was likely to be involved with somebody else. Flustered, she put the glass down on the nearby table.

'Please, don't apologise. I'd love to chat. I'm more comfortable doing it in person. Would you be able to join me for a drink? Or a meal?'

Warmed by wine and his invitation, her heart fluttered. She crossed and uncrossed her legs. 'Sure. Yes, please. I mean. Of course.' She cringed, tongue-tied. Playing a recital was less nerve-racking.

Ethan chuckled, a low rumble that he quickly brought under

control. 'I'm sorry. I shouldn't laugh. You seem surprised. You don't have to treat it like a date. We can talk and see where that goes.'

He handled the conversation with the same deftness he had handled the heavy tyres. She needed a practical man and one who was at ease with her, too.

'When?' she asked.

'Tomorrow. The King's Head is popular—'

'If you don't mind, could we go somewhere else?'

'Not a pub; okay.'

She hadn't meant pubs in general, only the King's Head. She might bump into Kyle or one of his friends.

Ethan clucked his tongue. 'Do you know that cafe, the one off the market?' He described the location perfectly and she knew it. Neutral territory and walking distance.

'Eight o'clock?' she suggested.

'Looking forward to it, Naomi. Sleep well.'

'Bye.' She stared at the phone, the wine and chocolates forgotten. She'd done it, and whether he said it or not, this was a date.

The next day, she stood in front of the wardrobe and dithered. Skirt? Probably the best way to hide her thighs and make the most of her dainty ankles. A baggy top? No, too frumpy. What about... she selected a shirt that was cut a little low, enough to show a touch of her cleavage, while not emphasising her breasts too much. Tasteful, decent and, what the heck, she looked good in it.

It wasn't really a cafe, more of a tame wine bar with a one-page menu and a smattering of tables and chairs. The warped floorboards glowed orange, as if the owner was attempting to recreate a warmer climate. In the day it sold paninis and pastries, and at night, little dishes resembling tapas. The limited range of vintages kept out the heavy drinkers.

Ethan waited by the door, wearing the same rugged jeans from the previous day, a plain white shirt with the top button undone, and loafers, not boots. Classic masculine stuff. She liked it. He folded his arms across his chest and paced. She wasn't late;

he'd arrived in plenty of time. He hadn't bought a jacket, but neither had she. The air was balmy and close, thick with unwelcome summer humidity. God, she hoped she didn't start sweating. She paused on the corner to catch her breath and admire him. He had to be an American; even with the extra accent, she was pretty convinced that he was. What would he make of her own connection to his homeland and the diaspora of the Liddell family? Did she tell him how close she'd come to living over there?

# The youngest sister, caught unaware

## 2004

Naomi was struck dumb when her father announced to his three daughters that he and her mother were emigrating to America. She failed to articulate a word of protest and fumed in silence, her lips expressively forming a pout of adolescent displeasure.

Paul Liddell convened the family meeting around the kitchen table on a chilly Sunday evening. Sanguine Nancy had laid out marshmallows with hot chocolate sauce, cheese dips, canapes and champagne flutes as if it was a cocktail party. The combination instantly killed Naomi's appetite and as she slumped despondently into her seat, the single white rose in the centrepiece crystal vase seemed to wilt in sympathy.

'A lucrative and prestigious offer of a post from Harvard University is too good to turn down,' her father explained, 'I've accepted the position. Your mother is fully supportive.' With twins Leia and Rebecca comfortably adults, only juvenile Naomi remained a loose end.

'Naomi has yet to reach maturity,' he said, as if Naomi were a bottle of Beaujolais Nouveau resting in a wine cellar. 'And, because of her age, she still needs plenty of guidance.' Paul's decree was greeted with a nod of agreement from Nancy, Naomi's deceptively quiet mother, who possessed the tenacity of a prosecuting barrister when stoked into action. What she lacked in maternal instinct, she made up for with her organisational prowess and astute thinking. The idea to re-locate was likely to have been hers and not Paul's.

The condescending remark about her immaturity hit Naomi hard; it was so untrue that she wasn't ready – she'd just turned sixteen. And she was supposed to be performing a solo in the school's spring concert. Her music teacher would be most disappointed if she left. Naomi's heart sank. She wasn't the one with a special talent; that honour belonged to the one sister who couldn't care less where she lived. She stared at Leia, who poked at the dips with her finger and scowled when Nancy told her to pull her finger out, both physically and metaphorically. 'Get on with your doctorate, Leia.'

Naomi, whose personal opinions were rarely voiced, was the inconvenient thread hanging from the completed tapestry of her parents' life. Her parents had everything mapped out, and were ready to go to Boston the following summer and start a new life in the leafy suburbs: Paul had his Harvard professorship and Nancy would eventually carve out a path as a legal consultant to human resource specialists.

Graciously, and equally unexpectedly, Rebecca fought Naomi's corner, arguing that it was unfair to take her out of the British education system at a crucial moment in her life. Music, Naomi's chosen career, was not a soft subject that could be picked up anywhere – Rebecca presented her case with the eloquence of a newly qualified solicitor. Leia, who was rarely home, agreed. She might have skirted the edges of family life, showing apparent unease at the concept of sisterhood, but she offered to help Rebecca look after Naomi and suggested they could both act *in loco parentis* until Naomi left school.

The twins were six years older than Naomi, and throughout her childhood they had treated her as an accident their parents had dreamt up one night and who'd subsequently, and inconveniently, hung around their bedrooms, listening to their music and stealing their makeup. Regardless of the bumps in their relationships, it was apparent to Naomi that her father had foreseen such a solution and, not wanting to force the twins to adopt their younger sibling, he'd stayed neutral. To Naomi's relief, Paul took little convincing. However, Nancy remained reticent, especially when Paul pointed out that Rose would offer support and advice.

'Naomi should be with us,' Nancy said. 'Rose is in her own little bubble since Frank died. Imagining silly things. She won't cope with the girls. The twins are only twenty-two, Rebecca works long hours, and as for Leia, she's demonstrated her utter inadequacy by losing her purse yet again.' Leia's lax attitude particularly riled her mother.

Leia shrugged off the criticism and scooped out a dollop of cheese sauce using a squished marshmallow.

'There's never any money in it,' she grumbled.

Nancy ignored her. 'I don't want you to worry, Naomi. Just concentrate on your school work and we'll work it out.' She reached across the expanse of polished wood and patted Naomi's hand.

Rebecca offered Naomi a sympathetic smile, as if quite aware how her younger sister felt, which she couldn't possibly know. How could she know? Rebecca was the gold star girl with curly locks of hair and glossy full lips, which were shinier than ever now that she'd met Howie. She went all dreamy-eyed when she said his name.

In the end, after Nancy had consumed two glasses of champagne and half the canapes, Rebecca convinced her to let Naomi stay in England. Naomi, far from celebrating, felt akin to a piece of luggage left at the lost property office of a railway station; she had little influence on the final arrangements. She'd move into Rebecca's flat in Cambridge, where her sister had started to practise law at a small firm of solicitors, and study music at the local college, enabling her to qualify for a diploma in instrumental teaching. Meanwhile, post-grad Leia would remain close by, studying for her PhD.

'Excellent.' Paul concluded the family meeting with a satisfied look. Nancy poured herself another glass of champagne and Leia and Rebecca presented a united, if frosty partnership. Side-lined, and forbidden to even touch the champagne, Naomi had nothing to look forward to in the coming years.

Six months later the family house, which was located in a tiny, idyllic Cambridgeshire village was sold, upsetting Rebecca the most out of the three sisters. Her childhood memories were locked inside its medieval timber walls and crooked windows.

She held a proper farewell party for her parents a week before everything was moved out into storage – eventually, the furniture was sold and the other possessions dispersed to family and friends.

Paul and Nancy claimed very little for themselves. Leia confessed relief as she hated the thought of maintaining the geriatric house with its dry rot and infestation of beetles. Naomi was too busy saying goodbye to her school friends to care. For those final months before her parents left, she despised them for putting their careers first and Rebecca for turning into a matriarchal figure with a heavy handed approach to guardianship – she insisted on a curfew every weekday. As for Leia, Naomi had no clue what her sister was plotting, but she'd no doubts that Leia's gigantic brain was computing something behind her seemingly vacant eyes.

The decision to rebel against Rebecca nearly cost Naomi her freedom to stay in England. A few months after her eighteenth birthday, she stayed out all night at a friend's house without telling her sister. She hadn't deliberately set out to deceive Rebecca. She'd drunk too much cider and fallen asleep on a chair while the rest of her friends partied. She'd no mobile, because strict – but fair, her sister believed – Rebecca refused to pay out for one and considered it an unnecessary luxury for a teenager. The following morning, Naomi turned up with a hangover, feeling unpleasantly delicate. The emerging adult Naomi had come as something of a shock to Rebecca, who threatened to send Naomi to their parents in the USA.

The incident led to Naomi acquiring her own mobile phone. However, she was sent to Leia's chaotic apartment as punishment. Leia lived precariously with two students who might be studying either art or anatomy, given the drawings they left lying around, Naomi couldn't tell which. Neither of the young men had any ability to clean or tidy up. Leia left them alone and practically lived in her laboratory. Or the pub across the road.

'Punishment for who?' Leia whined in sympathy with her younger sister. 'Let's go to the pub.' She dragged Naomi out to spend the evening with her postgraduate friends who talked about the science of blood-sucking leeches for the whole evening.

The next day, Naomi begged Rebecca to take her back. Her sister relented.

'I was never really worried about you,' Rebecca said. 'But, I nearly called the police to teach you a lesson.'

'That's unbelievable coming from you, isn't it?' Naomi thought Rebecca possessed unearthly standards.

Rebecca was already the perfect wife before she married and with Howard calling at the flat nearly every evening, often staying over the weekend, the role suited her perfectly. Naomi was the useless thread in the tapestry once more and sending her to Leia was a strong hint of what was to come.

'Why don't you find some digs with another student for next term?' Rebecca suggested, not knowing Naomi's newest friend was hankering for companionship that extended beyond dating. Kyle was a year ahead of Naomi at West Anglia University and likely to move out of expensive Cambridge once he graduated, but Naomi wasn't sure if she was ready to live with a man. Heather, a mature student at the university, whom Naomi trusted, had suggested a violinist as a suitable flatmate. Even before she graduated, Naomi was keen to start teaching to supplement her stipend.

She didn't actually mind leaving Rebecca's shrinking flat; she was ready to go and had been for some time. Rebecca had fulfilled her role as guardian with commendable competence and if Nancy had any criticisms, Naomi never heard about them. She packed her flute, a box of music, a suitcase full of clothes and moved out. She was finally free to live her life the way she chose.

\* \* \* \*

Over a glass of wine, Ethan told her a fragmented story about his time in Australia, how he scored high points on his visa application because of his specialist background in farming equipment and how he'd traversed the length of the country for several years. To her surprise, the tales of kangaroos, huge flocks of sheep herded by helicopters, the red-rock mountain ranges and scorching deserts, enthralled her. He'd even snorkelled in the Great Barrier Reef.

'I've never been,' she said. 'Never done anything that exciting.'

'Mostly, I sold stuff.' He shrugged off her disappointing contribution.

'And now you're here in the UK. You're not a Brit though.' She had to clear up his status; was he an immigrant who'd settled or was he staying for a few months on a work permit?

He shook out his napkin with a brisk snap of his wrist. 'No. My grandmother is Irish. I have an Irish passport.'

'Oh.' She heard Aussie, but no Irish lilt.

Her attempt to pry further into his past failed. Other than to confirm he'd been born in America, he deflected her questions, especially when he mentioned he had no siblings.

'Twins,' he repeated, when she told him about Leia and Rebecca. 'Older and wiser.'

'Oh, please, don't put yourself down, Naomi. You've amazing talent. You teach.'

She childishly craved compliments – when was the last time anyone had told her she was good at her job? The wine slid down her dry throat along with the cheesy nachos and spicy salsa dip; she hoped the glow she felt wasn't just down to the food. She wiped her mouth with the paper napkin and tried not to appear hungry for attention.

However, he'd compared her to her sisters; she hid a scowl. 'But Leia has so many papers published about this squitty little superbug she's obsessed with. The complete genome of la-di-da, whatever. And Rebecca, well, she studied law, reaped in a small fortune, then reeled in an ambitious banker and now has two gorgeous kids.' She halted, her lips pressed together. She'd said too much for the first evening.

'Children?' For a split second his eyes darkened.

This time, she wasn't going to pretend she was interested. From the outset, she and Ethan were going to be honest with each other. If she was to avoid the mistakes she'd made with Kyle, then from tonight, there would be no compromising on her feelings. At least not until she had a measure of Ethan.

'Yes. A niece and nephew. I love them to bits, but I'm relieved they're hers and not mine.' She ringed the top of her wine glass with a trembling finger.

He reached over and took her hand. 'We've only just met. I hardly think your opinion on kids matters at this moment, does it? You can't hate them, you teach them.' He squeezed her hand, steadying it. 'Don't say things you don't mean. Seriously, if you're in to kids and families, then say so. I'm not, it's just not my thing. But don't pretend you're not—'

'But,' she matched his gaze with an unwavering one of her own, 'I'm not the maternal type. Kyle, my ex, he waited and waited.' She glanced away. 'Sorry. We're supposed to be getting to know each other, not raking over my past screw-ups.'

'Agreed.' He let go of her hand. 'Let's move on, shall we?' He ordered another drink and topped up her glass.

She'd blown it. He seemed distant, staring over her shoulder to the bar and the rows of bottles and the line of clean glasses. There were only two other people left in the cafe. Naomi regretted not going to a pub where they could have hidden in a crowd. In that din, less would have been said and they could have simply grown accustomed to each other's company without complicating things with too much personal information. Fortunately, once she started to sip on the wine and smiled at him, he refocused on her face.

'Tell me how you came to be such a fantastic flutist.' Another re-direction; she didn't mind this time.

'Flautist. We say flautist on this side of the pond.'

'I didn't know there was a difference.'

'Oh, it's a common error,' she said, hastily. 'It's not important.'

'Why do you enjoy teaching? Do you get a kick out of it?'

She leaned forward, encouraged by the shine in his eyes. 'I hope I inspire. I like enthusing my students with a love of music. It's like teaching a language. It's incredibly satisfying giving somebody that ability.'

'I can imagine. I only speak the one.' He grinned. One language with many dialects, many twists of the tongue that hinted at a journey. She wanted to know more about that journey, but for now, she opened up about herself.

Naomi settled back into the chair. 'When I teach, I hope the kids get what the composer intended. But also, their interpretation is important.'

'Like a cover artist?'

'Kind of. I open up these kids; some of them are very shy. A few go on to join orchestras, bands. It helps them socialise.'

'Sounds great for them. Do you play with a group?'

'No.' Shyness wasn't always a hindrance to success; sometimes it was simply self-belief. 'I used to but... struggled to find the time.' A little lie. 'I'm a teacher, not a performer.' Ethan had no inkling of the inner battle she'd fought over that distinction.

She had performed with a wind quartet, which she'd joined towards the end of her degree. They had considered touring and making a thing of it. But in the end it wasn't to be. Unprepared, shockingly naive in her approach to performing, she'd faltered and lost her way. The circumstances that had brought the group together changed and they'd disbanded. She missed the camaraderie, mixing with other musicians, and she fancied giving it another go. This time she'd keep her ambitions in check and concentrate on personal pleasure, and not ridiculous goals.

'You'd look very pretty on a stage,' he said softly.

She lowered her eyes. 'It's not my strength.' A humble rebuttal, borne out of genuine shyness; behind the docile facade, she soaked up the praise.

'You should make that time. Me, on the other hand, not a musical bone in my body. According to my sax teacher.'

The throwaway remark surprised her, and she lifted her head with a jerk. 'Really?'

'Long time ago, but you know, perhaps I should start again.'

'Yes, you should. I don't own one, I could find you one—'

'Nah.' He waved a dismissive hand. 'I'd rather listen these days. Listen to you.' His eyes twinkled.

Naomi left his remark hanging in the air, unsure how to handle it.

'Why are your parents living in the States and not you? Don't you fancy living abroad?'

So she told him the tale of teenage Naomi and her overly maternal sisters, and he agreed, she'd made the right decision staying in England. 'Imagine though, if you ever had the chance to perform in the Carnegie Hall, would you take it?'

She laughed off his far-fetched idea. 'The most I've managed is a church or classroom. Hardly the beginnings of something great.'

He shrugged. 'I've learnt to expect the unexpected. I'm optimistic for you.'

She felt it again, the warm fuzzy feeling. Even though he'd not heard her play, he genuinely believed she had potential, something that she had failed to foster during her time with Kyle because she focused on money and teaching, the continuity of knowing every day offered security. With Ethan, perhaps she might embark on her abandoned journey, the one her parents had derailed with their emigration.

The offer to walk her home was for now sufficient. Next time, maybe, she'd invite him in and she might even serenade him. She suspected, though, he was on the path to something different. There was certainly a bounce in his feet, a rhythm to his walk, and she stepped along with him.

# eight

## Naomi

Ethan kept his beard neatly trimmed around his square jaw. Naomi loved the way little blond bristles framed his chin and upper lip. They tickled when he kissed her goodbye. They'd only kissed so far. She was warming to the idea that they might do something else, and soon.

Staring across the table in the White Hart pub – they had cleared up the misunderstanding about the pub during a spate of text messages – she was drawn to exploring his face as he talked. She wasn't that interested in sheep farming, but she wasn't going to put a dampener on the evening by cutting him off mid-flow.

Instead, she planted her elbow on the table, rested her chin on the heel of her palm and continued her inspection. She shifted her gaze from his stubble, passed the two slightly flared nostrils to the narrow pinch of the bridge of his nose, between two startling pale eyes. She hadn't cared much for Kyle's dark ones, but Ethan's moonlit pupils mesmerised. He rarely blinked, or so it seemed.

She worked out he'd spent quite a few years in Australia – seven or eight, maybe more – and had only been in England for a year.

'Why come to dull old England?' she asked when he paused to take a mouthful of ale.

'Better beer.' He winked.

She waited, hoping he might actually answer her question.

Ethan swirled the amber liquid around the glass and sighed. 'It's hard to settle in a big country. I came from one. I thought I would like Australia, but it reminded me of home sometimes. Not the scenery, just the vastness. England is neat. Pretty.'

'Quaint, you mean.'

'The farms are closer together. Less travelling.'

'The weather is wetter.'

'The sun doesn't bake you to a crisp.'

They both smiled.

'Fancy another drink?' he asked, pointing at her empty glass.

She declined. 'Packet of crisps would be nice, though.'

He walked over to the bar and fished out his wallet from his back pocket.

There was plenty of things about Ethan she didn't know and she'd love to know more. Her reticence remained. While Kyle might have been lazy and unimaginative when it came to talking, which wasn't Ethan's problem, the new man in her life wasn't an open book wanting to be read. He kept the covers closed and ensured that each volume about an earlier stage in his life was filed on an inaccessible shelf. He especially deviated around questions connected to his education and upbringing. One small query about his elusive Irish granny and he blanked her out. Ethan required a level of trust in her that she secretly admired. Why should he open up to her? She needed to be patient.

Each time they met, she noticed other little things about Ethan. He rarely dressed differently, always carried his wallet in his back pocket and his keys in his jacket next to his iPhone. The years of farm work were obvious in his broad shoulders and muscular forearms – no tattoos, though. He had a jagged scar in the fleshy part of his lower thumb. Sometimes, he absent-mindedly stroked it with his middle finger.

Ethan returned with a packet of salt and vinegar crisps and she tore it open.

'I spend too much time in a car these days.' He patted his stomach.

'Me, too. All that sitting in poky music rooms isn't good for me.' She envied his slight paunch. Hers needed working on, but finding the time to exercise alluded her. 'I'm going to reform the wind quartet I once played with,' she said, then licked the salt off her fingers.

'Quartet. That's four flutes?'

She shook her head. 'A flute, clarinet, oboe and bassoon. They balance really well. I'm hoping Heather, she's the clarinettist, will come along. And if she does, we'll have an oboist, too, because Mal is secretly besotted with her. However, the bassoon player, that's going to be a challenge. We might find a music student at the university who can help.'

'In Cambridge?'

'Yes. I'll have to drive over there for rehearsals. I don't have the space in my house,' she said, barely hiding her disappointment. The house had become a millstone weighing her down. Kyle wanted his money and who could blame him. She couldn't squat forever in something that really belonged to them both. The estate agents had sent around several viewers and one couple were particularly keen.

'No luck finding somewhere to move to?' Ethan asked, quite aware of the circumstances as it was often her sole topic of conversation. 'I'm sure things will work out,' he said, his gaze intense.

He walked her home. They held hands and said nothing. Words were starting to become an unnecessary obstacle to progress, especially due to Ethan's lack of interest in revealing his past. Years and years in Australia and not one girlfriend? She found that hard to believe.

Stopping by her front door, she turned to face him. 'Thanks for a lovely evening.'

He hovered, still holding her hand, the pause stretching into another spell of uncomfortable silence. Things would snowball if she invited him in and she wasn't ready to handle the fallout. The need was powerful though; it sank into the pit of her lower belly – an uncharacteristic ache for more than his hand.

Ethan dropped his arms to his side. 'Her name was Eileen,' he said abruptly. 'We met in Melbourne, where I was based much of the time. She rode horses. Liked to camp, which I hated. We met up and had good times. But that was it. A bit like you and Kyle, we never really got anywhere for all the effort of trying.'

'I see,' she murmured. 'And you left Australia to get away from her?'

He pulled a face. 'No,' he said sharply. 'I left after we split. She moved to Perth and I wasn't interested in going there; too far.'

'I see,' Naomi repeated. 'I guess we both have the same kind of baggage.'

Ethan stiffened. 'There's nothing wrong with our past.'

She'd upset him, somehow. 'I didn't mean... in any case, Kyle wasn't a casual relationship.'

'No, but he's dragging you backwards all the time, Naomi. Let him go, eh?' He took her hand and squeezed it. 'I have with Eileen. I'm not interested in where you came from or what you did when you were a little girl. Can't we think about the future?'

He stepped closer. The beard brushed against her cheek and he whispered, as if the walls of her house had ears. 'I like you, you know.'

Her heartbeat quickened. They'd only been seeing each other for three weeks. She wasn't sure if she felt the same. She and Kyle had taken... she was doing it again. Ethan was right – she had to put a stop to reminiscing.

'Not tonight,' she whispered back. 'I still need a little time, sorry.'

'Don't apologise. I didn't mean to push you. I'm just saying, I know where I'm going. When you're ready to catch up,' he kissed her on the lips, 'then I'll be here.'

'Thanks.' She grinned. 'That was intense, wasn't it?'

He stepped back and laughed. 'Yeah. Way too much for a man.'

She fished out her front door key. 'When do you want to meet up next week?'

'Wednesday, I'm back this way. Why not come to my house? If you want to practise, you can bring your flute.'

She nearly said no. She glanced at the "For Sale" sign impaled in her miniature front lawn. In a few weeks, she'd be moving out and there didn't seem much point in making her home a nest for Ethan to enjoy. She was already starting to clear out cupboards and pack non-essential things into boxes.

'Sure. That would be nice,' she said.

'Wednesday. I'll text you the postcode. I'll cook.'

He started to walk backwards, scrutinising her face. He nearly caught his heel on a crack in the pavement.

'Take care, Naomi,' he said softly into the night's breeze.

* * * *

'Malcolm is on board,' Heather told Naomi over the telephone. 'He wants a goal though. He's very driven that way.'

'He means a concert?' Naomi simply wanted to reconvene the group. Concerts meant resilience and coping with pressure. 'We've not even settled on style. Last time we were very baroque and traditionally oriented.'

'Why not mix contemporary with popular? I'm happy to do the arrangements.'

'Would you?' Naomi's voice lifted. Magically, Heather found the time to compose, teach and bring up two kids on her own.

The last concert they'd done together had left Naomi deflated and confused about her musical talents. Consequently, after a long hiatus, she'd been apprehensive about prodding Heather. Four years was a long time and Naomi wasn't expecting the enthusiasm that greeted her. Heather was honest enough to admit she wanted to escape the repetitious nature of home life. She'd bitten off Naomi's hand the moment she mentioned the quartet.

'I've contacted the graduate coordinator at the university,' said Heather. 'He's putting out feelers for a bassoon player.'

'Good. It's a pity Clive isn't around.' Clive had been the original bassoonist for Seasons Quartet – the name had been his idea. He now lived in Dorset.

'Well, we've got Malcolm back, which is a blessing. He's very busy, so we need to bait him with a concert. I'll see if there are any slots at St Mary's we could fill.'

St Mary's Church in Cambridge was less of a church and more an informal venue for classical concerts.

'In a few months' time, though. I really just want to get out of the house and have fun.'

'Sure,' said Heather.

The next day, Naomi drove the few miles out west toward Newmarket and an old 1950s estate. There were red bricks and slate roofs lined up in uniform rows and they were nothing like the cottage of her childhood. The semi-detached houses had all begun with the same original features: bay windows and canopy porches, and then over time each had acquired a degree of uniqueness, whether it was an extension to the side or the addition of double glazing. Ethan's house had none of these things.

He answered the doorbell within seconds and ushered her into a hallway. The flooring was laminated, as was the staircase. The sofa in the living room was worn on the arms and covered in scatter cushions in various shades of blue. A flat screen TV was mounted on the wall and, next to it, empty rows of book shelves. The back of the house offered a small dining room, kitchen, and a delightful sun lounge.

'Wow,' she said. 'It's deceptive. It goes back some way.'

'I was pleasantly surprised when I moved in,' Ethan said. 'Please sit.'

She chose a wicker chair by the double patio doors. The garden was small and overgrown along the borders, but the grass had been mowed recently.

'You didn't view it first?'

He disappeared into the kitchen, shouting his reply. 'Well, no. I took it on faith.'

Intrigued, she followed him into the kitchen. The beech cupboards were stained and faded, the freckled granite worktop and a glass splashback scarred like the furniture. The more of the house she saw, the less it fitted with Ethan. He was living in a home that had been used and abused by a large family.

'You're renting?'

'Yes. I met this guy out in Queensland. He's working out there, fell in love with the country. He decided to move his family out. But he's not ready to sell until he's absolutely sure. So I offered my place for him to rent and he's given me his.' He opened a cupboard and retrieved a sauce packet. 'Sorry, I only do pre-fabricated food.'

'That's okay. It's nice. Roomy.'

'That's what I meant about you practising. The acoustics in the sun lounge are sweet.'

She wandered back into the room while he threw together something in a pot. With the exception of the wicker sofa and chairs and a low coffee table, there was nothing else in the room.

If they pushed everything back against the walls, there would be enough space for her and the rest of the quartet to practise. But would Ethan want strangers in his house?

She had to tell him her other piece of news. She re-joined him in the kitchen.

'I've something else to tell you,' she said.

'Yeah?' He stirred the pot, his nose twitching as he inhaled. 'Pasta sauce.'

'I've accepted an offer on my place.'

He looked up. 'Great. I mean,' he wiped the smile off his face, 'I know it's not what you wanted, but it's a step in the right direction.'

A direction of sorts. Her stomach rumbled, and she tasted basil floating in the air. Outside, the evening sun ducked behind the houses at the bottom of the garden and an elongated shadow cast its mark on the lawn.

They ate in the dining room – spaghetti and something with tomatoes and peppers, and tuna. It worked taste-wise but lacked finesse. She didn't require culinary masterpieces.

'I think I've found a house to rent near the railway station.'

'Okay.' He dipped some garlic bread into his bowl.

'But it won't be available for a couple of months. And I think these buyers of mine are going to move fast, so—'

'So, move in with me. I've plenty of room, as you can see.' He waved his arm around at the bare walls.

'No, I couldn't. It's too soon.' She said the words, but she wasn't thinking them. Instead, she was playing the "what if" game. What if this was the moment her life was going to change for the better? What if this man, with his confidence and charm, provided her with the stability she craved? And then there were the counter points. What if she liked dating him and hated living with him? What if he left the toothpaste tube top off or the washing up in the bowl overnight? How many annoying habits of hers would he detest?

He lowered his fork. 'I'm not asking you into my bed, Naomi. It's a roof over your head until things are sorted and if, while you're here, we get on, then you're welcome to stay.'

'You're very chivalrous for a yank.' She grinned; he didn't, so she wiped the smile off her face. Any reference to America was often met with disdain.

However, his frown swiftly morphed into a smile and he patted the back of her hand as if to accept her unspoken apology. 'My armour is upstairs and you're a damsel in distress. Kinda.'

The accent slipped in when he was at his most charming. She liked the American in him. Why did he hide it?

The meal progressed to dessert – waffles and ice-cream. She wanted him to say, 'Like my momma made,' or something like that, but he didn't. She had to stop, put the whole Ethan the American to bed. If he didn't want to be bound by nationality, why should she force it upon him? Her own parents were devout Brits living in the States, whereas her sister had taken US citizenship and forsaken any interest in returning to England.

Dusk cooled the sun lounge. He played music on his iPod, mainly fifties classics from the days of Elvis and Buddy Holly, a few country and western songs that she didn't recognise. The genre suited him. He slouched and she, feeling colder, inched closer to him until he hooked his arm over her shoulder. She felt secure and happy. Ready, too. So ready, she ached for it.

'You know about the bed thing,' she said quietly.

'Um,' he murmured, staring directly ahead.

'I don't mind exploring the idea.' She tensed. Did she sound demanding or whining, like a clingy schoolgirl on her first date?

'Well, I reckon, it's one worth exploring. You can stay over. I have to be up at six to get to Stamford. Gives you time to go home before lessons start.' He stretched his arm across the back of the sofa, flexed his fingers and cocked his head to one side. The pose was supremely relaxed and self-assured; he didn't expect her to turn down the offer.

\* \* \* \*

Naomi lay next to him, a little hot and sweaty, and very pleased. Ethan sighed in a happy way and tucked his hands behind his head, apparently equally satisfied. She looked up at the ceiling, then around the bedroom, only now really taking in her surroundings: the metal poles of the headboard, which she'd clung onto in that precious moment; the solitary chest of drawers upon which she'd left her wristwatch ticking quietly; the chair where he'd tossed his clothes, and hers too; and the slatted doors of the inbuilt wardrobe that stretched the length of one wall. She stroked her hand along the white duvet, which was spotless; a sea of linen that covered their breathless bodies. Ethan might have lived rough in the outback when necessary, but he wasn't slovenly. He was a minimalist, though. A little too spartan for her tastes.

Clearing her throat, she rolled onto her side and tiptoed her fingers across his chest, weaving them between the soft hairs. He opened his eyes.

'You could do with some pictures on the wall,' she said.

'Probably.'

'I have a few. Tasteful. Should I pack them away or bring them?'

He turned to face her, propping his head on his arm. Now he was wide awake and quite aware of the implication of her question. 'Bring them.'

'So, the offer stands?' After what they had done that evening, it was inevitable that she was moving in. No turning back now. Addictive and fortuitous, the familiar fuzzy feeling of falling in love was brewing unhindered. Ethan was quite right: look forward, not back.

He ran his forefinger along her cheekbone. 'Sure does, baby.'

She squealed at the silly endearment.

He reached towards her and kissed her lips, silencing the sound. 'Come stay this weekend. Test me out. Us out.'

It was a good idea; she'd withdraw her interest in the property by the railway station and embrace the selling of the house and what it represented: a fresh start.

Ethan was a strange composite of cultural nuances and simple mannerisms. For a long time she'd sought a superficial, unhindered life with Kyle and it had suited her, or so she'd thought. Now, with Ethan, she saw a more complicated future with a complex man. Her twenties had been about frivolous fun and building her reputation as a teacher; maybe now that the quartet was reforming she could try to be more adventurous. Turning thirty was going to be about risk taking and no more cruising in neutral waiting for something to happen. She'd wasted her time with Kyle; she planned to make every moment with Ethan count.

# nine

## Naomi

## July

*Too quick!* Rebecca's imaginary warning rang in her ears. The motherly sister who'd insisted on three years of courting before she allowed Howard to propose would consider the way Naomi was handling Ethan as unwise, especially after Kyle.

Naomi's anxiety was heightened by the news she had to impart to Rebecca. Not only had she slept with Ethan, she now had done so several times and spent two weekends with him. The sale contract on her own house was about to be signed and the removal van was booked. Most of the larger pieces of furniture would go into storage, while her personal stuff would be delivered to Ethan's house. The best approach was to tell her sister the news in person.

She played her flute for Ethan on Sunday afternoon in the sun lounge. It was her first performance for him and he listened as she meandered through different pieces, some short, others long. It didn't matter whether the audience was many, one or none, she played with the same passion, the same expressive need of tonal quality and energy. She closed her eyes, as she couldn't see the dexterity of her fingers; she could only command them to move as she breathed around the pattern of the rhythm. She called upon her extensive repertoire and played from the heart without the aid of sheet music.

When she chose to play the elastic music of Erik Satie, she stretched the languishing notes and gave strength to the start of each phrase with the tip of her tongue flicking the roof of her palette. Error-free and fluid, she knew she was playing at her best, so when she opened her eyes and saw his glazed eyes, as if in state of sleep, she'd stopped.

'I'm listening,' he said, regaining his focus. 'I'm chilled. Take it as a compliment. Go on, don't stop.'

Remembering his taste in music, she blasted a furious hornpipe at a fiery pace. His eyes stayed open and fixed on her, his foot tapping. After she cleaned the flute and put it away, he snatched her onto his lap for an appreciative kiss.

'Have you ever been to a live concert?' she asked.

'A couple of rock concerts in Sydney.' He scratched his beard. 'Guess that's not what you like.'

She chuckled. When it came to live performances, she was thoroughly classical in her music tastes; she also valued her ear drums. 'No.'

'So what's with the shyness? Don't you want to be seen? Can't you release a recording, go on YouTube?'

She wasn't like Kyle. He'd once suggested the same thing and she'd dismissed it with an eye roll. He failed to grasp the concept of a live, reactive audience.

She shrugged. 'Just not for me.' She changed the topic. 'I'm going to my sister's next weekend.' Over in Huntingdon, Rebecca was waiting anxiously for news. In their last conversation, Naomi had described the house by the railway station and had told her nothing about Ethan.

She bent over to slip on her shoes. She had to leave soon – there was plenty still to sort out back at her house.

'You don't have to explain anything to her,' Ethan said, coiling his arm around her waist.

'She's not going to change my mind. If she tries, she'll get short shrift. She interfered too much with Kyle.' Naomi painted a less than flattering picture of Rebecca, which wasn't fair.

'So why stress yourself?' Ethan asked.

She freed herself and rose. Ethan's forehead had furrowed; talking about her family was the only thing that seemed to irk him and produce that particular expression. He'd have to learn to cope with Rebecca's good intentioned meddling.

'She's a romantic at heart, believes love solves everything. She wants me to be happy and I'm going to convince her I am, so don't worry.' She leaned down and pecked his cheek. As she straightened up, she came face to face with a poster painting: a large framed picture of a Monet landscape she'd hung in the sun lounge. She wasn't sure why she liked it but seeing it in Ethan's house helped her adjust. Males were supposed to mark their territories; Naomi intended to stamp her presence on the bland house with colour and music.

'Look,' she said. 'I'll come back here on Sunday, on the way back from Huntingdon, and we can have lunch at the pub you suggested.'

The incentive was sufficient; the furrows dispersed into smoothness. He walked her to the front door.

'Oh, I've something for you.' He rifled in the pocket of his denim jacket. 'Here.'

A shiny brass key. She remembered the day she'd given Kyle a front door key. He'd slipped it into his pocket, along with the loose change, and said nothing, as if it was an insignificant event. She'd taken offence at his lack of excitement.

'Thank you.' She reached up and hooked her arms around Ethan's neck.

He wriggled slightly and she brushed her lips against his fuzzy cheek. 'I better go.' She picked up her overnight bag and flute case.

'See you on Sunday.' He held the door for her.

By her car, she shouted, 'I'll be here by lunchtime.' She wasn't sure if he heard her, but he did wave.

\* \* \* \*

By the time Naomi drove through the gates of Rebecca's palatial mansion, she had concocted umpteen variations of what she planned to tell her and none of them sounded robust.

Naomi deposited her bag and car keys on the breakfast bar and glanced around the immaculate kitchen where Rebecca seemed to live in perpetuity wearing her sporty leggings and white cotton smock that floated with her; she drifted from the island counter to the kettle as if on casters. Naomi wondered yet again why a woman so talented in debate and legal prose had surrendered it all to such a humdrum life. she often feared Rebecca was too reclusive. Other than school runs, she lived the life of a hermit. The groceries arrived in a van, clothes were bought online and if she entertained, she always hosted. Things couldn't be that bad though: the children were sociable and happy.

Rebecca poured the tea into a cup and placed a homemade biscuit on the saucer. 'There, that will help. Poor thing,' she said, 'It's never an easy journey.'

'I'm fine, Becca,' Naomi said dryly. 'It's not that bad. Just tedious.'

'How are your lovely pupils?' Rebecca often asked about the children, as if she could embrace them as her own.

'Doing well. Three distinctions this term. And one, Hazel, you remember her, turning eighteen next month, she wants to go the Royal Academy.'

'Well done.'

Naomi accepted the compliment. They moved onto her niece and nephew's latest exploits, then briefly detoured into Howard's domain of banking, which made no sense to either of them other than he made heaps of money.

'Off to Hong Kong next week.' Rebecca frowned and poured herself a second cup of tea.

After a few sips, Naomi judged the preliminaries were concluded and took a deep breath. 'I've met a man.'

Rebecca's teaspoon clattered against her saucer and the colour seeped out of her cheeks. 'Tell me more.'

The enthusiastic tone was fake. Naomi had an excellent ear when it came to Rebecca's role playing and the omens were never good when Rebecca spoke one way and looked another. Sometimes, she seemed lost in a distant place, right in the middle of a conversation, and other times she hung onto every word spoken. Today would be the latter. Naomi braced herself and pushed aside the half-drunk tea.

'He's called Ethan. Ethan O'Reilly—'

'Irish. Black hair, like the Celts?'

Naomi rolled her eyes to the ceiling. Rebecca had the irritating habit of pre-empting anything Naomi said with romantic imagery. 'No,' she said. 'He's not a red-head either. Quite ordinary light brown hair with a beard.'

Her sister clucked her tongue disapprovingly. 'Howie prefers a goatee.'

'It's more like lengthy stubble. It suits him. Short hair...' Naomi fumbled in her pocket for her phone. 'Look, this will save you the lengthy descriptions. Here's a photo.'

It was a selfie of both of them – one of those distorted pictures where their chins seemed huge and their eyes popped wide open. The dreary sky behind them formed an ugly frame. Fortunately, Ethan had presented himself better than she had; she looked chubby cheeked.

Rebecca inspected the photo for several seconds, zooming in on his face. 'Not bad,' she said finally.

'He's an American, who's lived in Australia and has an Irish passport.'

'I see,' said Rebecca slowly. 'What does he do?'

'Sells farm machinery. Spends a lot of time on the road visiting farms and depots. He used to work on farms in Australia too.' She took back her phone.

'A proper job.'

'If you say so,' Naomi said icily. She was determined not to rake over Kyle's limitations. Since she'd partially moved into Ethan's house, she'd spent less time wondering what had happened to her ex-boyfriend to the extent she didn't care about his subsequent dating habits.

'Now, now, don't bite my head off.'

'I'm not. He's very different from Kyle. He thinks starting up the quartet is a great idea. I thought that would please you.'

Rebecca tipped the contents of the teapot down the kitchen sink. 'There's more to it than that, or why else did you come here in person.' Now, the sharp solicitor reared her head.

Naomi rose – she was a couple of inches taller than her sister and she used it to her advantage. 'I'm moving in with him.'

The teapot slipped out of Rebecca's hand and crashed into the sink. She fussed, making sure it wasn't broken, using the mishap as a cover while she regained her composure. Her hands shook as she carefully placed it on the draining board.

'So soon?' she said. 'Why the hurry?' Her mouth gaped open and she stared right at Naomi's belly. 'You're not, are you?'

'Oh, for... No! I'm more than careful in that department.'

'But you have slept with him?'

The little trap had caught Naomi out. She often wished her sister wasn't so seemingly dozy or sweet-natured, because when she switched out of motherly mode, she was more than a match for most people. Except for Leia, and perhaps their mother.

'I have slept with him,' she answered, in the tone of a defendant in the witness box. 'More than once. I'm about to sell my house. I've nowhere convenient to go and he invited me to live with him. It might be a long term thing, it might not. We're experimenting.' She winced at the choice of wording.

'Gracious. This is not what I expected. I thought, after Kyle, you'd take your time and not gallivant off with the first man you bumped into. Kyle was one long silly experiment and he burned you. Now, you're about to make another mistake.'

Naomi turned on her heel and went to collect her handbag from the breakfast bar. She'd go to Ethan's right now. Rebecca, with her whimsical view of love and romance, her unachievable fairy tales and Hollywood movie scripts, was once again dictating Naomi's relationships.

'Don't go.' Rebecca dashed to the door and intercepted her. 'Please. I'm sorry. I'm just shocked. You know I want the best for you. I worry... I always worry because I can't always see where things are going. I live in the here and now, where it's comfortable.' The words tumbled out, fraught and surprisingly insecure. 'You just fly with things. A bit like Leia. You two are so alike sometimes.'

Naomi didn't think so. How many chalks and cheeses could there be in one family? How many divergent traits could a small gene pool create? From the time they were little girls, they'd struggled to bond and find common ground. Leia's tepid displays of emotion juxtaposed Rebecca's exuberant ones and Naomi, where was she? The one in the middle or simply better at masking her feelings?

Rebecca looked genuinely apologetic. She wrung her hands into a ball. 'Stay. I'm sure he's a lovely man. Why wouldn't he be? Kyle wasn't a bad man. I suppose I aspire for you to find somebody like Howard—'

'I don't want a Howard. I don't need money or a big house or holidays in the Caribbean. I don't want what you want. If I'm making a mistake, another one, then it's mine to own. He's not going to hurt me. He's a bit of a cowboy. You know, one of those polite American types, all charm and manners. Hard worker too. So don't complain about that. He's not into computers, doesn't even have one. He watches a bit of sport and likes going to the cinema.' Naomi paused. 'I'm making him more at home. He's only been in England for a year or so.'

The fretful hands relaxed and dropped to Rebecca's sides. 'If you're happy.'

'I am,' Naomi said firmly. 'There's a chemistry between us. I can't describe the magnetism. The sexual tension… it's doesn't matter. Do you know, we argue? I never argued with Kyle. Oh, we disagreed, but more like friends do when they don't want to fall out over something. With Ethan, it's different. I think that's why I feel good about him.'

'All this emotional outpouring is quite intense, isn't it? How many weeks have you been together?' Rebecca said. Her eyebrows rose simultaneously into neat arches.

Naomi waved a dismissive hand. 'Oh, please, just trust me. Now, where have you put my niece and nephew?'

Rebecca laughed. 'Nowhere. They're watching some Disney film in the games room. I told them to give us a little time together.'

'Then let's go join them.'

Naomi had survived the inquisition. For now. Rebecca would no doubt inform Leia, who in turn would tell their parents, and then the emails would arrive and the text messages, and then she'd finally pluck up the courage to do some face time with them over the Internet and apologise for not telling them sooner that she'd fallen in love.

She checked her rambling thoughts. Fallen in love? Had she, or was that the message she wanted to convey to her family?

She'd no chance to explore those feelings because Eleanor and Toby barrelled into her.

\* \* \* \*

Naomi feathered Ethan's home with a few pieces of furniture, her computer and boxes of music. She added more of her pictures to the walls, and things she liked to have in the kitchen: a smoothie maker and spice rack.

Arriving home from the pre-arranged meeting with Kyle at the King's Head, she bolted the door shut behind her and smelt food – a pot was on the stove and the contents were bubbling away. Ethan was pleasantly domesticated. He cooked, ironed and sorted the rubbish ready for collection. He happily mowed the grass and washed her car. She contributed by running around with the vacuum cleaner and polishing the taps in the bathroom. So far they made a good team. Only money matters remained an issue.

Ethan came downstairs with damp hair, a trimmed beard and wearing a tight fitting t-shirt that stretched over his chest and shoulders. He claimed the wooden spoon from her hand and stirred the saucepan.

He sniffed the steam. 'So you gave Kyle the money?'

'Like we agreed. Kyle and me.'

Ethan frowned and abandoned the pan. 'Jeez. I just don't get why.'

'He paid half of the mortgage.' She had explained this to him several times.

'But why give him money for the other stuff?' He leaned back against the worktop and folded his arms across his chest.

She tried to ignore his unnaturally severe stance; he'd not kissed her or given her a hug, which he usually did after they hadn't seen each other all day. She huffed, both irritated and hungry. 'Because we bought things together.'

'All of it?'

'Most of it.' On her initiative, she had to admit, especially the king-size bed and wardrobe. Kyle wasn't bothered with matching bath towels or the dinner service. They were the kind of things Rebecca was given as wedding gifts and Naomi wanted them for the same reason – they signified an established relationship, or so she'd thought.

'But he didn't care. You said yourself, you wrote the list without any input from him. If he hadn't seen it, would he have asked?' Ethan's frown deepened into a scowl. 'He walked all over you.'

'It's the decent thing to do. For nine years we had a partnership. We might not have been married but no way am I going to get embroiled in a bitter argument about who owes what.'

Ethan snorted. 'You should have kept the money. I would have,' he said quietly, turning his back on her to stir the contents of the pan.

'Well, you're not me,' she snapped, frustrated by his interference.

Money was a serious issue. She had hoped to recoup sufficient funds for a deposit on a new house. However, the current housing situation meant she had to stump up a larger deposit than when she last bought a house. She was in danger of being priced out the market and she also needed somewhere suitable to practise. She couldn't rely on Ethan's sun lounge indefinitely. The landlord was unlikely to come back and eventually the house would be sold.

Ethan paid all the bills. When she asked to contribute, he brushed aside her request. 'You're my guest.'

For the time being she was happy with the status quo, but for how long? He showed no inclination to look at houses, and if she broached the subject he steered her away from it. 'You're with me. I'm taking care of things. It's about time you had somebody look after you.'

He implied Kyle had been a passenger in her life. Regardless of Ethan's opinion, she refused to be one in his. She would at some point in the future insist on helping out by contributing to the rent and bills. Perhaps the terms were so good he wasn't keen on moving. Everything about Ethan was speculation because of his refusal to open up to her.

Early days yet, as Rebecca had crudely pointed out. She needed to stay patient. As she spooned the stew onto her plate, she gave him a sweet smile. He generously acknowledged it with an endearing one of his own.

Forget about the money, she decided in silence. Concentrate on the quartet, instead.

# ten

## Rebecca

'He's called Ethan.' Rebecca braced herself. 'She's moved in with him.'

Leia's look of a surprise arrived on the screen a second later. 'Already? Kyle's hardly gone and she's hooked somebody? How?'

Rebecca's lack of information would disappoint Leia. 'He changed her tyre when it blew. So, I suppose he's practical. He has a steady job. Travels a lot; something to do with selling farming equipment.'

'Regular kind of guy, then?' Leia preferred the irregular kind. She was curled feline-like on a chair and the only light came from a lamp on her desk. Leia lived nocturnally even in the daytime.

Rebecca glanced out of the kitchen window at her children who were playing something that involved running from one end of the garden to the other neighing – horse racing? Their imagination was boundless and free to explore, as it should be.

'He's American.' Rebecca added the wildcard last.

Leia uncoiled. 'Which state?' Her pretty nose zoomed closer to the webcam. Rebecca never envied her brains, but her eyes, her shaped neckline…

'Dunno. He lived in Australia for years, but he's got an Irish passport.' Rebecca's supply of facts was exhausted. She blamed Naomi's reticence to divulge.

'He's not a gaming freak, thank God.' When Leia grinned the smile fractured into hundreds of disorganised pixels. 'And he's not Frederick.'

'You remember that then?' Was it wise to bring it up? The kitchen clock ticked louder.

Her sister's pixelated face settled into a benign expression. 'You do, obviously.'

It had played on her mind a great deal since Naomi had split up with Kyle. Rose had issued a warning about Frederick and the wording of it bothered Rebecca more over the years. Was it because he might be dangerous or simply a bad choice for a husband? Why the emphasis on his name – names were rare for Rose. If Ethan was the current choice, what if some other suitor sprung up and supplanted him? For all Rebecca knew, there could be a few contenders out there eyeing up her sister. Naomi's beauty was not in the shape of her figure or her generous height, but the gentle features of her promising face and magnificent blue eyes. Rebecca coveted their lightness and also Naomi's wavy hair. She sighed – the comparisons had to stop. She was thirty-five, not fifteen.

Something in the garden caught her eye. She opened the back door and stuck her head out. 'Oi,' she yelled at Toby, 'don't pull up the flowers.'

Leia's laughter crackled over the speaker. Rebecca retreated into the kitchen and looked at the phone in her hand. Something moved behind Leia, a black shadow skirted from one side of the screen to the other. She heard somebody mutter – a sexless voice, neither deep or feminine. Rebecca opened her mouth to ask who was there and hesitated.

There was something unnatural about Leia's unamused face – the interruption had upset the flow of conversation, as had Rebecca's reprimand of Toby. The silence lingered awkwardly. If only she could share Leia's sight; shouldn't twins have a deep connection? The back door was still open, and she edged her toes into the afternoon sunlight. She could pretend she and Leia were breathing the same air, seeing the same thing, but it was just that – her imagination. Nothing happened. Shutting the door, she opted for the direct approach.

'Who's with you?' she asked.

Leia glanced over her shoulder, then back at the webcam. She slid forward on her seat, filling the screen with her pointed nose and plucked eyebrows, neatly hijacking Rebecca's view.

'Nobody.'

She'd lied. The obstruction prevented Rebecca from prying into the dark scenery, but the whispering continued. Whatever was happening in the background was none of her business: the

Liddell twins didn't meddle in each other's affairs. The agreement was born years ago when adolescent Leia's flair for mischief began to drive them apart.

'I have to go,' Leia said abruptly. 'Bye.'

Rebecca huffed and placed the phone down. There wasn't any point in ringing her back. With the children drained of energy, it was feeding time. She opened a cupboard, located a packet of penne pasta and tomato sauce and cooked the bland meal on autopilot, paying little attention to fine-tuning the dish. The kids wouldn't care as long as she sprinkled grated cheese over it.

She worried. Should she invite Naomi and Ethan for dinner at the weekend? Probably not. Too soon and with Howard away all week, she had to put his needs first – he'd want a quiet spell of recovery. She could visit them? But that meant leaving the house and coping with something other than the supermarket or school. Howard drove the longer journeys. It left the usual option of calling the couple over the Internet. Once she'd seen Ethan, maybe she might be able to connect with him remotely, like she did with her father or the neighbours. If not, he'd join the ranks of her sisters and Howard; they were immune to her gift.

Her father wasn't, though. Whenever she drifted far across the sea and found herself by his side, he acted as if he knew she was there watching and observing him as he typed or read. He'd pause in mid-thought and smile, then return to tapping the keyboard or turning a page of a journal. Every day, she missed her father. Less so her mother and her side of the family. They'd scattered across the isles, blown like confetti in the wind, and wherever they'd landed, they'd stayed and not budged. She hadn't been angry or bitter when her parents decided to go, nor when Leia joined them. There was, however, a profound sense of loss that was akin to grief, like a hollowness. Was that why she pined to be near him? But what difference could her gift make to the pain his absence caused her? Perhaps it made it worse.

She sent the children upstairs to bed and, after reading to them, she kissed them goodnight and returned to the lounge with a book. The pages flapped uselessly on her lap – her concentration sapped. The night drew in and she waited, checking her watch from time to time. He'd be home soon.

How would she broach the subject of Naomi? There was Leia, too. Who was the hidden companion? Vetting Naomi's boyfriends was a legacy of her early responsibilities, but she never gave Leia the same treatment. Paul and Nancy were supposed to keep Leia in check and rein in her wilder moments. Had they given up trying to contain her sister? More unanswered questions to add to her growing list. She had things to tell him too, outstanding issues that she'd parked and left unsaid.

She fetched the phone and dialled the number.

'Hello?' Paul answered gruffly.

'Dad.'

'Oh, Becca. How are you?' His tense voice relaxed with each syllable.

She focused for a while on his grandchildren and her husband, ensuring her father first heard good news. 'Toby has passed his first stage of swimming lessons. Regular little dolphin.'

He talked, saying something about his book, but the words floated away.

'Dad,' she interrupted him. 'I've been thinking about Gran. It would have been her birthday recently, and … I suppose I miss her still.'

'Well, we all do, darling.'

'It's been eight years.' Rebecca paused and waited. Paul let the silence stretch on, so she continued. 'You remember all those things she said. I wrote them down and thought about the stories they might tell.'

'I know,' he said, so quietly he was a whisper in her ear.

She soldiered on. 'Except, there was one year I didn't know what she'd said and you couldn't remember either, which I've always thought was odd, because you remembered the others.' She snatched a breath. 'You see, I checked on them and do you know what, she wasn't far off with her predictions.' She tried to sound glib, as if amused by her discovery.

Paul exhaled heavily. 'Which year are you missing?'

She swallowed hard. '1994. I would have been about eleven, I think. I must have been ill or something, because you didn't take me. Any of us.' Meaning her sisters. 'The thing is, Dad, she had this knack of projecting ten years into the future. A bit of crystal ball gazing. I thought it was a crazy Gran thing. One whole decade, rather odd isn't it, that time frame?'

She gripped the phone tighter and her hand shook. Was he at his desk or reclined in his favourite armchair? She couldn't see. Maybe he was watching the baseball match on TV; he missed cricket dreadfully, according to Nancy.

'What do *you* think happened ten years later?' he asked finally.

'Granddad died, didn't he? Heart attack.' Her voice squeaked nervously. 'During that football match.'

There was another deep sigh from Paul and an even longer pause. She shouldn't break it, mustn't – it was his decision. 'Can you imagine it, Becca? An eminent chemist, a Harvard professor, believing his own mother could predict the future? Your mother was adamant I should never say anything to you and your sisters. That it was a big coincidence and for a long time, I convinced myself that was it: a play on words.'

'What words, Dad?'

'She rarely mentioned names.'

'I know,' she said. The name of a horse had fooled her for a while.

'Especially family ones, so you can imagine this cold feeling struck inside me when she said it.'

'What happened, Dad? What did she say?'

# Frank, wearing black, puffing and panting

## 1994

Rose pulled the extinguished candle from the cake, her face was pasty white.

'What's that, Mum?' Paul asked.

'Nothing, son. Perhaps forget that one.' She picked up the knife. 'Carrot cake. Your favourite.'

He'd gone alone, out of duty, and left Nancy at home in the cottage with Naomi, who had chickenpox. Nancy had insisted the twins shouldn't go either, something about catching shingles. Nancy generally had an excuse.

After hearing Rose's bizarre description of his father, it was a blessing that she'd kept the girls away.

'Wearing black? Like a suit? A funeral? Is that what you're talking about, Mum?'

Rose opened the fridge door, her back to him. She kept the milk in a small china jug ready to pour into the tea cups. He was witnessing something akin to a Japanese tea ritual; everything his mother did was with a gentle purpose and conducted at a leisurely pace. Except her hand shook a little as she poured the tea out of the pot. Something wasn't right.

'Mum?'

'They're just words, Paul. Don't pay any attention to them. I'm getting old.'

'Don't be daft. You're fifty-four. You're a sprite compared to the geriatrics you nurse at that home.'

She clucked her tongue, disapproving. 'Residents.'

'Well, if it's not important, then why are you white as a sheet? Usually you make sure I repeat it several times so Rebecca can write it in her book. You know she'll want to know.'

Rose's eyes narrowed, and she wagged her finger at him as though he was a little boy again. 'Do not tell her this one.'

'Why ever not?' He wasn't interested in cake or tea or a cosy chat.

'I think I heard it wrong. It's not come out … right.'

She collected her teacup and walked into the sitting room. He followed her.

'When will Dad be home?' he asked.

Frank worked shifts at an engineering plant. Most of the inhabitants of Chatteris worked in agriculture. Frank had begun working for the company as an apprentice and stayed through numerous shake-ups, downturns and layoffs. He'd climbed the ladder, then stopped halfway and refused the post of manager. He preferred to work with his hands and his brain, as he liked to joke.

'Late. We don't celebrate. You know we don't.'

For years Frank had worked on her birthday, while on his, which was unlikely to involve the wider family, he chose an evening out at a restaurant or the movies. Rose never minded not having her husband's company on her special day.

'He doesn't know what to do on my birthday,' she'd told Paul years go.

'But seriously, Mum, aren't you a bit old for candles?'

'Never too old for a bit of frivolity.' And because she'd used that word, Paul assumed that was why she said those things on her birthday, those crazy little sentences. He treated the whole thing as a game and she joined in, making a big thing of it as she lit the candle and dimmed the lights.

The other mums he met as a young boy weren't anything like his mother. They washed football kits and read "Women's Weekly". One knitted pullovers, another sang in the church choir, a few worked to supplement the household income. Those mums were too busy to bake cakes. Paul accepted there were worse things than a slightly eccentric mother who blurted out weird things and produced unnecessarily large quantities of cakes every week using mysterious recipes that she claimed incorporated a secret ingredient that made them special. Frank told his son there was method to her madness and it was best to go along with the birthday pantomime.

Gradually, as he grew up, and accepted he was an only child, he focused on school work. His teachers had convinced Frank his son was going to be a great scientist and able mathematician. Rose found work, spent less time at home and whether that was the reason or not, she had less to say. By the time he was in his late teens, the birthday routine was settled and less fraught and when he brought along his own family, she muttered things that only Rebecca noticed. The arrangement suited all of them. Then, as the years went on, Nancy went from disinterest to irritation at the thought of attending the gathering, and he continued to visit with his daughters or went alone.

Now, seeing her mental state, he had let it go on too long. 'Perhaps it's best you don't do the candle thing any more, Mum, if it upsets you.'

She turned on the spot and a look of horror crossed her face. The tea spilt over the side of the cup and the cake nearly slid off the tilted plate. 'Please, no, I have to. Frank...' She blinked, fighting the tears. 'Dad doesn't want to know in case...'

Paul intercepted the crockery before she dropped it. 'In case of what?'

'They mention him.'

She eased herself into the armchair. The kitten raced into the room from somewhere in the house and hopped onto her knee. She petted it, and the stroking calmed both her and the ball of fluff.

'There, there, Samwise,' she said softly.

Paul placed the cup and plate on the table next to her. 'Mum. You know you just mentioned him?'

She nodded, her head cocked to one side as if to listen. 'He'll be back soon. Don't say a word. Just let this one go, will you, Paul?'

'Okay, if that's what you want. I'll tell Rebecca I can't remember. We were too busy eating cake and I forgot.'

'Thank you.' She managed a weak smile.

He fended off the lack of rationale behind her prophetic statements. His mother was convinced that they would come true and that was what mattered to her. And had they? He really didn't want to know; the world would spin for him if they did.

He pictured Rebecca and her exercise book, the neat lines and the jagged handwriting she hadn't fully mastered. Should he tell her to throw it away?

'She's going to find out one day,' Rose murmured.

'Who?' he asked.

'Little Rebecca. She's writing them down for a reason.'

'How do you know?'

'Back in 1980, before she was born, I heard a whisper in my ear.'

He felt nauseous – why involve the children? 'What did you hear?' he asked, exasperated.

'She'll write then down and keep them safe.' Rose closed her eyes. 'I'm so tired. Wake me up when Frank comes home.'

'Mum…' He puffed out his lips and retreated.

\* \* \* \*

'Granddad wore a black shirt on the football pitch,' Rebecca said. 'He was the referee. Oh, God, poor Gran.'

'He refereed lots of games,' her father said. 'I think she hoped it wasn't exactly that, but it was.'

'Poor Gran. Poor Granddad. Imagine knowing—'

'All she knew was that he wore black and ran out of breath. Not exactly a bad omen.'

Rebecca disagreed, especially as they had kept it a secret from her. But now wasn't the time for recriminations. She'd filled a blank in her notebook and years later the significance of what Rose had said actually meant something.

'Dad,' she said slowly, 'I need to tell you what Gran said to Naomi. What she said ten years ago.'

Paul's voice sharpened. 'Tell me exactly.'

So she did. Far away in America, there was nothing her father could do. He reassured Rebecca that Rose might have meant somebody else, reiterating the feeble excuse Rebecca had conceived herself. However, in light of what she'd just found out about Frank, she no longer believed it.

'Ten years. I know something is around the corner. I feel it.' What if she told him about her visions? She bit on her lip and suppressed the desire to be spontaneous and open. It wasn't the right time. When would it ever be? Probably never. Some secrets were best kept buried.

She drew her finger along the arm of the chair. 'Dad. Did Gran ever mention my name?'

'No,' he said. 'Nor Leia. But…she did call you by different names.'

'What do you mean?' She straightened her back, her fingers cramped, aching from gripping the phone.

'This is something from years ago.'

'Let me guess, ten years before Leia and I was born.'

'Probably. It's a bit vague. Back then, she wasn't into the candle and birthday cake thing; she just blurted things out.'

'And?' Rebecca asked impatiently.

'Chalk and cheese need chocolate sometimes. Make sure you have three.' It was important: he had remembered it.

'Oh my God. Dad, Naomi is the chocolate, isn't she?'

'I guess. My three girls. So different. So clever. Leia… I worry about her, Becca. She's not coping.'

'What about her?'

There was a noise in the background. 'I'll tell you another time. Mum is home. She really doesn't get any of this.'

'But you do?'

He laughed. 'No. I just gave up trying to rationalise it. Take care of yourself, darling. We shouldn't have left you with so much responsibility. I do love you, you know that. I know it's hard to believe sometimes.'

She believed him. Perhaps there was hope he'd believe her too when she finally told him that Rose wasn't the only one with a special gift.

* * * *

Rebecca sat partially upright on the bed, her sleep disturbed by the dream. Next to her, Howard lay like a log, unaware of her troubled thoughts. She twisted the bed sheets around her fingers. Was it possible for Frederick to be a nutter? An idiot? That was it... a stranger on the street or in the pub, and he makes a joke of asking to marry her. If only... her grandfather's death wasn't a joke.

Carefully, so as not to wake Howard, she slid out of bed and crossed the room to the bay window. The moonbeams snuck in between the curtains, forming intrusive daggers of light that illuminated the stripes of the wallpaper. With delicate precision and as quietly as possible, she opened the bottom drawer and fished out the notebook. Tiptoeing out of the room, past the children's bedrooms, she switched on the light in the guest room and closed the door behind her, hushing the creak with a finger on her lips. Sitting on the bed, which was always made and ready for an unexpected and rare guest, she turned to the page with the solitary question mark.

It shouldn't be blank any longer. Rummaging around the bedside table, she found a biro. She printed the missing prediction neatly on the first line, obliterating the top of the question mark.

*Frank, wearing black, puffing and panting.*

Underneath she wrote a curt explanation, unlike the elaborate stories she'd written on the other pages.

*Heart attack. Football match. Referee.*

Hardly a poetic end to his life and one that Rose might have hoped was wrong. There were plenty of reasons for wearing black; for instance, attending a funeral. Or maybe she expected him to wear a formal dinner jacket, and the puffing and panting was due to dancing or... With a heavy heart, she laid down the pen and closed the book. According to Barbara, who'd been with Rose when the policeman arrived to pass on the bad news, Rose had obviously been upset about something from the moment Frank failed to come home at the appointed time. He'd left the house wearing a black shirt and she must have dreaded every time he had gone to referee a match that the fateful day would come. And yet she'd never stopped him going out. Rose had been resigned to his fate.

Rebecca flopped back on the bed and tried to stop worrying. There was nothing to do but wait for time to pass and for Frederick to emerge and make himself known. Then, when he did, the situation would be dealt with appropriately. On the plus side, although Rose had predicted tragic events, she'd never foretold violence or murder. The only criminal amongst her friends had been Neil, and he hardly counted as dangerous. She had to hope that nobody was out to harm Naomi.

Creeping back into the master bedroom, she returned the notebook to its drawer and slipped under the covers. Howard muttered something under his breath and turned onto his side. She shuffled over and moulded her body around his; he snored softly in reply.

She waited for sleep. It came belatedly and fitfully, leaving her tired and grumpy in the morning.

Howard shook her. 'Wakey, wakey.'

She burrowed deeper under the duvet. 'Get off.'

He folded the cover back and a stream of sunlight dazzled her. 'What's up?'

'Nothing,' she muttered, blinking.

'Hardly.' He snorted. 'Another one of those sleepless nights?'

She sat, drawing her knees up to her chin. 'Dreadful.'

'Oh, poor thing.'

'Dad and I chatted about one of Gran's premonitions. He told me something and I couldn't stop thinking about it.'

'Oh.' Howard straightened. 'I thought you found out everything.'

'There was one, remember, the year I was ill.'

He pursed his lips. He didn't remember, of course, why would he? When she'd shown him the notebook, he'd scanned the pages, chuckling at her childish block letters, and treated it like an artefact of dubious provenance. After his cursory glance, he'd handed it back to her without comment. He hadn't exactly dismissed her research but neither had he congratulated her. There was nothing of interest for a man steeped in currency and numbers; Rose never mentioned the stock market. If he'd been disturbed by the one that referred to him, he never said so.

'And?' he said warily.

'It relates to Grandad.'

Howard hadn't met Frank. He rose, offering her his solid back. 'I'll go put the kettle on.'

'Don't you want to know?' She threw off the covers.

'He died a long time ago. So, I can't think it's relevant now.' He swept his dressing gown over his shoulders. In another part of the house, the children shouted and slammed doors. They weren't friends in the mornings.

Rebecca marched across the room, opened the drawer and dug out the notebook. She waved it at her husband. 'It matters because Rose predicted his death. Don't you understand? She saw how he died, her own husband. Now I'm worried about Naomi. She warned her about this man—'

'Who she's never met.' He tied a knot in the cord without looking up.

She slammed the notebook down on the dresser. 'It's not too late. Ten years, assuming that's what it is. We only know about the birthday ones.'

Howard's chin shot up. 'What do you mean? You said they were the only ones.'

'I... don't think they are. I hope they are.' Where had that thought come from? 'Why does she get them right on cue.' She snapped her fingers. 'And mine are all over the place.'

'Because, sweetheart, you're not your gran.'

'Meaning?' She stared at him and he flinched. 'You think—'

'God, I meant nothing by it. You're different, that's all.'

She stormed past him, out on to the landing. 'Kids. Get dressed, or we'll be late.'

'Mummy, he flicked toothpaste at me—'

'Toby!'

Howard took over, herding the kids downstairs. Rebecca returned to the bedroom and threw herself onto the bed. It was just an idea that had dropped into her head, she hadn't seriously considered it before now. Rose kept her birthdays special for a reason and anything else wasn't worth contemplating. Rebecca wished she'd never said it. Howard needed to believe there was a future with fewer or no visions, when she could stand out in the open, unafraid.

'Oh, Becca,' she groaned into the pillow. 'What if she heard things all the time?'

# eleven
## Naomi
## September

The wood panelling spirited Naomi away to a different era, a time when women wore corsets and men breeches and stockings. The surroundings nurtured her through the pieces, especially those written for baroque instruments. She perched on the edge of the cushioned chair, listening to the melodic cadences of the clarinet while she counted her rests. Lifting the lip plate to her chin, she drew a lungful of air and snatched the melody from the clarinet and owned it for herself. The room supported her high notes, embellishing them with a slight echo. The duet of reed and flute continued, gathering to it the other two instruments.

Opposite her was Pierre, a twenty-year-old student with sprouting hair and spider-like fingers that sprawled across the keys of his bassoon. Heather had done well to find the young man from France, an undeniably gifted undergraduate at the university's music school. He brought youthful vigour to the quartet, which contrasted with the dour Malcolm, who sat next to him with his oboe slotted between his pursed lips.

Whereas Pierre had the lung capacity of a whale, Malcolm puffed until his cheeks ballooned out and his nose turned red. Remarkably, for all the animation, he never failed to reach a breath mark and managed to produce an astoundingly haunted tone.

The tubular Pierre, a younger and graceful performer with dancing eyebrows, who swayed his dynamic body and elongated instrument in a hypnotic manner, was on the cusp of reaching musical maturity. In a year's time he'd be snapped up by a national orchestra, or if he met the right people, a solo career. Naomi tried hard not to envy his passion; she was past her peak and had missed the opportunity to break out.

Heather was reassuringly competent: she was a bit rusty too. The whole point of reconstituting the quartet was to move on from where they'd left off four years ago and continue to stretch each other with carefully chosen words of criticism. The trouble was that Pierre, being more accustomed to the harsh opinions of his university tutors, was borderline abrasive in his feedback and peppered his remarks with his strong accent and animated Gallic gestures.

'He'll make a great conductor one day,' Heather whispered to Naomi during a break.

'True.' Naomi sighed. 'He is spot on with his comments though. Very perceptive and erudite. You know we've a long way to go before we're ready to book St Mary's.'

An unusually frosty expression descended on Heather's face. Naomi could understand why, as it was her fault, her lack of resilience, that had caused them to drift apart four years ago.

'We have to agree a programme,' said Heather. 'So far we've ditched Handel.'

Naomi considered this a pity. She loved Handel's *Queen of Sheba* and it really suited the room. Ethan's sun lounge hadn't been needed in the end. Heather had pulled some strings at her school and wrangled free access to their lofty, panelled practice room that once had been the boardroom of a company until the preparatory school took over the premises.

'We should use this room for a concert,' Naomi said. Small, more intimate, it was unlikely to haunt her in the same way as St Mary's.

Heather pulled another face of disapproval. 'Not enough capacity. Pierre's keen to try some contemporary pieces, really take the audience out of their comfort zone. So is Malcolm.'

'Is he okay?' Naomi glanced towards Malcolm who was adjusting his reed and out of earshot.

'He's reaching the precipice of mid-life and intends to suffer accordingly.' Heather rolled her eyes to the ornately decorative ceiling. She'd known Malcolm for years. 'Honestly, he's fine. He runs five miles at the weekend. He just struggles to shift it around his tummy. His lungs are like inflatable bladders. I'm sure,' she said to an amused Naomi, 'he's like the TARDIS, bigger on the inside.'

They resumed playing and Pierre had his way. They tried a poetic suite and the piece went better than Naomi had anticipated.

At nine o'clock, they packed up and walked across the road to the pub. Heather was keen for Pierre to feel at home in the quartet and not assume he was a convenient, temporary guest to their little group. Naomi had to agree; he was too good to let slip and she was determined not to let her cautious approach deflect his zeal.

Over drinks, they debated what to play. The French student had the influence of his tutors and suggested compositions that hadn't existed when Naomi studied.

'I bring the music next week, oui?' Pierre's enthusiasm was infectious. They said yes.

Naomi drove home with her energy levels still fizzing and the music resonating in her ears. The quartet was back; her flute was no longer just for teaching. She could enjoy the company of versatile, worldly musicians and the accomplishment of mutual admiration. As long as that was it. It didn't matter what anyone else said about her musical gifts, she wasn't up to anything more and that was fine. What once had been her dream – performing with a national orchestra or something equally prestigious – was ruined.

She no longer needed accolades, at least not the paper kind. She'd a heap of them anyway: a distinction for both her teaching and performers' diplomas, a couple of competition wins, and a first class honours degree. 'You're special. Astounding accomplishments,' her tutor had said at the graduation ceremony. 'Find a sponsor, somebody to guide you.'

The Seasons concert, the one four years ago, hadn't been a disaster for the whole quartet – the audience applauded vigorously for those pieces. Naomi blamed her lacklustre solo for letting everyone down – not that anyone said anything overtly critical about it, but she'd expected a rapturous ovation and it never came. Intuitive Rebecca understood the issue went deeper than ability.

'If you don't feel comfortable performing, then don't,' she said, after a rib-crushing embrace in the back of the church.

'It's not about performance nerves.' Naomi had fumbled for words to describe her failings, how she wanted to touch the listeners with what stirred inside her and make them feel it too.

Nancy had admonished Naomi during a subsequent telephone call. 'Why are you still teaching? Your tutors should have pushed you harder.'

A disillusioned Naomi snapped back at her absent mother. 'I don't want to perform any more. Why is it so hard for you to grasp? What does it matter to you anyway?' She'd slammed the phone down. She'd lied. Of course, she loved to perform, but something undefinable needed to click inside her head and it simply hadn't happened.

'What went wrong, Naomi?' Leia had asked, attempting to pick up the debris of Naomi's fractured confidence after the horrendous telephone call with their mother. 'You seemed really keen to give it a try.'

# The first time is the hardest, the least rewarding

The concert had been well attended; each pew fully occupied. The university music department had provided much of the audience – a huddle of professional musicians and eager undergraduates eyeballing her from the wings. Their expectations of her ran deeper than simply being note perfect.

The quartet's pieces had been straightforward. They'd done the requisite *Queen of Sheba*, which everyone loved, and a few arrangements of well-known string quartets. The harmonies carried around the church effortlessly. There were a few mistakes; no obvious ones.

After the interval, Naomi smoothed down her black skirt with a steady hand, adjusted the head piece of her flute and warmed the lip plate ready to go. Having convinced Clive to let her have centre stage and with Heather's nod of approval, she had chosen a piece that was supposed to dazzle the audience. With her confidence riding high after the first half of the concert, Naomi rose to her feet.

The piece was contemporary and a fusion of Japanese and Western styles. She always loved playing the composition – she'd never played it again after the concert. What went wrong wasn't stage fright – she'd performed for tutors and examiners and survived those encounters with her confidence intact. Something else happened and she put it down to the lack of connection to the notes that flew out of her flute. She'd done all the right things while practising and still, on the day, she'd struggled to share with her listeners the passionate love affair that existed between her and music.

She'd closed her eyes. She always did when performing a solo and playing from memory. The shutters came down and the audience was blocked out. They might cough or sneeze, but she heard nothing, and if they fidgeted or stared back at her, she was oblivious. The distance she believed was necessary. Why be distracted when all that was required from her was music? She wasn't an actor or a dancer, and her movements were limited by the positioning of her instrument. She wasn't attempting to be flamboyant or extrovert. If people wanted to see action, they could go to a rock concert or a musical. Yet, even so, there was the possibility that she had appeared too wooden and unanimated. Had she held something back, never quite gifting the listener the experience playing out in her head?

Perhaps the flaw was the lack of accompanist – the piece didn't require a pianist. Every note, just like her standing alone on the dais, was exposed. It wasn't a limp performance though, she sang the melody as confidently as an acapella singer. As for nerves, over the years she'd mastered the art of controlling the adrenaline kick that came with performing. She needed enough of it pumping through her body to focus the mind, but too much, and the untimely snatches of breath would ruin the crafted pattern of lyrical phrases.

Maybe she'd misjudged the acoustics, but the church wasn't a bad auditorium and musicians frequently used the location. So it had to be her. She failed to shine, to lift the piece to a higher plain where some magical transcendence happened and left the gathering awe struck and in a state of rapture. 'A bit like great sex,' Leia would say. In the past, Naomi had laughed off the remark, but now she hated the reference. However, Leia was right about the level of passion needed to succeed as a professional performer. Naomi wanted to communicate with the audience and after their polite, mediocre applause, she knew she'd fallen short of their expectations. She was nothing special. The rest of the concert fizzled away into a blur of forgotten sounds while the disappointment she felt hung around for an eternity.

The other members of the quartet knew she had issues with performing, and though they offered her congratulations, they sidestepped any thorough critique, all too aware of her own misgivings, except Malcolm, who lazily packed away his things at the end of the concert and tried to communicate something. Her own post-mortem had left her in a fragile state and she wasn't in the mood for anyone else's.

'Maybe something more challenging next time?' Malcolm said. The departing audience were pooling by the church door, their backs to the dais.

Her tongue and fingers disagreed; they had worked damn hard. What could be more challenging than that particular piece of music?

With a flushed face, he gathered his music, glancing in Naomi's direction, then over to Heather, who was chatting to a friend. His stand refused to collapse until he forced it with a grunt of annoyance. She might have misunderstood his frustration and gone on the defensive.

'That was the best I've played that piece.' Naomi rammed the cleaning cloth into the hollow body of her flute.

'It was, you played it well.' Malcolm paused. 'I meant challenging for the ears and eyes of the listener. Something that triggers feelings.' He gave a small shrug and disappeared behind the organ pipes.

Clive left the quartet not long after. Heather got pregnant and Malcolm without Heather wasn't interested in continuing. The concert turned into an unplanned swansong for the group. Naomi regretted her eagerness to take centre stage and often wondered if they blamed her for the break-up. She was too uncomfortable to ask anyone's opinion.

Following the performance in St Mary's, nobody badgered Naomi about the teaching, even her disappointed mother gave up while her father remained on the side-lines, aware but inert, as if he was waiting for something to happen that would nudge Naomi into achieving her full potential. That potential began life when she was five years old and dazzled her primary school teacher with a fluent, and tuneful, solo on a plastic recorder. Nobody had taught her how to play it and she'd learnt to read music before any words, an instinctive process that prodded her astonished parents into action. The day she was big enough to hold a flute in her hands, they started her with lessons. She liked the flute, the choice was a natural evolution after the array of recorders she'd mastered, and no other instrument appealed to Naomi in quite the same way as that shiny tube of metal and its smooth tone. She loved making up her own ditties and writing them down in a scrap book. Whenever the family went shopping in Cambridge, she dragged them along to the music shop and chose pieces she liked to play. There was at last something that she had control over; when she closed the door of her bedroom to practise, the taut Liddell life took a back seat. The recognition she achieved with her swift progress was also advantageous. Up to then, it was the twins who had monopolised their parents' attention.

However, only Rebecca had attended the concert. Leia had concocted an unsurprising feeble excuse for staying away. Her parents weren't expected to fly over especially – it was only one item on the program and hardly a breakthrough into the world of solo artist.

'Cheer up, Naomi,' Rebecca had said at the end of the concert. 'You were fine, honestly. A pretty piece, not my cup of tea, maybe… I should get going. Howie is baby sitting and… it's a long drive.' She'd hurried away, pulling a cowl over her head as if ashamed to be associated with her sister.

Kyle, the one person who might have lifted her morale, was worlds away from Naomi's dilemma. He excelled at doing things in the isolation of the online world and if he sought adulation, he never boasted about it. He quietly gathered a throng and cultivated that relationship in private. What Naomi wanted was the instant gratification that came with a live performance: an audience captivated by the hot-blooded display of an accomplished artist. Instead, she'd been passive. 'Disconnected,' she told him.

'A bit like when the Wi-Fi goes down?' Kyle's bad joke increased the growing divide between them.

Nobody understood that the yearning was still there, awake and hungry to be fed, so she gave up trying to explain. She hid her feelings so well that everyone assumed she was over the whole performing thing. They spoke of it in hushed tones, alluding to the concert in the politest of ways. 'You gave it a go, it's not for you.' Except it was exactly what she wanted to succeed at doing.

* * * *

Whatever the outcome, re-forming the Seasons was a step in the right direction for her, and Ethan. Unlike Kyle, Ethan could whistle in tune and stamp his foot along to the beat. He had some appreciation of her talent and that had to be a tick on Rebecca's invisible checklist of boyfriend requirements.

The previous weekend, she'd plucked up the courage to introduce Ethan to Rebecca over a quick Skype session so that Rebecca could listen to the potpourri of accents he'd accumulated. During the polite conversation, Naomi realised she adored Ethan for his quirks and damned if anyone was going to derail their relationship. Rebecca had said very little, which meant liked him better than Kyle. A good omen.

She said goodbye to the rest of the quartet and slipped out of the pub. By the time she reached Newmarket, she was drained of energy. However, when she spotted Ethan's Audi in the drive, a spike of adrenaline woke her.

A crowd was cheering, whooping shouts that rose and fell into silence. Naomi shut the door behind her, hurriedly kicked off her shoes and walked into sitting room.

Ethan was sprawled across the sofa, watching a baseball game with a beer bottle in one hand and TV remote in the other. Turning his head, he acknowledged Naomi's arrival with a piercing stare that was darker than usual. Something had gone wrong with his day.

'You're back at last,' he said. There was a minor key slur to his tone, a coolness that augmented her anxieties.

While she stood clutching her bags, stunned by his abruptness, he switched off the television. He didn't budge to make space for her and remained stretched along the full length of the couch. There were two empty beer bottles on the coffee table. He wore the same blue shirt she seen him put on that morning and there was an oily smudge on the sleeve.

'I came back early.' He pressed the bottled to his mouth and swallowed. 'Didn't seem any point in staying. It's all stuff I know.' He was supposed to have been attending a training day on some new machinery.

'Won't you get into trouble?' She perched on the edge of the armchair, bone weary from the long day.

'Nah.' He shrugged. 'I've spent my life on farms. You'd think I'd know about basic safety by now. All this equipment with their glossy manuals telling you what to do, but when it comes down to it, it's all common sense. The guy running it was a condescending drongo.' The Aussie accent had gone up a notch, which it often did when he drank. 'The trainer knows jack-shit. It's ridiculous. These machines have numerous warnings and safety grills stuck all over them. You'd have to be stupid to fuck up.'

She flinched at the rare curse. She and Rebecca had a low threshold for tolerating swearing. Leia was four-letter-word factory.

He tapped his watch. 'You're back late.'

'We went to the pub afterwards to plan things and welcome Pierre to the quartet.' Eleven o'clock wasn't late; she pressed her lips together.

'I texted you.'

'Oh.' She extracted her mobile from her handbag. There was one message from him, stating he was coming home. 'I set it to vibrate. Didn't want to be disturbed during the practice.'

'Pierre?' He lifted his disdainful eyebrows, expecting her to say something.

She refused to believe he was jealous. Rising to her feet, she detoured around the sofa, intending to get a drink of water. But the extending reach of Ethan's fingers caught her wrist above the watch strap and he tugged, halting her with jerk. She shook her arm free. It wasn't the first time he'd snared her, but usually it was her hand and done tenderly. The way he touched her now fell far short of a show of affection; he wanted to trap her, ensuring she had to stay put while he talked.

'Don't,' she snapped. 'Don't make it an issue. He's twenty, French, enthusiastic, looks like his bassoon and is too arrogant for my tastes. Why do I have to even explain this?' She stormed out of the room.

He followed her into the kitchen, hovering by the door as she poured a glass of water. Her hand trembled.

'I was worried when you didn't reply,' he said.

'You don't sound worried.' Swallowing, the icy water hit her belly and she shivered. The house was cold and unwelcoming. 'You're pissed.'

'Just three drinks,' he said indignantly.

'I meant you're pissed with me.'

He frowned. 'I'm not. I said I was worried. Why don't you believe me? Do you think I'd lie about that?'

The awkwardness hung limply between them. 'Then why mention Pierre?'

'I don't know him.'

The answer was weak and hypocritical. She rinsed the glass under the tap. 'I'm going to bed.'

When Naomi had been at college "Trust is the cornerstone of a good relationship" had been the subject of one of Rebecca's sanctimonious lectures. It had led to an unfortunate quarrel over Naomi's independence. Naomi had taken Rebecca's remark as a lack of faith in her judgement. She had pointed out that Rebecca's view of relationships was clearly tainted by the stream of divorce cases she handled at work. 'From which I learn,' Rebecca had said. Leia had left the room, which she often had done when the two sisters battled. The irksome memory rose to the surface as Naomi undressed.

Was this a trust issue? Had Ethan wanted her home so he could keep her under tabs, or was it simply that he wanted to protect her? And was jealousy such a bad thing? It implied his feelings toward her were strong enough to evoke the green-eyed monster. She lay stiff on the bed, unsure whether to wait for him to join her or just switch off the light. The rumble of the excited crowd drifted upstairs – the television was back on.

Ethan questioned her about one man and when she walked away, he acted hurt. It was such a ridiculous conversation; Pierre was ten years her junior. The little rift would heal overnight.

\* \* \* \*

She woke to find Ethan lying next to her, his bright gaze resting on her semi-covered body. The room was bathed in hot morning sunshine, the kind that conjured up the smell of summer roses and freshly cut grass. It was autumn, though. She stretched and fabricated a noisy yawn.

'I'm going to work,' she said, shutting her eyes. 'I'll be back later in the day. If you stay sober, perhaps we might—'

'Sober?' he said sharply.

She opened her eyes. He was bolt upright with his arms across his chest. 'Last night,' she said. 'You didn't come to bed—'

'I didn't think I was welcome.'

'You were hardly conciliatory.'

They both glared at each other. Three months into their relationship, three joyous months had suddenly hit a barrier and it had been constructed out of such a trivial embryonic feeling, a mutual distrust. Perhaps Rebecca was right: Naomi needed to demonstrate she trusted him and then, hopefully, he would respond in kind.

'I'm sorry,' she said. 'I hadn't realised I'd upset you that much. I went for a drink with friends instead of coming home, and then I was tired. I switched off the volume on my phone and didn't check it. Yes, if I hadn't done those things it might have made it a different evening. But you were distant, Ethan, acting like I'd done something terrible. I felt hurt by the questions.'

He relaxed, letting his hands fall into his lap. She was relieved to see the fiery display of irritation in his silvery eyes was extinguished.

'We're learning, aren't we?' she said, leaning over to drop a kiss on his slightly parted lips. 'It's how relationships develop. We hit a wall of misunderstanding and—'

He pulled her down and she collapsed across him with her head nestled in his arms. For a second, she nearly panicked. However, he cradled her there, and engaged her in a protracted kiss that unravelled the last knot in her taut belly. His moist lips tasted of bitter hops. When he released her, she ran her thumb along her lower lip. It had been a bruising, passionate embrace of mouths and a message had been transmitted in its midst – a promise of something later in the day.

She gathered some clean clothes from her side of the closet and backed out of the room. 'I'll shower. Bring up a coffee. A bagel or something?' She offered the peace offering and he accepted it with a smile.

Only later, as she drove across town to her first lesson of the day, did she wonder if she'd acquiesced too easily. She'd fallen for Ethan because he wasn't anything like Kyle and perhaps, given the disquiet that plagued her, she was tumbling too far along a less than idyllic path.

* * * *

Leia's face flickered. Her lips weren't syncing with her speech and her voice was distorted and delivered in fragmented phrases. Naomi ignored the customary glitches; they'd chatted many times before using video messaging.

'So, he's not called Frederick.'

The glib remark wasn't welcome. However, Leia wasn't snickering when she brought up Rose's ridiculous birthday premonition. The odd thing was Rebecca had made the same comment, and she was the one who had told Naomi to forget all about it. The three of them hadn't forgotten, not even sceptical Leia with her condescending view of spiritualism. The birthday remained fresh in Naomi's memory, including the buttery taste of the cake and Rose whispering in her ear.

'No,' she said curtly.

'Okay,' Leia drawled, mocking Naomi. 'He's American though, isn't he?' Leia wanted to meet him, but she wasn't due to visit the UK for a few weeks. In the meantime, she remained the primary conduit to Naomi's parents, leaking information to them, so that when Naomi contacted them, they were well-informed and already armed with opinions. To date, Ethan had fared better than Kyle on the approval front.

'He was born in America, but I don't think he considers himself an American, not any more. He's closer to an Aussie.' To her finely tuned ear, Ethan's soup of dialects favoured the southern hemisphere, rather than the western one. 'Irish, too.

He's mentioned an Irish grandmother who left Ireland to live in America.'

Leia's dark eyebrows rose a fraction. 'How odd. Americans are proud of their nationality. I wouldn't call him typical, but there again, he doesn't live over here, so perhaps he's happier living elsewhere. I'd like to know why, though. Wouldn't you?' Her grin was comically lopsided as she aired her more vicious nature. 'I can't wait to interrogate him. What state does he come from?'

Naomi quietly winced. The thought of Leia grilling Ethan unnerved her. Leia's approach would not be cerebral. For a genius, her sister could be blunt and uncouth, oblivious to the nuance of gentle probing, and she often blurted out inappropriate questions that caused ripples in the middle of otherwise polite discourse. Nancy called Leia the cuckoo in the nest, the one that nobody recognised – a heartless swipe at Leia that summed up their mother's attitude toward her daughter's intellect. It seemed that Nancy expected the whole package of brains, good looks and social elegance. Leia managed the first with enviable ease, the second because it was natural, and failed dismally to even attempt the third. Regardless of her failings, when Nancy summoned her, Leia had leapt across the Atlantic and taken up residence right next door. Naomi had duly lost her uninhibited sister at a key moment in her life. Rebecca's alarm at her twin's migration had been short-lived. It wasn't as if she went out of her way to spend time with Leia. Rebecca held court in Huntingdon and everyone was supposed to visit her. Naomi's next visit was overdue; she would fit one in at the end of the month.

'I don't know,' Naomi said truthfully. 'He's very cagey about his past. It's like he wants to forget. He's not past centric, he's forward looking. Rose would have liked him.'

The flickering image jumped a few times as Leia's face caught up with her words. 'Rose liked just about everybody she met.'

Their grandmother often cropped up in conversations in a compensatory fashion; she was a person who could heal wounds even in her absence. Nobody blamed Leia for failing to spot Rose's deterioration on that last day of her life. Although medically trained, Leia's immersion into the world of laboratory research had filled her head with equations and graphs, rather than symptoms. The day after Rose's had died, Leia wept openly, almost inconsolably; a disconcerting display of grief that ended as abruptly as it began – Leia had brushed off Rebecca's arm around her shoulder. Naomi remembered the day clearly, especially the way Leia kept staring at her, asking if she was alright. Leia, if she tried, could be very kind-hearted.

Naomi pushed aside the nagging concerns she had about her boyfriend. He continued to show affection, buying her little gifts – mostly chocolates and flowers – and exhibited a tender competence in his love-making. What annoyed her was his increasing need to track her whereabouts. The incident over Pierre had surprised her, and since then, she'd become more aware of his questions regarding her timekeeping and habits. Going out shopping might seem a superficial event to Naomi, but Ethan treated it as if she was heading into a dangerous jungle. He asked her to text when she arrived at the supermarket and when she left. Jokingly, she reminded him that England wasn't a gun-toting society.

'I don't think your safety is funny,' he said with a granite face.

'Why?' she asked. 'Are you going to follow me around? Checking up on the competition?' He backed off, but she had provided him with a list of locations because she hated the way he ignored her until she did as he asked.

She wasn't the spell-binding type, neither beautiful nor blessed with a shapely figure; she had unruly hair and two large earlobes, or so she thought, although Ethan liked to nibble on them. She hated her breasts – her smaller sisters were envious of their size. When Naomi passed a mirror, she glanced away, and assumed it was best not to know if her hair was unkempt or whether her waist needed sucking in. However, regardless of her faults, she occasionally attracted attention.

If she and Ethan had a little holiday away from work, he might relax and not see so many false threats surrounding him. For all their teething problems, she still couldn't stop thinking about him or wanting him. She'd developed quite an addiction to Ethan and his dramatic moments because invariably they at least made her feel alive, and for some odd reason she was able to respond to him in kind. Drama was exciting.

# Visits to the bakery don't always involve bread

The pattern of nights and days marched onward through the summer months and into autumn, and still no Frederick. Rose's premonition was nothing to do with Naomi; Rebecca clung on to the assumption, hoping it would reel in her anxieties, especially those odd thoughts about domineering types who preyed on nice women. Rose's unfulfilled warning remained a haunting echo, and in the absence of an obvious candidate, Rebecca sought to know more about Ethan. However, Naomi wasn't keen on bringing him to Huntingdon, for reasons she couldn't articulate beyond the excuse of being simply too busy.

The alternative solution had been a quick chat online and Rebecca had seen for herself that Ethan had a roughly hewn handsome face with a tawny beard and eyes that blinked so infrequently, the pinpricks of his pupils transfixed her. His accent was not Irish, nor for that matter was it solely Australian. Alongside him, shoulder to shoulder, Naomi glowed, apparently happy, and a little less chubby around the cheeks, which meant she wasn't comfort eating; her way of coping with stress.

What pleased Rebecca most was the news about the wind quartet.

'Jolly good,' she said when she told Howard. 'She needs to embrace her talents.'

*Why can't I?* Howard no longer referred to her "gift" unless she forced it into the conversation. His hopes that she might blank them out had failed. She'd not stopped her intrusive visions into other people's lives and she despised herself for retreating inside the house for hours upon end, only venturing out when necessary.

The school run should have been the least problematic element of Rebecca's weekday, and for the most part it was manageable. She had crafted a procedure that involved the car, a parking spot near the school gate and a location under a tree for shade. Each day, she arrived with plenty of time to park, bribing the kids with some last minute dose of sugar so that they waited in the car with her, before herding them as quickly as possible into the school yard just as the main entrance opened.

The rest of Rebecca's day was less predictable. She travelled to her designated locations — shops, primarily — weaving between parked cars as if driving in a chicane. An unremarkable day meant nothing happened and if she arrived home burdened with shopping bags, but no other emotional baggage, she congratulated herself. For a while nothing visionary happened until she bumped into Fran Williams outside the bakery — Rebecca preferred freshly baked bread even if it meant walking the three hundred yards from the town centre car park.

Fran waved. Rebecca ignored her and stared into the distance beyond. Unfortunately, Fran was persistent.

'Yo-ho!' she yelled. 'Rebecca, hi. It's me.'

Rebecca gripped the handle of her carrier bag and smiled in reply, hoping that would be sufficient. It wasn't. Fran intercepted Rebecca before she reached the bakery door.

'Will you be there tomorrow evening?' Fran asked.

Rebecca knew exactly to what Fran referred. The school fete was in two weeks and the PTA was in panic mode. The committee had been convened to bring order and Rebecca, as a nominal helper, was expected to attend the meeting. The start of term meant fresh parents, loose change in pockets and the opportunity to twist new mums — dads weren't excluded, just invisible — into joining the PTA. She didn't mind the meetings, which took place in a cosy front room of the chairperson's house, but the fete was a problem. Rebecca prayed for rain so that the stalls had to be set up in the school hall.

'Weather is set to hold,' Fran said, dashing Rebecca's hopes.

'Jolly good. Yes, I'll be there at the meeting.'

Chin-wag was a more accurate description and it explained the lamentable lack of productivity. But there again, she was out of the house and in company. Howie would be pleased.

'Excellent,' Fran said gleefully.

The conversation in the street was unnecessary and frustrating. Rebecca loved texting – it was her salvation, being able to converse in the comfort of her home.

'Will you make those delicious cakes?' Fran asked. Fran possessed chubby cheeks, rather like her sons.

'Of course. Red velvet and walnut.'

'Delicious.' Fran patted her stomach. 'I love nuts.'

'I'll put in extra. Maybe you'll win it in the tombola.'

'Oh?' Fran's lips sunk into a frown. 'You're not on the cake stall?'

'Not this year.'

Last year she'd nearly succumbed to a panic attack standing under a gazebo on the playing field thinking that any moment she would turn into a laughable zombie as her mind whisked her away to some distant place. In the end, she had seen nothing out of the ordinary, but had to sit under the shade of a tree while Eleanor fanned her with a comic book that Toby had bought with his pocket money. The intervention of her young children shamed her.

'Oh.' Fran pouted again. 'Everyone loves your cupcakes.'

'Thank you.' She edged closer to the shop door.

'Does Eleanor help you?' Fran had three football mad boys. 'Must be lovely.'

Thinking about Eleanor so intensely was a mistake. With her hand reaching for the handle, Rebecca braced herself for the heralding burst of adrenaline and flurry of icy shivers. For the first time she was with her little daughter, who was standing by the wall of the playground and alone, or so Rebecca thought.

A ginger-haired girl, slightly older than Eleanor, entered stage left and thrust her freckled face into Eleanor's, stuck out her tongue and said something accompanied by a disapproving wrinkle of her pert nose. The first word resembled "smelly", the second word possibly "knickers". Eleanor's body went rigid, her fingers clenched. The other girl giggled, her front two teeth missing.

Rebecca's hands formed their own fists, ready to punch, but the scene ended, fading out into greyness, the "open" sign on the door substituting itself over the girl's snarling grin.

'Are you okay?' Fran asked. 'You're very pale.'

Rebecca shot an unfair glare over her shoulders before relaxing her face with well-practised control. Nevertheless, the horror of the vision, seeing her child being bullied, remained vividly stamped in her mind, captured for eternity along with the sense of hopelessness that it conjured up.

'Quite alright, thank you. See you tomorrow.' With her hurried dismissal, she entered the shop.

She was far from alright. She leaned on the counter and ordered a granary bloomer.

Uninterested in the shop assistant's banter, she reeled in the latent images of her vision, analysing them and finding them horribly real. Eleanor, her beloved child, was the victim of teasing. What should she do? Charge into the school, demand to see the headteacher and insist she was shown Eleanor, so that she could talk to her daughter and ensure she was safe…happy?

'Two pounds, please,' said the woman behind the counter.

'Sorry.' Rebecca thrust the money into the woman's hand.

She glanced at her watch – ten to one. Lunch-time. If she walked quickly, she could reach the school by quarter past one. She dropped the change into her purse. Lunch break would have finished by quarter past, she realised as she turned. Eleanor would be back in class. If she pulled Eleanor out of the classroom…

'Your bread!' the assistant called out as Rebecca opened the door. 'You've forgotten it.'

A red-faced Rebecca retrieved the still warm bread and plopped it into her shopping bag. In the midst of fretting, she hadn't noticed the aroma of warm yeast, nor the flickering blue light of the fly trap or the ice capped buns lined up on the display shelf. Her senses were focused elsewhere while her empty stomach churned. The air was sickly sweet and hot.

Stepping outside onto the pavement – Fran thankfully gone – Rebecca stopped. How stupid to even think she could intervene on Eleanor's behalf; the child would be mortified and the teacher quite rightly would send Rebecca away. She had no grounds, no evidence to show what had happened to her daughter, and how could she possibly explain her ability to "imagine" so convincingly what had occurred? Eleanor would be upset, confused and likely to want an explanation. So would Howard. He wouldn't be pleased.

She sank onto a warped bench, the shopping bag squeezed between her feet, and there she remained, fighting tears, unaware of pedestrians and traffic. *The kids, oh God,* she shivered, *please not the children.* What if this wasn't a one off, and they came to her frequently? All those moments of their lives played out in mental videos, but not captured on a phone, like most people. What if she saw Eleanor in an accident or Toby in a fight? If only she could believe she would be shown moments to cherish: Toby scoring a goal or Eleanor reading out one of her delightful poems. Invariably, she witnessed far more lows than highs in her visions. She projected the timeline into the future: when they left home, would she follow them to university or work? What if they drank too much or were tempted by drugs? She could pretend to be their guardian angel and reach out to protect them, but they would hate her for interfering, even if they understood the reason why – for now they were too young to tell. She could speak to Howard, but how many crises could Howard take? She had tried, she really believed she had done what she could to stem the visions, but she had failed. The children would learn to fend for themselves, and so would Rebecca.

Eventually, when a spot of rain tapped her nose, she stirred from her melancholy and walked back to the car.

Howard wasn't home – he was in London – but as he'd promised he called Rebecca at precisely two o'clock. Rebecca by then was back in the safety of the kitchen.

He was bubbly, congratulating himself on a deal. Her silence crept into the conversation and he noted it.

'What's up, sweetheart?'

Rebecca opened her month and shut it. What could she say to him? He could appreciate the dilemma – the need to intervene on Eleanor's behalf, but he would remind her, as he had done on countless occasions, that it was impossible to do anything. The critical moment had passed. She could mop up the mess of the aftermath, and he helped her sometimes, but by then they were dealing with consequences. His usual tactic was to gently steer her away from the emotional fallout and distract her with other things: his work, the kids. A kiss. In response to her husband's tactile tricks, she'd happily seek sanctuary in his cocooning arms.

But this was Eleanor. Their daughter.

'I saw something,' she said tentatively.

'Oh.' He recognised the opening phrase.

She told him, stuttering a little.

'So, some kid was picking on Ellie?'

'Yes.'

'Calling her names?'

'Yes.' She forced the word out of her dry throat.

'Did she hit Ellie?'

'Well, no, but things faded, like they do.'

'Has the school rung?' Howard asked coolly, so in control. She needed to hear the confidence in his voice.

'No.' They hadn't. But what if they didn't know; they hadn't seen what Rebecca had seen in her vision.

'Love, it's school. Kids.'

She stared ahead at the streams of rainwater pouring down the window and envied the raindrops. Her frustration was like a raincloud that never released its payload. 'It's Eleanor,' she snapped back.

Howard sighed. 'This was always a possibility. One day, you might see the kids. We agreed, didn't we, that unless the situation was dangerous we would let things pan out. Eleanor is a wise girl. She'll tell us. She doesn't keep secrets from us.'

Rebecca winced. He probably didn't mean to make it sound like a comparison, but it felt that way. 'What if she doesn't say anything or never says anything?'

'Then she isn't upset by it,' he said with infuriating casualness.

'How can you know that? She can be proud. Headstrong. She might not admit she had problems.'

'You saw a few seconds—'

'Something happened—'

'Things happen every day, Rebecca,' he said, exasperated. He called her Rebecca as if on the cusp of anger; a vocal gesture that alarmed her. 'You can't be there for them every day. Look, I've a meeting, I've got to go. Have a cup of tea or something and wait to see Eleanor at the end of school.'

She gritted her teeth. He referred to their kids as a "them", as if they were no different from the others she saw in her visions. No amount of tea was going to comfort her anxieties; she'd witnessed one slither of a moment in time and the crippling uselessness of her situation paralysed her. She believed in the butterfly effect; one event rippling on into another and the waves travelled far into the future with unknown consequences. While Rose had been worn down by the waiting, the anticipation of things to come, Rebecca had to deal with the immediate aftermath and its impact.

At three o'clock, she watched her daughter carefully as she exited the school gate, swinging her school bag. Toby was picking his nose. Rebecca collected Eleanor's hand, the cool palm embraced by her clammy one, and gathered her into a hug. Eleanor wriggled free.

'Mummy, don't.'

'Everything okay? Good day?'

'The usual,' she said in a grown-up voice. She was her father's daughter. How many times had he come home saying just that. Eleanor repeated it with ease; she liked to use the exact same phrase.

What now? Rebecca had to decide. Did she pick apart Eleanor's vague answer or accept she really had no ability to change the flow of events?

With a heavy heart, she chose the latter and the decision crushed her as it embodied an impotence that would define the rest of her life. She was imprisoned by her gift in a place with no escape. If she had control of it, then maybe she wouldn't fear for her children. She wouldn't fear losing Howard.

Later that evening, feeling lethargic and preoccupied by the day's events, she walked past the pile of clothes waiting to be ironed and ignored it.

# twelve

## Naomi

Pierre had mellowed over the weeks to such an extent he'd abandoned his bombastic approach and quietly flirted with Naomi, something she wouldn't tell Ethan. Fortunately for Pierre, his skills as a bassoonist still outweighed his less endearing mannerisms. During the practice on Thursday evening the group bowed to pressure from Malcolm and attempted a new piece that required the kind of furious finger action and tonguing technique Naomi hadn't utilised since her university recitals.

Heather frowned at her part and apologised frequently as she crashed through the piece, frustrated by her limitations.

'Sorry, I'll try to find the time to practise next week,' she said, scribbling over the music with a worn out pencil.

'Don't worry,' Naomi said. 'It's not easy.'

'The way you play it you'd think you'd practised all night, every night, but I bet you haven't.'

She hadn't, of course. She'd barely looked at the piece since it arrived in her inbox.

Pierre lifted his head above the music stand. 'It is difficult. But not impossible.'

Malcolm clapped his hands together. 'It's going to take a few sessions, but we'll do it.'

'I wish I was as optimistic,' Heather said, hunting for a fault in the clarinet's reed.

'Well, it's worth a go. We don't get anywhere if we don't give it a bash.'

'Bash?' Pierre looked troubled by the violent implication.

Naomi took a peek at Pierre's part. Plenty of twiddly bits, some unusual rhythmic cadences, but compared to hers, it wasn't virtuoso stuff.

'Why did you pick this arrangement, Mal?' she asked.

He settled into his chair. 'For you.'

'Me?'

Heather rested the pencil on the stand. 'He thinks you need to shine.'

'But we're a quartet.' Naomi hadn't reconstituted the group for the purposes of using it as personal vehicle. 'This isn't—'

'Yes, it is,' Heather said sharply. 'We're all agreed,' she gestured in particular to Pierre who nodded. 'You know you're special. We've sat here for weeks listening to you play and we all know this is all about you, this quartet is your chance.'

'Chance for what?' she asked, uncomfortably aware of the direction of the conversation.

'To shine,' Malcolm said. 'What happened four years ago shouldn't hold you back. You have to get your name out there, Naomi. You should be signed up to a record label, or join a national orchestra—'

'I don't like orchestras.' Naomi was a little overwhelmed by social order of the orchestral hierarchy. She had no means to influence the conductor stuck back behind the string section. She preferred smaller ensembles.

'Because, and don't deny it,' Heather said, 'you have that gift, the one all musicians crave.'

The gift, as defined, wasn't like Leia's genius that showed up the moment she started to add up huge numbers at the age of five or speak fluent French after watching a film on TV. What differentiated Naomi from other musicians was the entwining of three attributes. She could practise, if she put her mind to it, and those sessions had developed her technical abilities to a high level. She also enjoyed playing; it wasn't a chore. Whenever Ethan killed the television she shot into the sun lounge and, using her reflection in the windows, watched her fingers dance over the silvery keys. He invariably stayed to listen, tapping his foot to any semblance of rhythm and said little, as he hadn't the vocabulary to offer a meaningful critique. However, he appreciated the last key element of her gift: performing. No matter how much she denied it, she needed the pump of adrenaline that an audience delivered. The applause wasn't her goal nor the critical acclaim of her peers. She wasn't seeking adulation or fame. The love affair she had with music was more satisfying than words could ever describe. Now, with the combination of hard work and her beloved flute, the group had brought her here and were willing her to take the next step – an unequal role in the quartet.

She blushed, lowered her head, and muttered something that sounded modest. 'I couldn't do it without you.' Humility she could handle, but raising her profile in the quartet was tougher.

Nobody said anything for a few seconds.

'I disagree,' Pierre said. 'You are... held back by us, is that what you say?'

Naomi opened her mouth, but Malcolm beat her to it. 'And for the time being, we'll support you the best way we can by trying harder. Now, let's start from bar sixteen, shall we?'

She was too astounded by her friends' honesty to tell Ethan; she wasn't sure if he would appreciate that the quartet's aspirations depended on her ambitions, so she relayed the information to Rebecca in the kitchen on the Friday morning. Naomi's long overdue visit proved timely.

Rebecca merely smiled in that way that meant she wasn't surprised in the slightest by the quartet's ambitions for Naomi.

'I sometimes wonder if I would find it easier if I played a different instrument,' Naomi said.

Her sister blinked, caught out by Naomi's abrupt comment. 'Why?' she asked.

'A violinist, or a cellist, they move with their instrument.' She mimed the actions of bow sawing against strings. 'So can a pianist. Even a drummer. They can use their face to communicate their feelings. They can close their eyes—'

'As do you—'

'Shut out the surroundings, and well, their expression becomes part of their performance.'

'Not on the radio. Nobody sees the recording studio.'

'No, I suppose not. But you see, I can't change my face, my lips, it effects the tone, the quality of the sound. My flute is like an extension of my arms and the sounds it produces... is a creation born from the air in my lungs. I have to keep the flute in position, like so.' She held her arms aloft, the angle of the flute perpendicular to her body. 'See?'

Rebecca nodded. 'And your eyes? Eyes are full of expression.'

'I prefer to close them. Some flautists don't. But where do you look when you can't see your hands? The audience is right there in front of you, staring, watching.'

'You don't want to look at them?'

'I'm afraid if I do, they'll see I'm a fake.'

'Fake?'

'I'm not showing enough of me.'

A fleeting change of expression passed over Rebecca's face. She was bemused, perhaps annoyed, too. 'I think you don't want to see their reaction, in case they look bored.'

'I would hope they're engrossed,' she said indignantly.

'How would you tell the difference? Naomi, you're going too deep with all this emotional stuff. Surely, if you play brilliantly, so good you wow them, does it matter if eyes are open or shut? Aren't they there to hear you make music, to be entertained?'

Ethan had said exactly the same thing, she recalled, after he'd asked her why she kept her eyes shut. Then years ago, there was Malcolm's hint after the concert that she hadn't given the audience anything to see. How was she supposed to solve that conundrum when she preferred to focus on her musicality? Was she really afraid of her audience's reaction? The idea unsettled her further.

'Do you want to sit outside?' Naomi said, wary of the direction the conversation was going. 'It's quite lovely today, like an Indian summer.' When was the last time she had swum in that pool house? She should have brought a swimming costume.

Rebecca hovered by the sink and stared out of the window. The sun caught the side of her face and illuminated the greyness under her eyes. For some reason, Rebecca had forgone make-up and the lack of glow to her cheeks and the blunting of her eyes was disconcerting. Naomi always thought that when Rebecca tumbled out of bed in the mornings, her sister immediately applied a layer of foundation to her face and thick mascara to her lashes. Today, she looked brittle and on edge.

There were other odd things Naomi noted upon arriving at the house. The missing curtain hook gave the drapes in the bay window a drooping expression – Rebecca accused boisterous Toby of the act of vandalism, but she hadn't fixed it yet. In the hallway there was an alarmingly high pile of crumpled clothes left in a laundry basket at the bottom of the stairs and a trail of muddy shoe prints on the kitchen tiles. These things in most people's homes wouldn't warrant much attention, but in Rebecca's pristine oasis of calm, they were major incidents.

'Are you okay?' Naomi asked when Rebecca turned down the suggestion for decamping outside.

'Sure,' Rebecca said too sharply.

'Howie?'

'Fine.'

'Where is he?'

'Well, obviously not here,' she said, stepping over the footprints. 'He's flying out this evening. Shareholders meeting somewhere. He's a big stakeholder.' A typical working day for Howard. Rebecca could hardly resent his job as it enabled her to live comfortably.

'Ethan is on the road too. He's stretching his territory further north.'

'Doing well then?' Rebecca swept a lock of hair out of her face.

'Yes, I guess.'

Rebecca began to rearrange the fruit in the bowl. 'You really don't know much about him, do you?'

'I know enough.'

'It took Howie and I years to really know each other, to appreciate each other without judging.'

Naomi ignored the mini lecture. Rebecca had kept Howard at arm's length until she was convinced he could deliver her long list of requirements. Naomi wasn't that fussy.

'We're going to Bath for a weekend. I expect that will give us more opportunities.' Ethan had chosen the city, stabbing the map with his finger with the casual air of man who once travelled a whole continent in search of work. She hadn't quibbled his choice; she'd never been to Bath. He'd left it to her to book the boutique hotel.

Rebecca stony expression was unmoved. 'One weekend? Well, I hope you have a nice time.'

'We will.' Naomi stared at the muddy prints. They must have been there since breakfast. The sight of grubbiness in Rebecca's sanctuary continued to unnerve her. 'Let's go to a pub for lunch. Which one do you fancy?'

Rebecca's hand jerked, and she knocked an apple off the fruit arrangement. It rolled along the surface of the worktop. Naomi grabbed it before it toppled over the edge. Her sister's reaction was benign, as if one more thing on the floor wouldn't matter.

'Do you mind staying here? I've got a quiche. It won't take long to heat up.'

'Sure.' Naomi hid her disappointment as once more she failed to extricate Rebecca from her haven of false tranquillity. 'Do you ever go out? It's like you're always here, in this house, waiting for something to happen.' Years ago, Naomi had envied Rebecca as she flew out to exotic holiday destinations with the aid of Howard's bottomless credit card. The pair lay on sandy beaches drinking cocktails in the middle of the day. Then the kids had arrived, and they stuck to holiday cottages, secluded spots by the sea or Scottish mountains. The children disrupted Rebecca's life to such an extent, she lived vicariously through them, abandoning her career along with any other interests.

'I'm perfectly happy being here.' Rebecca snatched the apple out of Naomi's hand. 'I do leave, every day. I take the kids to school. I go shopping. Really, Naomi, what's this got to do with Ethan and you?'

'Nothing.' Naomi sighed. For once, things weren't about her. The kid's school was two minutes away and the shop was at the end of the road; hardly a great expedition. 'Let's eat that quiche.' She wasn't hungry, but cooking generally cheered her sister up.

Rebecca picked up the dishcloth and wiped the floor tiles. As she rose from where she had squatted, she glanced at Naomi, her cheeks rosier than before.

'I'm sorry, darling,' she said. 'I'm having one of those days. It's nothing to do with you. I'm just a little more disorganised than usual. It's very off putting.'

The darling was back. Soon, Rebecca would have the house shipshape and her mood would lift. Perhaps Naomi was witnessing the tail end of an argument with Howard, something domestic that had caused ripples in the fabric of Rebecca's ordered life. She smiled reassuringly at her sister, projecting a veneer of calmness around Rebecca. How easy life was for Rebecca. How dull, too. Naomi hoped she wasn't succumbing to the same state of domestic co-habitation that required sacrifice, rather than compromise. She would go home and practise her flute. Heather and the others were right; she should be proud of her talents and not hide them. It was time to take back control from all those who wanted to manufacture her happiness.

If only she knew what made her happy. Perhaps she should have gone to America, taken her chances and stayed under the rigid wings of her parents. Leia was happy there and everything fell into place for her, effortlessly, it seemed.

# thirteen
## Leia

Over the past year, Leia had sacrificed any semblance of a social life to spend dawn to midnight in the lab, rubbing tired eyes and poking things in tubes and dishes. Finally she'd cracked the code – the illusive answer to a genetic conundrum – following one long stretch of non-stop experiments. It hardly rated as a eureka moment; she'd formulated the hypothesis years ago while still at Cambridge University. Somewhere there was a key molecule, the product of a vicious organism, whose immunological weaknesses were waiting to be discovered and analysed for points of attack. Once she'd achieved that goal, then the next stage dragged on, and on. She had to get the facts verified, reproducible for others to witness, and for weeks she and her little team of night owls had eaten junk food, washed intermittently and written everything up. Leia produced a final report and submitted it for publication.

The article had gone the equivalent of viral in the online medical world, attracting the attention of the big pharma companies and popular science channels. Her endeavour was hailed as a major breakthrough. With the pressure mounting over the weeks and the resulting publicity close to triggering a breakdown, the foundation who'd provided the funding for her research owed her a break and if she felt the urge to up sticks and go some place different, she would, even if it harmed her career. She no longer gave a toss; sod them all.

As for her parents' overbearing behaviour, they were more worried about bad influences, like the unknown persons who slept her sofa after a night out. So what? It was Leia's dingy annexe and they'd promised her when she moved to America that they would leave her alone. But what a fake promise that had turned out to be. The arrangement was fracturing along fault lines. Infuriating Leia further, she knew that they trusted Rebecca more than her. Even Naomi had been allowed to fly the nest in her teens to join Kyle, although Nancy wasn't happy that Naomi had done the same again with some new guy on what seemed like a whim – why hadn't Naomi furthered her career at some grand European conservatoire and made a name for herself? Leia retorted, on behalf of her sister, that shoving Naomi into the limelight was counterproductive. It didn't matter what accolades Leia earned; the brightest star in the Liddell family, who had wowed her school teachers with her astounding acuity in every subject, was kept on a leash. It was insanely unfair.

Since she'd arrived in the USA, she'd done her best to act normal, and when it became apparent she wasn't capable of that, she revelled in being different. She chose clothes that weren't fashionable, and through sheer incompetence she unintentionally pre-empted trends by tearing holes in her jeans and pulling the threads out of hems. The nose stud had been self-inflicted during one daring, slightly drunken evening. Using an ice cube and sterile needle she'd stabbed a hole in her nostril. As for her hair, she changed colour as quickly as the months, dyeing it on whim from platinum to coal black. She always kept it short and cropped around her neck.

Her mother had despaired, threatening to shame her by dragging her into high end boutiques. As a rebuttal, Leia had visited a tattoo parlour and nearly went through with it, except, upon seeing her reflection in the mirror – punk style hairdo, goth make-up and a nose ring – she hadn't recognised herself. Through her determination to hide the very thing that made her special and unique, she had turned herself into a caricature of rebellious teenager when at her age, she should be worrying about mortgages and pensions. She walked out and underwent yet another makeover back to frightening normality. However, the hair she'd kept short for practical reasons and the nose stud stayed, just to rile Nancy.

The saving grace, the one thing that stopped her sinking into a pit of self-loathing and depression, were her colleagues at work. It didn't matter if she uttered irreverent words when experiments failed, they respected her brain and her ability to think so far out of the box; she was miles away from where they stood. She churned huge quantities of information in a matter of hours, calculated complex numbers in her head while visiting the canteen, and recited verbatim, and without errors, articles she'd read years ago.

'How do you do it?' her assistant once asked her.

'Fuck knows,' she said with a shrug. 'Just who I am.'

Who was she? A loner, and she hated the designation. Somebody had to salvage her happiness before she really did do something shameful. The rescuer needed to be a soul mate, the kind that listened properly and judged rarely. Sweet-natured Naomi? What could her young sister do from so far away, especially as her little world was circling around some strange guy. Leia had added him to her list of things to solve. She'd put him near the top. She felt she owed Naomi quite a bit. Rose would have... no, no. *No.*

As for Rebecca – an unrealised relationship, a failing on both their parts. Every attempt Leia made at seeing past her sister's crumbling veneer was bluntly executed. Something wasn't right about her twin. Rebecca had intuition written into her genes, rather like Rose...

*Don't think about Rose. Don't think about what she said.*

Leia drank instead. She returned to her favourite bar and lurked. Shunning the leer of men with equally rude glares, she only noticed one person, the woman who poured beer into her glass.

# Cherish friends. Hold on to them

Within minutes of meeting, for some inexplicable reason Leia and Ashley hit it off. The bar was one of Leia's favourites because it stayed open late into the night. Ashley was a new member of the bar staff. The two women took pity on each other – the tedium of serving drinks to loudmouth men paired to the relentless pressure of research protocols. When Ashley clocked off she stayed with Leia, who'd chosen the dimmest corner, and quickly demolished a few rounds of beers.

'Why are you alone in a bar?' Ashley asked, wolfing down a handful of peanuts.

''Cos my life sucks.' Leia slurred her words into a melancholy hiss.

'Tell me about it.'

Leia interpreted the empathic sentence literally and started to talk, which Ashley hadn't minded. By the end of her monologue, which resembled a miniature rant, Ashley's sleepy head was propped on Leia's shoulder.

There were things she said to Ashley, a stranger, she hadn't told anyone.

'My primary school teachers didn't know what to do with me. Give Mum credit, when they suggested I should go to some special school, she refused to let them treat me differently. But it didn't make much difference; I hated the way they singled me out for extra work, sending me to sit with the big kids when I showed any hint of boredom.'

'Primary, is that like elementary?' Ashley asked.

'Yeah. Like kindergarten.'

'So, you rebelled. Kind of thing I'd do in your shoes.'

'I wish I had. Life might have been different. No, I towed the line. I took my GSCE Math when I was eleven. Had to go to the local high school and sit with the teenagers in this echoey massive hall. I remember the table wobbled and the boy next to me kept coughing. It took me half the allotted time to do the test. I got an A star.'

'Wow. What's GSCE?'

Leia smiled. She'd spend many years in the USA, and for the first year or so she had to translate stuff nearly every day. The English language was transferable, but not the vocabulary that defined the cultural diversity of the British. She had to learn the American equivalents because nobody understood her odd expressions unless they were immersed in English Literature or BBC America. When she drank or became emotional, the unfamiliar slipped back into her speech.

Integration was something of a miserable starting point to her story. After a failing at both being a doctor and belatedly completing her PhD at Cambridge, she'd been determined to fit in at Harvard. She hadn't ever really; they accommodated her "English eccentricities", which meant little other than they tolerated her dry sarcasm and, in an attempt to normalise her, her colleagues professed that having such a talented person on their team was an accolade in itself and nobody would judge her otherwise. They hadn't anticipated that talent came with unpredictable baggage. At least the progression from associate to research fellow had cemented her role in the department and ended speculation that she wouldn't survive the transition.

'I'm a nerd.' Leia hated the word.

'You don't look like one.' Ashley leaned back to absorb Leia's appearance fully.

'You're thinking of films where nerds wear round spectacles and bowties. They walk around with awkward expressions, terrified they might commit a social crime, and of course, they stutter when they speak. That's not my kind of nerd. I'm socially adept, I think. According to my adviser, Lee Wang, I'm a contributor, an influencer of ideas and, God help me, a team player. I can talk fluently and appear quite engaged, you see. Inside, though, I'm fucking dying. My greatest talent isn't scientific theorising, it's acting. I could win an Oscar for being me, the Leia everyone sees.'

Ashley, who had shifted closer along the faux leather seating, dispatched a sympathetic frown and rested her hand on Leia's knee. 'Then just be you.'

Sweet thought. Leia wished she was as optimistic as Ashley. 'Now you're sounding Disney. I'm not sure I can anymore.'

'Seems to me you're asking for permission.'

Leia paused to swallow a mouthful of cold beer – she missed warm ale – and snorted. 'Guess, I am.'

'Then consider it given.'

Ashley in her short skirt and pinafore apron wasn't dumb. 'What did you study?' Leia asked.

Ashley's laughter was like Tinkerbell's fluttering wings; light and effervescent. Leia rather liked it. 'Psychology major. I dropped out after two years. I'm good at listening, shit at writing essays.'

'Words don't come easy.'

'So, what are you afraid of then?' Ashley looked up expectantly. Leia was caught for a second in the stare: the girl had burnished eyes and the tiniest of freckles on her nose. Leia wished she'd hadn't noticed, but she couldn't help being drawn to the finer details of her new friend. Poor Ashley was struggling to stay awake and at the same time was managing to make a lot of sense.

'Me.' Leia tapped her temple. 'My brain. The things I think up here that I can't express. I'm a computer with no output, no peripherals attached. I'm locked into the rational world. I don't do superficial.' Unlike unemployed Rebecca, who baked cakes, and pleasing Naomi; both of whom led conventional lives of domestic routines and cosy evenings in. Leia frowned: best she kept her sisters out of the conversation.

Ashley latched onto the analogy. 'Plug something in. How about a new hobby or—'

'Tried it. I did ballet lessons as a kid. The most inelegant pupil ever, according to Miss Sapphire. I tried photography, then smartphones came along and damn, it's so much easier to carry one of those around.' She grinned – the photos never made it to America and Rebecca had them stored in the attic along with other useless childhood things. 'I even went along to one of my grandmother's art classes to see if I could get inspired. The guy who ran it was an ex-con and was way more fascinating than the paintings.'

Rose had tried to help and she'd nearly reached the real Leia. Unfortunately, Rose didn't seem able to go the last stretch, as if she needed Leia to come to her and open up, which ten or so years ago was unthinkable for the sceptical twenty-something Leia. She regretted not trying harder; there was a lot of misgivings buried inside Leia when it came to her grandmother, things she could, and more likely should have said; information she'd withheld that might, in retrospect, have had validity. Was it too late to speak up? The question always left her in a quandary. The giant brain couldn't solve that one because thinking of Rose brought Leia to a major emotional hurdle, one she had never overcome; she refused to believe it had anything to do with cakes and candles.

Ashley shrugged. 'You're afraid of being different. Who isn't? We like to fit in and conform to peer pressure.'

It was Leia's turn to laugh. 'Now you sound like my father. I should have followed his model career.'

Professor Paul Liddell was a wordsmith more than a scientist. His degree in chemistry, followed by a PhD, then a post-doctorate at Cambridge had led him to a prestigious professorship at Harvard. However, all he wanted to do was write books. Having accomplished the transition to America with enviable ease, he supervised and lectured students, and gained a reputation as an eminent author of academic textbooks, the kind every fresher chemistry student would have on their book shelf. The money from the books supplemented his stipend and enabled him to buy the large house with the annexe for Leia. He tempted her over, knowing she loved the concept of research, the thrill of discovering the unknown. What she hadn't anticipated was the lack of ground support in an environment where winning was everything.

'I'm not the competitive type,' she said. 'Dad found his niche and exploited it. But he's wrapped up with his own projects, trying to distil every last drop of knowledge he has buried in his head.'

'And your mum? I take it they're together?'

The assumption of broken parenting was common amongst many she met since she'd arrived in Boston. Blame Mom and Dad was something of a badge of honour for the most dysfunctional children. It wouldn't be fair for Leia to blame them for everything, except perhaps treating her like Rapunzel locked in her tower.

'She wants to protect me. Ostensibly from those who'd exploit my genius. Really, she's protecting me from myself.'

'Are you that dangerous?'

'I'm a contained wild child.'

'Then go wild, Leia.' Ashley yawned, her head lolling to one side and landing on Leia's shoulder. 'And, if you don't mind an audience, I'd love to watch.'

That night was the first time Ashley slept on the sofa in Leia's bijou living room, snoring and grunting to herself. Leia slept in her bedroom, wondering if she was on the verge of crossing the relationship threshold or whether she was going to keep things in check, as she had done with so many other people, be they men or women. Every time Ashley visited, they talked into the early hours. Regardless of her lack of training, Ashley had the makings of a fine therapist. Leia bounced her poorly defined emotions off Ashley's broad shoulders and the perceptive young woman shaped them into more cohesive thoughts.

The secret liaison was busted two weeks later.

Unfortunately when Leia stole into the main house kitchen to raid the fridge – grocery shopping rated low on her priorities – she and Ashley unceremoniously bumped into her parents. Paul raised one awkward eyebrow and pursed his lips. He said nothing other than, 'Good morning,' before disappearing into his den. Nancy was less subtle. Her disapproval of the tattooed creature standing half-naked in her kitchen had been exhibited in a finely etched expression of disdain. Leia ignored her and helped herself to a milk and a bowl of cereal, encouraging the embarrassed Ashley to do the same.

Over several weeks, amongst Ashley's shifts and Leia's erratic timetable in the lab, they spent as much time together as they could allocate from their schedules. Ashley staying the night became a regular thing and Leia was too focused on utilising Ashley's excellent listening skills to risk ruining their flourishing relationship with the suggestion she simply move in. Gradually, and with plenty of heart to hearts, Leia's mixed up emotions started to unravel.

'I'm not a superhero,' Leia said one morning. 'Why do people think I am because I started out as a child genius? Am I still one? I can't cope with people's expectations when I'm carrying this genius label around with me.'

Ashley handed her a mug of strong morning coffee. 'You can change labels, y'know.'

'You reckon?'

Leia dropped Ashley off at her squalid apartment block and drove to work. Something was happening in and around the lab, a flurry of hushed conversations and furtive glances in her direction. What had she done now? The stupid label refused to budge.

# fourteen

## Naomi

## October

The idea to call in at Stonehenge on the way back from Bath had been Naomi's.

'That's the ring of stones, yeah?' Ethan asked. He drove with a slouched posture: one hand on the steering wheel, the other fiddling with the lid of the coffee cup, which he'd bought at the services. Having decided to call in at the Henge, he reprogrammed the satnav.

The weekend in Bath had been a successful interlude due in part to Bath's history providing some scope to tap into his marginal romanticism. He'd been fascinated by the neat rows of Georgian houses, especially the long arc of the Royal Crescent. She wanted to visit the assembly rooms, he preferred the Roman baths. They navigated an agenda that suited both their interests.

Driving home on the Sunday afternoon, Naomi kept a soft smile on her face as she stared at the line of cars speeding ahead of them on the carriageway. Bath had proved to her that Ethan could unwind. The only minor upset was that Ethan stole a bath robe from the hotel.

'Why not? We've paid a small fortune to stay in this place,' he said, stuffing it into his bag.

She hung hers back on the hook. 'You can't do that. They might charge your card extra.'

He'd shrugged off her protests. What could she do to stop him? He treated these occasional attacks of deviant behaviour as acts of mischief or games of chance. The ease with which Ethan broke the minor rules of society troubled Naomi, but not sufficiently to cause her angst. Part of her pined for a level of irresponsibility that enabled minor acts of disobedience without actually harming the balance of order. Her attention to detail, the way she obsessed over some small error on her part, held her back, and that weakness prevented her from connecting to people through music. If she could take a smidgen of Ethan's unique combination of work ethic and lax regard for rules, maybe it would help her overcome her doubts about performing.

They circled Stonehenge on foot and admired the hewed blocks from a distance. Naomi snapped a few photos. However, there was no sun to create shadows and the drizzle-filled skies formed a silvery backdrop behind the equally grey stones; it was a little bit of an anti-climax. What a pity there were no druids or strange pagan rituals being acted out accompanied by eerie music piped through the paths, as if to conjure up ghosts and spirits.

Ethan eyed the stone structures with an engineer's eye. 'How the fuck did they lift it up there without cranes?'

'The stone came from miles away.'

'You know, if this was Florida or Hollywood, they'd turn it into a theme park with rides and shops.'

She laughed; for once he'd referred to his home land without prompting. Perhaps, at last, he saw his past as something to share.

'Have you been there? Those places?'

He shook his head slowly. 'Not my thing, really,' he muttered. 'Let's keep walking; the rain's getting heavier.'

They completed the circuit. Abruptly the shower stopped and the clouds parted sufficiently for a slither of sunshine to poke through. The stones changed from grey to ochre as the sky turned an unearthly glow of orange. A rainbow struck the far side of the monument, touching the ground somewhere between the blocks.

'Wow, that's amazing.' She looped her arm through his and leaned against him.

'Sure,' he said. 'Mighty fine scene.'

'I feel happy,' she said spontaneously.

'Good. I am too.'

'Then let's go home.'

Walking to the car park, Ethan suddenly stopped and turned to face her. 'Are you really happy?'

She shaded her eyes from the low sun. 'I said I am. Are you?'

'Very.'

'I just wish...' She shifted her hands behind her back. The issue still bugged her and since they been getting on well for the last few weeks, she decided to broach the subject again. 'You know what would make me even happier? Paying my way. Like the rent.'

Ethan turned and started to walk ahead of her. She hurried to catch up.

'No? Why not? I've even saved enough for us to find somewhere different. A fresh start. Then you don't have to worry if your friend comes back or sells up.'

He continued to stride forward. 'I don't think he minds how long I stay. He's on the other side of the world.'

'But the rent?' Her heartbeat quickened in response to his change of pace and mood.

He snatched her hand and squeezed it. 'I don't want you to worry. I'm taking care of you.'

'I'm not a pet, Ethan,' she said abrasively. His grip pinched excessively. The sun vanished and an oppressive blanket of grey descended over the meadows of the plain.

'Let's do this differently.' He slowed his pace, slackened his grip and checked around. They were quite alone on the path – loitering far behind them were an older couple with binoculars trained on the stones.

'Do what differently?'

He sandwiched her damp hand between his and gave it a brisk rub. 'You're getting cold. Perhaps I'll ask another time.'

He'd stoked her curiosity and no way was he keeping her in suspense. 'No, tell me.'

'I agree, we should find somewhere to live together. But I want it to be special. I know you're not keen on the idea, but if you want to put the agreements or deeds in your name, I don't mind, but I want for us to be in this together.'

'In what together?'

'Marriage.'

'Are you proposing?' She attempted to retrieve her hand, but his grasp was steadfast. While her fingers trembled due to a thunderous mixture of both arousal and shock, his remained calm.

'I am. Please don't kid yourself you're not interested. This is about you and me, and nobody else. Your sisters don't have to know. We can marry in secret without an expensive wedding. Just a couple of friends as witnesses. Then we can put this financial uncertainty to bed. Does it matter who pays what when we'll be sharing everything?'

'I don't know, Ethan,' she stammered. No big church wedding. Not even a small family wedding. He'd framed the idea as a business proposition, one that would benefit both of them. His salary was generous compared to her irregular income and she assumed he'd gain from marrying a British citizen. She opened her mouth to ask and instead was deflected by his constant stream of words. He mentioned getting her furniture out of storage, finding a house with somewhere for her to teach, so she didn't have to travel everywhere. He'd planned quite a bit in his head; the idea wasn't entirely impulsive.

'You said yourself, you don't need the hullabaloo of a wedding. You can keep your name, I don't mind. I'll take yours. Names can change.' He grinned, cocking his head to one side. A drop of rain splashed against his nose. 'I can take care of you. You won't worry about money. And if things don't work out, then you'll have your own money stashed away just in case.'

And what about love? He'd not mentioned it. 'Can I think about it?'

'Babe, of course, you should. I've hit you out of the blue, haven't I? I'm sure I can wait a few days.'

Days? She might have suggested weeks. 'And if I say no?'

He stared at her, his unbroken gaze delving deep and twisting her nerves into a knot. Was she feeling uncomfortable, anxious or thrilled? She'd claimed to be the non-marrying type as far back as her teens, along with Leia. Although Leia's reasons had to do with her preference for bug busting, and, unsurprisingly, she'd analysed marriage and deemed it an institution controlled by society for commercial purposes. But, unlike her sister, Naomi viewed lifelong commitment as a necessity for happiness, as long as it involved the right person. She'd rather not live on her own. However, living with somebody had to have mutual benefits, or why do it?

Had she simply chosen to avoid discussing marriage with Kyle because he, in the end, wasn't the one for her? Did it matter that she'd adopted a new opinion? She was thirty next month. A new decade, a new impetus. Everyone was capable of change.

Ethan's trust in marriage surprised her, as did the spontaneity of his proposal. Marriage wouldn't entertain him or her every day. They'd argue – they already did argue, and after the harsh words had been spent, the guilt racked her. But he always managed to bend her back to him, folding her into his arms, often literally. Those tense moments had so far strengthened their relationship. Rebecca quarrelled with Howard; her sister admitted that they didn't see eye to eye on everything, and Leia had thrown one of her boyfriends out on to the street when they'd disagreed. The Liddell sisters each in their own way sought a perfect equilibrium of emotional outbursts and quiet reasoning. Perhaps they were too fickle.

'I don't think you want to say no to me,' Ethan said. 'I know I need to get out more. Stop moping around the house at the weekend. I've lived too long with men, you know that. Lots of muscle men in bars who drink and smoke, boast about sex and women. The sheilas I knew, like Eileen, weren't interested in settling down either, but you are. You're not like them. And being with you, I reckon I'm more like you than I thought. I think I'm becoming a Brit.'

'You're admitting this will help you gain permanent residency? But you're Irish. You don't need it.'

'It'll consolidate my status – I'm only Irish by heritage. But that's not the reason I'm asking. You know why I'm asking to marry you and after your reluctance with Kyle, I'm not going to let you dither and regret things. If you can't see where we're going, then perhaps we don't have a future together.'

His bluntness was medicinal. He spoken quickly, almost arrogantly, but also honestly.

'You're a bit mixed up. I am too.' She reached up on tiptoes, the rain now showering them in heavy droplets, and she found his mouth amongst the wet whiskers and kissed it. 'I'm not saying no. I'm not saying yes either. But, you know what, this crazy secret wedding plan kind of appeals to me. I've always wanted to be a dark horse. My sisters, they would be horrified if I didn't tell them. My parents, too. I've spent my whole life being watched, appraised and guided by them. Damn it. I want to be free.'

'Then that's nearly a yes.' He lifted his jacket over his head. 'Let's run. I'm fucking soaked.'

They sat in silence in the car. Ethan overtook everyone as he sped along the fastest lanes, drumming his fingers on the wheel, impatient and restless. Naomi replayed things over in her head, wondering if she was thinking irrationally and allowing her heart to lead. How quickly the shape of her thoughts had altered over the last few months since she'd met Ethan. He'd ensnared her with promises of security and home comforts, things she should find condescending and controlling, and yet she didn't want to leave him. Infected by the affliction of love, like a disease Leia would say, she was infatuated by Ethan's mercenary approach to gaining her heart.

At home, she threw the laundry into the washing machine and he cooked steak. Naomi picked at her food; she wasn't hungry. She felt feverish, but not ill. Ethan's eyes were wilder than usual and he stabbed a slab of bloody meat.

'You didn't say whether you love me,' she blurted over her half-eaten dish.

He paused, the fork almost reaching his mouth. He lowered his arm, leaned forward so that his nose was level with her. 'I love you.' He said it without embellishment and with his eyes fixed firmly on hers.

She believed him. 'I love you, too.'

She wasn't entirely sure they were the right words, yet, but they spilled out easily. Rebecca must never know how Ethan tempted her by suggesting she kept their marriage a secret. A relationship begun on a lie wasn't a good foundation: the trust lecture lingered on. Rebecca would remind her that love came in many forms. Music should be the key to Naomi's heart and soul, but Ethan had found another way in.

He reached across the table and took her hand. 'Then let's go to bed.'

The night's activities added a glow to her cheeks in the morning and even her most observant pupils noticed the energy in her playing when she accompanied them during their lessons.

'What's made you cheerful, miss?' one child had the gumption to ask.

'Life,' she replied. 'Now, let's play that one more time with gusto, shall we?'

# fifteen
## Leia

Before Leia made it through the doors into the atrium of the main laboratory complex, a troupe of her colleagues barrelled into her, enthusiastically shaking her crushed hand or opting to thump her on the back. The unwanted intimacy was claustrophobic and startlingly in its ferocity.

*Breathe, dammit, breathe.* A sea of bodies, and even though she knew every one of them and valued them as equals, they weren't her friends.

'You did it, Leia. You've won the immunology prize,' said somebody in the throng of people circling her.

'I have?' she said with disbelief. The entry was a last minute thing by the wily Lee Wang. He'd not sought out her opinion on entering the competition, and to her dismay, her permission either, because he knew she'd try to wriggle out of the nomination.

'You know what that means?' The familiar boom of his voice forced her to turn to face him. His eyes twinkled with tiny sparks of exuberance. 'The keynote speech is all yours.'

She edged her way out of the huddle. The nausea had already started.

'The gala dinner?' she said. 'God, no.'

The lavish dinner was held in a luxury hotel with the popular science press in full attendance and dignitaries handing out platitudes and money, lots of money, especially as the gala was a fundraiser for medical research. Under the chandeliers, people in tuxedos and evening gowns, clutching champagne flutes and plates of hors d'oeuvres, would circle around each other, chasing smiles and greeting each other loudly. The small talk alone would be unbearable, never mind the podium and lectern where she would stand and deliver her speech.

She elbowed her way to the restroom and threw up in the toilet bowl. A cool splash of water on her face ended the panic attack. Had Naomi ever felt this assault of nerves before she played her flute at a concert? Unlikely; something else bothered Naomi. Regardless of the definition of stage fright, Leia envied her sister's ability to breathe though her nerves, just that alone would be an advantage. As for her twin, Rebecca may have given up court appearances, but before then, she had battered the opposing team with calmly delivered arguments and, although Leia had not witnessed the trials, Howard had spoken with great pride with regard to Rebecca's commanding presence. Leia's sensible sisters possessed coping tactics that required no acting.

Cornering Lee in his office, she leaned her back against the door, barring anyone else from entering. 'I can't do it.'

Now the twinkle was gone. 'You've done lots of seminars—'

'To other researchers, scientists. People like me.'

'They'll be there.'

'And lots who aren't.'

He shrugged off her concerns with a bemused expression. 'You deserve this, Leia. Enjoy it,' he said earnestly.

'I can't,' she said, pathetically. 'I just can't stand there and talk about me, my story.'

They'd want wit and anecdotes. She'd be expected to speak with passion about her work as if nothing else mattered, which for years might have been true, but now she'd met Ashley and for once something else mattered and it wasn't an obsession with a nasty superbug. Lee couldn't see or understand her fear. Being different sucked, and hiding that genius rating had influenced her whole life. She dreamed of a having a calm mind, a total emptiness in her head where frivolity and fantasy reigned. The concept of mysticism alluded her. Imagination was for artists, like Naomi, while romance was Rebecca's domain. What Leia excelled at after years of burning the candle at both ends was dogged determination.

She spent the rest of the day hiding in store cupboards or a cubicle in the library.

Upon hearing the news, her mother wanted to take her for a dress fitting – the ridiculous idea was the first thing that spouted out of Nancy's mouth. Leia's jaw locked into a grimace. Her father, sensing her lack of joy, offered to help write the speech; the author's solution and it lacked empathy just as much as her mother's insensitive suggestion.

*Go away. Go away!*

She harried them out of her study. Alone, she kicked over a pile of books left on the floor. There was paper everywhere: piled on the desk and crammed onto shelves. Then the rest: dirty plates, Coke cans, stained wine glasses, the detritus of her existence. Work had wreaked stress into every cranny of her life. She retreated into the bedroom and crushed a Valium into a glass.

The next day, instead of facing work, Leia sent a brief email reminding Lee of the vacation she was owed and that she was taking the days in lieu immediately. Let him threaten her with ending her contract, she didn't care, she'd earned her right to live in the country and work wherever she chose. Her team could accept the award on her behalf and lap up the praise themselves; it belonged to them just as much as her. Leia was going to take a rest…somewhere.

She threw up again, mostly wine and vodka.

'I'm coming,' said Ashley from the sofa where she lay stretched out, pale faced and still slightly inebriated from the previous night. The drinks at the bar were less of a celebration and more of a spiral into a state of inertia. The more Leia drank, the less she cared about the consequences. Everyone deserved a mini breakdown now and again.

Leia stuffed clean underwear into a holdall. She threw in her passports – the privilege of possessing two would come in handy if she decided to go as far as Canada. 'You can't. You're working.'

'I don't give a fuck about that job. It's always been a temporary thing.' Ashley glugged a pint of water down in one go.

'You don't have anything to wear—'

'I've cash, I can pick up something on the way. And we're the same size. I can borrow something of yours.' She picked out a few things from Leia's wardrobe. 'We nearly have the same tastes.' She grinned and held up a skull-faced t-shirt.

Two hollow eyes stared at Leia. Death was something she'd seen many times. It never used to torment her until it involved somebody she loved. She'd closed those eyes, kissed them goodnight.

*I'm thirty-five years old and I'm running away.*

At least she'd known one person who had approved of letting fate taking charge.

'Take it,' she said. 'Let's go.'

# sixteen
## Naomi
## 24 October 2018

Half way through the week, Ethan packed his overnight bag for a trip north and drove off a little after dawn. Naomi had hardly any lessons to teach. Most of the schools were closed for half-term, and Ethan had graciously offered to cover one of his colleague's patches for a few days. In his absence, she spruced the house up with a thorough clean.

She polished the inside of the windows, emptied the kitchen cupboards and wiped the shelves down, before restocking them in neat rows of tins and packets; creating a uniformity that calmed the fluctuating emotions caused by the Ethan situation. There was something of an unspoken "yes" in her response to his proposal rather than an outright verbalised "no". Ethan had gifted her a new, unusual emotion – trepidation – and she was thriving on the emergent sense of adventure.

She set about the cleaning with a burst of energy. Outside, autumn was well established, yet in her heart, it was spring and as fledging love budded and grew, the copper leaves outside died and tumbled to the ground.

Upstairs, she dusted the bedroom, shook out the rugs, then turned her attention to the closets. Hers was in a reasonable state with her shoes neatly lined up on the floor and the clothes arranged in colour groups. Ethan's was chaotic with creased shirts mixed with jackets hanging limply. Above her head was a shelf and stuffed into the gap between the shelf and the ceiling, spare pillows and towels. Arranged haphazardly, they teetered precariously close to the edge. When she attempted to shut it, the door wouldn't close properly. Standing on tiptoe, she pulled on the pillow, hoping to rearrange things. However, it shot out so fast it brought down a heap of towels with it. And something else.

The square-shaped box dropped onto the rug. An elastic band, which had held the lid on, snapped and the contents settled in a circle around her feet. Crouching down, she picked up two folded sheets of paper, then let them slip between her fingers. What attracted her attention were the two passports, each one stamped on the front with the emblem of a country: USA and the Republic of Ireland.

She picked up the Irish passport and thumbed through the pages. There were no stamps, nothing other than a picture of Ethan and his name. The date of his birthday was familiar and she'd already marked it in her diary. The other passport was chewed around the edges and older. Carefully, she opened the pages. He'd taken a day trip to Canada years ago, then a long gap before an exit stamp from Mexico. And a day later, an entry visa for Australia with a smudged date. No exit date, but then, he'd already said he'd used his Irish passport to obtain entry to the UK.

When she opened the American passport to the identification page, she recognised the younger version of Ethan, because although he'd no beard and lighter hair, she saw the familiar startling grey eyes and shape of his nose and forehead. She glanced at the details next to the photograph and her heart skipped a beat. She swayed and dropped onto her knees. The nausea sent waves of terrified butterflies from her belly to her mouth. A torrent of unpleasant sensations unleashed itself.

She fumbled with the folded pieces of paper. He'd earned a degree in agriculture engineering from University of Southern Queensland in the name she knew, but the other education certificate wasn't in that name and had been issued ten years ago by the Ohio State University in Wooster – a double degree in power machinery and agronomy. She was faced with an increasingly confused picture of Ethan. She lay the documents on the bed and raked her fingers through her hair.

*Who the hell is this man?* She covered his name with her hand, unable to contemplate the implication that a mystical prophesy had come true.

*Breathe… breathe.*

She had to find out the truth, ask awkward questions of him, and who else? Who really knew him? She fetched her phone and snapped images of the relevant pages. She kept coming back to the American passport and the grainy photograph of a young man with silver eyes and tight lips. Without his beard, he looked gaunt and pale. In the Irish one he had a fuller face and tanned cheeks. Time had passed between the two – how much?

There was a scroll of paper, much like a cigar and she unrolled it to reveal a birth certificate bearing the name Dorothy O'Reilly born in 1922 in Limerick. Ethan had acquired the copy in Australia and used it to manufacture a different identity, but why? Was Dorothy really his Irish grandmother?

None of Naomi's friends were suitable sounding boards in a crisis; they were mostly the musical kind, whom she'd gathered over the years of teaching, and they were scattered all over the region. The obvious candidate for advice was somebody with legal training and that meant contacting Rebecca. What Naomi needed though wasn't the sweet-natured repertoire, the currency of "goshes" and "jolly goods" with which Rebecca peppered her speech, but the sharp insight of the woman who'd once shielded an adolescent girl from the pitfalls of starting out alone in life. Back then, Naomi had ignored her sister's codified dislike of Kyle, now she yearned to hear the soothing words of wisdom from her solicitor sister.

She called Rebecca on her mobile, pacing the bedroom as the trills pierced her ear.

'Becca,' she gasped, fighting back the tears.

Rebecca latched onto the distress the moment Naomi used the diminutive name. She might as well have said 'Mum'. 'Naomi, what's wrong?'

'He's lied to me.'

'Who? Ethan?'

Naomi took a deep breath. 'His real name is Frederick Nieman, not Ethan O'Reilly.'

Rebecca gasped. 'Frederick?'

'Yes. And, there's something else I haven't told you. We were going to keep it a secret, and I... I'm sorry. I shouldn't have.'

'What?' Rebecca asked impatiently, 'Tell me, I won't be cross.'

'He's asked me to marry him and I've basically agreed.' She fingered the necklace and the tiny pendant hanging between her collar bones, something Ethan had bought her in Bath.

The pause stretched on; the silence horrified Naomi. She'd upset her sister so much, Rebecca had lost the ability to speak. 'I know I should have said something,' Naomi said through her parched lips.

'How did you find out?' Rebecca asked, equally hoarse, her voice shaking with either disappointment or rage. Both possibly.

Naomi swallowed a dry lump in her throat. 'He's got documents in a box. He hid it from me. There's a US passport in one name. It's definitely his photo, a younger man with no beard, almost a boy. Then there's another Irish one with this other name, which he must have got in Australia.' The art of forgery was surely too costly for a farm worker. Assuming he was ever a farm worker.

'When did he become Ethan?' Rebecca said, her tone hardening.

Naomi opened the passport and checked the dates. 'There's a stamp in the US one for when he arrived in Australia. It's about ten years ago.'

'Ten years.'

'The Irish one is about two years old, issued after the US one expired. Becca, it's the name.'

'Beware Frederick and his offer of marriage. Yes, I know, quite unbelievable.'

Bringing up Rose's daunting exclamation was unavoidable. She had to agree with Rebecca, the coincidence was beyond remarkable.

'It can't be true. She can't have known. How could she? None of those silly things she said came true.' The birthday was fresh still. She smelt the candle flame, tasted the sweetness of the cake. The puff of smoke.

There was a rasping sigh from Rebecca. 'They do, Naomi,' she said. 'I wrote them all down, even the ones Dad heard before we were born. I've nearly twenty years of her birthday predications documented. From what I've found out over the years, they do come true.'

Blood rushed to Naomi's head, clouding her vision. 'What? Why didn't you tell me?'

How could anyone deduce anything from Rose's cryptic sayings? They were a few words with no meaningful context. Twaddle, according to Leia. The scientific twin would have laughed her head off unless she was shown indubitable evidence. Naomi doubted Rebecca's information had that level of validity.

'I really didn't think Gran meant you when she said it,' Rebecca began in a frantic deluge of words. 'I know it seemed that way at the time and I convinced myself she was just looking at you. But, you see, I now know she heard things about people she knew, not strangers, and they come true after ten years, almost exactly as she said. I kept quiet, because they're generally minor things. So I didn't think she really meant you when she mentioned Frederick. We said it was a silly name, didn't we? Darling? Say something.'

Naomi's head ached with the repercussions. Would it have made any difference to her time with Ethan if she had known what Rebecca suspected? There hadn't been a hint of Frederick before her discovery.

'What do want me to say? He's called Frederick and he's asked me to marry him, and Gran warned me about it. Does that mean I shouldn't? She didn't exactly imply I shouldn't marry him. Perhaps she warned me because he's unlike any other man I've met before. Which is the very reason I like him.'

'Please think carefully.' Rebecca was on the move. Naomi heard her footsteps crossing the kitchen floor. There was rain splattering somewhere. The reception flickered, then improved. Rebecca wanted to hear things clearly, so had gone outside. 'Forget Gran. Why hasn't he told you?'

Conversations with Ethan typically swung between innocuous interactions and heated exchanges. She hated arguments and misunderstandings, yet they drew them closer together. She'd become addicted to the drama of emotional displays. She and Ethan – his name was irrelevant, surely – would work it out.

'It's probably an innocent thing. People change their names for lots of reasons – there's deed poll. He might hate being called

Frederick, that's what Gran meant – and I can't blame him, it's a daft name—'

'Naomi—'

'Ethan proposed to me, not Frederick—'

'Listen to me—'

'It's just a play on words, isn't it? I don't need to worry.' She stretched her imagination as far as she could.

'Just get out, please. Come here and we'll check it all out.'

She'd not convinced Rebecca. 'No,' she said, firmly. 'I have the right to know what the hell his going on. He owes me the truth.'

'Naomi, I really think you should leave—'

Rebecca hadn't met him; what could she possibly know? Rose just said things; feelings went deeper. She started to gather the documents up. 'Let me talk to him first—'

The phone clicked a few times, as if the line had gone dead. 'Oh, Naomi,' Rebecca's pained voice whispered through the rain and the rustle of dying leaves. 'I wish I'd told you. I wanted to so many times.'

'What do you mean?' She rammed the lid back down, squashing the papers inside the container.

'Gran heard things, that was her gift.' Rebecca cleared her throat. 'And I, well, I see things, that's mine.'

Naomi paused. 'Your gift?'

'I didn't think I had one. But... Naomi, he's coming. I see him now. He's bound to you, so I see him, too.'

What the hell did she mean? Rebecca's obsession with Rose's birthdays had gone too far.

The line hissed and clicked. The rain had ceased. Outside the house a car was approaching. She rushed to the window in time to see his car swing into the drive. She caught a glimpse of his baseball cap and sunshades. It wasn't sunny.

Naomi spoke, breathlessly. 'Becca, he's back'

His deep voice called out a greeting.

'Becca, I have to go. I'll ring you later.'

She hung up.

# seventeen

## Rebecca
## 24 October 2018

The raindrops pattered on the kitchen window. Rebeca grabbed the key, half listening to Naomi, and opened the back door. Standing in the rain, she waited, opened her mind to whatever was out there. Something relevant, she hoped, nothing trivial. Now wasn't the time to be with her father at his desk. She had to know, had to see for herself. To her amazement she honed in on him, acquiring her target with spectacular ease. The implication scared her – her talent had just gone up a huge notch.

White knuckles. A puckered scar by his thumb. Hands on the steering wheel. When he glanced in the rear view mirror, she saw his reflection even though the peaked baseball cap hid his eyes. She wanted more, she needed a window into his soul, but there wasn't one.

The rain soaked into her clothes. Goosebumps rippled along her arms and she shivered. He was still driving. How far away was he? Her sister was determined to confront Ethan… Frederick, this man who had clawed his way into Naomi's life and allowed her to become infatuated. Now, in wondrous hindsight, Kyle seemed innocuous and acceptable, an ordinary man who, after years of waiting, had given up on Naomi.

Rebecca pleaded with her sister to leave the house, but Naomi wasn't listening. What Naomi wanted was a simple riddle, a play on words. It wouldn't be like that. Rose had always been remarkably accurate in her choice of words.

She had nothing prepared to explain her visions. She'd only done it once before, years ago with Howard, and he grasped the nature of her gift instantly when she described what she had seen, as if he'd always known in some way that she was different, 'A special lady.' His words, not hers or Rose's.

The line crackled, interrupting her as she attempted to explain her intrusive talent for seeing things that she should not. The rain abruptly stopped and so did the conversation.

For a few frantic minutes, Rebecca battled the urge to drive to Newmarket. She couldn't; she had to collect the kids from school. What else could she do? She paced the kitchen like a caged animal afraid of life on the other side of the bars.

Would the police listen to her suspicions? She knew the answer to that: there was no crime to report, not even harassment or bullying on Ethan's part. As for her husband, Howard was miles away, incommunicado, and due back after nine o'clock. What support could he offer? Since her call about Eleanor they'd spoken little about her visions. She'd been walking on eggshells around him, trying desperately to convince him she was fine. She lied to him almost daily; she was far from fine. She was an emotional wreck every time she left the house.

In the meantime, she'd wait for Naomi to ring back and update her on Ethan's deception. The minute hand on the kitchen clock crept its way round slowly, taunting her with its ticking.

She drove to school and for once, as she parked by the tree, she wanted to be somewhere else. But nothing materialised. It was like that – haphazard and unpredictable. Sometimes weeks might pass between visions. Was she trying too hard, because after the incident with Eleanor she'd wondered if thinking hard was the issue. Waiting in the playground, she hurried past the huddle of parents and stood as close to the entrance door as possible, ready to intercept her children. In the car, the kids screeched their news: the yucky dinner, the horrors of a spelling test, the annoying friends at playtime. She paid them woefully scant attention and left them in the sitting room, squabbling over the TV remote. There was tea to cook, clothes to iron and later Howard to feed.

The arguing died down and the television took over. She opened cupboards and grabbed at things until a tin toppled onto tiles by her toes.

'Damn it,' she shouted, then picked up the dinted tin. The choice at least was made – baked beans on toast.

She stirred the contents of the saucepan with jagged movements. Her patience was worn out. She'd ring Naomi back; she couldn't leave it another minute. Snatching the phone out of her back pocket, she swiped the screen. Naomi had texted her; she'd not heard the ping over the kids' racket.

*He hates the name Frederick. I want to believe him. Do I believe him? We're talking.*

That was it? Naomi's brevity provided no relief. The anxiety merely seemed to hunker down ready to do battle.

Of course people changed their names. As a solicitor she had encountered many who altered their identity, people wanting to get rid of a ludicrous name their parents had foisted on them or change it to something equally silly, like a celebrity's. Or they were running away from somebody or something. Ethan didn't strike Rebecca as a crazy fan, nor was Frederick that daft a name. If the process was legitimate, there'd be a paper trail in some government department. Ethan wasn't running away, he was only hiding the documentation, not himself. As for Naomi, she was happy and if her sister had learnt any lessons from her relationship with Kyle, it was not to waste time on superficial things. Naomi seemed prepared to stick by Ethan and give him the benefit of the doubt.

Naomi's lack of curiosity frustrated her inner solicitor.

Her phone bleeped once followed by a barrage of pings in succession. Her sister had sent a string of messages and each one contained an attached image – a screenshot of a document. Ethan's two passports and the certificates. Zooming in, she spotted the holograms and watermarks. They looked genuine and the two photographs illustrated a boy turned man without losing Ethan's distinguishing features.

However, she spotted something Naomi hadn't mentioned – his birth date. There was a discrepancy between the two passports of three years. Was that a clerical error or had he deliberately misled the issuing office? She was on the cusp of calling Naomi when the children charged into the kitchen.

'Mummy, Mummy, where's tea?' they chorused.

A mush of baked beans had stuck to the bottom of the pan. 'Oh, bugger.'

After the kids were tucked up in bed, she tried to ring Naomi, but there was no answer. The call went directly to voicemail.

She was left with one other option; contact her father and let him decide whether Naomi's relationship with Ethan was sufficiently worrying to intervene on her behalf.

Nancy answered the phone. Rebecca cursed in silence.

'Your father is out looking for Leia,' Nancy said, cutting through Rebecca's request to speak to him.

Rebecca's rapid heartbeats quickened into a symphony of pounding drumbeats. 'What's happened?'

'She's only gone and run off. We don't know where.' Her mother sounded more cross than alarmed.

Hardly a sin. 'She's not a teenager,' Rebecca said, her pulse steadying.

'She might as well be one.'

'Why has she gone?' Leia falling out with her parents wasn't exceptional.

'She's been awarded a prize. A prestigious medical award for her research. She'll need to attend a dinner and give a keynote speech.'

'Oh.' Rebecca smiled. Leia would detest every second of such an event; she'd turn up in jeans and t-shirt, chewing gum and showing off her shiny nose stud.

'It isn't funny, Rebecca. There's money wrapped up in this. She's letting down the rest of the research team.'

'Does it have to be her?'

'It's her idea. Her brains, her hard work that has got them this recognition. Why shouldn't she go?'

There were a hundred reasons why Leia couldn't care less and none of them would mean a thing to her goal-driven mother. Nancy rated bonuses and tick boxes, and other meaningless measurements of success. Rebecca was partial to such requirements in a business setting, but she appreciated Leia wasn't driven by them. Like Paul, Leia's fascination with science ran deeper than doing a job or making a name for herself; she loved solving an unsolvable problem.

'So why is Dad chasing after her?'

'She's gone off with Ashley.' The tone of disapproval was obvious. 'She works in the bar Leia hangs out in. He's gone to see if anyone knows where Ashley lives.'

Rebecca sighed. There was so much about her sister that her parents kept secret. 'Who's Ashley?'

'Somebody she's let into her life. She's… enamoured with her.'

Another thing that didn't surprise Rebecca, but clearly had upset her mother. 'Enamoured? As in they're—'

'She's in love, yes. I don't have a problem with *that*, but she could have picked somebody who's less of a sponger. She's a big distraction in Leia's life. She'd rather swan off with this Ashley instead of focusing on her career.'

Thankfully, Nancy couldn't see Rebecca's grimace of sympathy. 'She is thirty-five, Mum. Her career is pretty much established. She's a success and when she wants to publicise her findings, she does. She goes to conferences and gives lectures. She's hardly shy about it.'

'Then why not—'

'Because it's an award just for her. Just her. She's not the loner you make her out to be; she wants to be liked and not treated as something extraordinary.' Rebecca paused, aware of her own shortcomings. It had been eight years since Leia left England, years of separation from her twin, and not once had she actually asked what Leia wanted out of life.

'She's miserable,' said Nancy, 'that's for sure. Can't cope with all the attention this award is heaping on her. If this Ashley gets it wrong, I really fear Leia will tip into a truly dark place.' The doom and gloom appraisal didn't sum up the Leia Rebecca knew. Her twin had amazing determination and resilience. What she lacked was emotional support. Companionship.

'And maybe Ashley is exactly what Leia needs right now.'

'What did you want Dad for?' Nancy asked belatedly, dismissing Rebecca's opinion at the same time.

'It doesn't matter,' Rebecca said. What was the point in troubling her parents with Naomi when Leia was causing them grief. 'I'll speak to him another time. Have you tried texting Leia?'

'Of course,' her mother said. 'You try. Perhaps she'll answer you.'

Rebecca poured herself a glass of red wine, draped a woollen wrap around her shoulders and stepped outside. Leaving the back door ajar, so she could hear the kids if they called out for her, she sat on the swing chair on the patio and sipped on the Chianti. Howard would be home soon. Should she try again to explain her fears, her ineffectiveness in handling her family? What comfort could he really bring her? A horrible silence was starting to engulf their love.

She rocked the seat, anchoring the heels of her sandals on the crack between the paving stones. Closing her eyes, she practised the closest thing to meditation she'd ever managed to achieve, which was nothing like what her yoga teacher had taught her. She breathed in a lungful and thought about Leia in a positive way – laughing her head off. The chances of reaching Leia or Ashley, a woman Rebecca hadn't met or seen, were slim...

Leia was laughing, raucously and silently at the same time. She was driving a car and a litter of empty coffee cups and candy wrappers was scattered around the dashboard and foot-well. On her right, in the passenger seat, was a pink-haired woman with tattoos ringing her arm from wrist to elbow. She too was laughing.

Rebecca wasn't expecting it. Twice in one day was exceptionally rare, and it was Leia, too – her elusive twin right with her. Rebecca clung onto the view. Where they were driving? The dusty windshield was covered in the splattered corpses of flies. Lining the road, the brown leaves of the trees, tinged with brilliant oranges and yellows, formed a shady avenue. Leia could be anywhere in the north eastern corner of the country. The blurred road signs came and went too quickly for Rebecca to decipher the exact location.

It was as if she was perched between them, an invisible passenger. What a pity she couldn't touch Leia's shoulder and whisper into her ear. Slowly, the view began to fade. Rebecca opened her eyes and blinked, struck blind by the darkness of her night compared to the brilliance of Leia's day. She finished her wine and went back indoors.

Leia was on a road that could take her anywhere she liked – contrary to Nancy's alarming assessment, Leia wasn't on the verge of a crisis. She seemed fine.

Rebecca checked on a map and located Wooster in the middle of Ohio. There was nothing to lose if she sent Leia the images and appealed to her sister's latent maternal instincts. The cumbersome screenshots had to be transmitted one by one, which was a nuisance. On the last one she added a brief explanation. She was banking on Leia's innate curiosity and tendency to apply logical reasoning to irrational things, an infuriating habit that Leia often used for selfish purposes. Rebecca also prayed that Leia wouldn't judge her motives for delving into Ethan's private life harshly or cast aspersions on their grandmother's peculiar wisdom and foresight. Ethan's past and Naomi's future were intertwined in some way and only Leia had the means and opportunity to find out why he'd lied.

*Naomi has met Frederick. He's asked her to marry him. Why would Rose warn her? Please, find out who he really is. Go to Wooster.*

# eighteen

## Leia

### 24 October 2018

Ashley's eyes reminded Leia of charcoal; the burnt ashes of a smouldering fire. Pink highlights streaked her tangled straw hair and she wore a faded work t-shirt with the bar's logo across her chest. One of her ears was covered in a cluster of studs, while the other had a solitary hoop in the lobe. Her full lips – she had a cute little dimple under the bottom one – were painted a deep cerise and she'd plucked her eyebrows into a thin line of inky hairs. Completing the portrait: the tattoo that extended from her right wrist to shoulder.

Given Ashley's unconventional appearance, it was no big surprise that Leia's parents didn't approve of her new friend. When Leia had deposited the stupefied Ashley on the sofa, she knew she'd done it again – broken one of those unspoken rules of "living with your parents". Although Leia had never lived in the main part of the house or bothered her parents much when at home – especially her dad who kept himself locked away in his study, always writing something – there were conflicts of interest that her parents considered were symptomatic of her failure to fit into their little world. Their understated disappointment extended to her choice of friends.

The solution to all her problems, old and new, lay in running away, or, since it was more practical, driving away.

She slammed the car into reverse and the wheels squealed in protest. There was nobody home to watch her fly down the drive and back out onto the side street. Maybe a nosey neighbour or two might twitch their curtains and take a peek.

'Are you sure about this, Leia?' Ashley asked for the umpteenth time since Leia had started packing her bag.

'Fuck, yes. I should have done this ages ago.'

'So where are we going?' Ashley asked.

Leia paid little heed to the flow of traffic and weaved between cars, stopping at the interchanges with a pump of the brake.

'Jeez, calm the fuck down, will you.' Ashley gripped the edge of her seat.

Ashley was right. Bagging a speeding ticket was a bad idea. She eased back on the gas pedal.

'So,' Ashley asked again. 'Where are we going? Got any plans?'

'Nope, not really.' Leia focused on the road. Rubbing her temples, she tried to soothe her throbbing head. She'd taken Advil before they left and the tablets hadn't kicked in yet. There were other props available to her – sleeping pills and prescription drugs. If she enquired, someone might slip her something, tell her it was okay, better than burning out and falling off the edge of a cliff. Having given herself permission to fracture along well-defined fault lines, bolting was easier than she anticipated. Even amongst the fatigue and delirium of jumbled thoughts, she knew exactly what she was doing and why. However, she was adrift, unfettered from her usual routine.

'Let's go to Philly,' she said.

'Never been.' Ashley relaxed into her seat, propped her knees up on the dashboard and popped a stick of gum into her mouth and offered the pack to Leia.

'No, thanks. What route is best?'

Ashley shrugged. 'I don't know. Via Hartford?'

Leia aimed the car west. 'I feel like I'm a fugitive.'

'Why? You're not a prisoner. You said you're owed a vacation.'

'At least two weeks. Philly it is then.'

Hopping from one town to the next, the scenery shifted from urban to semi-rural. Fall in New England was the most awe-inspiring time of year. Foliage peeping had been one of Leia's earliest adventures when she arrived in America. She and her parents drove west, then up into Vermont and New Hampshire, just to take snapshots of the rainbow of auburn maple leaves and golden ashes. The fascination remained, but the adventures had ceased. While her parents took weekend vacations, she stayed behind in the city. In hindsight, as she admired the unfolding beauty of Connecticut, she should have tried harder to escape the confines of the lab. Ashley cheered her up with jokes about the difference between folks from Maine, where she had grown up, and other states. They laughed, hearty chuckles that flushed away the stresses of the last few days.

The onset of guilt was abrupt. Hearing Ashley's observant and generous descriptions of her co-workers, Leia knew she was handling her own situation crudely and possibly maliciously. Her father would be beside himself with worry if she didn't contact him. And as for her colleagues, she'd dumped a load of grief on their shoulders with her sudden departure. The least she could do was tell them she was safe

'I need the restroom.' Ashley fidgeted in her seat, pre-empting Leia's request for a break.

'We'll pull over at the next service stop. I should really text Dad and let him know I'm okay.'

It was on the outskirts of Waterbury that Leia's phone started to beep in spurts as the phone picked up a signal then lost it again. Somebody was bombarding her with messages.

# nineteen
## Naomi

Surrounded by a heap of towels and pillows, and clutching the tatty cigar box to her chest, Naomi stayed rooted to the spot by the closet. Ethan bounded upstairs and halted on the threshold of the room, his cheeks flushed an unnatural hue of red.

'What are you doing with that?' Ethan grabbed the cigar box out of her hands and shoved it back on the shelf. His anger was evident in the stark whiteness of his eyes. There was something else there too – a reflection of disappointment? Regret?

Naomi refused to shrink under his glare. 'We're supposed to be getting married and I find out you're not who you say you are.'

'Clearly, I'm me.' He stormed out of the bedroom. She hurried after him, abandoning the phone on the bed. Rebecca would have to wait.

'Speak to me.' She caught his sleeve with her fingertips.

He stopped at the top of the stairs. Now his peculiar expression resembled anguish – what had she awoken?

'It's just an identity. A name. It's what's in here that counts, isn't it?' He thumped his chest. 'I love you.'

If it wasn't that important, why was he so upset? She followed him downstairs where he continued his explanation of his namesake, Dorothy O'Reilly, and how she was the only one in the family who, 'Got me.' He spoke of his great-grandfather, another Frederick, an ambiguous figurehead who was admired by his relatives and also despised for his domineering attitude. 'He wasn't the best role model for fatherhood.'

Standing in the kitchen, making himself a coffee, Ethan tried hard to explain to her why he didn't want to be aligned with the man who'd founded the farm in Ohio. She listened, but didn't really hear. The explanation was irrelevant; water that had passed under the bridge decades ago.

'So why do I have to find it out this way? Don't you trust me?'

He slammed the mug down. Coffee splashed the cream worktop. She jumped to one side; she wanted drama, she was certainly getting some.

Cursing at the mess, he wiped it away with a dishcloth before answering. 'I've been Ethan since I left home. Fred isn't somebody I know any more. It isn't important. Why should I tell you when it doesn't matter to anyone? And as for the passports, I admit, I wanted the Irish one for immigration purposes. I left the US to become someone extraordinary, someone different to a simple farmer. The opportunity to change my name just seemed,' he reached out with his hand as if grasping for a word, 'too good a chance to miss.'

'And that's it?' she asked, touching his sleeve.

'Yes,' he said, without flinching or drawing back.

Another impassioned argument. Or was it more of a heated conversation about a misunderstanding. Or a dispute about trust and honesty? All those things. It annoyed her, knowing that he had created a crisis out of an issue that should have been dealt with months ago.

'Let's go out to eat,' he said, softening the lines of his face in an attempt at pacification.

She accepted the offer of a meal out; a neutral and public location meant staying level-headed and civil. However, awkward silences and empty pauses punctuated the evening meal as they struggled to find something to talk about that wouldn't stretch the chasm between them.

Remembering how she'd abandoned Rebeca in a state of panic, Naomi texted her sister, hoping to deflect her sister's curiosity with a comment about Ethan's choice of name. People changed their names for all sorts of reasons. However, when she revisited the captured images on her phone, they illustrated a process that couldn't have been simple. Rebecca knew things; behind her pretentious mannerisms, she had witnessed the darker side of society far more than Naomi. She had to ask for help, even if it meant worrying Rebecca further. She forwarded the screenshots to her sister without explanation. Becca would know what to do. She generally did.

* * * *

The next morning, Naomi remained in a fragile state with regard to Ethan. Her confidence slipped further when, not long after he left for work, Rebecca mentioned in a telephone call the passports and erroneous dates.

'Isn't it all a bit odd?' Rebecca asked.

Naomi wondered if Rebecca was toying with her.

'I suppose.' The irritating flock of butterflies in Naomi's stomach was back. 'He's not said anything more about it.' It was a feeble excuse and unlikely to convince a solicitor.

'You are sure about him?' Rebecca asked.

No, she wasn't. But she wasn't prepared to give up on the basis of a name change.

'Naomi?'

Naomi had hesitated for too long before answering, 'Yes. I love him.'

Rebecca said nothing, which was wise of her.

'I'm holding off on the marriage idea, though,' Naomi said.

This time, unlike with Kyle, her decision to wait had nothing to do with finances, neither was it about babies. The excuse was a fundamental one – was Ethan the right man for her? Rebecca might continue to check up on her, but Naomi had nothing further to add to the topic of Ethan's dual identity. What perturbed her the more than anything was the memory of Rose's haunting voice projecting a warning directly at her face. How could her grandmother have seen the future so accurately? Improbable; no, impossible. So how had Rose known and what else had she foretold? Naomi had paid a little attention to those birthdays and for years she had chosen to ignore them. She'd lost that blissful state of ignorance due to the ramifications of meeting Ethan. Now she wished she could embrace it again. Instead, she picked up her flute.

Naomi began her practice session in the hope that the soothing melody and breath control would ease her anxious thoughts. She closed her eyes, blocking out the smoking candle and the glazed, tired eyes of her grandmother. Gradually, the music won over and she concentrated harder and harder on the trickier passages. After what felt like an eternity, she regained a quietness in her mind. Ethan wasn't there to hear her practice, which was something of a relief. She'd rather play for herself.

# twenty
## Leia

Halloween lanterns it up the roadside diner. In the evening darkness, the glow of lights was a welcome sight. Ashley ordered steak and fries. Leia chose chicken salad. She wasn't hungry and, rather than eating, she sent an email to her father explaining she was safe, taking a holiday with her friend and would check back in every couple of days. To her surprise, there was an email from Lee Wang. He'd agreed a vacation was needed and deserved, and she shouldn't worry about the awards evening until she returned. Clearly, Lee and Paul had been discussing her "stress" and had decided to give her space. As for her mother, the lack of direct communication was a relief.

'Well, that's good, isn't it?' Ashley poured water into their glasses. 'I guess this foundation need you more than you think.'

Having dealt with her guilt, Leia turned her attention to the thread of texts from Rebecca. 'She's sent me photos of passports and a birth certificate.' She flashed one at Ashley. 'She's obsessed with Naomi's boyfriend.'

It was the first time she seen him. Ethan appeared unremarkable, somewhat handsome, although beards weren't her thing. The final text was a message from Rebecca. Leia spluttered on a mouthful of water. 'She can't be serious.'

'What?'

Leia sighed. 'Naomi has this guy called Ethan who it seems is also called Frederick.'

'Okay.' Ashley shrugged off the fuss.

Leia really didn't want to have to explain about Rose's quirky birthday habits in detail. 'My gran warned her not to marry anyone call Frederick.' She gave a non-committal shrug, hoping to cast herself as indifferent. 'Crazy, I know, but it's become a thing for Rebecca.'

She scrolled up and down the message thread and assimilated each document fully; she had a photographic memory, something that was a both a hindrance and a help when it came to learning new things. Each newly acquired fact glued itself into her brain and stuck there, adding to the accumulated clutter. Sometimes she'd just like to forget a piece of information. Her genius had more to do with this talent than any other ability, and although Lee relied heavily on her analytical skills to decipher problems, without her memory she would have floundered years ago.

After so many years – ten years – why was this happening now? She recalled perfectly the flatness of the Fens, the marble cake, falling asleep in the middle of *Enchanted*. Nothing of importance was supposed to happen on those birthdays other than humouring an eccentric woman with a panache for making dramatic statements. Back then Leia's medical training had suggested a diagnosis, a reason for Rose's references to voices in her head: schizophrenia or a similar disorder. The candle was irrelevant, a smoke screen behind which Rose hid the truth about her affliction. Leia stayed quiet. She wasn't a qualified shrink; she was Rose's granddaughter.

But now she knew differently – the proof was surely right in front of her. Realising that the impact of those voices stretched far beyond Rose's life, she would have to tell her sisters, starting with level-headed Rebecca, about Rose's last day. She deserved to know. However, for the moment, she had to deal with the enormity of Naomi's situation. She needed more evidence, data, something tangible before she said anything to Rebecca. For now, she would concentrate on her strengths: analysing the facts, speculating and testing, utilising what little she knew about Naomi's boyfriend.

She zoomed in on the numbers, which were easier than letters to decipher. Her mental capacity was huge and slightly disorganised. She often funnelled her thoughts one way, then the other, shuffling personal things in amongst the molecules of genes and proteins that would one day cure terrible diseases. Today, those remarkable ideas of hers were not useful in the slightest. Her stomach churned itself into a knot because she spotted what Rebecca might have seen too.

Ashley reached out and touched Leia's hand. 'What's up?'

'The dates on the passports don't match.'

'Is that a big deal?'

'Dunno. Rebecca wants me to go to Wooster.'

'Wooster? Where the hell is Wooster?'

Geography wasn't one of Ashley's strong points, but the States were huge and the names of towns and cities so numerous they repeated themselves up and down the country.

'Ohio. Frederick obtained a degree at the Ohio State University campus in Wooster. They have an Agricultural Institute there.'

'Farming is a big thing in Ohio.' Their food arrived, heaped on two large plates. 'Thank you.' Ashley greeted the waitress with a smile. The two chatted while Leia tried to build a picture of Ethan based on her limited knowledge.

Frederick Neiman born in America, possibly in Ohio where he'd gained his degree, had gone to Australia, and, by adopting his grandmother's name, had become Ethan O'Reilly, then he'd travelled to England on an Irish passport. Did Rebecca suspect Ethan forged one of the passports and constructed a fake identity? Leia nudged those issues to one side; her primary concern was Naomi. Was she safe? Had Ethan threatened Naomi? Was he a troublemaker? Leia needed more information. She needed to find somebody who knew Frederick Nieman. Which meant going to Wooster.

Having barely touched her salad, Leia trampled it with her fork. 'Do you mind a change of plan?'

'I'm hardly in a position to tell you what to do. It's your vacation.'

'If you don't want to come with me, I can drop you off at a train station or a greyhound stop.'

Ashley frowned. 'Are you dumping me—'

'No,' Leia said swiftly. 'You don't have to ride along if you don't want to. It's just I have some family issues to resolve and it's a long way.'

Ashley waved a chip at Leia's phone. 'You're going to Wooster then?'

Leia nodded.

'Why not ask Naomi what's going on? I mean, surely she knows why he has two IDs?'

Ashley had some inkling of Leia's sisters, but her view of them remained portraits that lacked depth and perception. Leia's complicated relationship with Rebecca and Naomi would intrigue a psychologist, the rifts they had created, the years of bypassing awkward questions about Rose, her parents and the differing coping strategies they had adopted after Paul and Nancy had moved on with their lives. Leia screwed her face into a ball. Her headache had bounced back.

Leia hated anyone meddling with her life, and yet for years her parents had convinced her they were protecting her from exploitation and she allowed them to control her – or more likely, she caved in to their methods. The conclusion they fostered was that geniuses were emotionally crippled by their gift and after three decades of claustrophobic guidance, Leia's parents treated her as if she was a fragile, defective person who needed constant supervision. Was she about to treat Naomi as equally juvenile?

'It's not that easy to explain. If I go prying into Ethan's past… Naomi really doesn't like anyone interfering with her life.'

'Who does?' Ashley said sympathetically, focusing her sharp eyes on Leia.

Naomi had been so excited in the days before their parents announced they were leaving England. She'd been selected to play for a national competition. Her excitement collapsed when she realised Rebecca was engrossed in work and Leia wouldn't lift a finger. What followed was self-indulgent and hurtful. Leia had gone back to her digs in Cambridge and smoked pot while writing a delirious conclusion for her dissertation; it had failed to impress her tutor. She'd laughed it off, she laughed off everything back then, and decided there had to be another way to exercise her mind. Years later, she was going to make things up to Naomi by doing something she'd always wanted to do: play detective.

'I let Naomi down. Rebecca, too. I was supposed be a big sister and agony aunt rolled into one. Our parents entrusted me to guide Naomi into adulthood. But I avoided her, went out of my way to be awkward and gauche. I didn't even go to her concerts. Rebecca did. Rebecca knows she has this amazing capacity to use music to reach out to people, as if she was playing to an audience of one, not many. But I fucked around, drank, partied… I'm selfish. I couldn't even care about my patients because I don't want to feel. I'm a selfish kind of bitch.'

'So this is as much about you as it is finding out about this guy she's dating?' Ashley asked.

'Yeah… you're right. But I'm intrigued. I have been since I found out about him weeks ago and I knew it.' She thumped her hand on the table. Perhaps there was something of Rose in her after all, and because of that she shouldn't fear resurrecting memories of her grandmother. 'I knew something wasn't right. I guess I want to show Naomi I care. Is it too late?'

Ashley said nothing, which was a blessing. Leia's perceptive companion knew exactly when a question was rhetorical.

Leia picked up her phone, licked her sticky thumbs, and composed a reply to Rebecca.

*Going to Wooster. Is Naomi okay? Send more info.*

\* \* \* \*

With the unfamiliar roads to navigate and Leia's headache re-emerging, they agreed to wait until morning. The friendly waitress suggested a motel a few miles further along the road.

The bland room was under-furnished, but it was clean and cheap. Leia drew the curtains and took two more Advils, washing them down with a soda. Ashley crashed on one of the beds and immediately fell asleep, rattling off her familiar gentle snore. Leia retrieved her laptop and hooked it up to the motel's weak wi-fi signal. She couldn't sleep, not until she'd fathomed some elements of the Ethan mystery.

She started with assumptions and hypotheses. Firstly, that Dorothy O'Reilly was a paternal grandmother who came to America and married somebody called Nieman and secondly, Frederick was born in Ohio and his family still lived there. If she could find somebody who knew him, maybe that person could explain why Frederick had left America and gone to Australia, and in doing so, shed a glimmer of light on the change of name and discrepancy over birthdays. Ten or so years wasn't a huge timeframe.

She hunted the Internet for evidence of a Frederick Nieman and drew a blank. There were no social media accounts matching the information Rebecca had sent her. Would Ethan's grandmother turned up better results? Had she made it into any publicly available records? The latest census records were for 1941. Leia searched the database, but Dorothy O'Reilly wasn't listed anywhere in Ohio with her birth date. So, Leia kicked assumption number one into action – she'd married somebody called Nieman. Dorothy Nieman pulled up one relevant record close to Wooster – there were several Niemans in the area, too. The age was right, a young woman of eighteen, and she'd married Henry Nieman of Nieman Farm, Knox County, Ohio. The census records stopped there, but at least Leia now had a possible location for the Nieman family home. Ethan knew a lot about farming equipment and had worked in Australia as a farm labourer. The two lives of one man fitted together nice and snug. Tomorrow, they'd check the newspaper records in Wooster's city library for information about the Niemans in and around Knox County.

Satisfied with her progress, Leia switched off her computer. She was tempted to lie next to the oblivious, semi-clad Ashley and feel some body heat reach out across the bed into her own cold limbs. However, she wasn't ready to tamper with a blossoming friendship. It wasn't that Leia needed any physical intimacy with Ashley; what she wanted was for her friend to acknowledge that Leia was worthy of her love. All her life, Leia had craved the simplicity of unconditional love and, contrary to the impression that she behaved promiscuously, she rarely slept with anyone and often regretted it when she had. The roadblock to successfully integrating with people was her tendency to over-analyse everything. According to Nancy, Leia was an emotionally undeveloped icicle who drove herself into other people's warm hearts and then ran away when things got too tough. Her mother could be damn cruel sometimes, but unfortunately, horrifyingly accurate.

She might have slept. She couldn't always tell as she never remembered her dreams, not even the nightmares that produced cold sweats.

Leia took advantage of the dawn light leaching through the venetian blinds to check her emails. Rebecca, ahead by half a day, had replied. The substance of Rebecca's email relayed what Ethan had told Naomi and it was flimsy. Somehow, Ethan had convinced Naomi that the name change was merely a forgotten moment in his past, something that he conveniently cared little about and, although the couple had argued, according to Rebecca, they'd kissed and made up. Rebecca used the word "infatuated" with regard to Naomi's flipping from shock to acceptance. In Rebecca's rosy world, Ethan's appeal should simply be romantic, but it wasn't and she was clearly worried. In contrast, Leia, never one for complicating situations with emotions, was stuck at the first logical hurdle: why bother with the hassle of a bureaucratic process in a foreign country? What had he really gained from being Ethan and not Frederick? It couldn't be Naomi; she hadn't been part of his life back then, and the Irish passport would have been issued on his Irish ancestry alone. The switch to O'Reilly wasn't necessary, either.

She bought coffee and waffles from the breakfast bar across the road. It had rained in the night and with it had come a frosty northerly breeze. Unlike England, which never truly grasped the bitterness of winter nor the scorching heat of summer, New England did them all thoroughly. Shivering, she hurried back to the motel room. Ashley was singing loudly in the shower and, after emerging wet and unashamedly naked, she swallowed the hot beverage in a few gulps.

Leia turned away and gathered up her things, stuffing them into her bag. 'Still okay to move on?' she asked. People changed their minds in the cold light of a new day.

'Sure. Let me throw on some clothes and we can get going, yeah?' Ashley scampered around the room, picking up her abandoned bra and yesterday's socks. 'I guess we could share the driving, then we might get there by evening?'

They set off shortly after nine o'clock. Ashley made up rap songs based on every town they drove past or around. Leia laughed more than she had in a long time.

\* \* \* \*

Since she'd selfishly been the subject of many of their conversations since they'd met, the journey gave Leia the opportunity to find out more about Ashley, who'd described her childhood as 'uneventful and ordinary'.

'Well, except for my kid brother. He got into trouble with the law. Criminal damage. He's got anger issues.' Ashley's gentle laughter tickled Leia once again. 'Poor kid got quite a shock being locked up. Shook him up. He's okay now.'

'And you? No run-ins with the cops?' Leia asked, staring at the road ahead – the highway was mind-numbingly boring.

'Me?' Ashley exclaimed with mock indignation. 'An angel. But I left Maine 'cos what's a girl to do up there when the bright lights of a big city beckon?'

'How old are you?' Leia hadn't thought to ask because in her little world age was irrelevant – she'd been accepted into Cambridge at sixteen years old, although her parents wisely insisted waiting until she was an adult before attending university. During the intervening two years, she'd taken another four A levels, just for the heck of it.

'Twenty-eight. Do I look older?' Ashley asked, glancing at her reflection in the mirror on the back of the sun visor.

'Do you want to look older?'

Ashley grinned. 'Nah. Forever young, that's me. A kid at heart. You have that air of youthfulness about you, too.'

'I do?'

'Sure. I would never have guessed you're in your mid-thirties. Don't you want to settle down?'

'Settle into what?' Surprised at how Ashley's question disturbed her, she lapsed into silence.

By the time they reached the outskirts of Wooster, the day was nearly over. Their stomachs rumbled and heavy eyelids drooped. There was no point in pursuing any line of enquiries. They checked into the slightly more upmarket hotel and collapsed onto their beds. With no news from Rebecca, Leia concluded there was nothing to report about Naomi and Ethan: which had to be good?

# twenty-one
## Leia
## 26 October 2018

The public library in Wooster was a predictable dead end – Leia was in the wrong county. The librarian recommended going to Mount Vernon in Knox County and looking at their local newspapers. It meant another hour or so drive south. The route took them through forests and back again into fields and small valleys. Leia saw signs to Fredericktown.

'Do you think he was named after there?' asked Ashley.

'According to the librarian at Wooster, a lot of Germans settled in the county. Irish, too.' The combination of immigrants that created Frederick Nieman.

The satnav located Mount Vernon public library in the centre of the city. The rain that had plagued them during the morning's drive had stopped. Golden leaves, which floated down in the breeze, formed a carpet on the sidewalk. Leia couldn't describe the city as beautiful or even pretty; she'd grown up in Medieval East Anglia. But for what it was – a mid-west urban centre – Mount Vernon didn't lack charm. It was pleasantly tidy and compact.

'We'll try the newspapers first. Find some obituaries, birth records,' Leia said as they entered the single-storey building.

'What are you looking for?' asked Ashley.

'I don't know,' she replied. 'Something mentioning the Niemans, I suppose.'

The older newspapers were on microfilm. Fortunately, her ability to read quickly and snatch individual words out of heaps of text proved invaluable. Beginning her search around the time of the second world war, she discovered Dorothy's arrival in America in a brief account of the Catholic wedding in Mount Vernon.

At the ridiculously tender age of sixteen, Dorothy O'Reilly married Henry Nieman in 1939 just before the outbreak of the war. She was related to other O'Reillys in the county who had emigrated decades earlier. A cousin had arranged the courting, initially by exchanging letters until Dorothy arrived in person. The local reporter who wrote the brief paragraph called it a match made in heaven and the wedding day was well attended by both families.

'Look.' Ashley pointed at the screen. 'Henry is the son of Frederick Nieman, who arrived from Germany and bought land south of Mount Vernon.'

'The younger Frederick's great-grandfather, I assume.' Leia continued to scroll through films.

Dorothy's children had eight children and their births were announced every two or three years. By the sixties, the obituaries began to appear, starting with the old man, Frederick Nieman, who'd died in his sleep. The archive of old newspapers gradually dwindled over the next couple of decades as newspapers went out of business or ceased recording the finer details of family life. Nobody cared to know; which was kind of sad. With social media in charge of people's lives, the formality of announcements had been swept away.

'That's that then.' Ashley leaned back in her chair and rubbed her eyes. 'Hardly a breakthrough. This guy, Ethan, he's not showing up because there is nothing. Your sister met a man who hates his name. Maybe he got bullied at school.'

Leia wasn't about to give up. 'According to the USA passport, Frederick Nieman was born in 1987. We know Dorothy's youngest son, William, was born in 1957 when Dorothy was thirty-five. I'm guessing, hoping, that William is Fred's dad and that William is still alive. Let's shift forward and go for the online records.'

She hunted the archives of the Mount Vernon News, church gazettes and Knox News websites. The name Nieman popped up several times in 2008 and 2009. The headline of the first article quickened the pace of her heartbeats.

'Look, look.' She gestured at the screen. Ashley, having lost interest, was swinging on her chair.

'Local farmer killed in freak accident,' Ashley read slowly.

Leia's lightning quick eyes scanned the article. 'Robert Nieman, aged 20, lost his foot in the mechanism of a potato harvester and bled to death while trapped under the wheels.'

'Poor guy.'

'His father, William, found him but was unable to revive his son due to loss of blood. Details of the funeral, blah blah.' Leia read to the end of the article and the last sentence stuck out. 'The sheriff's office in Mount Vernon were notified and an investigation is under way.'

'Now this is more like it,' Ashley said, perhaps too loudly – the man opposite their table gave her a stern glare of disapproval. 'Isn't it?' she whispered into Leia's ear.

'If the sheriff is involved, there'll be a coroner's report.' Leia clicked on the next article link – a preliminary coroner's report that added nothing to the original one other than that the family were deeply in shock having lost their beloved son. No mention of a Frederick. She began to wonder if she'd got the wrong family and if another one of Dorothy's sons had produced Frederick.

The last entry was several months later. The coroner's final verdict had concluded Robert had died through misadventure; an accidental death as a result of failing to turn off the tractor's engine, poorly maintained brakes and Robert's choices; he ignored the safety procedures.

Leia's mouth dropped. 'The sheriff was quoted as being disappointed with the verdict. Disappointed? Meaning he was expecting something different?'

'Possibly criminal?'

Leia hogged the screen, and scanning rapidly, she reached the last paragraph. Impatient Ashley plucked on Leia's sleeve.

'Robert's family agreed with the verdict and are satisfied no further action is necessary in locating their other son, Frederick Nieman, who went missing after the accident. Frederick Nieman had just completed his degree at Ohio State University in Wooster and was due to return to the farm to help his family. It is not known if Frederick knows that his brother is dead as he did not attend the funeral or contact the family after the accident. While the sheriff could not provide any clear evidence of Robert's death being anything other than a tragic accident, he expressed disappointment in not being able to trace Frederick Nieman's current address.'

The man opposite glared again as Leia's voice rose with excitement. 'Oh my God, Ashley. You know what this means? He's on the run. He has to be involved in his brother's death and he's on the run. We need to find this sheriff and speak to him.'

'What about the family? Shouldn't we ask them first? Maybe they've been in contact with their son since then. It's ten years since Robert died.'

The address of Nieman's Farm was given on an earlier article referring to the funeral. Leia noted it down. 'Out by Martinsburg. We're getting further away from Wooster.' She glanced at her watch. It was past lunchtime and she was hungry. 'Let's eat first, then drive out there. Just have to chance it that they're in and will talk to us.'

The need to solve a mystery drove Leia further along the roads of Ohio. Being a so-called genius enabled her to think in unusual ways, and just like anybody else, she loved the unravelling of threads, rather like the DNA she mapped in the lab. But unlike those hours of sifting through tortuous data hunting for clues about a microbe, Leia was rediscovering the frailties of people. Humans were unpredictable and infuriating, their choices warped by emotions and relationships. People defined each other and in doing so they corrupted or spoilt those they loved, or, as in Leia's experience, they caged a loved one in order to protect. In retrospect, Kyle had been benign. Ethan, from what little she understood of him, was malignant. Leia feared that the longer Naomi was with her American lover, the greater the risk she would cease to be the precious Naomi, the girl with a gift that Leia could never match. Naomi brought joy and pleasure through her music. She needed people to listen to her, not shape her.

# twenty-two

## Naomi

## 27 October 2018

He bounded into the house, enthused with energy and kissed her brow before inspecting the lasagne in the oven.

He clapped his hands together. 'Excellent. I'm starving.'

'You're happy.' The episode of the cigar box was forgotten and the question of his identity mothballed. There seemed little point forcing the issue to the surface when he clearly had no intention of discussing it. Did it matter? Who Ethan was was surely evident in other ways and not determined by documents.

The grin on his face widened. 'Bonus arrived today. My bank balance just rocketed.' He wrapped his arm around her waist and drew her into an embrace. He smelt a little of engine oil – not unusual – and his lips tasted of Coke, which he drank in the car.

'I've been thinking,' he said, releasing her mouth. 'About Ireland.'

'Oh,' she said cautiously.

The sparkle in his eyes was especially vibrant. 'Perhaps we should go and visit my ancestors' homeland.'

Ethan's volatility slammed into Naomi, battering her with its suddenness. 'You want to go to Ireland?'

'Yeah, babe.' He sidled closer to her, brushing a hip against her and nearly pinning her to the worktop. Her heart quickened and her skin prickled with goose bumps. The chemistry between them hadn't imploded because of that box. However, she shouldn't be feeling this way; she should feel... what exactly?

'Whereabouts?' she asked.

'Limerick or Cork. Maybe a nice cottage by the sea. Just us two getting to know each other better.'

A sensible suggestion. She relaxed a fraction, imagining the charm of an Irish summer's day and a walk along a beach. Except, it wouldn't be like that. 'It's nearly winter.'

'We can light fires and cuddle.' He cocked his head to one side and the halogen spotlights optimised the luminescence of his eyes. 'What do you think?'

Okay, an Irish winter – did it matter? 'When?'

'Soon.'

She'd some plans, but nothing that couldn't be re-arranged. 'There's Christmas. I don't have to go to Boston.' The only time she ever did go out there was for Christmas. New England offered the appropriate seasonal weather far better than damp old England.

He blinked. When he blinked it signalled something wasn't right. 'That's just one or two weeks. How about longer?'

She shook her head. They'd had this debate about school terms before. 'I can't, you know that—'

'It's a business. Your business. Take a break.'

A break would damage her reputation.

'I've pupils.' Not only that, each week with the quartet, she edged closer to reclaiming her confidence. Leaving now would blow it away, just like when her parents left England. 'What about your work?'

'I can get another job.'

The blasé manner in which he brushed off employment, especially after earning a bonus, alarmed her. She took a step sideways, creating space between them.

'Exactly how long do you think we're going to be away for?'

The oven timer started to bleep. 'The lasagne is ready,' he said. The relaxed slouch of his shoulders and the presentation of her favourite dish were carefully crafted to alleviate her concerns.

'Ethan?'

'Think about it.' He fetched the oven gloves.

She'd thought she understood something of what motivated him – work and money - and now she realised she still had no clue who Ethan really was. He blanked her questions, twisted her around his little finger by heating up her emotions, then blindsided her with a decision that he assumed she would readily accept. Her parents had done this to her years ago, but she wasn't sixteen any more.

'I will,' she said softly, soothing him with smile. 'I'll sleep on it.'

She needed time and the opportunity to ring Rebecca in private.

After eating, Ethan offered to wash up, and he gathered the dirty dishes and cutlery and balanced them on one arm.

'Ta-da!

His excitement wasn't derailed by her subdued response. She polished her flute while he hunted the Internet for cottages to rent. He wasn't interested in the weekly holiday ones; he filtered his results down to the long term lets. There was a flightiness to his taps and swipes, an exuberance that he'd not shown in any other activity he'd initiated. She mimicked his enthusiasm to the best of her ability as she rubbed a sheen into the lip plate, but tucked out of sight from him, she was unnerved, almost afraid of his ever-changing moods. Why couldn't he settle and be happy with her, here, where she had friends and a purpose? Why the sudden need to uproot again when he'd only been in England for a year?

He showed her pictures of stone-clad cottages in the middle of green fields – Ireland had an emptiness to its pastures and fields that even the Fens couldn't mimic. Perhaps he wanted the space more than he'd realised.

'You could teach out there too,' he said, between mouthfuls of beer.

'I can teach anywhere.' But what about the possibilities of performing as a soloist? That deep-seated need remained unresolved and she had to find out one way or the other if she could stretch her talents to their fullest potential. She just needed to crack it, win it. A remote spot in Ireland was hardly going to conjure up an awe-inspired audience.

# twenty-three
## Leia

By the time Leia and Ashley reached Martinsburg the sun had set, leaving the ploughed fields bleached of warmth. A thin layer of misty coldness drifted up from the valleys and along the banks of the rolling hills. The farm was a challenge to find in the evening's long shadows. Each farm they drove past had to be checked for a name. Eventually they saw a sign swinging from a cock-eyed wooden post – Nieman's Farm.

'What do you think?' Ashley asked, chewing on her lip. 'It's a bit spooky isn't it? Coming out here and not knowing what we might find. What if they're armed with shotguns?' In other circumstances, Ashley's over-active imagination might be entertaining, but not when the rain had been beating down on the roof of the car for most of the journey; it struck Leia as a tad too melodramatic.

Leia was accustomed to the bleak landscape of the Fens with its isolated little villages and farms dotted along the criss-cross network of tracks and dykes. There was nothing especially lonesome about this one farm and there were others just a mile or so further up the road. She turned the car off the main road and onto the bumpy track.

'It's just a farm,' she said.

The sun-blistered barn might once have been a glorious shade of reddish-brown. Not any longer – one dilapidated wall had nearly collapsed in on itself. The picture of neglect continued with the silo tower that leant slightly to one side. A ring of tall grass circled its base and creepers climbed the rusty ladder that clung to the cylinder.

As for the house, the timber had suffered. The whitewash had faded or flaked away, leaving the silvery wood exposed and the window frames rotting. All the curtains were drawn shut, blocking any inquisitive visitor from seeing inside.

Leia parked by the front porch. 'I can't see any lights,' Ashley said.

Leia pointed at the battered pickup truck. 'Somebody must be home.' Unperturbed by the stillness within the house, Leia climbed out of the car and Ashley reluctantly followed.

The porch creaked as it bore their weight and enormous moths flitted around the broken porch light, perhaps lured by the memory of hazy sunshine. Ashley swatted them away. Leia smelt the premature decline of the house – damp, musty mildew and traces of creosote and some kind of insect repellent. An attempt had been made to salvage the structure. Having lived most of her childhood in an old Medieval cottage she knew what she sensed was not entirely due to the passing of time but something to do with a lack of energy; the house appeared tired and fed-up.

She opened the screen door and rapped her knuckles on the door. Ashley attempted to peer through a window.

'Perhaps—' Ashley began to say, but halted, hushing herself with a finger pressed to her lips.

The footsteps came closer and a key turned in the door. Slowly it opened, and a small pool of light fell across the gloomy porch. The man who'd opened the door was stooped and shuffling his feet; he formed an impenetrable silhouette.

'Mr Nieman?' Leia asked.

'What do you want?' he asked gruffly.

'I'm sorry, I know it's late, but I hope if you let me explain the reason for our unannounced visit that you might understand why we've called by so unexpectedly.' Leia hadn't really rehearsed what to say during the hour-long drive from Mount Vernon; perhaps she should have done.

'You're not from about here,' he said. 'I mean, you aren't American.'

'No, I'm English. A Brit. I'm Leia.' She pointed at Ashley. 'My friend Ashley comes from Maine.'

A cold blast of wind caught the screen door and it rattled against the wall.

He snorted. 'That's a long way to come to see me.' He remained a fixture in the doorway, barring their entry and ensuring his face stayed in the shadows, undefined and foreboding.

Ashley shifted backwards, closer to where the car was parked.

Leia decided pleasantries were unlikely to work and opted for a more abrupt approach. 'I'm here to talk about your son, Mr Nieman. You are William Nieman, yes? Father of Frederick Nieman?'

He swayed and clutched the door frame. For a second Leia thought he might tumble. She dashed over and took his arm, steadying him.

'I'm sorry,' Leia said, 'I didn't mean to startle you. Can we come in? I don't think you're very well.'

'I'm fine.' He shook himself free. He waved them into the kitchen. Leia expected the smell of food, whether fresh or rotten, but it was a surprisingly odourless room with cupboards at one end and a rickety kitchen table at the other. The table was bare, except for a vase of wilted wildflowers, the sink clean and empty, and the worktops wiped down. There were cans lined up next to the stove, cheap food and not exactly the most nutritious. It explained his fleshless build, the belt drawn tight by his hips, and his hollow cheeks.

He wore a woollen shirt with a button missing. The stubble on his chin was wiry and grey, his lips pale and blemished with sunspots, as was the rest of his mottled face. At the centre of it was his crooked nose, which ended with a bulbous, thickly covered nest of bloodshot capillaries. He'd lived most of his life out in the sun. He looked older than his fifty-plus years, and haggard, too. Nothing covered the peeling skin of his bald patch, not even a wisp of hair, and what little hair he did have was snowy white and circling the back of his head.

'What about Fred?' He glanced from Leia to Ashley, cautiously eyeing her ear studs.

'I think I know where he is,' said Leia. She clutched her handbag. 'He's alive, if that's what you're wondering.'

While his eyes widened, his lips remained turned down and sour. The frown transformed his cheeks into jowls of slackened skin. The swaying worsened and he swept the back of his hand over his brow. Leia feared she might be called upon to act like the doctor she nearly once became, but he stayed upright and unsupported.

'Come this way,' he said abruptly, and led them out of the dimly-lit kitchen, across a narrow hallway into another room.

The couch was covered in quilts and crocheted blankets, reminding Leia of Rose's small front room. The dresser, which lined one wall, displayed dinner plates, china cups and saucers that looked European in origin. In the centre were framed photographs of a young man. Leia had never seen him before. The youth – presumably Robert – was smiling, happy and standing next to his father William in one photograph, and in another, a motherly-looking woman. There was no evidence of Ethan, or Fred, as his father had called him.

Almost indistinguishable in the low light was a woman in a wheelchair. Her droopy face was lopsided, her lips chewing on nothing. Coming out of her nose was a feeding tube, the stoppered end of which hung down the side of the wheelchair. Her eyes though had a brilliance still to them. Fred's mother, if that was who Leia was looking at, was very much alive and imprisoned in her body.

'ALS. Been like this for a few years now,' William said. He patted his wife's hand. 'Somebody who knows Fred.'

Her eyes blinked rapidly as if to convey a message. William nodded; he understood. 'She wants to know more. Don't be put off by her appearance. She can hear. She can think for herself.'

'I'm sure she can.' Leia smiled a greeting.

They all sat, forming a little circle that included the wheelchair. William had switched on another light. The only other electric appliance in the room was an old television, not even a flat screen one. Everything in the room belonged to another generation and not a couple closer to her parent's age. She couldn't imagine two young brothers with boundless energy cooped up in house that resembled a crippled nursing home.

'I want to show you something before I say anything else.' She hooked her handbag off her shoulder and retrieved her mobile. She quickly found the photograph of Ethan from his Irish

Passport. Holding out the phone, she held it up in front of William.

'Is this your son?'

William pulled out a pair of reading glasses from his top pocket and balanced them on his nose. He stared for a few seconds at the image before nodding slowly. 'Yes. That's Fred. He looks older.'

'It would have been taken two or so years ago. In Australia,' she added carefully. 'It's from an Irish passport which bears the name Ethan O'Reilly.'

Mrs Nieman sucked hard and jerked in her chair. William leaned over and stroked her arm. 'It's him, Susie. Got them eyes of his and colour of his hair too. He's got a beard.' He turned to speak to Leia. 'Ethan's his middle name. He preferred it. When he went to study in Wooster, that's the name he used, and his friends called him that.'

'So only you called him Fred?'

'Me, his mom. And Rob,' he added quietly, the glasses slipping forward. 'And his cousins, too. We were close family until...' A shadow of intense sadness passed across his craggy face.

'I'm sorry about your son,' Leia said quickly.

'Yes,' said Ashley, chipping in. 'I'm so sorry.'

William glanced over to the photographs. 'Fine young man, Robert. Hardworking. Loyal,' he said with a marked tone of bitterness.

'O'Reilly was your mother's maiden name?' Leia edged closer on her seat.

'Dorothy O'Reilly. Lovely, generous soul. Died back in 2000. Fred took it badly, her dying. He was never one for close relationships or speaking his heart, but he cried that day. I think it was the only day I ever saw him cry since he was a small boy.'

'Would that explain why he chose that name? You see, he changed it in Australia.'

'You're not Australian though,' he said. He straightened and inspected them with wary eyes. 'So how come you're here?'

'He left Australia about a year ago and came to England on an Irish passport. It means he has leave to stay and work, otherwise he'd need a visa. It's perfectly legitimate,' Leia explained. 'Except, he's now Ethan, and ... he's dating my sister, Naomi. In fact, he wants to marry her.'

'That doesn't sound like my boy.' He waved a dismissive hand.

'It doesn't sound like my sister either. She wasn't keen on marrying her last boyfriend, even though they lived together for nearly a decade. Which brings me to why I'm here. Why would your son, Fred, go to such lengths to change his name, get a passport in that name, when it wasn't necessary? I take it he hasn't contacted you since ... he left?'

Susie gurgled a weird sound of despair.

'No,' he said, his face hardened into a fossilised expression of contempt. 'We didn't part on good terms, you see. Since then, with Rob gone, I can't manage the farm on my own and we had no money to invest, so I leased the land to a neighbouring farm and they work it, give me some rent and that keeps us going. The only way we can get our land back is with help and Fred isn't here. He left.'

'Why? What happened that day, Mr Nieman? I read the newspaper reports.' She paused. Had she said too much about the research she and Ashley had conducted hours earlier in Mount Vernon? What if she alluded to hers and Rebecca's fear that Ethan might harm their sister? What William had told her so far matched the information Rebecca had relayed to Leia. Was her sister really in peril when Naomi herself had insisted she was okay with Ethan's explanation? The mystery remained – what had kept him from making any contact with his family for ten long years?

'Why?' William repeated. 'He finished studying at Wooster, turned up one day for an hour, maybe not even that, and after that, we never heard or saw from him again. You're the first person to say they've met him since then.'

Leia shook her head. 'I've never met him. I live in Boston. I'm a US citizen. It's my sister who's living with him. I need to know what happened that day.'

William squeezed his wife's hand. 'I'll tell you, but I don't think it will help your sister. For all these years, we thought he was dead.'

# twenty-four
## Ethan
## 5 August 2008

A hazy cloud of dirt billowed behind the departing bus. He'd forgotten the dust, how it swept along the roadside and up into the air. Adjusting his sunglasses, he swung the duffel bag over his shoulder and started walking.

After two miles, Ethan was sweating. He paused under the shadow of a sugar maple and took a few sips of Coke out of a bottle. He could have called his dad, William, and asked him to collect him from the bus stop, but Ethan wanted his arrival to be a surprise. He'd not been home for nearly nine months and he hoped their last quarrel had been kicked into the long grass.

A Chevy pickup truck drove past, slowing as it went past Ethan. When it stopped, Ethan caught up with it.

'I thought it was you.' The bearded driver pushed back his cap until his mouse-like eyes were visible and greeted Ethan with a smile. The two dogs in the back barked and snarled; they'd forgotten Ethan's scent. 'Shut it,' the man snapped over his shoulder.

'Mr Murray,' Ethan said.

'Ignore them bitches. Both in season, driving me crazy.' He leaned over and opened the passenger door. 'Lift?'

'Thanks.' Ethan heaved the duffel bag up on to the seat and squeezed in next to it. 'Bus dropped me off.'

'So, you're back?' Murray pulled away. The air conditioning was welcome and Ethan turned the vent towards his flushed face.

'Don't know,' he said truthfully. 'Done studying. Got my degree.'

'Well done. Good for you. Mrs Henderson said you're a bright kid.'

Ethan was twenty-one, hardly a kid, but it was sweet that his old elementary school teacher remembered him given how much trouble he'd caused in class. She'd mislaid more pencils and rules during that year than any other. He'd done a good trade in selling them in the school yard after lessons were over.

'Your folks are good,' Murray said. 'Although, your grandfather don't come to church no more.'

Ethan stared out of the window at the straight road ahead, the gentle rise and fall as it undulated its way into the distance. 'Henry's a proud man. He hates being in a wheelchair.' Ethan hadn't seen his grandpa for a while.

Murray slowed the truck; the brakes squealed. The farm was visible through the small cluster of trees. 'Okay dropping you here?'

'Sure. Thanks for the ride.' Ethan dragged his bag out and waved goodbye to Murray.

With his back to the sun, he walked along the rutted track until he came to the first barn, the oldest, built from timber, and leaning slightly to one side. He detoured around it, past the hen coop and the silo, before emerging by the back porch of the house.

He dropped the bag on the swing chair and inhaled deeply. The pungent smell of sickly honeysuckle. He'd nothing prepared, no explanation for his return or why he'd stopped calling or sending letters. There was no such thing as broadband at the Nieman farm. He'd never had the imagination to write in long hand on paper. Penelope had offered him some notepaper – pink and scented – but he'd politely declined. She wrote her essays using sharpie pens and stencilled headings, the kind of puerile thing that annoyed Ethan.

She'd dropped out after two semesters and taken a job at a bar. Ethan had continued to see her until she wriggled out of a date with a flimsy excuse about shifts. He'd seen her later that day with an insurance broker.

Ethan had never fitted in at the Agriculture Institute. He flitted on the edges, kept his head down, and worked hard when needed, usually when an exam approached or a teacher called him out for lacklustre essays. The only thing that interested him was graduating and proving to his parents he'd made the right decision – leaving home, going to college and widening his horizons. But here he was, back at the farm, unemployed, tired of college, no money beyond what he carried in his wallet; the leftovers from two jobs minus rent and what he'd used to keep girls like Penelope happy.

What he had to offer William Nieman was everything he'd learnt. He'd gained new skills and was bursting to share the latest agricultural developments, the new machines that toiled in the fields. It was time to drag the Nieman farm into the 21st century.

He opened the screen door and sniffed: home-cooking and cut flowers.

'Who's there?' his father bellowed from somewhere further inside the house.

'Me,' he answered.

The silence lasted as long as it took for William to assimilate his arrival. By the time his father was in the kitchen doorway, Ethan had poured himself a glass of water from the jug on the table.

'You're back.' His dad spoke slowly, drawling the words with no enthusiasm. He'd shrunk, it seemed, or else his shoulders were especially stooped that day. He wore a red shirt and a Cleveland Monsters ice hockey cap, his jeans hung below his beer paunch and the whiskers on his chin were unkempt. Central to his features was the broken nose he'd earned as a young man during an unevenly matched fight; talking about its origins were taboo. Ethan suspected a family member.

'Where's Mum?' Ethan asked.

'In town. Groceries. She'll be baking.'

His mum made good pumpkin pies and macaroni cheese.

'I miss her cooking.' He attempted a smile; his father didn't reciprocate.

'Rob?' His younger brother; William's favourite and the sunbeam in his mother's eyes.

'By the creek. We'll be harvesting the first crop of potatoes soon.'

Ethan nodded. He guessed as much. 'It's good to see you, Dad.' He tried the gentle approach, smoothing the way forward, making it feel like he'd never been gone. He stared at his father, watching his face for a reaction.

William snorted and looked away. 'I doubt it. You're broke, aren't you?' He walked over to the sink. Water splashed over the back of his hands as he rinsed them.

Ethan licked his dry lips – he'd not touched his drink. It wasn't going well.

'I worked, like I said I would. I didn't need a cent from you. I came back to help, to share what I've learnt. Just like I said.' He repeated the promises he'd made – ones that, for once, he wanted to keep. Mostly he said what people wanted to hear because it was easier that way and he could deal with the consequences of changing his mind in the aftermath.

William turned off the tap and spun on his heels, his cheeks flushed and eyes hooded by the furrowed lines of his forehead.

'We needed you a year ago when the storms came. We needed you when your grandpa fell and broke his leg. He's in a wheelchair still. Your ma needed you when she took sick and couldn't cook or sew or drive.'

'You've Rob.' A weak response, and Ethan knew it.

'Rob has worked so hard to keep this place going, the skin on his hands is a thick as cowhide. Your degree, them debts and college friends, don't make a difference out here.' He planted his hands on his hips and straightened up. He had an inch advantage over Ethan, nothing more than that. What William had gained were years. Age had worn him to the bone: loose leathery skin that wrinkled around his bare forearms and gaunt neck. His once bold jaw now hung slack, as if the earth was dragging him to the ground.

Ethan wasn't cowed though. When had he ever been by his father or any other man? He could use his fists if he had to, he knew how to shoot a gun and he'd wielded an axe a few times. Annoyingly, so far, he'd blustered his way through the role of prodigal son and failed to pull it off. There was no hint of a fatted calf or party to mark his homecoming. Instead, he anticipated resentment from dawn to dusk, being shunned by his father, harangued by his mother for not courting their neighbour's daughter, and sneered at by the golden boy, Rob. Ethan would spend his evenings alone in his childhood bedroom, just like his last disastrous trip home when everyone shut him out, even his mother. She had no backbone for standing up to William and her spoilt son, who never went anywhere. Rob wallowed in his mother's pandering and adoration, and as boys, he'd boasted to Ethan about it, adding spiteful remarks about Ethan's inability to play by any rules at home or in school.

'I'll go wash.' Ethan backed away from his father's uncompromising stance.

'That's it – hide. Useless, you are, boy. We never wanted your fancy ideas. We needed your brawn, the hours in the night when the harvest is due, the backbreaking digging when the culverts collapse. The time when the bull broke out and trampled the corn. You weren't there, then.'

Ethan stormed back into the kitchen. 'That's goddamn unfair and you know it. I never took money, I paid my own way. I went to find out how to save this farm, give us all a chance to survive. You've Rob, the loyal dog at your side. What can he do but work, and work, for your sake because he's too damn stupid to realise there is life out there, better places to go and see than this shithole of a farm? I don't want to work myself to an early grave.'

He wouldn't be like Frederick Nieman Senior, who'd left Germany, tilled the land, married and died having never had a day's holiday. A God-fearing man who instilled a family tradition that ensured a stranglehold on every Nieman's life ever since. The custom of self-sacrifice had infected the women, too. Ethan's grandmother, fresh out of Ireland, married within days of landing at Ellis Island. The mother of eight children, five of whom had their lives cut short by disease and the Vietnam conflict. Her two surviving daughters had been given away to farmers to bear sons, and her youngest boy, Ethan's father, married into one of oldest families in the county. The pattern of life continued alongside the relentless changing of the seasons. From the baking sun to the bitter snow, the family toiled. Ethan had gone in search of something different.

He clenched his hands into fists. 'I could have gone to any one of those big machinery companies, worked in an office, travelled—'

'And you think coming back absolves you of going in the first place?' William gripped Ethan's collar, hauling him up so their noses nearly touched. Ethan braced himself, expecting a blow, the kind that sent him spinning across the floor into a heap. 'You thought of your own selfish hide.'

'We can turn the farm around.'

'We can't afford to—'

'You can get a loan from—'

'I'll not put more debts to my name. We can't go on forever—'

'The increase in productivity will pay—' He'd done the calculations.

'Promises? More promises. Guaranteed is it?' William let him go and staggered back. The purple veins on his temples pulsated.

Ethan trembled with a rage that could easily equal William's. He turned his back on his father and walked out of the house. He left behind his bag and hurried away. What had he expected? There was no way he could simply return and carry on as if he'd never been away.

# twenty-five

## Leia

William showed immense restraint as he recounted his son's tragic death. What tears he might once have shed had long ago had dried up, however, his soft voice shook as he spoke. He clasped his white-knuckled hands into a trembling knot of fingers and rested them on his knees. Ten years had passed since Robert died and mourning his loss was now an integral part of William and Susan's lives. Leia saw it in every aspect of the house – the memorial on the dresser, the lack of interest in maintaining the buildings and the loss of farm land – the heart of the family's existence given over to others. William had surrendered to grief and given up.

Ashley leaned over and wiped a tear from Susie's face with a tissue from her pocket.

The recollections of that day were visceral for William as he relied on his imagination to fill in the blanks of how his son came to be fatally injured. He described the scene: the lifeless body lying hidden in the shadows.

'I hadn't realised how muddy it had got down there. We'd had problems with culverts and flooding in the creek.' William's head was bowed and he examined his bony fingers and dirty nails.

'I'm sure it was just a freak accident,' Leia said, but she wasn't saying what she actually thought – was Ethan involved in a nefarious way?

Undeniably, there was a sense of grotesque fate that he lost two sons in one day under differing circumstances. William had come close to blows with his eldest son and dismissed him. Later, after he'd tended to the hens in the coop and given feed to the small herd of cattle sheltering in the barn, he'd regretted his harsh judgement of Ethan's modernising ideas and went in search of him in an attempt to yet again bridge the chasm that existed between father and son. However, Ethan and his bag had gone. What led William to explore the fields was the crowing of birds, the black harbingers of doom that squawked in the treetops above where Robert lay prone. The horror of the scene obliterated his argument with Ethan – he recalled the emergency services arriving and then the deputy from the sheriff's department.

'Terrible. To die alone. Helpless,' he muttered. 'They treated us with kindness but all the same, the cruel way Rob died branded me as a careless farmer. The rumours meant I wasn't in a position to advertise for help. My machinery was ancient and poorly maintained. Fred was right, I should have listened to him. I'm partly to blame for what happened.'

Susie made a guttural sound of distress. William turned his face away.

Outside, the rain rattled against the window panes. They needed to return to Mount Vernon and find somewhere to spend the night. But in churning up the past, she had drawn an irrepressible sadness out of the couple and leaving them distressed was unkind.

Ashley glanced at her watch. 'We have to go,' she said.

'Stay,' William said abruptly, lifting his head.

'Oh, we couldn't,' Leia said. 'It would inconvenience you.'

'We don't use the upstairs. There are plenty of beds, all made up… in case,' he ended lamely. 'The downstairs was converted to help look after Susie. We've a bath with a hoist and another one in our bedroom, haven't we, love?'

She gurgled again.

Leia cast a more professional eye over the paralysed woman whose grey hair was matted in places. Her limbs were stripped of fat and the muscles had atrophied. The sallow skin hinted at jaundice. She probably didn't have much longer left.

'Do you get support?' she asked.

He lowered his eyes. 'Most of our savings went in the alterations. Somebody comes out twice a week to help bathe her and sort out her meds and feeding tube.'

'Just twice,' Ashley said, aghast.

'Neighbours help too,' he added, 'with visits to church and town. We're not lonely. God always provides.'

Susie said something that sounded almost like "amen".

Leia stopped her eyes from rolling in despair. Faith hadn't given them much and the devil had taken an awful lot more from them. 'We can stay a night, thank you.' She nudged Ashley. 'Ashley can cook you something, yes?'

'Oh, um. Yes,' said a startled Ashley.

'And, if you like, I can help bathe your wife and check her feeding tube.'

William's eyebrows furrowed.

'I'm a doctor, well, I trained as one. I work in medical research, mostly in a lab,' she said, apologetically. The last time she'd been with a patient who wasn't part of a drug trial had been years ago.

The decision made, Leia retrieved their bags from the car and Ashley inspected the contents of the cupboards. She waved Leia over to the fridge.

'There's mainly cabbage. Some potatoes and lots of tins of beans. My God, the man must pass wind like a trumpet player.'

Leia chuckled. 'Make him some bubble and squeak.'

'What's that?' Ashley asked.

'Like hash. If there's some tinned meat, you can add that. Just boil up some potatoes and chop up the cabbage.' She left Ashley rummaging around cupboards for saucepans and a chopping board.

Treat patients with dignity. Leia recollected the sage advice the nurses had often given her during her days as a medical student on the wards. With William's help, she peeled away the layers of clothing that kept Susie warm. The hoist was bolted to the bathroom ceiling and it bore the burden of her pathetic body without complaining. The rose-scented soap masked the unfortunate odours of a body that could no longer control its functions. William had done this many times and Leia's medical training was of little use compared to a practised carer.

Susie was in better shape than Leia had first thought. Her medication was up to date, and administered correctly – William kept detailed notes – and the feeding tube was functioning as it should. While her skin appeared pale and undernourished, Susie's eyeballs were white and pure, also alert. She communicated with William in the form of grunts and other peculiar noises, which he seemed to understand. He directed the proceedings in his soft voice and touched his wife gently and thoughtfully.

By the time they had her washed, dried and dressed in clean clothes, Ashley had mastered the bubble and squeak. They sat around the table with Susie in her wheelchair, watching and mumbling.

William's curiosity about his guests grew during the meal. Leia now had to explain, quite rightly, a little more about herself. William also wanted to know more about his absent son. Unfortunately, there wasn't much she could tell him.

'He's living in Newmarket, which is famed for horse racing. He sells farm machinery. Travels a lot.'

'And they're going to marry?' he asked, eyeing the bubble and squeak suspiciously as Ashley served it onto plates.

'I'm not too sure, but that's a possibility,' she said. Where things stood between Ethan and Naomi was already a couple of days out of date. She'd not heard any news from Rebecca, which was worrying, but then her cell phone had refused to pick up a signal for most of the day.

'And he's never spoken about us?'

She shrugged off her ignorance of Ethan. 'To be honest, Mr Nieman, I came here to make sure he's a decent kind of man. My other sister, Rebecca, has concerns, because Naomi found two passports in different names for the same person and called her in a panic. But your son claims he changed his name while working in Australia so she calmed down. Rebecca is more cautious. She's a lawyer.'

William puckered his lips. 'He always wanted to travel. Never liked the name Frederick because it meant comparing him to my grandfather. He came here from Germany after the First World War. Lots of prejudice. Made him a tough old bastard.' He chortled. 'My father wasn't that fond of him either, but I thought we should honour his legacy. So me and Susie chose Frederick.'

'And the surname? Why do you think he changed that too?'

'Fred loved Gran. She often talked about Ireland to him, but he never expressed an interest in going there.' He started to shovel the food into his mouth as if he'd not eaten in days.

Leia sampled a mouthful. 'Not bad.' She winked at Ashley.

Ashley rolled her eyes to the ceiling. 'It's just hash. Anyone can cook it.'

William scraped his plate clean. 'He's not said anything about us then?' It clearly bothered him.

Leia felt ill-equipped to handle his questions and selfishly hadn't considered what he might ask. 'To be honest, I don't know much about him. He seems settled in England. Would you welcome him home if he came here?'

He lowered his fork. 'Frankly, no. For ten years he hasn't contacted us once. I doubt he even knows his grandpa is dead either. He knew back then that Mom was suffering. He's selfish. Something not quite right in the head – a cold, calculating boy. He might as well be dead to us still.' He pushed the plate away.

Susie slumped in her wheelchair. Her fiery eyes spoke of anger.

William blushed, apparently ashamed by his outburst. He cleared his throat. 'If he comes here, if he turned up here today, I don't know. There's a lot to forgive.' He dragged his chair back. 'She's tired. I'll take her to bed. Your rooms are upstairs, on the left.'

As he wheeled Susie out of the kitchen, he turned. 'Thank you for the food. It's the best meal I've had in a long time.'

Ashley blinked. 'It was only hash,' she whispered to Leia.

Leia wasn't paying much attention. William's comment about Ethan being a little crazy had stunned her. Given he had only one son left in the world, she would have hoped he might reach out to him. However, he'd not asked for contact details or suggested healing the breach. Whatever he said openly about how Rob had died, part of William blamed Ethan in some way. Maybe, if he hadn't been arguing with Ethan, he'd have been out in the fields with Rob? Hindsight was a terrible perspective upon which to foster an opinion.

The damp bedroom was charmless. On one wall hung an ebony crucifix surrounded by small framed pictures of famous scenes of biblical parables. Leia recognised them if only because she'd studied Religious Education and not because she'd ever attended church. Each image had been cut out of a book or magazine. Hardly works of art; the illustrations had faded in places. How long had they been up on the walls? They looked like they might be from the days of Dorothy or even the first Frederick.

Collecting her toothbrush and toothpaste, she walked past the bedroom Ashley was using and entered the green tiled bathroom. Its cleanliness seemed to stem from lack of use rather than regular housekeeping. The magnolia bar of soap was cracked and the plastic shower curtain was missing a few hooks; she daren't touch it. She quickly brushed her teeth.

The door to the bedroom opposite hers was slightly ajar. She pushed the door open and stuck her head around. Unlike her room, this one had no hint of religious overtones, unless baseball pendants counted as icons. There were posters of football players stuck on the walls and an ice hockey stick propped against the wall. The bed was made, the sheet tucked neatly underneath the mattress and the pillow was plumped up. On the chest of drawers was a photograph of Robert and his mother. The room was a mausoleum to a dead boy. She doubted Ethan had been honoured in quite the same way.

Leia backed out on tiptoes and closed the door behind her. She'd invaded the holiest of sanctuaries and it wasn't anything to do with God.

Laying under the cold sheet, she switched off the lamp, and was cast into pitch blackness – no streetlights or moonlight. What a sad house. No wonder Ethan stayed away. The legacy of tragedies and mismanagement had broken the Nieman family. Leia held the assumption that ordinary families were just like the Niemans: unburdened by gifts, nestled in a close-knit community and God-fearing enough that they always followed some form of moral compass. Her assumption had flaws. That very ordinariness had torn this family apart.

The trip to Ohio had created unexpected ramifications in her own life. She should stop trying to twist and bend away from uncontrollable events, but embrace them as opportunities. Why not celebrate her achievements?

And as for her parents, they had done their best to protect her from self-destruction. She'd been manipulated by them possibly, but certainly not ignored, unlike Ethan who had been cast aside for the favoured son and consequently despised his parents. There were no excuses for her to feel the same way. If anything, she was the favoured daughter. Ethan's over-bearing father lacked ambition and inspiration whereas Paul and Nancy had carried her with them as they pushed her to achieve greater things. They'd picked her to go with them.

Given the strangeness of the house and the accompanying noises of a wild autumn night, she slept well. In the morning she refocused her attention on Naomi's boyfriend. There was one last question that her over-analytical brain refused to erase – why had the sheriff been disappointed?

# twenty-six
## Ethan
## 5 August 2008

He chose the path that clipped the edge of the cornfield. The tops of the corn swayed in the breeze. Beneath his feet, the ground was cracked and hard, sapped of its moisture by the thirsty crop. In the distance, he heard the rumble of the beast – a tractor. He ducked under the branches of a tree, climbed over a wooden fence, and walked another hundred yards to the corner of the potato field. Unlike the sun-baked maize, the periphery of the field was puddle-strewn – the creek had flooded recently; it often did when a summer storm struck.

The tractor was lurching precariously to one side and the trailer, an antiquated potato harvester with flaking blue paint, was slipping into the mud. Ethan approached and spotted his brother in the cab. Robert thumped the wheel in frustration; he'd attempted to cross the creek and the back end of the rusting harvester had skidded to one side.

Rob ignored Ethan's wave and clambered down to inspect the trailer.

'You're back,' he shouted over the engine.

'I can help.' Ethan moved towards the tractor.

Rob glanced over his shoulder. 'I don't want it. Just go back to Wooster and your pretty girls.' The sun had burnt the end of his nose into a peeling mess of flaky skin. Boyish freckles clustered around his cheekbones.

'I'm back,' Ethan repeated, louder. 'To help,' he added.

Rob yanked a lever and tried to unhitch the harvester so that he could realign it with the tractor. The tractor's wheels weren't quite locked and they shifted further down the bank. Ethan could shout a warning, but he didn't; Rob wasn't blind.

'How's Mum?' Ethan asked.

'Worn out,' Rob replied. 'Doc thinks its rheumatism or something degenerative, I don't know. She won't talk about it.'

'And you?' A foolish question – Rob let go of the lever and spun around to face him.

'I should've missed you. I didn't.' The wind collected the scruffy ends of his hair and tossed them around his shoulders. Rob, only eighteen, had lines beneath his weary eyes that clashed with his boyish cheeks. Both were as lean as their father, but only Rob had added muscle to his frame and the bulge in his bent arms stretched the fabric of his plaid shirt. 'You'll not get him to change his mind. You can take your stupid plans and shove them where the sun don't shine. God will see us through, not you.'

'God might have sent me; did that not cross your thick skull?' Ethan stepped forward, his shoes squelching in the quagmire.

The rains had washed away the grass verge and the crossing needed boulders to hold back the flow of brown water that frothed along the trench. Angry surges of water were ready to catch somebody unprepared. Their father had often warned them as boys that the creek could easily turn into a torrent as water tumbled out of the faraway hills on its long journey to Lake Erie. The tractor wallowed deeper into the embankment.

An agitated Rob, distracted by Ethan's arrival, snatched at the crank and pivoted. He slipped in the glutinous slurry that lay under the wheel of the harvester. As his foot sank beneath the tyre, he fell backwards. A split second later, the weight of the shifting harvester trapped him there.

'Fred,' he hollered. The harvester rolled several inches, dragging Rob with it. His anklebone broke with a gut-wrenching snap.

Rob screamed. Ethan froze. The tractor and harvester were now leaning at forty-five degrees at near right angles to each other, and moving not forward, but down the bank, pulling Rob with them and further rotating his brother's crooked leg. Rob flailed his arms in a futile attempt at extracting his shattered limb.

'Fred,' he cried. The lines of agony contorted his face into that of a wizened old man.

Ethan's heartbeats remained strangely unaffected, almost placid. He should be feeling something, like a rush of adrenaline or a burst of energy. The beloved son of William, favoured from the moment of his birth, spoilt at every birthday, the star of the local fairs and the constant companion of his father and grandfather, writhed just a few feet from him. Rob was at Ethan's mercy. Unfortunately, Ethan lacked the necessary empathy to deliver that mercy.

He moved, but not to Rob's side; he took a simple step back, out of the shadows of the trees into the penetrating sunlight. Here, under his feet, the sun had done its work and dried the ground, and yet, only a few yards away, the sticky mud had swallowed his brother. All he had to do was switch off the tractor, find something to prop the harvester up and let it stabilise – something like the branch of a tree or a plank, or even a few large rocks by the wheel would do the trick.

Unable to grip anything, Rob slithered down the bank. The machinery of the harvester was just above his head, ready to spin and churn up the potato plants with its spikes and chains. Rob, panicking, thrashed from side to side, oblivious to the pain in his crushed leg. Ethan saw the red ooze into the earth where it quickly congealed with the filth. The jagged edge of white bone stuck through his torn jeans, just above his mangled boot. The blood ran in rivulets, a livid crimson stream, full of Rob's life force.

Ethan knew time wasn't on his side. If he ran for help, would his father make it to Rob's side in time to save him? Or did Ethan stay and shore up the harvester?

The dilemma might have been an interesting conundrum in the safety lessons of the classroom. A debate amongst college students about farming accidents and risk assessments, but played out for real, the predicament was hampered by raw emotions.

'You bastard,' Rob shrieked. 'What you standing there for? Help me!'

Tears poured down his pale cheeks. With a low moan, he suddenly flopped back and began to shiver. So quickly it happened; one moment he was fighting for his life, and the next, Rob was drained of energy and paralysed by blood loss. Two minutes after the accident had started to unfold, Ethan's brother went into shock.

Ethan had no strength to lift the harvester – it would weigh many tonnes – and he had probably left it too late to run for help. He checked his cell phone; no reception, which was no surprise.

With the peculiar onset of a familiar calmness that often came when a crisis struck, he switched off the engine. Immediately, birds interrupted the silence, a melancholy chorus of crowing rather than the joyous chirps of the songbird. He should go closer, hold Rob's hand and reassure him somebody was coming. He could tell lies like that so easily; he had no qualms about hiding the truth when needs must. Instead, he hung back and watched the life bleed out of his younger brother.

Would William want Ethan now? He speculated about how things might play out, once they'd all stopped grieving. His father would have to take out that loan, buy equipment to replace the treacherous tractor with its now proven faulty brakes and a new potato harvester with better guards and an emergency shut off switch. Ethan would guide him through the changes, while lamenting with him about the lost son. He'd depend on Ethan, not at first, but slowly, then William would let go and hand over the management of the farm to him.

Rob sighed, a low exhale of breath that sounded almost peaceful. Finally, Ethan crept forward, so not to disturb the last breaths of a dying boy.

'Don't hate me,' he whispered.

Rob's eyes flickered, and a dark veil covered the flat irises. In the shadows of the harvester and glued to the ground, he was already entombed in the earth.

There'd be a funeral. Plenty of mourners, a troop of neighbours and friends, plus those distant cousins who only came for weddings and funerals. They'd parade past the open casket and touch Rob's youthful face, his trimmed hair framed around his chubby cheeks and his hands neatly folded on top his Sunday suit. Their mother would weep inconsolably, dredging up pitiful sobs from her heartbroken belly. His father, bitter and morose, would go every day to Rob's grave and talk to the tombstone.

Horrified, Ethan realised he would always be blamed for this accident and, regardless of the chances of successfully extraditing

Rob from underneath the wheels or halting the flow of arterial blood, his father would never believe that Ethan on his first day home wasn't responsible for Rob's cruel fate. Faced with the likelihood of being held accountable, he finally acted. He'd no belt to make a tourniquet, nothing to staunch the flow of blood. The corner of a white handkerchief poked out of Rob's shirt pocket. Ethan whipped it out and attempted to mop up the blood around the jagged tear of flesh. The last-ditch attempt at first aid was futile.

Ethan grabbed Rob's wrist, hunting for a pulse. 'No, no,' he cried. The limp wrist was silent. He cradled his brother's head in his hands before gently laying it back down in a halo of dirt.

He couldn't stay. He'd never be a prodigal son – the bible told it all wrong. He'd be judged a failure. Even if his parents ever found out the truth of what had happened by the creek, they'd never understand the reality of the situation – what could he have done to save Rob?

Clutching the bloody handkerchief, Ethan ran, crashing through the corn until he reached the backyard and the porch where his bag lay on the swing chair. There was no sign or sound of his parents. Catching his breath, he steadied himself and wiped the mud off his shoes. The crimson blood had congealed on the square piece of cloth and was nearly dry. He stared at the flecks of blood and dirt, the dark patch in the middle of the handkerchief. He should throw it away, but he couldn't. The crimson spillage was part of his brother. When they lowered his body into the ground, a little part of Rob would stay with Ethan wherever he went to remind him he had no choice but to keep running, and he intended to go as far away as he could, perhaps towards Pittsburgh, then farther – Mexico. He folded the handkerchief and slipped it inside the duffel bag. He passed the old decrepit barn and walked along the dust-covered road. A bus would come by eventually, but for now, he walked.

Sirens wailed. Half an hour had passed since he'd left Rob's side. Somebody, probably his father, had found Rob. Poor William; but Ethan felt no sympathy. Both had ignored his advice about respecting machinery.

As dusk arrived, his stomach rumbled. He stuck out his thumb. A bus wasn't coming, and he needed to leave the area as quickly as possible. A car stopped. Thankfully, he didn't recognise the driver.

'Where you going, son?' the grey-haired man asked. He wore a white shirt and no tie. His GPS demanded he drive on.

'As far as you can take me, sir,' Ethan said with courtesy.

He lay his duffel bag on the back seat, amongst the discarded paper cups and crumpled forms and invoices.

'Long drive?' he asked the driver.

'Yeah. Going to Philly.'

Philadelphia. Even better. 'That's a big coincidence. I'm off that way to visit my aunt.'

'Then be my guest. I'm on a tight schedule. Got to drive through the night.' The man took a slurp out of a covered coffee cup and offered Ethan a bottle of water.

Ethan swallowed and wiped his dry lips. 'What do you do?'

'Sell machinery, mostly the big harvesters. Pickers, stuff like that.'

Ethan nearly laughed aloud. The irony. 'Make good money?'

The conversation flowed back and forth easily. The image of Rob's bloody leg faded. Escaping the scene had cleared his head. He tried to appear as unremarkable as possible. He wanted to be forgotten by all who met him in the coming days and weeks. He'd wipe out Frederick with a proper beard and trendy clothes.

'What's your name, son?' the man asked as they hit the lights of the next town.

Ethan opened his mouth, then thought of the consequences of saying his name. He grinned and quickly re-instated the strategy he'd used at college to distance himself from his past.

'I'm Ethan. Ethan O'Reilly.'

One day, he'd find a way to make that name real; he'd permanently marry his middle name and his grandmother's maiden name and then he wouldn't have to ever be Frederick Nieman again.

# twenty-seven
## Leia
## 27 October 2018

Leia and Ashely said goodbye to William on the rickety porch of his tired house. Susie remained in bed. Leia suspected the news about Ethan was the source of that excessive fatigue.

William's opinion of his son hadn't shifted in the cold morning light. Over breakfast and when they shook hands with him, he didn't ask for Ethan's specific whereabouts.

Just before reaching the car door, Leia turned to ask him one last question. 'Mr Nieman, did you agree with the coroner's verdict about Robert's death?'

He stiffened and glared as if her question was an effrontery. 'There's no Cain and Abel story here, miss. If that's what you came searching for, then you've come on a wasted journey. Whatever happened was an accident. My son left the engine running and the brakes failed.' He spoke mechanically, delivering a message that had probably been said many times.

'So, there are no grounds for suspicion?' Leia recalled the newspaper report word for word. She homed in on the sheriff's unanswered question – *Where was Frederick Nieman on the day of his brother's death?* She wasn't asking that very same question for herself, though, nor was she solving a problem for the benefit of society. She was here to help Naomi and reassure a fractious Rebecca.

William's expression wasn't comforting. It was like witnessing an experiment going badly wrong; it produced a sinking feeling in her belly. William hadn't convinced the officer and years later, the question still troubled Ethan's father.

'None,' he said firmly.

'So, if we go speak to the sheriff—'

'Sadly, Bill Jones is dead.'

'Dead?' said Ashley.

'Cancer took him two years ago. Mighty fine officer. Lots of folks came to his funeral, my family included.'

Leia took the hint. Probing the investigations of a deceased elected officer of the law was not going to provide her with answers. Who else would remember the events of ten years ago except the family affected? The conversation was over.

'Goodbye,' she said. 'And thank you for your hospitality.' She offered one last pause for him to fill, but he nodded an acknowledgement instead.

Ashley broke the silence in the car as Leia drove north.

'What sad folks. I kinda wish there was something we could do. Maybe a crowdfunding, raise some money that way for them.'

'Perhaps,' said Leia, uncertain the proud Niemans would take strangers' money. She drummed her fingers on the steering wheel. 'None of this make sense.'

'You mean Robert's death or Frederick's disappearance?'

'Well, both. The sheriff obviously believed they were linked. The coroner described a gruesome scene with blood and crushed limbs. Anyone witnessing that spectacle is going to be left traumatised.'

'So he ran off—'

'And never came back?' Leia shot a glance at Ashley. 'Ever? He must have known his parents were upset. Mourning Robert, then losing their other son, it would rack a decent man with guilt.'

'So, what we know is Frederick comes home full of new ideas, argues with the father about running the farm, makes no attempt to speak to his brother, and vanishes. I suppose he might not have had the chance to talk to Robert,' Ashley said.

'According to William, somebody gave him a lift from the bus stop, and the bus driver remembered him, too. But nobody came forward about picking him up after he left the farm.'

'The sheriff would have been bothered by that,' Ashley said. 'What else was in the newspaper report.'

'Footprints. Lots of footprints around the tractor.' Leia wondered why forensics hadn't stepped in. There again, Mount Vernon was a small city, not CSI Miami, and accidents were bound to happen. 'Robert left the engine running and he should have switched it off; the coroner's verdict was accepted.'

'And the footprints?'

Leia shrugged. 'Who knows.'

She could appreciate the sheriff's disappointment now. He believed a jealous brother had witnessed the last dying screams of his brother and done nothing. Leia's fear sank deeper into her belly and stuck there, churning away. What he speculated seemed plausible, although hypothetical, and she wished it didn't paint Ethan as being so cruel. What exactly had he done?

He'd run away from his responsibilities. A familiar trait. She was equally weak and when faced with surmountable pressure she'd bolted. The big difference – nobody had died because of her actions. Quite the contrary, people were going to live due to her hard work. All the same, she'd acted lily-livered and immature. Running away wasn't going to solve anything for her, or Ethan. What he'd done troubled Leia: he had manipulated Naomi into sticking by him, offering him a chance at redeeming himself. Unfortunately, Naomi had no clue as to what Ethan had done and whether he deserved reconciliation with his family. Just how cold and calculating could he be?

'Would you be okay driving the car back to Boston on your own?'

Ashley started in her seat. 'What?'

'If you drop me off at Columbus airport—'

'What?'

Leia made the decision: she and Rebecca would have to present a united front in person.

'I'm going to England. I have to put a stop to this marriage. I don't care if I'm guessing, he could be dangerous. There is no way my little sister is marrying Frederick Nieman.'

She also had to tell Rebecca about her other secret, especially as she'd gone to great lengths to paint herself as a sceptic. Would Rebecca believe the story she had to reveal?

# twenty-eight

## Naomi

## 28 October 2018

In the morning, lying in bed next to the sleepy Ethan, she whispered in his ear. 'Let's go to Ireland.'

The offer bought her time, breathing space without him hassling her.

Ethan was thrilled and leapt out of bed, punching the air. The moment he left for work – how long would that be his job, his income? – she contacted the school she was due to visit and apologised. 'I've got a migraine.'

Naomi lay in bed until lunchtime, plagued by deepening anxieties about Ethan's mysterious past. After showering and forcing down a mediocre lunch, she pottered around the house with a duster and pretended that she was having a normal cleaning day. The uneasiness eked itself inward, tampering with nerves and her heart rate. In a fit of pique, annoyed that Ethan had twisted the direction of her life out of her hands and straight into his, she threw the duster across the dining table.

There had to be a reason why he'd come up with the Ireland idea so suddenly and her meddling with his things was the obvious one. Had it been a mistake letting Rebecca see the photos? Apparently not, given Rebecca hadn't exactly badgered her with questions, which surprised Naomi. As for the rest of her family, her parents might worry but wouldn't do anything unless Naomi was in peril or there was the chance of, God forbid, unwanted publicity. Emotionally detached Leia was naturally inquisitive but unlikely to ring up and demand to speak to Ethan given the effort involved. Leia remained on the periphery of Naomi's life. She refused to harbour any animosity toward Leia, although some days, like today, she felt annoyed at the lack of involvement. There was only one thing to do – sort it herself, which meant examining the authentic documents again and not the grainy images on her phone. Had she missed anything in the cigar box, something that would alarm him if she found it?

She threw open the wardrobe doors, stood on tiptoes and scoured the shelf for the cigar box. Four days on, the box was gone. She tried the drawers and every cupboard in the house. She checked his box files, where he kept his sales reports and receipts for expenses. No passports.

She rang Rebecca. The call went straight to voicemail.

'Becca, ring me.' She immediately regretted the alarm in her voice. It wasn't fair to upset Rebecca. She was determined to handle Ethan herself.

She paced around the house. She'd looked everywhere, hadn't she? Pivoting on her toes, she glanced upwards to the ceiling and snapped her fingers at the discovery.

The loft. She fetched the stepladder and torch and carried them up the stairs. The loft hatch was in the spare room. She had to hit it hard to force it open. Shoving the hatch to one side, she climbed higher up the steps and switched on the torch. Feeling around the perimeter of the hatch, she skated over the cobwebs and sticky insulating layer until her fingers stumbled over a bundle of rough cloth. Yanking on it, a billowing pool of dust came down with it – a faded khaki duffel bag, the kind soldiers used to carry their things while on manoeuvres.

She lowered it between her legs and climbed down the steps. There was something rustling inside it. Taking the bag into the bedroom, she untied the drawstring and tipped it upside down and shook. The cigar box dropped out first, the contents scattering once again. She gave the bag another shake and a folded sheet of paper floated out onto the rug.

Kneeling on the floor, she flattened out the creases. The yellow paper was slightly damp. The printed text was of a website page and it referred to unknown places and the side column of advertisements listed unfamiliar brands and products. The headline of the Knox County News was stark and gut-wrenching.

*Local farmer killed in freak accident.*

Underneath she saw the name – Robert Nieman. The month – August 2008.

Covering the rest of the article was a square piece of stained cloth: a handkerchief monogrammed with the initials RN in one corner.

The stains were dark crimson, almost black. No attempt had been made to wash out the blotches of blood nor the dirt that had stiffened the greyed fabric. The handkerchief was a trophy that commemorated something gruesome. Sliding it to one side with the tips of her fingers, she read the rest of the article. The coroner described the scene, how Robert had been crushed to death under a potato harvester, his bloody body discovered by his grief-stricken father. The journalist paid special attention to the sheriff's disquiet at the verdict of accidental death. The sheriff believed somebody else had been there; he recalled another set of footprints, partially destroyed by the subsequent activities at the scene. The absence of Frederick Nieman, Robert's older brother, was noted. Naomi knew he'd been there; the evidence lay in her hands.

She cried and her love bled out in those despondent tears as they splashed onto the paper. The truth added details to a poorly defined portrait: Ethan had abandoned his family in a time of crisis and hid himself behind a new identity. He'd changed his name and the date of his birth for a purpose that had nothing to do with his treasured grandmother. He'd wantonly corrupted, possibly forged documents, in order to create a false trail. In Australia, he'd moved from town to town, job to job, so that he never established a presence anywhere long enough for him to be discovered.

He'd always implied he had plenty of money. But was that true, too? He'd arrived in England with only the clothes in his duffel bag, the bloody relic and cigar box stuffed out of sight. He quickly established a new career with his Irish passport and rented a house from a friend who never needed to check up on him. All this to escape what? Even if he wasn't culpable, were his actions those of an innocent man?

With the duffel bag on her lap, the contents once more hidden inside it, she sat on the edge of the bed and waited for Ethan to return home. He was still running. Only now, he wanted to take her with him to Ireland and start over again. What had become the pattern of life for him would be a momentous upheaval for her and he selfishly assumed she'd follow him there. Had he ever loved her? He exuded an increasingly claustrophobic passion for her and no longer was it comforting in its nature because now she saw him for what he truly was – a consummate liar who had controlled her from the day he'd changed her tyre.

If she'd not found out about his past, or seen those passports, or known he was Frederick, they might be getting married, possibly going to Ireland. Accepting his plan, she would have given up the dream of performing and lived by the sea, teaching the flute in a local school while he sold his stuff to Irish farmers. It might have worked, except the scenario would have been built on his lies and her crushed dreams.

What she had with Ethan was over. Finished. There wasn't any point in salvaging her splintering heart. The trust between them was shattered, too. Could she ever trust again?

She shivered, nauseated by the idea he might be responsible for harming Robert, a brother Naomi hadn't even known existed. Was Ethan really capable of violence? How would he react when she confronted him with the contents of the bag and the stained handkerchief? Up to now, he'd never lashed out at her in anger, but this was no longer about faking an identity. Ethan might have committed a crime.

She should leave right then, pack her things and go to Rebecca's; the sensible option, the one her sister had wanted from the outset. However, Naomi wanted closure. And answers. Looking back, she'd missed the opportunities to dig a little deeper into his past, to pay heed to the warning. Poor Gran had foreseen the heartbreak and pain. What powers Rose possessed were a mystery to Naomi. Along with Leia, she'd dismissed the birthday game. However, Rebecca had written them all down and accounted for each one. Rebecca's muted assessments of Naomi's choice of men were rooted in her belief in Rose. What else had she foretold?

The memories of that day were vivid, and Naomi revisited the emotions, especially her response to the troubled look on Rose's face as she woke from her slumber. Her gran had made sure Naomi received the prophecy, memorised it. Now, years later, the decision as to what happened next was down to Naomi — Rose had put her faith in her youngest granddaughter.

Was she truly in peril? During their brief time together, Ethan's behaviour was hardly that of a man who wished her harm: he had supported her, given her a comfortable home and left her in peace with her music while providing her with a constant audience of one devoted fan. She believed those aspects of Ethan were genuine acts of kindness. The newspaper report speculated, whereas the coroner was conclusive: Robert's death was a terrible accident and the whereabouts of Frederick a separate matter. Only the sheriff drew attention to the anomalies of the scene and that was his job — to theorise and spot the evidence of a crime.

The dilemma remained — what should she do?

He wasn't due back for half an hour or so, which gave her the opportunity to plan something less confrontational, shift the focus from him to her. She needed a means to end things on her terms. She would take back control, even if she presented herself as the flawed character in their story; a story that had begun with Rose's warning.

# twenty-nine
## Naomi

Naomi waited for Ethan in the kitchen. No birdsong penetrated the window, only the ticking wall clock broke the silence. A little past six o'clock the key turned in the lock and the door hinges squeaked; noises she usually greeted with enthusiasm. Today, they instilled a sense of foreboding.

She had one last chance to steady her shaking hands, control her stuttering exhales and ignore the thumping of her racing heart – the rhythm of her body was telling her something was profoundly wrong. She was about to step onto an imaginary stage and give the performance of her life. Every turbulent emotion needed to be contained so that he only heard what she wanted him to hear – a pack of lies.

Lies were necessary. A man on the run was always afraid of discovery. Ethan, though, had never given her the impression he was unstable or crazy. What he did exhibit, and how apparent that was to her now that her emotions were charged, was the way he had conducted their relationship as if he was waving a baton and directing every change of pace and mood. She'd allowed him, just as she had let her family shape her relationships.

'Hi, babe, I'm home,' he called out. His keys jangled on the hall table.

The babe didn't work any longer. It grated. So did all those other words of affection he used. She bundled them into the back of her mind, treating them with the contempt they deserved.

Wiping her hands on a tea towel, she stepped out of the kitchen. She clutched the towel, using it to hide her trembling fingers. Ethan kicked off his boots and left them on the door mat. She kept her distance and hovered by the kitchen door. It was the last opportunity to admire his incredible eyes and the neat curls of beard that were trimmed to the line of his firm jaw. However, those favoured charming attributes of his immediately became irrelevant, superficial.

'Can we talk?' Meaning we have to talk. She gestured towards the living room.

'Sure,' he said warily.

She waited for him to pick a seat and then chose the armchair across the room from him. Scrunching the tea towel into a ball, she held it like a stress ball, squeezing it with her fingertips.

'What's up?' he asked.

She inhaled deeply and avoided his sharp eyes. 'I have to come clean. I'm sorry, I can't go on like this.' She'd not lied, so far.

He started to rise to his feet, but she stopped him with an open palm. 'Please, let me talk. Explain.'

Lowering himself, he perched on the edge of the chair, his hands clasped between his knees, his gaze honing in on her. She had to say this to his face or else he might not believe her.

She swallowed a lump in her dry throat and tried hard not to stammer. 'I've been lying to you. In fact, using you.'

His long spine jolted upright. She had expected this response. The conversation was coming from out of nowhere and she'd had no time to rehearse or practise her lines. It was rather like sight reading a new piece of music. With luck, she'd trick him into thinking this was all about her, and not him.

'What? I don't get what you're saying.' He scratched his beard, scraping his nails against the stubble like a saw. She gritted her teeth.

'I'm not been honest with you. I've realised, since last night, that it's wrong of me to lead you on. Please, let me finish.' She snatched a breath. 'You've given me a roof over my head, paid for everything, and it's been good for me. But it's not fair. I never really expected this, us I mean, to go so far. When you asked me to marry you, I thought, let's give it a go, but the more I think about it, and then with Ireland popping up out of the blue, the more I realise we're wrong.'

'Wrong?' he said sharply. 'How can what we have together be wrong?'

'Well, I'm wrong for you. I can't go on thinking things will work out between us just because I fancy you, because you're... sexy. I've lied. I don't want to go to Ireland, at least not in the way you do. And I don't want to get married. I never have, music is my… well. I don't think I love you, not the way...' She examined the pattern on the tea towel and briefly closed her eyes. Telling lies hurt more than she could have imagined. Back at Stonehenge, she'd accepted his proposal in good faith and pictured a future together, living somewhere new – although Ireland hadn't crossed her mind – and based on both of them paying their way as a partnership.

'Faking things. Naomi, what are you talking about?' The aggressive tone went up a notch; she had to stay focused on not apportioning blame because she'd no clue as to how he might react if she dropped a single hint that it was his fault things had gone so terribly wrong. There might have been an opportunity for him to come clean when he'd seen the cigar box on the bed, but he hadn't; he'd slung it back up on the shelf of the wardrobe and walked out of the room.

'I really like you, Ethan. But when you admitted to the passports and name change, it made me realise I've not been honest with you either. I moved in to save money. I know it's beneficial to me to keep that arrangement. And I lied about how I feel. The idea of quitting everything and moving to Ireland, it's just not going to work—'

'We can go elsewhere. Anywhere you like,' he said, leaning forward. 'Naomi, I love you.'

'But I don't love you.' She forced the words out through chattering teeth – the shivering was in contrast to her burning cheeks.

The necessary gap between her and Ethan elongated, grew heavier with mistrust, and was entirely of her making. Breaking up wasn't easy. The courage she'd found she would use again, she would take it along with her to future venues. If she could tell lies to the man who had broken her heart, she could communicate her true feelings to a willing audience through the passion of music.

He remained frozen as if locked into his seat, then suddenly he sprang to his feet and clenched his fists. She'd misjudged him; perhaps he was capable of violence towards her. Her flight-fright instinct was about to kick in when suddenly his square shoulders drooped, forming a rounded hunch of unexpected submission. He shook his head, as if to reign in a tiny disagreement he'd had with himself.

He circled the spot, his head bowed. During the interval of protracted silence he seemed to cast a longer shadow over the furniture. With the light behind him, he looked shady, a criminal. Who exactly was this man? Ethan, who'd helped her change a tyre, or the unknown Frederick in Rose's warning? Two characters in her story who bore no resemblance to each other. The absconded brother described in the newspaper had been treated as a suspect by the sheriff and that possible assailant might actually be standing in front of Naomi. But she had no sense of Frederick, no measure of that man, only Ethan.

'You faked it? All of this?' He gestured around at the room. There were her pictures on the wall, her books on the shelves, the music stand in the sun lounge, the silvery flute waiting for her to breathe life into it. The objects crystallised a thought: there was still nothing of his in the house that was permanent. He'd never intended to stay put. Because of what he'd done ten years ago, he had to move on whenever suspicions dogged him.

'Yes,' she said firmly, building the momentum; the tempo of the conversation was under her control; Ethan for once seemed lost and confused. 'The money was a good bait, and then the fun things we did. As for the wedding, I thought I could put it off, kick it into the long grass. I did it before, you see, with Kyle; I kept him strung along and waiting. I'm good at it. I'm good at lying to people about my feelings. I'm so sorry, Ethan. But when you started to make plans, big plans, I knew I couldn't commit and my deceit tormented me. I feel awful stringing you along. Call me a selfish bitch, whatever you like, but I have to go, move out and—'

'No, don't.' He stepped towards her. 'We can sort this out. I get what you're saying. We'll think again about the options for getting married.'

She refused to shrivel and held fast to her plan. 'You need this marriage, you said yourself. It's important to you to belong somewhere. And your work? What's with the quitting? I'm not worth it, trust me on that.'

His face was a portrait of confusion. He grasped a handful of his hair and yanked on it – he wasn't to know she had rejected him based on a bloody handkerchief hidden in the loft, and if he never spoke of that day, there was no way of knowing the truth of it. Regardless of what had happened ten years ago, Ethan had constructed his own selfish creed, and upon it, he'd built layers of lies. As for the destructive wake he'd left behind him, her fractured heart would heal in time – she had to believe this.

'You're all the same. Everyone I meet, they take, take from me.' He thumped his chest, as he had done a few days ago, but this time there was no passionate gaze accompanying it; he stared at her until she flinched. 'I really thought you were the one. I really did.' Ethan inhaled sharply, as if pained. 'You're like the rest – using me, then ignoring my feelings, my say in how things should be done.'

Naomi rose – she had to leave and now; she wasn't sure who he was addressing. It didn't seem to be her. The startling eyes that had once mesmerised her when he changed the tyre were devoid of shimmer and narrowed into slits.

'Perhaps you should stop running away from your problems, from people, and start facing up to the consequences of your actions.' She'd alluded to his past too much, so she quickly added, 'I'm going to Rebecca's until I can sort out a place to live.' Where, she wouldn't tell him; she couldn't risk him stalking her.

'Then go,' he snapped.

He spun on his heels and stormed out of the room. The keys jangled and she waited for the door to slam shut behind him. Instead, there was a low groan and he re-appeared under the architrave, his expression dour, his cheeks drained of colour.

'I would have been a good husband. But for the wrong reasons.' He pursed his lips.

'That would have been true for both of us.'

A faint smile of amusement crossed his face then vanished. 'You don't understand. Every day I battle with demons. They keep me from opening up and being honest with my feelings. I can't speak the truth if it doesn't serve any purpose. Lies come so much easier – I think you understand, you're just like me.'

She smothered a gasp with her hand. That grotesque remark pained her more than anything else. She'd always until that hour spoken the truth to him. But that was the point of her strategy. If he believed she was a liar then he had no excuse not to accept her excuses. The circle was complete.

'There are things I've done that…' He sucked in air between his teeth and shook his head, leaving the end of the sentence dangling – yes, there were things he'd done, she only wished he hadn't. With his anger quelled, she risked one question.

'Why did you change your birth date on your Irish passport?' It bothered her because it was the only obviously illegal thing he'd done.

His cheeks flushed this time with a shade of embarrassment. 'I wanted to claim a few years back off my life. I hoped they wouldn't notice. They didn't. Lucky for me.'

'And if they had?'

He produced a pathetic shrug which told her all she needed to know. 'I'd have corrected it.'

His lie was crystal clear and easy to spot: he'd paid to have records falsified and covered his tracks, just like the plan to go to Ireland. Criminal or not, he had no intention of taking responsibility for his past mistakes. She said nothing. What was the point? It was up to him to seek reconciliation and redeem himself; she wasn't his moral compass.

'Good luck with the flute. I know it's your future.' He turned on his heel and left the house. The Audi roared into life and only when the rumble of engine died away did she move.

Naomi slumped into the armchair, exhausted, her nerves frayed. Her performance was over. There was no audience to applaud or critique her; she'd given her all to one man and every moment of it had required exceptional willpower to sustain her deception. However, Ethan had quickly given up. In the end, nothing bound them together and he hadn't bothered to win her back. If it was the wrong decision, fate had delivered its verdict and she accepted it.

She wiped the tears away with the tea towel. She'd just enough time to pack some clothes and her music. She wasn't leaving anything important behind for him to hold hostage.

She dashed upstairs and began the frantic process of emptying drawers and pulling clothes off hangers. There was no order to her packing. As she zipped up her bag, a car pulled up outside, the engine ticking over.

My God! She gasped, horrified. He was already back. Was he expecting a second chance, a change of mind? She dug her nails into her palms and braced herself once again. If she had to tell him about the duffel bag this time, she would. She wasn't going to lie anymore.

# thirty

## Rebecca

Rebecca couldn't find Ethan. She searched through the dimmest parts of her mind, hoping to catch a glimpse of him. Trying to have a vision while driving wasn't a good idea.

She swerved, avoiding a parked car and spotted her sister outside the station. Leia was propped against a pillar and with her eyes shut; she resembled a walking corpse. Leia's long journey from Columbus to Cambridge had taken most of a day and she'd given Rebecca little notice prior to her arrival. Rebecca had scrawled a message for Howard and stuck it to the fridge: a list of things to feed the kids and another one listing not what to feed them regardless of how much they begged. Howard didn't always discriminate between the two.

Leia collapsed into the passenger seat. 'I think we might be too late,' Rebecca said.

'Don't be so damn pessimistic,' Leia said curtly, then sighed. 'Sorry. Jet lag. I'm somewhere still over the Atlantic Ocean.'

'Tell me again about Frederick. Ethan, whoever the bloody hell he is. You could have warned me about him while you were in Ohio. Why did you wait until you were at the airport?'

Prior to picking up Leia, all Rebecca knew was snippets of information sent by email and text messages. The collection hinted at something felonious, but not sufficiently detailed for Rebecca to make an informed decision whether to wait for Leia to arrive in England or to rescue Naomi from Ethan's house with the police leading the charge.

'I didn't want to alarm you. I don't think he'll harm her,' Leia said.

'You don't think? Oh my God. Please tell me he's not some fantasist serial killer.' Rebecca pressed her foot down harder on the gas pedal.

'No, he isn't like that. And please slow down. You're making me feel sick.'

How could she possibly know? Rebecca snapped her fingers at her handbag in the footwell. 'Get my phone out and check it again. I've not heard from her today.'

'Watch the road, will you!' Leia rummaged in the handbag and located the mobile. 'The battery is flat and the screen is all sticky.'

'What? Plug it in now.' Toby had borrowed it to play some game.

'Yes, ma'am.' Leia plugged it into the phone into the charging cradle. 'It'll take a few minutes to boot up again.'

Rebecca drummed her fingers on the steering wheel. 'What did you find out about him, Leia?'

The story of Frederick Nieman wasn't the worst she'd ever encountered as a solicitor. It fell into the category of dysfunctional families and bitter rivalries between loved ones, which often warranted pity, but rarely anything requiring legal intervention.

'Ethan was jealous of his brother. This is what the sheriff thought? So he's negligent by failing to intervene and help his brother, or,' she paused to consider, 'did he deliberately cause the accident? There's a big difference.'

Leia hid a yawn with the back of her hand. 'Sorry. I'm fighting my body. My mind is wide awake, honestly. I'm just as worried as you are, Becca. She's got herself involved with a compulsive liar, a sociopath, who's moved from place to place, never allowing himself to create ties. He's not just running from his mistakes, he's making sure he doesn't make any more by becoming attached to somebody who will give him a clean reputation. He can become a British citizen, change his name again to Liddell, do what he likes while he has Naomi to unwittingly protect him.'

'He wants to marry her, the very thing Gran warned her about.'

'Gran.' Leia released a long breath between her puffed out lips. 'Yes, I suppose she did see things quite clearly.' She spoke without sarcasm and with a note of regret. Quite unexpected.

'Hear things,' Rebecca corrected. Hearing was so much easier, wasn't it? She refused to be envious of her grandmother. The journey to Newmarket wasn't the best time to reveal secrets and probably not the wisest place either. She had planned it so differently.

A quick cough cleared her dry throat. 'Leia, I know you don't believe in Gran's gift, but I've something to tell you about me.'

'You?' Leia said with incredulity. 'Oh, no, please don't tell me you've inherited—'

'Yes. I have.' Rebecca unleashed everything she wanted to say in a tumble of disjointed phrases. 'I have a piece of Gran in me. Unlike you and Naomi. I didn't get the brains of Dad. Nor am I blessed with Naomi's ability to inspire. What I do is see things. Visions that belong to other people. People I know, friends, mainly. Even neighbours. But not you though. Well, just the once. I saw you in the car with Ashley surrounded by paper cups and sweet wrappers. I saw you laughing on the road to Ohio, just after Mum told me you'd gone.' Rebecca stopped talking, aware that Leia hadn't interrupted her in any form, including with a sneer of derision. The silence hung heavily between them and she dared not glance over in Leia's direction. She focused on the car in front.

'You saw what I saw in Ohio?' Leia said quietly, her voice almost lost to the sound of the wind brushing against the car and the wheels hurtling along the tarmac.

What would make something so unreal actually feel real to Leia's rationalist view of the world?

'No. I think I was closer to Ashley's mind – oh, I like her by the way. Sometimes I'm in somebody's head, but never yours, or Mum's or Naomi's. Howie isn't a conduit either, well, he was just the once. But Dad is. It's confusing and I can't control it and since I had the kids, the frequency and potency of them has intensified. They don't happen indoors or at regular times. They're pretty random.'

She was rambling. This was never the way she wanted to reveal her secret to Leia, or Naomi for that matter. She wanted to do it over a glass of excellent wine and a home-cooked meal with Howard next to her, her hand in his and the kids tucked up in bed. She wanted her sisters to appreciate how scary her visions were and how wondrous too, especially when it meant she could help somebody or solve a problem. She planned to tell them when she'd finally embraced her gift and ceased fearing it, and most importantly, she would reassure her family she wasn't mad, only extraordinarily lucky to possess something so special that it had to be given to her by nature and not an omnipotent power. The last sentence would be to respect Leia's lack of faith. Rebecca believed it came from God. She suspected Naomi preferred the mystical option of, "Who knows, does it matter?" Rebecca pictured that improbable day often and it was nothing like the disjointed conversation in the car.

'You see visions of things to come?' Leia asked. Her question calmed Rebecca; her sister wasn't trying to humiliate her. Something had changed her – Ashley? Rebecca welcomed the influence.

'Oh, no. Not like Gran. I see things that are happening right now. It's called remote sensing.' This was according to the research she had done on psychic abilities. She slowed the car down, the traffic was building as they approached the town centre. 'I guess you think I'm crazy, too, like Gran.'

Leia sighed. 'Before I went to Ohio, I would have said yes. But now… Let's just say I'm suspending my scientific reasoning, all the logic my brain tells me, and I'm just accepting what you tell me is true. Can you see him? Ethan?'

'Only the once, a few days ago, before I contacted you. He's hard to reach, like concrete, his vision can be dark and murky.'

Leia chuckled softly. 'You make it sound almost poetic.'

'I can't describe it any other way. So you believe Gran's prediction?'

'It seems to be the case, doesn't it?'

'Then, I need to tell you—'

Her plan to reveal the notebook was cut off by the bleep of her phone catching up with messages. Leia snatched it off the cradle and swiped away.

'There's a voicemail.' She thrust the phone to Rebecca's ear, enabling her to listen.

'Becca, ring me,' Rebecca repeated to Leia. 'She sent it two hours ago, Leia. Two hours!'

The car shot forward and nearly collided with the one in front of them.

'Cool it,' Leia said. 'We're nearly there, aren't we?'

'It's somewhere down this road. I haven't been before... she's very reticent about having visitors.'

'I wonder why that is,' Leia said dryly.

The only car parked outside was Naomi's small Ibiza. Rebecca abandoned her car nearly a foot away from the kerbside and hurried up the path to the front door.

She rapped her knuckles on the door and rang the bell with an agitated press of her finger. 'Naomi, it's me,' she yelled through the letterbox.

The door was flung wide open and a tearful Naomi crash landed into Rebecca's waiting arms.

'Oh, thank God, it's you. I thought Ethan had come back.' Naomi snivelled into her shoulder.

'I'm here, darling.' Rebecca patted her on her back. 'Now, chin up, not a moment to lose. Get your things, we're taking you home.'

# thirty-one
## Rebecca

Naomi stood rooted to the spot, her pale cheeks and watery eyes illustrated her miserable episode.

'I've left him, Becca,' she croaked, her shoulders deflated.

Rebecca pitied Naomi. Everyone needed a soul mate like Howard. Naomi had had two boyfriends, but Kyle and Ethan had represented the polar opposites of each other. What Naomi needed was someone in the middle.

'I lied to him,' Naomi said.

'Shush, darling.' She patted Naomi's quivering hand, keeping her close, while Leia rushed about the house, gathering up Naomi's handbag and suitcase.

'We should go,' Leia whispered into Rebecca's ear.

'I told him I didn't love him, Becca.' Naomi hugged her flute case to her chest. 'I had to go. He's done something terrible, I think. Something he did ten years ago. You do understand why I did it?'

'I'll tell you what I found out in the car.' Leia nudged Naomi's arm. 'Do you want me to drive?'

Naomi shook her head and finally seemed to notice the presence of her sister. 'What are you doing here?'

Rebecca steered Naomi through the front door. 'She's been helping you.'

'Helping me?'

Leia locked the front door, handing Naomi the keys. 'I went to Ethan's home. I met his father and he told me about their son, Robert.'

'You went to Ohio?' Naomi's eyes widened. 'Why?'

'Because you deserved to know the truth about him. And I had the time.' Leia smirked. 'I ran away.'

'To Ohio? Alone?'

'No. I went with my friend Ashley. She's been helping me find myself and I think I have.'

'In Ohio,' Naomi repeated, the disbelief unfettered.

'I had to know why Gran warned you.'

'You don't believe in—'

Leia sighed. 'I believe there are many things that can't be explained adequately, but, whatever.' She waved a dismissive hand. 'Gran saw—'

'Heard,' interrupted Rebecca. 'There is a difference,' she muttered.

'And I went to find out for myself,' Leia said. 'Get in your car and I'll tell you everything I found out.'

The journey would give Leia enough time for her to tell the story of Ethan. And it was simply that, a tale, since nobody knew the real Ethan.

Rebecca arrived home first. Howard greeted her on the doorstep with a kiss on the cheek and a gentle embrace. Of all the places she wanted to be, it was here with her husband, the rock of her life.

'Is everything okay?' he asked, eyeing her up and down with a puzzled expression. 'I got your message about picking the kids up from school.'

'Oh, thank you, darling. I'm sorry to spring that on you,' she said. 'We've company. My sisters are staying with us for a while. I hope you don't mind.'

He followed her into the house. 'Of course not. Free childcare, isn't it?' His tense face momentarily broke into a smile. 'You three could do with a good heart to heart. Where are they?'

'In Naomi's car. She insisted on driving herself here.'

'Is she okay? What's going on?'

Rebecca squeezed his hand. 'I'll tell you later. Naomi will probably be with us for a while until she sorts out somewhere to live.'

Howard's eyes widened. 'Now you've got me intrigued.'

She followed him into the kitchen, where he filled the kettle.

'I saw him, I made myself see Ethan and I knew I had to do something.'

'I thought you couldn't control it like that?'

'It appears I might be able to.'

'Honey, this is great news, isn't it?' Howard cupped her face in his hands. 'You know this could be a breakthrough?'

She nodded, battling the tears. 'I was so afraid, Howie. So worried you would give up on me.'

He pouted, forming an artificial frown of disapproval while his eyes twinkled. 'Me, give up on you?' He adopted a sincere expression. 'Never, ever, Becca, and if you think that again, you don't hide it. You tell me straight out that you're struggling.'

'The kids… the day I saw Eleanor in school and you… I thought you brushed it off.'

'I didn't mean to.' He looked offended. 'Did I?'

She shook her head. She internalised her fears so much he couldn't possibly have known. 'Did you notice things weren't the same after that?'

He closed his eyes, nodded slowly and opened them. 'Yes, I did, but I thought if I pushed you to explain why you'd stopped caring about the little things, you would bite my head off. I mean, does it matter if the house isn't pristine or dinner is late?'

She laughed in surprise. 'No, I just made them important to keep me happy, I suppose. I've become beholden to the art of distracting myself.'

'I admit, I do like a tidy house, but you know we can afford a cleaner. We can hire somebody to iron—'

'Oh, for God's sake, give me something to do in life.' Outside, a car ground its wheels into the gravel. 'I'm going to own this part of me, I know I will,' she said quietly as the engine cut out. She stared right into his sparkling eyes.

'Yes,' he said, drawing her closer.

He hugged her and kissed the crown of her head. She crushed her body against his crumpled shirt and tie, feeling the weight of her burden dissolve in his arms.

Soup revived both Leia and Naomi, although Naomi remained agitated. Her world was off-kilter, thrown into confusion, and she had a heap of questions. Rebecca put the gas fire in the sitting room on, brought in a tray of hot chocolate and cookies and left them on the hearth. Howard joined them, sitting in his favourite corner armchair – the old dependable, she called it – under a lamp with his newspaper, which remained folded on his lap. He looked the part of a youthful curator at a museum, guarding his treasured possessions, which she knew to be her and their children. His presence, Rebecca believed, was essential; a witness to the remarkable foresight of Rose Liddell.

'I can't believe Ethan would really leave his brother to die,' Naomi said.

Her eyes were red-rimmed and a touch feverish. Rebecca despised what Frederick had done to Naomi. Frederick. Ethan. A name was merely a label. Character went to the core. Naomi, so pale, needed comfort from someone. 'He's not that callous, surely?'

Leia shrugged. 'You say he kept a handkerchief?'

Naomi hugged her hands under her armpits, as if a chilly wind was blasting through the house. 'I found it in a duffel bag in the attic. It was wrapped in a newspaper report describing Robert's accident. Ethan put the cigar box up there too with the passports; he didn't want me to find them again. I found them today, and that's why I left him. It wasn't anything to do with the name change.'

'The handkerchief is a trophy,' Leia said. Her tired face was drawn and her eyes were heavy lidded. The nose ring was absent. 'A memento of his brother's murder?'

'Maybe,' Rebecca murmured. She glanced at Naomi, the poor girl would be distraught at the thought of living with a killer. Given the insubstantial evidence, there was nothing to indicate he was one. She drew Naomi closer, letting her rest her head on Rebecca's shoulder, something Eleanor might do when she was older. Rebecca wished there was some way to soothe her younger sister's shattered nerves.

She offered her verdict, hoping it would bring closure. 'Or perhaps it's a relic, something he keeps to help him deal with the grief of seeing his dead brother. We don't know if he was there when Robert died, or arrived shortly after. He might have got there before his father, used the hankie to staunch the bleeding, and then ran away, fearing he would be blamed.' According to Leia, the sheriff believed something different. But who would ever have known the truth? 'Why didn't you ask him?'

Naomi's pallor was slowly returning to normal. 'I'd no idea if I confronted him about this and the article whether he'd go ballistic on me. So I made out that I was finished with him because... because I didn't love him. I fed him a pack of lies to protect myself.'

'I'm sorry, sweetie, but it's for the best,' Rebecca said. Opposite her, Leia nodded in agreement.

'He's still on the run, then?' said Leia.

'He suggested we go to Ireland.' Naomi folded her hands over each other, pressing them into her lap. 'God, I nearly said yes. The last thing he said before he walked out was that he struggled with demons and that lying comes easier than opening up. But, honestly, he never laid a finger on me or threatened me. I don't think he's a criminal. Morally unsound, maybe, but not evil.'

Rebecca doubted Ethan's need to hide was due to false accusations – he had left a dead boy alone in a field; he was guilty of that simple fact.

'The blood-stained hankie will have Robert's DNA on it,' said Rebecca. 'Although after all these years it might not stand up in court as valid. And, it only proves Ethan was there but nothing about culpability. So we don't know what he did, only that he ran away and never contacted his family again. Hardly the actions of a saint.'

'No,' Naomi murmured. 'He's not a saint. I don't want to see him, but I'll need to go back and get the rest of my stuff.'

'I'll hire a van and come along, just in case he makes trouble,' said Howard. 'It's Saturday and the kids can go to friends for the morning.'

'Do you have the address of the farm?' Naomi asked Leia abruptly.

'What?' Leia blinked. 'You want to visit—'

'No. I want to write. You said in the car they didn't have email. I'm going to write to William and tell him that his son was here.'

'What will you say?' Rebecca asked. The solicitor in her wanted to advise Naomi to do nothing. It wasn't wise to stir up a tragedy that had happened ten years ago or interfere with people's grief. Rose had probably learnt this lesson a long time ago. Whatever she foresaw, once it happened, she clearly hadn't rubbed salt into wounds nor offered latent sympathy. She merely acted as a bystander, an observer. Rose had been the perfect member of the audience watching stories acted out on a real stage, never criticising or altering the performance. Rebecca envied Rose's ability to hold back from judging. She wasn't sure if she could follow those steadfast footsteps of her grandmother. She'd try, she promised herself.

'I'll tell him the truth,' said Naomi. 'I'll tell him how his son loved me. How he hid his real identity and the hankie. But I shall also say that I loved Ethan, too, that he never harmed me and that he worked hard at his job and was well respected by the farming communities. He might have had his demons, but largely, he kept them at bay. I think, deep down, he's desperate to go home and start again. He carries this guilt with him and unless his parents welcome him home, he won't go back.'

'Unfortunately, his mother doesn't have long,' Leia said. 'I'm not sure I could be as magnanimous as you, Naomi.'

Naomi's face fractured slightly. 'It's nothing to do with generosity. It's about his family, especially if his mother is dying. They can decide what to do with the information. I'm tired of being the passenger in my own life. I know everyone wants the best for me and I'm truly grateful for what you did, Leia, but it's time for me to step up and not be dependent on relationships.'

'Good for you.' Leia folded her arms.

'What will you do?' Rebecca asked.

'Go back to Bury. Heather and Malcolm have given me this opportunity to perform at a concert they're planning, something for me to showcase my talent. They're talking about inviting prominent players, people with connections. I'm terrified. I'm also humbled by their encouragement. I'm going to take all this heartache and unleash myself, like a cork flying off a champagne bottle. The audience won't know what's hit them.' Naomi grinned. Rebecca liked the nature of the smile; it exuded confidence and purpose.

'Finally,' Leia murmured softly. 'Do you know how fucking hard it's been having to carry the weight of my damn talent on my shoulders. I'm handing my duties over to you while I bugger off round the world with Ashley.'

'What?' said Rebecca.

'That's right. I'm taking an extended break. I'm going to unplug my elephantine brain. You,' she pointed at Naomi, 'will do something that makes Mum and Dad regret every day they weren't around to watch you become the wonderful person you are. And you, Becca, can stop pretending you're nothing special.'

'I am not agoraphobic—'

'I didn't mean that. I meant being a mum and wife.' Leia looked over Rebecca's shoulders to where a bemused Howard sat.

'She's not just that, you know,' Naomi added. 'She's got this amazing gift. Gran would be so proud.'

Rebecca brushed away a tear. 'Oh, do shut up the pair of you.'

'Both of you have to work things out. Becca, you went out of your way to find the truth about Ethan after I dismissed your concerns, told you not to bother, but you persevered. You two have got more in common than you think.'

Naomi lectured beautifully, thought Rebecca.

Leia pressed the tip of her finger to a vacant hole in her nose. 'Fancy one of these, Becca?'

The laughter healed. Rose often laughed, even when she must have known things that nobody else could ever have imagined.

'I'll go write that letter.' Naomi rose.

Howard stretched out his legs. 'I'll find you some good old-fashioned letter paper and a pen.'

Naomi smiled. 'I think I can remember how to hold one.'

When they left the room, Leia turned to Rebecca and folded her arms across her chest. 'Now, sis, what were you going to say about Gran in the car?'

Damn her memory. Now, Rebecca would have to explain about the notebook and everything she'd found out since Rose had died.

# thirty-two
## Leia

Leia listened without interrupting. Of course, being the analytical type, she was tempted to pick apart much of Rebecca's assumptions. However, undeniably, there were many intriguing facts and coincidences that didn't add up, which meant it was hard to ignore the truth: Rose definitely had gifts, both as a kindly lady who helped people out and a clairvoyant with a good ear for listening. Frederick masquerading as Ethan had silenced Leia's noisy scepticism. She allowed the acceptance to sweep over her and she relished the pleasure of not caring if something was right or wrong.

What came as a real surprise, as her sister shifted the story of Rose's birthday to her own visionary acuity, was its extent and frequency.

'So that's why you're stuck in the house?' Leia said. 'You gave up your career to live like a hermit on purpose?' The revelation explained so much about Rebecca's demure lifestyle and Leia privately regretted every sassy remark she'd made about her sister and Howard. Rebecca's constant companion – her wan complexion – was due to a lack of sunshine. Leia's eye for detail had served her poorly when it came to her family.

'Not on purpose,' said Rebecca. 'I have the kids to raise, that's a job in itself. Regrettably, I've grown comfortable being behind these walls. I never intended to use this house as a crutch.'

'So, here we are. Me, with my planet-sized brain and you with your visions. We're quite a pair.' Leia retrieved a cookie from the plate. 'I'm so hungry again.'

Her sister chuckled. 'You need to eat. You're a waif.'

'You sound like Mum,' Leia muttered under her breath.

Rebecca handed her the whole plate of cookies. 'Eat up.'

Between mouthfuls Leia asked Rebecca how she coped and Rebecca described instances with neighbours and friends, some entertaining, others had clearly caused awkward moments for Rebecca and Howard as they sought excuses for Rebecca's spy-like behaviour. Leia detected something else behind the jovial recollections. Rebecca was afraid of her gift.

After she'd demolished a third cookie, she asked a specific question she'd held back in reserve. 'Why don't you control it, like Gran?'

'What do you mean, like Gran?' asked Rebecca sharply.

Leia put the plate to one side and chased the crumbs off her lap. 'Do you really think she had these so-called happenings once a year, right on cue when she blew out that pink candle?'

Rebecca placed her half-drunk mug of hot chocolate back on the hearth with a trembling hand. 'Leia, what is it you know about Gran?'

Leia tried hard not to look sheepish. Rebecca had every right to be cross with her. Leia had said nothing to anyone for years about the day Rose had died. This was Leia's little secret and she felt terrible for keeping it. If Rebecca had known, she might have found a means to control her visions, and if Naomi knew what Rose had said, then her future might be filled with optimism.

She twisted her hands in her laps and glanced over her shoulder. She didn't want Naomi to hear, not unless Rebecca thought it right.

'You have to appreciate, Becca,' Leia said quietly, 'I didn't believe her, back then. I brushed it off as I always did. It wasn't until this Frederick business—'

'Leia. Tell me.'

# Rose sleeps forever, a doctor by her side

## May 2010

As Leia drove the rental car to Chatteris, she hummed. Two years on, she didn't regret the move to the States. The headhunting, orchestrated by her mother, had been carefully crafted to appeal to Leia's specific expertise. The decision to uproot, though, ultimately had been hers. However, she actually longed a little for England, especially the spring, which was cooler and prettier than she remembered. Blossom blew across the windscreen, the pink and white petals caught in the wind, and swirled like mini tornadoes on the roadside and pavements. Soon she'd be sweltering in the heat of a New England summer and the constant blast of air conditioning. The lab she worked in was enclosed, windowless and polar white. She'd adapted to the clinical environment and odd smells so much, she often perceived the outside world as unbearably dazzling and invasive. Travelling remained an odd diversionary activity. She missed the security of knowing her place, the routine of work. However, she didn't pine for the house she lived in, which was a different kind of prison; a smothering one provided by her parents.

The disquieting row she'd had with Rebecca was one of many they'd had since she'd arrived back in the country. They simply did not get on. Leia wanted to throw a party and invite her old friends from her Cambridge days, but pregnant Rebecca was horrified at the thought of strangers in her pristine house. She'd turned it into a nest and treated her body like a temple, fastidiously eating healthy food while reading every baby book and magazine that crossed her path. Leia couldn't have picked a worse time to visit. But it didn't matter, she'd be gone soon enough.

In three weeks' time Rose would be sixty-nine years old. Leia wasn't planning to be there on her birthday. She was flying back to Boston in a couple of days. It was something of a relief that she would miss the annual candle blowing party. Rebecca would attend, naturally, and Naomi, perhaps, although she was busy with a music group that should finally give her the publicity she deserved.

Oh, to have a gift that was embraced and considered a blessing. Leia was the freaky, geeky lab hermit, envied and pitied in equal measure by her colleagues.

When Rebecca found out Leia was returning to America before Rose's birthday, she'd been furious with her sister.

'You could have waited. You know she's not good at the moment.' Rebecca's acidic tongue lashed Leia and she shrugged it off. Staying with her sister was convenient for the purpose of visiting her friends and her maternal grandparents, the ones up north who never came south of the Wash and stuck to the notion that families functioned better apart than together. The day trips kept her occupied and helped the two week vacation zip along nicely.

Chatteris sat alone in the middle of flat, shapeless fields. She might as well be in Kansas, except the sky wasn't blue. It was more of a muddy grey. Turning into Rose's street, she parked outside the house and braced herself. Rose would fuss over her, complain about her being far too thin around the waist and insist she eat a slice of stodgy cake.

'You're not getting enough sun,' Rose declared on the doorstep, then angled her cheek for the obligatory kiss.

Rose was the paler of the two. Her walking stick seemed necessary – she swayed and nearly careered into a wall. She glared at Leia's hand around her arm and shook it free.

'I'm quite alright,' she said, but her voice was thready.

Putting aside Rose's tendency to babble on about silly things, Leia missed her occasional grandmother moments. There was nothing more satisfying than hearing about the trivial comings and goings of a small town on the edge of nowhere. The gossip was meaningless; the folks strangers. Compared to the bustle of university life and the long hours Leia worked, a visit to Rose's home offered her a quietness and a few possibly sage words of observation that she could take or leave. She relished the pleasure of treating words as inconsequential and forgettable.

Leia closed the front door behind them and wandered into the living room. She was immediately stuck by the bareness of the book shelves and the absence of the usual stack of magazines.

'What have you been doing? Where is everything?'

'Been tidying up. Such a nuisance cleaning around all this stuff I never touch.' Rose waved her stick in mid-air as if holding a magical duster.

'They're your things, Gran.'

'I don't need them.' She sat heavily in a chair and sighed. 'You don't mind helping yourself to tea, love. I'm awfully tired today. These damn voices, the headaches...' She closed her eyes.

Leia resisted the temptation to take her pulse. 'You should be in bed.'

'Maybe,' Rose muttered. 'Soon. I've something to tell you.'

'Gran, you don't have to remind me about getting out. Finding love, la-de-da. I'm quite happy.'

Leia began to walk to the kitchen.

'No you're not.' Rose's eyes sprang open. 'You have nothing but that brain of yours. Brains aren't always the best thing in life.'

'Now you sound like Rebecca. Nobody knows what it's like to be burdened with a gift. It's not easy, you know. I have to put up with stupid people—'

'Oh, do be quiet, Leia,' Rose said bluntly.

The bark stopped Leia in her tracks.

'Sorry,' Rose said, shrivelling back into the chair. 'I didn't mean to snap. I don't have much time, you see.'

'Time? I'm here for the rest of the day, Gran. If you like I can take you out in the car. Have a cup a tea somewhere.' The bare house unnerved her. It felt cold too, even for a spring day.

'Actually, I'd quite like a lie down. I've a bit of a headache.' She wrestled with her stick.

Leia helped her to her feet. 'What's wrong?'

Rose's blue tinged lips worried her.

'I'm worn out, dearie. You're the doctor, work it out.' The dwindling grin was almost lost amongst the wrinkles.

Arthritic maybe. Worn out by what? 'Come on then.'

It took several minutes for Rose to shuffle upstairs. One side of her body was definitely weaker than the other. Leia contemplated ringing her doctor.

Rose lay on the bed and Leia removed her slippers. Sitting next to her, she held Rose's hand.

'Gran, I'm a bit worried—'

'Don't be. I'm not afraid. For once, I can just let them chatter away and be done with it all.'

She'd lost the plot completely, poor thing.

'Who are you talking about?'

Rose closed her eyes. 'If I told anyone, they would have carted me off to one of those nasty hospitals and drugged me. That's what happens when you tell people you hear voices. But my voices aren't like that.'

Leia decided to humour her. 'Like what, Gran?'

'Demanding. They simply whisper. I learnt to ignore them. When I first met your grandfather, it was very hard, so I turned the volume down, so to speak, and concentrated on him. Then Paul came along. Such a difficult birth. He kicked his way out of me.'

Leia found that hard to imagine. 'Dad isn't the most active of people.'

'He was on his birthday. I told them to shut up. And that gave me an idea, and I knew it would reassure Frank if I could. I only listen to those whispers on my birthday. Just once a year. It's my head.'

'Of course.' Leia patted Rose's withered hand.

'I know you don't believe me. Rebecca does, of course. She's got her own worries. And little Naomi—'

'Less of the little, please.'

'I still think of her as that chocolate-haired baby. So sweet. So innocent. Somebody will gobble her up. That's what I fear.'

Leia lowered her head; Rose's voice was tired. She reached over and pulled a cover over her legs. She noted the loss of weight. Something wasn't right.

'I'll go make that cup of tea, shall I?' She'd never had the makings of a doctor, but today she managed to be a nurse, just like Rose, who'd specialised in taking care of the infirm – something she needed herself.

Leia would speak to Rebecca when she returned to Huntingdon and they'd sort out a carer and investigate sheltered housing with an on-call warden. It wasn't as if Rose had much to take with her.

She'd nearly reached the door, when Rose spoke. 'Trust David.'

Leia leaned over the bed. 'What's that?'

'Trust David.'

'Who's David?'

Rose didn't answer. Her lips were puckered, cracked and dry, from a lack of fluids. She chuckled softly. 'Good,' she said, as if addressing somebody else.

'Gran, who is David?' Leia repeated.

'Oh, it's not for you. You'll know what to do. I'll let you decide whether to tell her or not.'

The confusion was worsening. Rose was delirious, obviously sick. 'Tell who?'

'Naomi, of course. This time she'll be happy. I know it.'

Leia rolled her eyes to the ceiling. 'I'll get that tea, now. You rest up.'

Downstairs, she boiled the kettle until it whistled and pumped out steam. The teapot was cracked and when she opened a cupboard door, she found only one box of tea bags, which was nearly empty. An alarm bell rang in her head, triggering a horrible sickening sensation. She yanked open another door – the shelves were empty – the fridge had next to nothing in it too, just milk, some eggs and an unopened block of cheddar cheese. Rose's larder was bare. She had no food in the house; it explained her weight loss. On the back of the kitchen door hung a blackboard, the kind children used in Victorian schools, and attached to it a piece of chalk on a length of string. The board was titled Shopping List. There was nothing written beneath the faded heading.

'Oh, God,' Leia cried, despairingly. The situation was more urgent than she'd realised.

She bounded up the stairs, ready to tell Rose that she was taking her to Rebecca's right then and there was to be no arguing about it. She froze on the threshold of the bedroom.

Rose stared up at the ceiling, her hands neatly placed on her chest. The wedding ring glinted in the waning light. Leia sat on the bed and was careful not to touch her. She wept. When she had her emotions under control, she reached over and closed Rose's eyes.

'There,' she said softly. 'No more silly voices.'

She wasn't leaving after all. She'd have to cancel her flight home.

\* \* \* \*

Leia waited while Rebecca dabbed at her cheeks with a tissue.

'Don't tell Naomi,' Rebecca said.

'I agree,' Leia said. 'The aneurysm… there was nothing I could have done to prevent it from happening.'

'I know.' Rebecca sighed, her relief palpable in its depth. 'So you believe all those things I wrote down?'

Leia nodded her acknowledgement. The detailed accounts in Rebecca's notebook had added significant substance to the brevity of Rose's strange sayings. 'The prediction about Ethan, I mean Frederick, was the only one she actually said directly to the person involved. Am I correct?'

Rebecca rubbed her chin. 'The one about Grandad, wearing black, he wasn't there. Dad heard it while Grandad was at work. You know, he never liked to hang around on her birthday. Always said he celebrated with her in their own way, which I took to mean…' She blushed.

Leia laughed. 'Me, too.'

'But he didn't want to hear, just in case it was going to be him. All the others – Babs, Neil, the stable boy – they never had an inkling; she never told anyone what she heard. Their fate was never in her hands. Naomi was the exception.'

'We can't tell her about this David – my God, another name! It's not fair, and even if Gran seemed happy with it, she was pretty confused and I might have it wrong—'

'I'm sure you heard it right.' Rebecca pursed her lips. 'No. Let's just wait. It will be another year or so, assuming the ten years apply.'

'Or maybe not. Who knows. She left me with the impression she heard voices more than she let on. I suspect toward the end she must have struggled to contain herself. She was very unwell, years of struggling with those things she heard had taken its toll.' A lump formed in her throat. 'She knew she was going to die that day.' The idea of predicting your own death wasn't one she wanted to contemplate.

'I'm glad you told me, because I think I'm going to take a leaf out of Gran's book. I'm determined to control this, like she did.'

'Like on your birthday?' She grinned, rather too enthusiastically.

'Well, no,' she said, frowning at Leia's attempt at humour. 'I think it's more likely to be a place that works for me, rather than a specific time or event.'

Leia wasn't going to be thwarted by her sister's dull approach. 'The bottom of the garden?'

There was a pause, while Leia tensed, waiting for Rebecca's barbed response. Instead, her face cracked into a much needed smile.

'The vegetable patch?' she suggested.

They both laughed, and the mood lightened.

'I have to try something, don't I?'

'And Naomi?'

'Naomi will make her own way. She proved she can handle herself with this Ethan business. She gave him the boot, even before she'd heard what you found out. I don't think we should worry.'

Leia stretched her arms above her head. 'I'm glad.' She yawned. 'I got to tell you. I never intended to keep it a secret. I just assumed it was the ramblings of a dying woman. Her last words, who would believe a thing she said?'

Rebecca pulled her up onto her feet. 'There's nothing to forgive. I never told you about the notebook, because frankly, I wasn't convinced until I found out about Grandad.'

'I probably wouldn't have believed any of what you wrote, you know that.'

'So much for my painstaking research.'

'What about the birthday after I went to America, the one before she died? Did you and Naomi go to see her? Won't that happen next?' All the others had been accounted for over the last ten years, and with little impact on the family.

Rebecca paused to think. 'Oh, very innocuous,' she said. 'Something to do with hens not laying eggs. Quirky, like most of them. Nameless and anecdotal. I'm not worrying about it. It was only ever Naomi's that bothered me.'

'Who keeps hens?'

Her sister shrugged. 'A friend of hers. Neighbour? I've met the farmer she knows at the art club... do you think I should warn ... no, perhaps not. Silly, really. It will probably be a fox or something.'

They looped arms and Rebecca steered the staggering Leia towards the staircase.

'Go to bed,' Rebecca suggested. 'Tomorrow, we might have to face Ethan and since we've never actually met him, I'm not sure I can keep my hands to myself. A jolly good slap around the face is what he deserves.'

'You can join the queue. I'm first.'

* * * *

Howard snorted. 'Scarpered again, hasn't he? A bit of a coward.'

Naomi walked around the icy house. There were boxes of her things piled neatly alongside a stack of her pictures. The fridge was empty, the sink drained, and any remaining unopened packets of food arranged in plastic bags. She raced upstairs and by the time Leia had joined her, she'd flung open chest drawers and the wardrobe.

'The rest of my clothes are here. His have gone. In fact, everything of his has gone.' She checked the bathroom. 'His toothbrush, too. I don't understand. I was leaving him.'

'Well, he's left you, I would say,' said Leia, slamming an empty drawer shut. 'I assume he's not left anything incriminating behind.'

If he'd been there, she would have pinned Ethan against the wall, her sharp nails digging into his arms and for once in his life make him cower. The reason why wasn't due to Naomi or Robert's death, but Susan. He'd not seen his mother speechless and paralysed, still hoping for reconciliation. Leia's memory of that broken body and Ashley's heartfelt wish to help Susan remained raw. The least Leia could do was send some of her prize money to the couple, if their pride would accept it. Leia was convinced Susan's eyes were forgiving ones.

'Oh, my God. The loft,' Naomi exclaimed.

Howard fetched the stepladder and climbed right up inside it to take a good look round. 'Nothing here.'

'Not even a duffel bag?' Naomi asked from the bottom step.

'No. He's taken it.'

'He could be anywhere,' Rebecca remarked. 'He's probably gone to Ireland.'

They reconvened downstairs, gathering all of Naomi's possessions in a tidy heap ready to load into the van Howard had hired. Leia spotted two sheets of paper on the dining room table.

One was a letter from a letting agent. 'Naomi. You said he was renting this house from a friend in Australia.' She held up the sheet. 'He's not.'

'What?'

Naomi read the letter and frowned. 'The lying bastard. He owes them rent. Why would he lie about such a thing?'

'Because, you said yourself, it comes easily to him. He's not a morally sound man, Naomi,' Rebecca said, her arm around Naomi's shoulder.

She crumpled the letter into a ball. 'Well, I'm not paying. What's the other one?' She held out her hand.

'Do you recognise the company logo?' Rebecca asked.

'Yes. It's his employer.'

'What does it say?' Leia asked.

'It's his bonus award. He got the top sales figures in the whole country. It's a letter of commendation.'

'And he left it here?'

'He's hardly going to get good references now that he's up and left them in the lurch.' Naomi turned the sheet over. 'He's written something.'

Leia waited impatiently, her fingers itching to snatch it out of her sister's hands. A little sob escaped from between Naomi's lip.

*I lied about some things, but not this. And not my feelings toward you. I'm sorry.*

'Don't cry,' Rebecca said swiftly. 'He's still trying to manipulate you—'

'No,' Naomi said. 'I don't think he is. I think this is genuine Ethan. And I'm not crying.'

'Let's get this stuff loaded and go.'

'And then?'

Leia took the letter and folded it carefully, knowing at some point Naomi might want to read it again for one last time. 'We're here to help you in whatever way you need. You decide, Naomi. What do you want to do?'

'Play my flute. Play to anyone who will listen.'

'We'll listen.'

# thirty-three
## The Three Sisters
## November 2018

The frost lingered all day, keeping the spiny grass white and the leaves crisp. Autumn had hardened into a premature winter. The three sisters didn't care what was happening outside as they basked in the warmth of the pool house. They swam and chatted, using the banter to shape their relationships into something steadfast. The accumulation of events that began on the other side of an ocean with the tragic death of Robert continued to ripple on days after Ethan vanished. For years they'd carried their gifts like burdens, hiding them from themselves as much as each other. Consequences meant re-evaluations and discussions, some were intense, others light-hearted and genial.

'I'm going back to Boston,' Leia announced after finishing a lazy length of awkward breaststroke. Her short hair formed spikes and her nose stud twinkled under the bright lights. 'I'm going to accept that award. I've already written the speech and sent Dad a draft copy for him to check over.'

In the deepest part of the pool, Rebecca applauded, splashing water everywhere. 'Jolly good.'

Naomi climbed out and grabbed a towel. 'Mum's forgiven you?'

Leia laughed. 'She doesn't have much choice. Ashley turned up with my car and they had, according to Ashley, a bit of a heart to heart. You know how Mum needs time to get to know somebody and Ashley is such a good listener.'

'You'll need a dress,' Rebecca said. 'Something elegant that will fit around your bony bum. My mission is to fatten you up before you go back.'

Leia groaned. 'More cake. Jeez, woman, you should be on that TV show with what's-her-name. The one in the tent. Halle Berry?'

Rebecca and Naomi laughed so hard, they cried. 'So much for your remarkable memory.' Naomi sniggered. 'You're a con artist.'

'That's me. A million dollar con artist.' Leia had been informed of the extent of the prize money in an email from Lee Wang. Her esteemed adviser not only was still urging her to accept the prize, he'd agreed she should take an extended vacation afterwards. She and Ashley planned to travel.

'As soon it's over, the photographs taken, we're off,' Leia said. 'And I've told Mum, I'm going to find somewhere to live with Ashley. It's about time I had a roommate who's my friend.'

'So.' Rebecca swam up to Leia. 'Can I help you buy the dress? Please, pretty please. We can go to Cambridge. Shopping,' she said the last word gleefully.

'Oh, okay.' Leia sighed with mock heaviness. 'The new me, the one that doesn't mind being labelled a genius, is going shopping with her slightly, very slightly older sister.'

Rebecca squealed as her twin tumbled backwards in the water, kicking her feet and splashing her with water.

* * * *

As they reached the end of the second week — the two weeks was the longest spell together in a decade — Rebecca struggled the hardest to let go of her sisters. Side by side they cooked in the kitchen, played with the children and ambled along the River Great Ouse, their coats buttoned up to their chins to keep out the brisk wind. For the first walk, Rebecca had pulled a hood over her eyes and looked at her shoes. Ignoring Rebecca's protest, Leia had swept the hood off her head, allowing the breeze to toss her hair around and the low autumn sun to warm her face.

'See what you want to see,' Leia said quietly. 'The holly bush over there. The red berries and hungry birds. The stuff of life in all its glory. Look, isn't that a kestrel hovering over there?'

Rebecca followed Leia's finger and the bird swooped down into a hedgerow. 'Yes. I can see.' It pleased her because that was all she saw and intended to see. They linked arms and giggled, slightly embarrassed by the harmony of thoughts.

For the duration of Leia's stay, they continued to reminisce about the highs and lows and missing their grandmother.

Speaking of Rose without judging her as an eccentric busy body gave Rebecca hope. She told Howard, just before he flew out to Hong Kong on a business trip, that she wanted to conquer her fear of open spaces.

'This is what you meant about taking back control?' he asked.

'Something like that. I treated this ability as a burden, like a gaoler locking me in. Thinking about it, what nonsense.' She straightened his already immaculate tie and flicked a piece of lint off his starched collar. 'Should what I see around us dictate my fears?'

'I don't understand.' He slipped each arm into the sleeve of his jacket. The next time he went for a fitting, she would go with him and watch as the tailors fussed around him. He deserved some pampering; he'd waited far too long for her to break free.

'I've been blinded by these visions. I should treat them like daydreams, something that drifts in and out of my thoughts, instead of letting them overwhelm me with emotions. Rose accepted her voices as part of her. I shall do the same. No more fighting back. I suppose it's bit like turning the volume down on the TV. The less intrusive they are, the easier it is to contain them.'

He looked visibly relieved. For the first time, he admitted he was comfortable leaving her alone. He kissed her farewell, drawing her into a tight embrace that crumpled his tie and left a smudge of red lipstick on his cheek. She said nothing. It wasn't just about the visions; she had to lighten up and cope with untidiness if she intended to implement her plan.

* * * *

Naomi secured the house by the railway station; the same one she'd rejected months ago was available once again. Fate moved in mysterious ways, she declared after the letting agent contacted her with the news. Leia agreed. She was flying home the next day and couldn't wait to see Ashley.

Rebecca explained her rationale for coping to her sisters across the oak dining table.

'I'm going to break out,' Rebecca announced, popping open another bottle of red. 'This prison is no more.' She swept her hands out, nearly knocking over her wine glass. 'And, I've discussed it with Howie, and we're both agreed: I'm going back to work.' She swallowed a mouthful of wine.

'When?' Naomi asked.

Leia had never enquired why her ambitious twin had given up her successful career, believing that the decision was a commitment she had made to Howard, which was unfair and caused Leia to judge him poorly. Naomi, in private, had admitted the same fault.

'I've approached my old firm about locum type work, like holiday and sick cover, and they're on board with the idea of easing me back in gently. They think,' she hiccoughed, 'That it's a wonderful idea. I'm following the Rose Liddell approach. I'm the boss, I get to say when others get to intrude into my life.' She drummed her palm on the table and knocked a fork off her dessert plate.

Leia was content to watch her sister stumble into drunkenness. It was an art that Leia herself had practised too often, too selfishly and with little consideration for those who cared for her. What a dazzling idiot she had been to think that losing control was the way to escape stress. Rebecca exemplified how fear paralysed and Leia wasn't going to fall into the same trap.

'You'll still have the visions,' Leia said. 'Gran did.'

Rebecca's eyes sparkled. 'Maybe. I guess I'll have to wait and find out. Probably in the potting shed.'

Naomi spluttered on her drink. 'What?'

Leia tilted her head toward her younger sister. 'She's going to pick a place, like Rose and her birthdays.'

'You're going to blow out a candle in the potting shed?'

'No candles,' said Rebecca. 'No cakes. Just me, and nobody else. And if I think I see something important, I'll act, otherwise, it's nobody business. You two will have to trust me.'

Leia held up her palms. 'Fine by me. Let's raise a glass to the new Rebecca. Or old. I don't think you know how much it means to me to see you so positive and full of hope.'

'I'm embracing my gift for what it is: a facet of me. It's like a place I go to. Somewhere I shall hang out from time to time.'

Naomi imagined her version of "hanging out": the thrill of performing to a captive audience. After the applause died down, she could be herself once more – Naomi the teacher, or perhaps even composer, who knew. The important part was reclaiming her future.

'What about you, Leia?' Naomi asked.

'Oh.' Leia waved a dismissive hand. 'Genius doesn't take me anywhere.'

'Nonsense,' Rebecca said. 'You think our brains are that different? Go find yourself, get lost in some place that doesn't know you.'

The twins merged for a second, or so it seemed to Naomi. In the haze of alcohol, she saw a blurring of interlaced hair and fiery eyes, imagining them as one person, split apart at conception, now together and bonded. A warm tingle of delight filled her, replacing the cold emptiness left by Ethan.

'Can't image you two without those gifts. They make you.'

Rebecca nodded. 'Without mine, I wouldn't have Howie.'

'Howard?' Leia said.

'I saw,' Rebecca dabbed two fingers in the air, 'him blow off another woman when we were dating. I plucked up the courage and told him what I saw and thanked him. He didn't laugh or call me crazy, instead, he looked me in the eyes and said I was special.'

Naomi tilted her head to one side. 'Oh, Becca. That's so sweet. You've got a keeper. One day, I'll meet somebody who gets me. I just have to be patient.'

'You will.' Leia winked at Rebecca. 'Trust me.'

'And you, Naomi, will you be able to move on after Ethan?' Rebecca asked.

'Of course,' she said confidently. 'Twice bitten and not shy. I know for certain now, I'm not the marrying type at all, but somewhere out there, there is a somebody special for me. Somebody who knows what I need.'

They sat and drank sobering coffee. Naomi put down her mug and took a deep breath as if she was about to hold a long note.

'I've some other news. I spoke to Heather yesterday and we're agreed: I'm going to perform a solo at our concert next year. I'm working on an incredibly challenging piece that's rarely performed. I'm determined to do it and enjoy every moment. I want to give performing another go. I guess it's more important to me than I thought.'

'I'm so proud of you, Naomi.' A tearful Rebecca wiped her eyes.

Leia leapt to her feet. 'Group hug!' They formed a huddle, arms resting on each other's shoulders. 'From now on, the Liddell sisters are winners.'

# thirty-four
## Naomi
## April 2019

Naomi heard the rumble of a passing train. For a few seconds it interrupted her playing, then she resumed. A quick session before she left for the first lesson of the day. In less than a week, she would be on the dais of St Mary's church performing her long awaited solo. She was ready; the practice almost unnecessary. After tidying up her things, her departure was delayed by the arrival of an envelope dropping on the doormat. She carefully examined the postage stamp and recognised Rebecca's handwriting – the letter had been forwarded from her address. Naomi tore open the flap with impatient fingers.

Smoothing out the thin blue paper, noting the date – three days ago – she knew the address, even if she'd hadn't been there. The handwriting was unfamiliar: the letter wasn't from Ethan. Part of her was glad. Part of her was disappointed. However, it was how it should be. He was out of her life and gone, and she had moved on and settled into a life on her own. Perhaps there was no way for him to apologise or reach out to her that wasn't painful for either of them. She had lied to him, too.

The name at the end of the page was William Nieman. The writing was linear and neat, with a hint of copperplate style that belong to another era.

Dear Miss Naomi Liddell.

I received your letter. I apologise for not writing sooner, but my wife took a turn for the worse, thank the Lord she recovered. Only now am I able to reflect on the past few weeks.

My son Fred returned home in December. He walked into the kitchen, just as he had done over ten years ago, but this time, he came home a broken man. Heartbroken. I don't blame you for ending things. His mother is deteriorating and I need him. I need his expertise. I need his ambition. This time, I let him in and he agreed to stay. My son is home. We have plans to save the farm. Plans that I should have implemented years ago when Robert was alive.

Fred gave me Robert's handkerchief. I burnt it. Why you might ask, given its significance, which I am sure you appreciate given what you wrote in your letter. That terrible day is carved into my heart. I went to the field, where the crows screamed, and found my poor boy trapped under the wheels of the harvester. I touched him, but he was gone. When I saw the state of the creek, I blamed myself for letting things get so bad. I also saw the footprints in the mud and I knew Fred had been there. I called for him, but I'd lost him too. He witnessed a terrible scene, and knowing my son, he would not have had the capacity to deal with it. Running is his weakness. So I covered his tracks.

It never entered my head that Fred would harm Rob, like the sheriff implied at the press briefing. They might have been like apples to oranges, but they grew out of the same tree. My tree. I switched on the tractor engine, hoping to free him, and immediately I could see that the pull of the tractor had caused the accident. I'd not replaced the brake disks. I should have done. As for Rob, he was young, reckless and wouldn't listen to advice. I'd spoilt him. Ethan should have been in charge of the farm.

Fred is not a honorable man. I guess you worked that out. I tried to help him when he was a boy to understand right from wrong, but I am not a good teacher and his mother was already fading. You wrote that he took care of you and worked hard. If you can forgive him, so can I. Soon, it will be just us two.

He speaks of you occasionally. He regrets some things, I can tell, but not meeting you. He says you play the flute. My sister played the fiddle for us in the evenings when I was a boy. Fred says you're going to be famous, at least to those who know about such things. Life here is very quiet.

He won't come looking for you, if that troubles you. I kindly ask that you leave us alone, too.

William Nieman.

Naomi folded the letter and carefully put it back in the envelope. No tears splashed her cheeks; she felt satisfied, almost relieved that the letter insisted on absolute closure on both of their parts. She wasn't surprised by the contents; she suspected Ethan was home and because Rebecca couldn't see him, Naomi knew he was truly gone from her life. What was a surprise was the part about William covering up the footprints in the mud. For years, he had known his son had been there and hadn't said a word to incriminate him.

Whether he stayed silent for the sake of family honour or for love of his son, she would never know. If the letter proved anything it was that family secrets were sometimes best left hidden. While hers and Leia's gifts were generous and easily shared, Rebecca's, just like Rose's, would never be acknowledged and the burden was harsh. She would help Rebecca carry it by not being a burden herself and facing her own challenges without fear.

As for the man she thought she loved, Frederick was getting a second chance. However, he would always be Ethan to her and if she kept one memory of him alive, it was his foot tapping in time to the pulse of the music.

\* \* \* \*

The flutter of her tongue, which was as fast as a hummingbird's wings, splintered the note into thousands of vibrating elements. Naomi flew to the rafters of the church and descended back down again with a swoop of cascading notes. She serenaded the audience with soft vibratos and complex trills. She paraded her ability to reach the highest notes effortlessly, then drop to the rich lower ones in one smooth transition.

She'd paid heed to the advice from her friends about what to play, how to engage using eye contact and not let her limited sphere of movement make her stilted in appearance. She'd chosen a piece that delivered settled harmonies first, creating a comfort zone for the ear, then lifted the emotions with subtle silences, changes of tempo and dynamics. Unlike her previous performance, she played as if she was the listener and imagined herself sitting there amongst her audience, relieved of tension and transported someplace else. The whole approach delivered everything she wanted, and needed.

She understood what the composer desired as if she might have been there in the room with him while he wrote the notes down. She imagined his hand touching the keys as he sketched out the themes, humming to himself under his breath as he played each one. It helped to commune with him and eased her mind to think that he alone would have understood how she'd finally broken free and found herself. She'd never fear to be on her own again.

The applause was rapturous. Heather was grinning from ear to ear, Malcolm, his ruby cheeks shiny with perspiration, nodded gravely and appreciatively. Pierre simply looked at her in awe.

With the concert over, the crowd dispersed, clutching their concert programmes. At the back of the church waited Rebecca, Ashley and Leia, who had recorded the whole performance to show to her parents when she returned to Boston. Paul and Nancy's absence in Naomi's life was no source of unhappiness; they had chosen their path and she hers. After hugging her friends and exchanging a few quick hellos to some of her pupils waiting in the wings to congratulate her, she packed away her flute and stand. She hurried over to her sisters.

Rebecca was sheltered under the wing of Howard's arm. She didn't need it; her resilience remained strong. She was living beyond the walls of her house, trusting others to take care of the kids, dating Howard again.

'I invited along my work colleagues. They thoroughly enjoyed it,' Rebecca said.

The church was packed. Naomi spotted other music teachers, her tutors from college and old friends of her parents who had known her as a child. The loyalty of many humbled her.

'Thank you for letting them know. It's been a good turnout.'

Leia, wearing a long dress, delicate eye shadow and her hair flowing over her shoulders, leaned toward Naomi. 'Almost as many as my prize-giving ceremony.'

Rebecca thumped Leia's arm.

Naomi laughed. 'Well, this isn't going to reap in any gold. How goes the trip?'

More than a trip. Leia and Ashley had interrupted their European tour to fly in for the concert.

'We're off to India next week. Then China and New Zealand. I need to be back for August for the new semester.'

Ashley's thick eyelashes framed her pretty eyes. Regardless of the subject, she spoke candidly. Naomi could see why Leia liked her so much. 'She's missing it,' Ashley said. 'She might say otherwise, but she's full of ideas of a new project. This break is good for restocking the grey cells.'

Leia mocked her friend with an eye-roll. 'You can't make new neurons.' Ashley playfully thumped her. 'They're giving me funding and new lab facilities.' Leia brushed her hand down Ashley's arm. 'And we've found an apartment we both like. Mum and Dad are moving too. Downsizing.'

Everyone had plans, except Naomi. This one concert had been her sole purpose for so long, she hadn't looked beyond it. She turned and headed towards the front of the church, where the rest of the quartet were huddled. From out of the shadows of a stone pillar approached a slight angular man wearing a polo neck top and jacket. He intercepted Naomi and held out his hand.

'Naomi, I'm so glad I had a chance to catch you,' he said, breathlessly. He pushed his dark spectacles back up his nose. They reflected her face and hid his eyes. She didn't mind. The eyes weren't the window to the soul for everyone, she'd learnt that the hard way.

She shook his hand, a brief connection that gave her an instantaneous buzz of excitement. 'I'm sorry, do I know you?' He had something of a familiar face.

'That was a fabulous concert by you and your friends. You really captured the mood of that last piece. Impressive. I don't think I've heard it played so passionately.'

She blushed. 'Thank you.'

'Which leads me on to ask, would you like to perform a concerto, something new and exciting? I've been seeking a flautist just like you to premier a new piece by—'

'Me?' She glanced behind her. 'Just me?'

'I wouldn't want to take you away from your lovely quartet, of course, but this is very much a solo project.'

The thrill of wanting to know more was too much to contain. 'No, no. It's okay. We're just an informal group. We can come and go as needed, like the seasons.' She smiled.

He laughed. 'I get it. So, we're putting together a concert in Berlin—'

'Berlin?'

'Oh yes, the Kingston Chamber Orchestra is visiting Berlin in the summer and we, I, would love it if you'd try us out.'

The Kingston! 'Nobody knows me.'

'Well, they will soon. I'm their music director and if I say you're the one, then you are. Oh, and it's being recorded, so you'll receive royalties. What do you say, Naomi? Interested?'

She glanced over his shoulder at her waiting sisters. They stood patiently, sensing perhaps something momentous was happening on the other side of the church. Would Rose have predicted it? Could Rebecca see his energised face and warm expression? And Leia, would she analyse and investigate, ensuring she was safe?

Whose instincts did she trust? Hers. Naomi Liddell was more than capable of taking care of herself and if it meant going solo, then fine, she was up to the task.

She took a deep breath. 'I'd love to find out more. I'm definitely interested.' She beamed.

'Excellent.' He clapped his hands together. 'Forgive me. I should have said up front. My name is Harrington. David Harrington.'

# About the Author

Are people born gifted? Can a natural talent be nurtured into something special? Whether gifts are real or imagined, how does somebody live with being a bit different or unusual?

These questions evolved from a conversation with my youngest daughter – then aged nine – about what you would do if your grandmother said something weird, namely an enigmatic and unconvincing prediction about the future. Would you ignore it or worry that it might come true? The topic was the spark and like many writers and storytellers it grew into a plot and I weaved into it the challenge of living with gifts, include magical ones, and the relationship between three sisters who compare themselves to chalk, cheese and chocolate – three women whom never quite understood each other.

Ideas often start as something simple and evolve into complex themes. I'm grateful to all those who have helped me along the way and turned them into a published book.

Some other notes – I play the flute, but I'm not a performer. I could never feel what Naomi feels when she plays. My limited knowledge comes from listening and watching others perform. In my past I worked as an information scientist with many amazing people with big brains and incredible ingenuity. However, Leia is unique and based on nobody I know. Rebecca and Rose belong to that magical world of "what if" and that is where I find most of my ideas for writing.

If you enjoyed my book, please leave a review; writing is a lonely business and hearing from readers is very stimulating. You can find out more about my writing on my website – rachelwalkley.com – or Goodreads.

For news about my future projects or the gift of a short story, then please sign up for my newsletter (link on the website).

# The Women of Heachley Hall

**Only women can discover Heachley's secret.**

"Beautifully constructed."
"Utterly loved this book."
"Highly recommended."

*~ Goodreads Reviewers*

The life of a freelance illustrator will never rake in the millions so when twenty-eight year old Miriam discovers she's the sole surviving heir to her great-aunt's fortune, she can't believe her luck. She dreams of selling her poky city flat and buying a studio.

But great fortune comes with an unbreakable contract. To earn her inheritance, Miriam must live a year and a day in the decaying Heachley Hall.

The fond memories of visiting the once grand Victorian mansion are all she has left of her parents and the million pound inheritance is enough of a temptation to encourage her to live there alone.

After all, a year's not that long. So with the help of a local handyman, she begins to transform the house.

But the mystery remains. Why would loving Aunt Felicity do this to her?

Alone in the hall with her old life miles away, Miriam is desperate to discover the truth behind Felicity's terms. Miriam believes the answer is hiding in her aunt's last possession: a lost box. But delving into Felicity and Heachley's long past is going to turn Miriam's view of the world upside down.

Does she dare keep searching, and if she does, what if she finds something she wasn't seeking?

Has something tragic happened at Heachley Hall?

**Miriam has one year to uncover an unimaginable past.**

Printed in Great Britain
by Amazon